Chords of Us

Donald Fortier

CONTENTS

CHAPTER 1

1st October 2020

London, England

Sophie Cartwright burst into tears as she physically tried to drag her eight-year-old daughter, Maddie, into Westgate Primary School.

Everyone was staring, judging, and looking down on Sophie as the dirty, little scrubber who was too poor and too stupid to be a good mum.

And goddammit, they were right. Sophie couldn't even get Maddie to go into school. She had only managed to get Maddie into school three days in the last fortnight.

"Maddie, please!" Sophie begged, on her knees before her daughter. "Please, just go inside. Stop fighting me!"

Maddie was glaring down at Sophie, her large, brown eyes flaring with hysterical anger. Sophie knew hers would mirror Maddie's exactly.

"NO!" screamed Maddie, with no care whatsoever for the scene that she was making. Sophie's own tears were not helping the situation. Maddie threw her backpack on the ground and folded her arms stubbornly. "I will not go! I hate school!"

Maddie had been academically challenged since nursery school. Her teachers had always told Sophie that Maddie was just away with the fairies and was never interested in school, no matter what they tried to do for her. Maddie was in all the support classes in school, and had reading, writing, and maths assistance. She had not progressed further than a Year 1 student in reading and was only being put up at the end of the year because Sophie had begged the school each time.

Maddie would certainly never return to school if she was not in the same year level with her friends.

Not that she had many friends. Maddie struggled socially, too.

Not being able to afford a tutor made Sophie feel like even more of a failure as a mother. All she could do at home was borrow simple books from the library to read with Maddie, but she had always refused to do her readers.

Maddie had been such a beautiful child up until the age of four when she had needed to start going to school. The next four years had aged Sophie dramatically. Biologically she might have been twenty-six, but she felt fifty-three.

"Maddie, please, I can't be late for work again," Sophie implored. "Do you want me to lose my job?"

Sophie knew that Pete, the owner of the bar where she worked, would never sack her, but that was beside the point.

Maddie just glared at her mum. "You cannot make me go inside. I will scream that you kidnapped me," she threatened.

Sophie just looked at her daughter with utter defeat. What on earth was she supposed to do? She couldn't just sit on the side of the road and cry. She climbed to her feet and grabbed Maddie's hand before picking up her backpack. She then started to drag Maddie back towards the tube station, and Maddie trotted along willingly this time, having won the battle.

Maddie won more than Sophie did these days, and Sophie knew that she was failing in that respect, too. Nobody needed to point that out to her, though many took pleasure in doing that.

Namely Maddie's arsehole of a dad, who thought he was entitled to an opinion because he put two hundred pounds in Sophie's account every month.

It didn't help that he frequented the bar where Sophie worked, though Sophie knew that was just to torment her.

Sophie and Maddie travelled on the tube into the city, getting off at Sophie's usual stop at Leicester Square. Maddie was decidedly happier now, and there was no evidence on her face that she had only just threatened her mother with shouting out to the public that she had been kidnapped.

Still holding Maddie's hand, they walked up Charing Cross Road, and turned onto Shaftesbury Avenue. Sophie loved this part of London. She loved how busy it was, how everyone seemed so much happier to be around the art and the excitement of the West End.

It had been her dream once to perform on the West End, but the closest she had gotten to a theatre was the West End Piano Bar.

Sophie had been studying a musical theatre degree when she had met Kyle Becker, known to his moron rugby mates as "Beck". But having just turned eighteen, Sophie was charmed by his handsome face and movie star good looks, and three months into their relationship, she had discovered that she was pregnant.

Beck could not drop her fast enough, and Sophie's parents wanted nothing to do with her either. Luckily Beck's mother forced him to do right by Sophie in financially supporting her as she found herself a tiny flat in a dodgy part of town, and a job at the only place in the city that didn't mind hiring a pregnant teenager. She had dropped out of her uni degree and had been working ever since.

Sophie would not ever change her mind about the blessing that had been Madeleine Jane Cartwright, even if Maddie did make each day a battle. She had learned over the years that while she would love her beautiful daughter endlessly and would trade her life for Maddie's in an instant, bloody hell she did not like her sometimes.

The West End Piano Bar was a cosy theatre pub, frequented by patrons coming and going to the many productions each night. As indicated in the name, there was a huge grand piano on the stage in the corner, but without a proper piano man. Pete had been advertising in the window for months and was too tech illiterate to try to source someone online.

Sophie sang every few nights, and was accompanied by a CD, rather than the live music that the setting of the bar demanded.

The scent of beer that had long since leeched into the timber of the bar, stools, and floor immediately filled Sophie's nostrils as she made her way into the establishment.

Still wildly stressed and upset, she immediately set Maddie up at one of the tables and began to unpack her school bag. She pulled out her lunch box and her reader that she had refused to read the night before.

Maddie also had a mindful colouring book in her bag, as well as her pencil case, and Sophie knew she would have better luck keeping her occupied with that.

As soon as she turned around, she met Pete's eye as he stood behind the bar with a disapproving look on his face. Pete Gregson was much like Sophie really, only twenty years older. He had once had a musical theatre dream and had channelled it into the bar when nothing had really happened for him. He was a kind man, with a sweet, round face, and baby blue eyes.

"I'm sorry!" cried Sophie hysterically.

"Sophie, sweetheart, that's every day this week, so far," Pete noted, frowning. "The kid's got to go to school."

"Really?" Sophie found herself retorting sarcastically. "I never thought of that."

Pete rolled his eyes and came out from behind the bar, before wrapping arms around her tightly. Sophie whimpered. She had really needed a hug.

She knew Pete would never really be angry with her. He was never really angry with anyone. He was the reason she had stayed working at the bar for so long. That and who else would put up with Maddie's shenanigans?

"Go and clean yourself up, sweetie. You look like shit. I'll go and give Miss Maddie a broom. If she's going to skip school, she'd better learn a skill." Pete kissed Sophie's temple.

Sophie scoffed. "Do you know, Pete? If you were twenty years younger, and, you know, straight, I would totally marry you."

Pete chuckled. "Get out of here."

Sophie disappeared into the backroom. It was very basic, with a vending machine, a tatty, old couch, and a few hooks for handbags and coats. Sophie walked through the backroom and slipped into the employee bathroom. God, Pete was right. She did look like shit. She looked like she hadn't slept in a week, which was entirely accurate. She looked like she hadn't washed her hair in a week. Again, accurate.

Sophie splashed her face with water and ran her fingers through her long, strawberry blonde hair, which was looking much redder with the grease. She looked pale, and her brown eyes looked dead.

If you ever wanted to see a picture of a failure of a mother, you needed to look no further.

Sophie stared at herself and watched as her tired, brown eyes began to fill with tears. How she hated crying, but she couldn't help it. She gripped the sides of the sink and sobbed for a minute, needing to get it out of her system.

"Pull yourself together, Sophie," she whispered to herself.

Sophie left the bathroom, and grabbed an apron from the backroom, before returning to the bar to start work.

Sophie worked double shifts five days a week. Usually it was only her and Pete during the day. She spent time cleaning, cooking, and preparing for the busier nights. The bartenders, waitresses, and bouncers all worked the nightshifts. Sophie usually left work at three to collect Maddie from school, brought her home, cooked her dinner, and fought with her about homework, before leaving her with a babysitter so that she could work the nightshift.

Their crappy flat didn't pay for itself.

But that was only the routine on the odd occasion that Maddie actually went inside the school building.

As soon as Sophie had picked up the bottle of spray and wipe and a cloth to start wiping down the surfaces, she noticed that

Maddie was not alone on the bar floor. There was someone sitting at the piano.

A man, who appeared very deep in thought, was scrawling all over sheets of music, some of which had spilled over onto the floor.

From across the room, Sophie could see that he was young, perhaps her age or a little older. He had shaggy, dark hair, and an intense stare. He looked tall and lean as he sat before the instrument.

No sooner had Sophie noticed him, he began to play the piano, and her jaw dropped. Maddie, too, stopped colouring and turned to stare at him.

She had never heard anything like it, not even on television. He sounded perfect, poetic and passionate, a true professional. His fingers flew across the keys as though he did not even need to think about what he was doing. The music just flowed out of him.

And then he stopped abruptly, slamming his fingers down roughly on the keys.

"It's crap, right?" he asked, an obvious American accent about him.

Just as Sophie was about to answer him, assuring the stranger that his playing was magnificent, a voice answered him, coming from the speaker of a phone.

"Yeah," said an American female voice. "Not your best."

Sophie's eyes widened. Not his best? How on earth could this man play if that was not his best?

The man picked up his phone, and Sophie saw that he was on FaceTime with a woman.

"I'm screwed, Tally," he told her, not seeming to care that he wasn't alone in the room.

"You're not screwed," the woman, Tally assured him. "You just haven't figured it out yet. You like this piano, right? Keep playing, and you'll find something you like. The right tune will come. It always does. Anyway, I've got to go. Call me later, okay? I love you."

"I love you, too," murmured the man, before disconnected the call.

"He knocked on the window at about five this morning," Pete whispered to Sophie. "American bloke, he is. He saw the piano man advertisement in the window and asked to see the instrument. He bloody looked over my piano like an antique dealer would over Queen Victoria's smelling salts. Didn't have the heart to tell him I bought it for fifty quid from a guy who was taking it to the tip."

Pete chuckled, shaking his head.

"Anyway, he asked for the job, and played bloody Rachmaninoff or something to prove to me that he was a pianist. Get this, then he offers to work for no pay."

Sophie raised her eyebrows in disbelief. "He is working for no wages?"

Pete nodded. "In exchange, he can play whatever he likes during the day. Looks like he's working on something." Pete shrugged. "Doesn't bother me. My piano bar finally has a piano man, and I don't have to pay him. It's like bloody Christmas."

"What sort of nutter would work for no wages?" Sophie asked him.

"The kind who is on a deadline and has perfectly good hearing," interjected the piano man, who looked up from his notes for the first time.

His intense, blue eyes met hers, and he stared at her, frowning, appraising.

Sophie self-consciously looked away, not wanting any sort of scrutinisation in her current state.

"Sorry," she muttered in apology.

The piano man said nothing more, returning to his sheet music, and sporadically playing passages of true art. He kept at it for most of the morning, and Sophie found that she quite liked having the sound of the piano in the background, even if the pianist lost his temper ever few bars and stopped playing.

It made her wonder what sort of work he did.

Pete kept to his word and put Maddie to work. Maddie obeyed him immediately, and that cut Sophie more than it should have.

She looked terribly cute with a broom that was entirely too big for her, as she clumsily swept the previous night's peanut shells into messy piles.

Just before eleven in the morning, when Sophie had unpacked Maddie's morning tea for her, Sophie's phone rang.

As soon as she looked at the caller, her heart sank. It was the school. She hit the answer button, and said, "Hello, Sophie speaking," shakily.

"Good morning, Ms Cartwright," said Ann Peddington, the assistant principal of Maddie's school.

"Good morning, Ms Peddington."

"Our records indicate that Maddie is absent againtoday," she said disapprovingly.

Sophie winced. She knew that the school was not judging her. They were not like the other gossipy mothers. They had put into place every method of support possible to help with Maddie's struggles. Nothing seemed to work.

"I know, I am terribly sorry. She refused again this morning," Sophie said apologetically.

"Yes, well, Maddie's start to the school year has been less than ideal. Ms Cartwright, I would like you to come into school tomorrow morning for a meeting with myself, the principal, and Maddie's teacher. Would nine o'clock be convenient?"

Oh, God, what were they going to say? Were they going to report Sophie to child welfare? Would she be labelled an unfit mother? Would Maddie be expelled from school?

"Yes," squeaked Sophie.

"Excellent. We shall try and get Maddie into the classroom again tomorrow morning, and then we will devise a plan moving forward."

Sophie's stomach settled a little as soon as Ms Peddington said "we". Perhaps she wasn't putting the blame entirely on Sophie.

"Thank you, Ms Peddington," Sophie said gratefully.

"Have a good afternoon, Ms Cartwright." The call then disconnected.

Sophie put her phone away in her back pocket, and immediately noticed that both Maddie and the piano man were watching her. Maddie more accusingly.

"What did she want?" Maddie sneered angrily.

"Eat your apple, please," Sophie encouraged her, walking out from behind the bar.

Maddie reluctantly took an apple segment. "I won't go tomorrow. You can't make me. I hate it there!" she cried.

Sophie needed to physically stop herself from swearing. "Maddie, it's school, not prison. They only want to help you!"

"They all treat me like I'm dumb," Maddie complained, stuffing some apple into her mouth.

Sophie slumped down into the chair next to Maddie. "Maddie, you are not dumb, and there is nothing wrong with needing a little help."

God knew that Sophie needed it.

CHAPTER 2

Noah Bentley had told his twin sister, Tally, that he would be going down to the store to buy some red vines in order to get him out of his funk.

Tally was the one to call it a funk.

Noah would call it block.

Well, Noah had gone down to the gas station and looked at all the different candy bars and had quickly realised that a sugar injection was not going to solve his problem. But a change of scenery might.

The next thing he knew, he was standing in the departure terminal at LAX, booking a ticket on the next flight to London.

Why London?

It was the first city that was listed on the departures board. Noah took it as a sign.

Tally had brought him a bag of clothes and his passport, and he was away.

Noah had never been blocked like this before. He honestly felt as though there was a dumbbell resting on his creativity that was just far too heavy to lift up. Everything he played sounded like pretentious garbage, and nothing that was coming to him was remotely suitable.

Noah Bentley had a reputation, a very, very good reputation, as a musician, lyricist, and composer. He was talented, gifted at what he did.

He wasn't being vain. It was the honest truth. Noah Bentley had a gift. He had taken his first piano lesson in his mother's church when he was five, and by the following week, he was teaching the teacher.

He could pick up any musical instrument and play it. He had a brain for music, and melodies seemed to follow him wherever he went. It had been Noah's dream to score movies, and he spent most of his freshman year of college burning CDs of his original compositions and sending them to movie studios. While studying at Julliard when he was nineteen, a producer found him buried underneath a pile of sheet music and gave him a shot.

That shot had given Noah his big break and had earned him his first Academy Award nomination for Best Original Score.

For a nineteen-year-old kid to be nominated for such a prestigious award opened a lot of doors for Noah. People started calling him. The following year he moved out to LA. His sister, Tally, moved down from their hometown in Napa, and they shared an apartment together. Noah was lauded again for his next score and was nominated for just about every award there was.

And he won.

At twenty, he set the record for the youngest ever composer to win an Academy Award, and to top it off, he took home the award for Best Original Song as well.

He had been working consistently for the last nine years in Hollywood, never failing to turn a score in on time, and never receiving one negative review for his compositions.

So, he had no idea why he was struggling so much with this score. It was due by Christmas, and he owed the studio an original song for the end credits.

He was officially nowhere.

Noah still lived with his sister, only now she and her girlfriend had bought a condo together, and Noah lived in their guest room. Really, his bedroom was his studio, and he slept on a pull-out couch in the corner.

He had been writing in there for months to no end, so it was no wonder he had spontaneously decided to jump on a plane.

Noah was working on a movie called "The Last Hope", a historical drama centred on the Irish Potato Famine, and the mass social and political change that went through Ireland in the mid-1800s. Noah's brief was a dramatic, intense, emotional score that would add weight and depth to the film. The film was to end on a positive note, which would feature the mass migration of the Irish for want of a better life, and the original song that Noah was meant to be writing would be an uplifting song of hope and triumph over adversity.

It sounded wonderful on paper.

But in reality, Noah was at a standstill, and his deadline was approaching even faster.

He had seen a show on the West End the night before, just wanting to listen to the music, and listen to the musicians who knew their craft so well. He had then been drinking in a bar and watching a sport on the TV that he didn't really follow.

And then he had found himself wandering down Shaftsbury Avenue at five in the morning. That was when he had spotted the "Piano Man Wanted" sign in the window of the West End Piano Bar.

Noah had always been a piano man first and foremost. And he did need an instrument to practise on when the inspiration hit. Noah had not expected to see such an incredible instrument in such an establishment, and the owner seemed to have no clue as to why Noah would be admiring it.

Did he not know that he owned a Steinway D-274? The beautiful instrument had to be worth something like two hundred grand. How on earth had he managed to get it into the bar?

Noah was desperate to play on it. He had not played on such a piano since his Julliard days. There was no way he was ever fitting this sort of piano into his little studio in Tally's condo.

"Do you play?" the owner, Pete, had asked.

"A little," confirmed Noah as he ran his fingers over the ivory. A shiver ran down his spine.

"I am looking for a piano man," Pete said casually.

"And I happen to be a piano man," replied Noah as he got down at eyelevel with the piano.

He knew he would have looked entirely ridiculous, but Rachmaninoff had recorded his all his sessions on this type of piano. God, it was a beauty.

"Give me a demonstration, and I'll give you the job," Pete gestured for Noah to sit down.

Seemed only fitting he played Rachmaninoff on a Steinway. He only needed to play the first four bars of his Piano Concerto Number 2 before Pete's jaw was on the floor and he was begging Noah to take the job.

"What on earth are you doing in a London pub, mate?" Pete asked him. "You could be making real money with skills like that!"

"I don't want your money, Pete," assured Noah. "I want your piano. I just want to play this piano, and I will work for free."

Again, Noah's actions floored the portly pub owner. "No wages?" he asked in disbelief. "You'll play like that for no wages?"

Noah nodded. "I am not entirely altruistic. I am in London to work. I am writing some music."

"You can have the whole day to play like that," Pete stammered. "I'll just need you to play the classic theatre songs at night. You know, "Memory", "The Music of the Night", and the like. One of my girls, Sophie, sings in the pub every few nights so she'll accompany you."

"That's fine," Noah replied. He could make it through a few show tunes in the evening. He would have ample time during the day to craft on this magnificent instrument.

The two men had shaken hands, and Noah had pulled out his sheet music to immediately get to work. He played, arranged, and jotted down ideas, as he tried to find the right sound for the movie.

Noah had a bad habit of getting lost in his work. Of concentrating so hard that entire days could pass by and he would forget to eat.

There was a reason why, at twenty-nine, he was still living in his sister's guest room. His mother depended on Tally to ensure that Noah didn't starve.

Noah then realised that he had left the country without telling his mother. Oh, that would not be a fun conversation.

Four hours passed, and shortly after nine in the morning, a red headed woman and her young daughter came into the bar erratically. The woman seemed hysterical, and he could see the emotion and tears upon her face.

If she was not holding the hand of a kid, Noah might have been afraid that she was crazy. So he did his best to ignore the distraction, and get back to his work.

He pulled out his phone, and FaceTimed Tally. She answered immediately, thought Noah could see that she was in bed. LA was seven hours behind him, and he just realised it was the middle of the night.

"Sorry," he apologised.

Tally looked at him disapprovingly. She lauded those three minutes she had on him as his older sister and liked to scold him. "You couldn't call when you landed?"

"I found a piano I like. Tally, it's a Steinway!" Noah said enthusiastically.

"Tell Noah to shut up," murmured Tally's girlfriend, Vanessa, who was in the bed beside her. "I have Pilates in like four hours."

Tally got out of bed and walked into their kitchen, turning on the light as she went. "So, you like this piano?" she prompted.

Noah smiled at her. "I've been playing around and written something. Can you listen?"

"Of course," Tally invited.

Noah placed his phone down on the stood beside him and began to play the tune that he had come up with. It was harsh, but passionate, his fingers flying over the keys. But no matter how well he played it, the music sounded generic, like every other emotive score there was. It wasn't original, and it certainly wasn't up to the standard that he was known for delivering.

Noah abruptly stopped, hitting the keys impatiently, before immediately regretting losing his temper on a Steinway.

"It's crap, right?" he looked down at Tally's face on the phone beside him.

He saw the honesty in her face immediately. Tally wasn't blown away. She pursed her lips apologetically, before agreeing, "Yeah, not your best."

Noah picked up his phone and slouched against the piano. "I'm screwed, Tally."

Tally frowned and shook her head. "You're not screwed," Tally promised him. "You just haven't figured it out yet. You like this piano, right? Keep playing, and you'll find something you like. The right tune will come. It always does. Anyway, I've got to go. Call me later, okay? I love you."

Noah would have to keep playing. He had signed a contract. And he did not feel like welcoming in the New Year with a freaking law suit.

"I love you, too," he muttered, before he disconnected the call.

Upon putting his phone away, he noticed that the red headed woman was now standing behind the bar with Pete, and her daughter was set up at one of the bar tables with a colouring book.

He wondered if there was a school break in England at the moment ... or if it was even legal to have a kid in a bar.

Now that he was not talking to Tally, he could hear that they were talking about him, and commenting on how strange he was. Noah knew that he probably seemed pretty eccentric.

But it wasn't strange to work for no wages if you were wealthy enough not to need them, was it?

"What sort of nutter would work for no wages?"

His ears pricked up as the woman spoke about him. Noah did not know what a nutter was, but he was smart enough to understand the context of her sentence.

"The kind who is on a deadline and has perfectly good hearing," Noah called out to them, catching them both by surprise, as though they weren't aware that being the only people in the darn room made their voices carry.

The woman looked far more alarmed than Pete, and Noah felt badly for embarrassing her. Noah found himself staring at her in her self-conscious state and looking at her more closely than he had when she had first walked in the door of the bar.

She seemed young, but she didn't necessarily look it. Not that she had wrinkles or grey hair, but the lack of sleep, and the redness in her eyes from crying did make her seem older than she probably was. Noah wondered why she had been crying.

She looked average in height, short next to Pete, and she seemed a little too thin. Perhaps the way she carried herself made her seem smaller. She honestly looked run down and exhausted, her shoulders rolled forward in defeat.

This poor girl was having a hard time.

Underneath everything, though, there was a vulnerability about her that Noah found a little endearing.

"Sorry," she uttered quietly, nervously playing with a section of her long, red hair.

Noah looked away from her then, bringing his attention back to his piece. Maybe if he played around with it a bit more, instead of abandoning it, he could find something in it to make it work.

Throughout the morning, Noah found himself looking up as the girl moved about the bar, cleaning tables and wiping down the chairs. He wanted to speak to her, to introduce himself, and to ask her name, but he felt bad for embarrassing her, and he didn't want to make it worse, so he kept his mouth shut.

She seemed to actively avoid him anyway, not once looking in his direction. Noah really had embarrassed her.

The little girl was called Maddie. That was what Pete called her when he handed her a broom that was nearly twice her height. Maddie took on the opportunity and got to work helping her mother, while being entirely useless.

Maddie did look very much like her mother. The same light red hair, only hers was brushed neatly into a pony tail. She wore a school uniform, which raised the question he had as to why Maddie wasn't in school.

Noah continued to play, only he got further and further away from his own work and started to play some of his favourites instead. It was how he procrastinated. Some played on their phones. Noah played Mozart.

Midway through the Piano Concerto Number 21, he heard her phone ring, and she answered it, finally giving Noah her name.

"Hello, Sophie speaking."

Noah saw the look of dread on her face. He had never been so curious about someone else's business before. He was worse than his mother.

He noticed Sophie look to Maddie as she spoke, and Noah deduced that the phone call had to be about her. From what Sophie was saying, Noah also assumed the caller was from Maddie's school.

Maddie had refused to go to school?

Sophie ended the call looking completely stressed. He found himself feeling really sorry for the poor woman,

As soon as she put her phone away, Sophie met his eye, and she saw that he was watching her. Noah immediately looked away, and returned his attention to his notes. He only pretended to write so that he could hear the next exchange. Dear God, what was wrong with him?

Was he really so uninspired that the business of a random Englishwoman and her daughter was important to him?

"I won't go tomorrow. You can't make me. I hate it there!" Maddie told her mother angrily.

If that had been him at her age, and he had spoken to his mother like that, he would have received a slap around the ears. Hell, if he spoke to his mother like that at twenty-nine then he would receive a slap around the ears.

But in hearing what Maddie was protesting, Noah could immediately empathise. There had been a time when he was a kid where school was the worst thing ever. Most kids felt like that at some point or another.

Sophie looked incredibly frustrated, and completely worn down. "Maddie's it's school, not prison. They only want to help you!"

"They all treat me like I'm dumb," Maddie moaned.

Noah watched as Sophie slumped down in her chair, looking like she was on the verge of tears. "Maddie, you are not dumb, and there is nothing wrong with needing a little help."

Maddie's poor mom looked done for. She was exhausted and emotional and no energy to check her kid for talking to her with such an attitude. But he did know how Maddie felt.

A lot of Noah's teachers had thought he was dumb, too, at varying points throughout his education. And having grown-ups look down on you as if you were stupid were some of the most demoralising times in Noah's childhood.

Noah forced himself to focus. He needed to stop playing the music of other composers, and he certainly needed to stop behaving as though he was a nosy neighbour peering over the fence for a bit of gossip. He was in London for one very specific purpose.

To write his damn score.

Sophie and Maddie's issues were none of his concern.

CHAPTER 3

As soon as the night shift started, Sophie moved Maddie into the backroom with her schoolbag, and left her with some fish fingers and oven chips for dinner, and Sophie's phone for entertainment.

Sophie got changed into her night uniform, which basically consisted of a white singlet top with Pete's logo, and a black, denim skirt.

Holly and Amy, two of Pete's waitresses, arrived promptly for their shift at five. The minute they walked into the backroom, Sophie could see the questions on their faces.

"Babes, who's the spunk? Pete reckons he's got himself a piano man. Certainly, a lot better looking than the last one," Holly giggled. "Being forty years younger doesn't hurt either."

Aside from Sophie, Holly had worked at Pete's the longest. She was a perpetual student, completing her third degree, this time around in environmental studies.

Amy had got a job through Holly. They both shared a flat with two other people. Amy was Australian and was in London on a working holiday. Sophie could not even fathom having the sort of freedom and a lack of responsibility to pick up one's life and move to another country.

"I don't know," murmured Sophie. "I haven't spoken to him. I sort of put my foot in it and embarrassed myself in front of him, and so I've been successfully avoiding him ever since."

Holly and Amy hung up their bags on the hooks.

"I am so jealous. I wish I could sing," Amy complained, "then I could slip him my Snapchat." She pursed her lips thoughtfully. "Might do it overtly anyway. You only live once."

Sophie had spent the best part of the day deliberately avoiding any sort of eye contact with the new piano man, and so she hadn't really taken the time to appreciate whether or not he was good looking. Both Holly and Amy seemed to whole heartedly agree that he was.

Oh, what did it matter if he was? There was a huge reason as to why Sophie had not been paying attention to the piano man today, and she was sitting contently on the old sofa, munching on a fish finger.

Holly seemed to read Sophie's mind as she noticed Maddie sitting quietly.

"You not at school again today, Mads?" Holly asked Maddie, placing her hands on her hips.

Maddie blinked, her large brown eyes a picture of innocence. "Nope. I hate school. I don't go anymore."

That was a new one, and it hit Sophie like a punch to the gut. God, when she was a kid, school was just where you went on a weekday! There was no debating! On the very rare occasion, she could successfully fake a stomach ache, but really, she would not have dreamed of simply refusing to go into school.

"Best get you an apron then," Holly said sternly. "Since waitressing is all you'll amount to with that attitude."

Sophie appreciated Holly trying to help, but Maddie would not grasp her meaning. Helping out at Pete's was a jolly holiday for Maddie. For Sophie, it was a terrifying glimpse into Maddie's future if she didn't find a solution to this refusal.

Sophie wanted so much more for Maddie than what she herself had managed to achieve.

"Holly, leave her," Sophie uttered.

Holly and Amy both offered Sophie looks of sympathy as they headed back out into the pub, leaving Sophie alone with Maddie.

Sophie knelt down in front of Maddie and lifted her chin with her index finger. It had been a hard day for them both, and it was far from over.

"I want you to have a go at your reader while I'm working. Miss Forster told me the other day that you should be able to work out the words. It's an easier level for you. I will read it with you again in the morning before we go to school. Do you think you can manage that?" Sophie did her best to sound calm and tender, without her usual frustrated, on the brink of crying, stressed voice.

Maddie's readers were the easiest ones her teacher could source. Lots of simple, repetitive words. But just getting her to attempt the sounds was like pulling teeth.

Maddie's innocent expression turned sullen, and she scowled at Sophie. "I don't want to read books for dumb people!" she hissed.

Sophie sighed exasperatedly and stood up. "I give up," she said in anger, and then immediately regretted it. It wasn't right for Maddie to hear her mum 'give up'. "Maddie, you're not dumb. Where are you getting this word from?" Sophie demanded to know.

Maddie glared at Sophie. "It's a dumb person book! And I only do dumb work. I am dumb!" she growled.

Sophie forced herself to take a deep breath. That word had to be coming from somewhere, and she would find out the source at the meeting tomorrow morning.

Even then, she knew it would only get harder and harder for Maddie. She was in Year 3 now. It was much easier to hide her modified work schedule when she was in Reception and Year 1. Kids her age noticed when someone was doing much simpler tasks.

God, if only she would practise, she might start to catch up!

"Your food is getting cold," she said quietly, before kissing the top of Maddie's head, and leaving her in the backroom.

The pub was much busier now. On any given night, but especially as Thursday led into the weekend, there were always large crowds gathering as they waited for their evening shows to begin.

Holly and Amy were already on the floor in their sections, collecting food and drink orders from customers. Sophie knew that she needed to keep her shit together now. On the odd occasion, if she was able to put a smile on her face, customers would leave her a few quid in thanks for her service.

Pete was working the bar, and shamelessly flirting with the suits who were in for a drink after work. She found that quite a lot of men didn't mind it when a gay man complimented them. It was good for their egos.

Over on the stage, she could see that the mess of sheet music had been collected and put away, and the new piano man was at work officially, playing the piano tune of "Can You Feel the Love Tonight" from "The Lion King". Oh, Sophie loved that musical. She desperately wanted to take Maddie to see it one day when she could afford it.

From in and amongst the crowd, Sophie could now properly look at him without fear of him noticing her obvious staring.

His hair was dark and unkempt, but in that fashionable way that told Sophie he had put some product in it at some point. He did have blue eyes. She had remembered those from when he had looked at her earlier in the day. Sophie had always liked blue eyes.

Beck had blue eyes. As much as she hated to admit it, she had always thought they were attractive. Unluckily for Maddie, she had inherited Sophie's brown eyes.

The piano man was dressed casually, wearing only a fitted grey skivvy, and dark skinny jeans. His trainers looked expensive, and they were expertly working the pedals of the piano.

He did look very fit, and she could see the definition in his arms through the sleeves of his skivvy. Gosh, Holly and Amy were right. He was a cutie.

Taking a deep breath, Sophie grabbed her notebook and pen, and worked her way through the crowd into her section, approaching her first table.

Four men in suits welcomed her with a smile.

"What can I get for you gentlemen?" Sophie asked cheerfully, plastering on a smile.

Sophie's shifts always ended at ten o'clock, even with the rush. She needed to relieve her babysitter, or, which was more often than not, she needed to get Maddie home to bed.

Maddie often fell asleep on the sofa in the backroom around her bedtime anyway, and Sophie always looked in on her. She hadn't told Maddie's school about this, as she was afraid it would make her look like an even worse mother than they already must have thought she was.

But really, what was she supposed to do? She was a single mother, and blessed Pete was the only employer who would ever put up with her coming and going as she did.

The pub was quieter anyway, but there always was an additional rush of customers when the shows finished at half past ten – quarter to eleven.

Sophie gathered up Maddie's things and packed them into her schoolbag, noticing, of course, that she had not touched her reader. Sophie then gently woke her and lifted her into her arms. Maddie wrapped her arms around Sophie's neck, and her legs around her waist, as she rested her head on her mum's shoulder.

Sophie struggled doing this now. It was much easier when she was smaller. But she would not begrudge the poor thing. It was late, and she was tired.

Sophie made the rounds, saying goodbye to Pete, Amy, and then to Holly.

Holly kissed Sophie's cheek. "See you later, babes. Text me when you're home, okay? I hope Mads is alright tomorrow."

"Me too," Sophie prayed. "I'll text you later."

Sophie hesitated at the door of the pub. It would be rude not to say goodbye to him, and she really was behaving like a child if she was still embarrassed over a silly, throwaway comment. She turned, juggling Maddie's weight, and made her way over to the stage.

He noticed her approaching, and he stopped playing to listen to her, turning his body on the stool to face her.

"I'm Sophie, by the way," she introduced herself. "I really am sorry about this morning. I didn't mean to be rude. I'm not a rude person, I promise."

To her surprise, he smiled. He had a nice smile, the kind that reached his eyes. "I promise you; I haven't thought anything of it," he assured her. "It's nice to properly meet you, Sophie. I'm Noah."

Sophie breathed a sigh of relief. "Well, I'm glad. Thank you. And welcome, I suppose. You play beautifully," she complimented him sincerely. "But I'm sure you hear that all the time."

Noah chuckled. "It's mostly my mom telling me, but it's nice to hear all the same. Thanks." He then changed the subject. "Pete tells me you're a singer?"

Sophie felt a blush fill her cheeks. "Uh, no, not really. I sing, but I'm not a singer."

Noah furrowed his eyebrows. "You sing, but you're not a singer?" he clarified.

"Well, a singer is a professional," Sophie said bashfully.

She could tell that Noah had an opinion on that subject, but he didn't press her, and she was glad for it.

"You'll be up here tomorrow night, won't you?" he checked.

Sophie nodded, adjusting Maddie.

"Any requests?"

"Well, what do you know how to play?" she asked.

Noah seemed to find this very amusing and Sophie had no idea why. "You tell me what you want to sing, and I'll play it. No problem."

Cocky. "Okay then, do you know "Memory"?" she asked.

Noah nodded. "You got it."

"Alright, well, I will see you tomorrow then. I had best get her home. This is Maddie, by the way. She's often with me." Not by Sophie's choice, but that was not a conversation to be having with a stranger.

"Are you okay carrying her? Do you need me to help you get her to the car?"

That was actually sort of gentlemanlike. Sophie was truly surprised. "Oh, no, this is London, Noah. We use the tube," she joked. Of course, a lot of people did have cars, but finding a parting spot that didn't cost half of your rent was a near impossibility, not the mention the fact that cars themselves were expensive things to own.

"You're going to carry her to the subway?" he asked in disbelief.

"We mums are stronger than we look. See you later then," she said dismissively, turning her back on him, and making her way to the door.

Chapter 4

S ophie manically spread some marmite on a bit of toast and shoved it in her mouth as she threw Maddie's lunch together.

They were late, all because Sophie thought it was a good idea to push her luck by trying to get Maddie to do her reader when she woke up. Maddie, being Maddie, had thrown the monster of all tantrums, and had locked herself in the bathroom, flatly refusing to come out if Sophie was going to take her to school.

After begging, pleading, and bargaining with a bloody eight-year-old for half an hour, Sophie had given in once again, and had promised to take her into the city to spend the morning with Pete while Sophie had her meeting.

That meant a trip into town, and back out again, and if they did not leave soon, Sophie was going to be incredibly late, and she did not want to start that meeting off looking like a bad mum.

It would end that way, but she didn't want it to start that way.

Sophie looked around her tiny flat as she searched for her hand-bag. God, it was a tip. She hadn't folded her sofa bed back up, and her bedding was everywhere. There were dishes in the sink, and baskets of washing everywhere. It was a perfect representation of the chaos that was her emotional state at that minute.

"Maddie, let's go!" Sophie cried, taking the piece of toast out of her mouth to shout.

Maddie trotted out of the bathroom having just brushed her teeth. She was not dressed in her school uniform and had instead picked out her own mismatch of floral clothing. She had fixed her own hair with butterfly slips and a flower crown headband, though her hair still needed a good brush. Sophie didn't have time to care.

She found her handbag in one of the washing baskets and she fetched her keys from the kitchen bench. Taking Maddie's hand, she locked her front door behind her, and they raced down the stairs together.

What was poor Pete going to say when Sophie arrived? She had never asked him to look after Maddie by himself before, and she did not have courage enough to text him on the off chance he said no. Selfishly, she needed to put him on the spot so that she could get to her meeting on time.

At twenty-five past eight, Sophie and Maddie rushed through the door of the West End Piano Bar.

Pete was standing at the till counting the takings from Thursday night, and there was music in the air as Noah sat at the piano, once again surrounded by his mass of sheet music. He did stop to look up at her when she arrived, and he offered her a small smile.

Sophie was too stressed to return the greeting.

"Pete, I'm in a jam!" Sophie panicked.

Pete frowned immediately, before he read between the lines as he looked down at Maddie. "No," he said flatly. "I can't be responsible for a child. There's alcohol in here. She needs to be watched by her mum."

"She's not going to get drunk, Pete!" exclaimed Sophie. "Please, I'm desperate. I've got to get back out to her school for a nine o'clock meeting, and I've already had a bloody terrible morning and I didn't even get to drink my tea!" she guilted.

Sophie did think regretfully to the cup of English Breakfast that was steeping by her kettle undrunk.

Releasing Maddie's hand, Sophie clasped hers together. "Please," she begged.

"Sophie, I've got things to do this morning," Pete said regretfully. "I've got to duck out in a minute anyway as I've run out of limes. Can't you take her with you?"

Sophie was about to lose it. Not out of anger for Pete, but just because it was like some people didn't realise that Sophie had already tried the obvious choice, and that had resulted in her angel daughter transforming into a demonic dictator.

"I'll watch her if you want."

Both Sophie and Pete turned around to look at Noah. Neither had noticed that he had stopped playing as their conversation heated with Sophie's anxiety.

Ordinarily, Sophie would never had accepted his offer. Noah was essentially a stranger, a man off the street from God knows where, who just happened to be a talented pianist.

The stress and panic had clearly compromised her judgement.

"Really?" cried Sophie.

Noah stood up from the piano and walked over to Sophie and Maddie. Sophie then realised that this was the first time that she had seen Noah standing. She had not realised he was so tall. He stood at least a head taller than her.

"You have no idea how much this means to me, Noah, really," Sophie gushed gratefully. "She won't be any trouble, she really is a good girl," she promised. Maddie was especially good when she got her way. It was for Sophie that she liked to be a terror.

"It's no trouble. I'm just going to be sitting on my a ... butt all day anyway." Maddie giggled at his near faux pas. Noah looked down at Maddie, a curious expression on his face. "You don't mind hanging out with me while I work, do you, kid?"

Maddie looked up at Sophie for an answer, and Sophie nodded encouragingly. "You've got all your bits in your bag, and I packed you some lunch. I won't be long at all. I'll be back just as soon as I'm finished at school." Sophie looked back to Noah. "Thank you so much. If you need to call me, use the pub phone. My number is the second speed dial." Sophie kissed the top of Maddie's head. "Alright, I've really got to go. Be good, sweetheart. I love you."

"Love you, too, Mummy," chirped Maddie.

Sophie shot one last smile at Noah before she took off in a run back out of the door and down Shaftesbury Avenue.

Sophie was late, but only just. The bell ran for nine o'clock as she dashed down the path into the school building. Sophie had run all the way to the tube, and she had run from the station to Westgate Primary School.

She was hot, sweaty, and looked every bit the picture of a useless parent who could not keep an appointment.

Sophie sucked in quick, successive breaths in an attempt to calm her pulse so as not to sound like she was dying as she approached the ladies in the office.

She tucked the hair that had fallen out of her twist behind her ears and smoothed out the navy dress that she had put on to specifically appear smart and professional.

"Good morning, Sophie," greeted Belinda, the school secretary.

Lovely Belinda did not know all the parents by name, only that Sophie was up at the school so frequently.

"Morning," puffed Sophie. "No Maddie today. I'm sorry to be a pain."

"No, no, not a pain at all," promised Belinda. "I'll pop it into the system now. If you head right into Margaret's office, they are waiting for you." Belinda pointed her around to the principal, Mrs Margaret Hibberd's office.

Sophie's heart was still thundering, and she was unsure now if it was because she had run so far, or because she was unfathomably nervous. The latter was more likely.

The principal's door was open, and as soon as she approached, she was waved in.

Three woman were convened in a pleasantly decorated office, all seated on the small arm chairs that was positioned around a coffee table before the large desk.

Margaret Hibberd was accompanied by Ann Peddington, the assistant principal, and Judy Forster, Maddie's classroom teacher.

Sophie was the youngest one in the room by at least twenty years, and so it was dreadfully difficult to approach such a meeting feeling like an equal. But she knew she needed to. She knew she needed to get on with it, just as she got on with everything else, and be an advocate for Maddie.

No matter how much that girl drove Sophie up the walls, she would always, always be a champion for her.

"Good morning, Sophie. How are you?" greeted Margaret. She stood and adjusted her glasses before she shook Sophie's hand.

Sophie hoped it wasn't sweaty. "Fine, thank you," she said quietly.

"Please, do have a seat." Margaret gestured to the empty arm-chair.

Upon sitting down, Sophie noticed the dozens of documents that had been collected and displayed on the coffee table for the meeting.

Madeleine Cartwright was on all of them.

Sophie's stomach clenched.

"How did you go with Maddie this morning, Sophie?" Judy asked.

It almost felt as though she were in a deposition, or a courtroom, as she had three pairs of eyes on her as she prepared to answer the question.

"She refused again," Sophie confessed, purposefully not disclosing the fact that she had locked herself in a bathroom for half an hour. "She is being minded by a ..."again, another iffy detail, "friend, while I'm here."

Judy's face fell, though both Margaret and Ann did not look shocked.

"Sophie, we wanted to have this chat with you this morning to check in regarding Maddie's progress. I know we only had a meeting like this at the end of the last school year where we did recommend to you that Maddie repeat Year 2," Margaret reminded her.

Sophie had not forgotten weeping in this very room at that thought, and subsequently begging that Maddie not be left behind.

"I assessed Maddie's reading last week, on one of the days she was at school," Judy continued, pulling out one of the documents. "It was a Reception level book, designed to help the students recognise high frequency words through repetition." Regretfully, she said, "Maddie couldn't read it. She had no idea, I'm afraid. I read the book to her to test her comprehension, and she couldn't remember any of the details of the book at all."

Sophie felt her stress and emotions rising, and she willed herself not to cry in this office again.

"I know you are well aware of Maddie's academic struggles," interjected Ann. She wore a sympathetic expression. "I know it can seem overwhelming, and confusing, and, of course, worrying when you hear that your child is not where they need to be."

Sophie did appreciate the effort of understanding.

"I know she is behind," Sophie replied as bravely as she could. "I am doing everything I can to encourage and motivate her to attempt her readers and try to work out words."

"We know you are, Sophie," said Margaret kindly. "I want you to know that we have no intentions of leaving Maddie behind, and letting her slip through the cracks."

Sophie's lower lip trembled as an unfamiliar feeling of relief bubbled to the surface.

"What Judy, and Maddie's previous classroom teachers have compiled here are key assessment pieces for you to have. Judy has also kindly put together some activities for you to do at home to work on each of these areas. There is simple reading/comprehension, letter/sounds, high frequency words, handwriting, maths," listed Ann as she began to sift through the folders.

And Sophie's heart sunk right back to where it had been at the beginning of the meeting. As much as she could beg, there was no way she would be able to get Maddie to do anything at home.

"Thank you," Sophie said tentatively. "But I should tell you that Maddie will be very reluctant to attempt this. She calls it 'dumb people work'. She's very aware that her work differs to that of her peers."

Reluctant was putting it nicely.

"With Maddie absent, I've been having several discussions with the class about respect for others, and compassion," Judy assured Sophie. "And Maddie is not the only child with differentiated work."

That told Sophie that some little snot had said something nasty to Maddie about her work.

The expressions on all the of the women's faces then changed, and Sophie tensed. This was not all that they wanted to speak about.

"What we also need to discuss with you this morning is Maddie's social development," Margaret continued delicately.

Her social development?

"Maddie's school refusal is clearly a very serious issue," Ann continued. "Her attitude towards school is uncommonly negative."

"Maddie also struggles very much in connecting with her peers," Judy added carefully. "Absences do not help, but she has yet to make any friendships within the class. Her teacher from last year held these same concerns about Maddie's lack of social interaction, and her lack of effort to engage with others socially."

Sophie was trembling as another weight was piled on top of her already struggling shoulders. Not only was she struggling academically, but now they were terribly concerned about her socially?

What the hell was she supposed to do for her poor child?

"Maddie doesn't follow classroom instructions, often because she is not listening. While her articulation is excellent, she often doesn't communicate effectively, and loses her temper at me or her classmates. Her lack of social interaction has meant that she often has no concept of how others are feeling."

Sucker punch.

Sucker punch.

Sucker punch.

It was right about now that she wished that Beck was not such a knob, and actually wanted to be a hands-on parent, so that he could shoulder some of this stress and anxiety.

"While we do have an excellent wellbeing officer at school, it is our recommendation that you seek advice from a paediatrician and a child psychologist about the possibility of assessing Maddie for autism spectrum disorder. We do have an association with an excellent child psychologist who we can refer you to in order to help start assimilating Maddie socially, with the hopes that it will assist in her school refusal and in meeting her academic milestones." Margaret produced a business card from amongst the documents and held it out to Sophie.

Sophie could not manage to get her brain to tell her arm to reach out for the business card. It was because she was quite certain that she had had a small stroke as soon as she had heard the word 'autism'.

Chapter 5

Noah had never seen a more panicked and stressed woman in his life before seeing Sophie like that, and that observation included his mother on Thanksgiving.

He was raised better than to sit by and watch someone in need, and the least he could do would be to watch the kid while she coloured so that her mom could do whatever was so important.

"I'm Noah," he introduced himself. "What's your name?" he asked, knowing the answer already.

Maddie looked up at him with a curious, but oddly confident expression. "Maddie," she replied.

Noah was still entirely unused to the English accent. The sweet way that Maddie talked seemed completely angelic, but his instincts told him that this kid could be a little hellraiser.

Although, the fact that she was wearing two different flower patterns on her clothes, and a gypsy crown on her head was entirely deceptive.

"Is that short for Madison?" he queried.

Maddie shook her head. "No, Madeleine," she corrected. "But Mummy only calls me that when she's really, really cross."

Noah chuckled. "I bet you never get your mommy really angry, do you?"

Maddie shrugged her shoulders. "You talk funny," she observed nonchalantly.

"So do you," Noah countered.

"No, I don't," Maddie protested.

"You don't sound like any of the kids from where I come from," Noah continued. "But all of those kids are in school right now. Why aren't you?" Before he gave Maddie a chance to answer his question, he turned his back on her, and walked back over to the piano. A quick check over his shoulder saw him notice that Maddie was trotting along after him.

"Because I hate school!" Maddie cried after him. "I don't go to school anymore because I hate it."

Noah knew that all kids hated school at some point. There might have been a hard test coming up, or studying for finals was sucking, or you had your fitness test coming up in gym and you were going to embarrass yourself in front of the entire cohort.

But why would a kid her age hate school? Wasn't school at her age all cutting and colouring and eating paste?

"You've got to go to school, Maddie. It makes you smarter." Noah pulled out a chair next to the table that was closest to the piano.

Maddie immediately settled in it, unzipping her backpack in the process. "They all say I'm dumb," Maddie replied, pulling out the colouring book that she had been doodling in the day before.

Noah knew exactly how that felt. Today, he knew teachers wouldn't use those words. Kids might. Kids could be assholes. But teachers wouldn't.

When he was a kid, teachers did use words like 'dumb', and even worse, 'retarded'. Noah had crapped out on every test there was. He had been the dumb kid that was in all the bottom groups with modified work that even a monkey could do. He had been this close to be held back before anyone had even bothered to ask why he wasn't performing well.

"There are a thousand different ways to be smart, kid," Noah told her. "You've just got to find what you're good at."

Maddie organised her coloured pencils and began to diligently colour in her complex picture of an owl in perfect rainbow.

Noah hopped up onto the stage and sat back down at the piano as Pete waved to him from the door.

"I'll be back in ten minutes," he called out. "Just heading out to get the limes."

Noah nodded.

Shuffling his notes, he found the piece of sheet music that he was currently working with, and that he did not hate in this moment. Using a pencil, he scribbled down some secondary ideas before he began to play, closing his eyes and imagining the movie as he did.

He had the raw footage on his computer. The studio didn't know that, and he would probably be fired if they did. He was supposed to score the film in the studio for legitimate legal reasons, but his reputation allowed him to bend the rules a little.

Or break the whole damn lot and steal an uncut production. Better to ask forgiveness than for permission.

He had been watching it in his hotel room last night. Without a score, movies, in Noah's opinion, had no soul. He could often hear in his mind what the movie needed to sound like when he watched scoreless scenes.

Sometimes, just quietly, he could hear what movies should have sounded like if they had been scored poorly.

The scene in his mind was between mother and child, and tender moment of understanding of the famine, and what that would mean for their family. In his head he could hear a dolcissimo tune, something sweet and soft.

Noah began to play, stopping and scribbling down the notes as he changed his mind. In five minutes, he had managed a full page of music, and he did not think it was total horseshit.

What time was it in LA? Noah checked his watch, wondering when he could call Tally to get her opinion.

"Can you play the song you were doing yesterday?" Maddie suddenly asked.

Noah turned to look at her and frowned. "What song?"

"The song," she repeated. "You know ..." Maddie proceeded to hum the exact melody of one of his discarded ideas from the day before.

Exactly.

How on earth had she managed to recall that? He had probably played it once, before cursing under his breath and chucking it.

"That one was nice," Maddie added wistfully as she selected her orange pencil to colour with.

Noah stared at her, still completely bewildered as to how she'd managed to hum something he'd written and abandoned within two minutes. "This one?" Noah played a bar, deliberately knowing one of the notes was wrong.

Maddie looked up at him and shook her head. "No, that's not right."

Noah played the bar again, this time correctly, and Maddie smiled.

"Yes, I like that."

Noah liked it, too, except it sounded more romantic that dramatic. He might put it in his bottom drawer for a rainy day.

"How did you remember that, Maddie?"

Maddie shrugged. "I heard it yesterday."

She heard it for all of two minutes, and then had probably heard a thousand other things between then and now. That still didn't explain how she was able to recall it perfectly and discern between an incorrect and a correct bar.

"Have you ever had a piano lesson, kid?"

Noah probably was barking up the wrong tree. It was more likely that Maddie has just really liked that tune and had had it stuck in her head for twenty-four hours. That happened to Noah all the time, and more often than not with songs that he hated.

But his curiosity was piqued.

"No," replied Maddie.

"Come up here with me," he encouraged, shuffling over to the left-hand side of the stool so that Maddie could sit on his right.

Maddie sat down excitedly, and immediately reached out her hands to start pressing down keys.

"Wait!" Noah said firmly.

Maddie hesitated.

"This is a holy instrument; do you understand that? This is a Steinway. And one day, you'll see a shi – cheap – keyboard, and think back to when you had the privilege of playing your first lesson on a Steinway."

Maddie blinked, and stared at Noah with an expression of confusion.

Yes, he supposed he did sound like an insane person. Noah's dad had a collection of wine and if he or his sisters so much as disturbed the dust on the holy relics there would have been hell to pay.

"Pretend the keys are like a kitten," he said, changing his approach. "Think of this piano like a kitten, and how softly you would pet it. That's how nicely you will touch the keys. Do you understand?"

Maddie nodded, and gently pressed her fingers down on the keys, eliciting a jumbled collection of sounds. She beamed as soon as she did it. Her reaction made Noah smile.

His mom had organised piano lessons for him when he was five years old. He was in kindergarten, had no friends, and his teachers believed that he was slow.

Cleverly, Joy Bentley had convinced Noah's father, John, that the motor skills he would be learning from taking the lessons would help him in learning to catch a football.

Noah had never picked up a football in his life.

The piano had been the thing to stick.

Kids didn't learn if people assumed they were stupid. Kids went on the assumptions of adults. If you taught a kid with high expectations, you were encouraging them to reach up, not to settle for someone else's opinion.

Noah pressed down on middle C. "This note here is middle C," he began, already having flashbacks to Mrs Novak as she taught him the first note in church. "The piano keys are like an alphabet from A to G. What comes after C?"

"D," Maddie replied.

Noah then pressed down the note to the left of middle C. "Which would make the note before C ...?"

"B."

"That's right," Noah commended. "Do you want to learn an easy song?"

Maddie nodded excitedly.

"This is the first song I learned to play on the piano when I was five years old. It's called "Heart and Soul". Have you ever seen the movie "Big"?"

"No," replied Maddie.

Noah tsked."What the hell is your mother teaching you, kid? Anyway, I'll play it for you, so you know what it is meant to sound like, and then I'll teach you the chords. Watch." He positioned his right hand. "On your right hand it starts, C, C, E, E, A, A, C, C ..."

Noah slowly played "Heart and Soul", and strangely enjoyed going back to his youth in playing something so nostalgic.

Maddie watched mesmerised.

Noah finished after a minute, and then removed his hands from the keys. Just as he was about to position Maddie's hand over the correct keys, she took it upon herself to place her left hand correctly on the notes.

She then started to play the higher section by herself, following the same rhythm that Noah had only just performed. She did not miss a note and played it exactly how Noah had.

Noah's jaw unwillingly dropped as he watched her, and as he did, his suspicions seemed more and more likely. But he could not help but join in, add in the lower bass notes with his left hand to complete the duet.

What was crazy was that it could have easily been him playing. Not a seasoned, professional multi-instrumentalist, and a child who had never even touched a piano up until three minutes ago.

"Maddie, how did you do that?" Noah asked in disbelief as the song finished.

Maddie's brown eyes were innocent, as though she had no real idea of how brilliant she had just been. "Do what?" she asked.

"How did you play that song?"

"I watched you and then I did it," she said simply, as though it was something that any person could do.

Noah quickly played a few bars of something random, this time a discarded melody of his, something that she could have never heard before. It was much more complicated than "Heart and Soul" and would truly test his theory.

Maddie watched, and moments later, she was repeating the same tune note for note.

The reason behind Noah being such a talented multi-instrumentalist was because he had an eidetic memory. In addition to his ability to recall images, he possessed and auditory eidetic memory. Every sound, every song, every conversation that he had ever had was stored in his mind. If he ever had an idea for a melody, it never left him.

These talents had bubbled to the surface when he had taken his first piano lesson with Mrs Novak. He did what Maddie had just done. He had watched, listened, and repeated exactly what Mrs

Novak had played, and absorbed the lesson book so quickly that he was teaching her by the next week.

"Maddie, how come you don't like school?" Noah asked quietly.

Maddie's excited expression quickly turned sour, and Noah hated to take that preliminary joy from her. "Because they all think I'm dumb," she stated plainly.

"Do you think you're dumb?" he countered.

"My teacher only gives me dumb people work. I hate it," Maddie complained angrily.

That didn't answer his question, and Noah had suspicions that Maddie didn't honestly know how to answer his question.

Noah had been labelled slow. He had been labelled dumb and stupid and was far behind his peers. Tally had been his only friend and were it not for his twin sister beating the shit out of anyone who picked on him, he might have refused to go to school just like Maddie was.

Only Noah wasn't stupid. He was bored out of his mind. And bored kids did not try.

It took a creative outlet, like learning the piano, to get him to actually want to use his brain academically.

Noah and Maddie continued to play together for the rest of the morning, with Noah abandoning his work in favour of songs that Maddie liked from her favourite Disney movies.

It turned out that Maddie actually had a beautiful, hauntingly innocent singing voice. It reminded him that Sophie would be singing tonight, and he gathered she was the source of Maddie's singing talent.

The door to the bar opened again just after eleven-thirty, and Sophie entered looking absolutely devastated. She looked like someone had just shot her damn cat. What the hell had happened?

Chapter 6

Sophie hadn't always lived as she did. There was once a time when she really had not understood the value of money.

She had grown up in a posh London neighbourhood, had attended one of the best private girls' schools in the city, and had been set up for great success by her obscenely wealthy parents.

While they had not been at all receptive to the idea of Sophie studying for a degree in musical theatre, they could still brag to their friends that Sophie had been accepted into the Royal Academy of Dramatic Art.

Of course, Sophie had only been there three months before she had found out that she was pregnant with Maddie, and her parents promptly had informed her that she was no longer welcome in their house if the situation was not quietly handled.

And so, Sophie had not spoken to them in eight and a half years, and for the first time since their last conversation, Sophie found herself standing outside of their Kensington townhouse.

She stared up at her childhood home in awe, wondering if it had always been so grand. Either way, it was home to two of the grandest, most pretentious people to ever walk to earth.

She could remember her mum, Susan Cartwright, screaming at her, telling her she was too stupid and too irresponsible to properly care for a child. Her father, investment banker, Paul Cartwright, had promptly threatened to cut her off completely.

As soon as she had left this house, he had followed through on his threat, with all her bank accounts emptied and cancelled.

Sophie had promised herself that she would never return to this house, especially to ask for money. She would rather drink toilet bleach then let them be right about her.

But Sophie knew that was selfish, and that Maddie's needs were more important that her pride.

The minute she had left the meeting at Maddie's school, she had phoned the child psychologist that had been recommended to her. If Maddie was autistic, as scary as that word was, Sophie wanted her diagnosed and put in whatever programs were necessary to help her to be where she needed to be.

Life should not be hard at Maddie's age, and Sophie needed to do whatever she could, even if that meant making her own life harder.

But that conviction went out the door when she was informed that without health insurance, the psychologist fees would be no less than eighty pounds and hour.

Sophie didn't have ten pounds spare at the end of the month, let alone eighty pounds a week for a psychologist.

It was this mindset that had almost put her into an emotional trance and had taken her off the tube at what once was her normal stop.

She needed to swallow her pride, and she needed to speak to her parents, no matter how hard it would be.

Sophie opened the gate, and approached the white front door, only made more intimidating by the brass door knocker in the shape of a lion's head. Sophie climbed the stone steps and took the door knocker in her hand, knocking twice. She could hear the sound echo within the two-storey foyer of the house.

A minute or so later, the door was opened, and Sophie was met by the face of her mother.

Susan Cartwright was every bit the proud society wife. Her life was dedicated to supporting her husband's career by throwing parties and schmoozing the wives of other rich men over ten o-clock in the morning champagne cocktails at the country club.

Her face was youthful thanks to the quarterly nips and tucks by her plastic surgeon. Her hair was once the same strawberry blonde colour of Sophie's, but she had long kept it a perfectly highlighted blonde, and it had not changed since Sophie had last seen her. It was styled into a perfect bob, with not a single strand out of place.

Her figure was kept by daily Pilates, and weekly tennis matches, and she accentuated it with a navy blouse and a white pencil skirt. She always wore heels, even at home, and today was no different.

"Sophie," she remarked, surprise in her voice, but not evident on her smooth face. "I was not expecting you. You might have telephoned."

"I need an appointment to see you, do I, Mum?" Sophie murmured.

"Do not mumble, child. I cannot cope with mumbling. Elocution is a virtue." Nevertheless, Susan opened the door, and Sophie entered into the house.

Considering she had lived eighteen of her twenty-six years in this house, it felt like she was walking into a stranger's house and she ought not to touch anything.

Her mother always entertained guests in the front sitting room off the foyer. Sophie was taken through to the back of the house and into the pristine kitchen.

It did not escape her notice that there were still pictures of her hanging in her parents' house. She didn't know how that made her feel.

Susan boiled the kettle, and it looked utterly strange to see her own mother doing that.

"Do you still take tea?"

"An English Breakfast teabag will do, Mum," Sophie replied, truly trying not to be any trouble.

A teabag, of course, was an offensive idea, and Susan disregarded it. She spooned tealeaves into her blue china teapot and collected the matching cups. She set them on a tea tray, before filling the teapot with boiling water from the kettle.

Sophie did have to admit that the aroma was comforting. She carried the tea tray over to the little breakfast table and set it down before Sophie, before she poured her tea through a silver tea strainer.

"How have you been, Mum?" Sophie asked nervously.

Susan arched a perfectly threaded brow. "How have I been?" she repeated. "Sophie, please do not insult my intelligence in leading me to believe that you have appeared on our doorstep purely for a chat," she sneered. "You look dreadful," she said bluntly, gesturing to Sophie's appearance. "That outfit looks like it came from an Asda bargain bin. Your skin looks awful. Your hair looks like it hasn't seen a stylist in a decade. You look underweight. Sophie, are you a ... street person?"

Sophie closed her eyes as each one of her mother's insults slapped her across the face. She couldn't be rude. She was here for Maddie.

"My dress is from an Asda bargain bin, Mum. Five pounds fifty," Sophie said dryly. "My skincare routine is washing my face with a flannel. I cut my own hair. I might be underweight, I don't know, but that's not on purpose. And no, I am not homeless." She did her best to keep her voice calm and her thoughts coherent. "Aren't you curious about your granddaughter?"

Susan did look taken aback before she collected herself. "A girl, was it?" she said nonchalantly.

"Yes," confirmed Sophie. "I named her Madeleine, but I call her Maddie." She took a sip from her teacup and hated to admit that it was one of the nicest cups of tea she had had in a long time.

"Shortened names are for children, Sophie," Susan said disapprovingly.

"Well, Maddie is eight," Sophie replied cynically. She could feel the tension rising between them, and Sophie knew that she needed to get her request over and done with before she lost it at her mother. "I came to talk to you about Maddie. She's having some problems."

"Is she ill?"

"No," Sophie replied quickly, not even wanting to contemplate the idea. "Maddie's teachers believe that she might have autism."

Sophie was still absolutely terrified of the idea that Maddie would have any sort of label, but she was glad that she was able to say the word without crying.

Susan's brown eyes widened. "Autism?" she repeated. "Your daughter is intellectually disabled?"

Sophie could not honestly tell if her mother was trying to be offensive or not. "No," she replied defensively. "She is not intellectually disabled. Autism is not a disability, and I do not even know if she has it. I've … I've been referred to a psychologist and a paediatrician –"

"Ah," Susan realised. "But of course, I should have known. You need money."

She said it in such a condescending way that it made Sophie's skin crawl, as though she was taking pleasure from making Sophie feel inadequate.

Swallow your pride, Sophie willed herself. Maddie needs this.

"Mum, I need eighty quid a week for the psychologist. I can't afford it, and Maddie needs it. Will you help me?"

Susan placed her perfectly manicured left hand on top of the table, on which a ring the size of Jupiter sparked on her wedding finger. She continued to appraise Sophie, looking over every inch of her with a holier than thou expression on her face.

"No."

She said it with such finality that Sophie was certain that she might have hallucinated the whole thing, but she could see it on her mother's face.

"What?" gasped Sophie.

"You have made your bed, Sophie. Now you must lie in it."

Sophie shook her head in disbelief. "Mum, I could feel down the back of your bloody sofa and find eighty quid!" she exclaimed. "It will be no skin off your nose! And it is to help your granddaughter! I am not here because I want to be!"

"Exactly," replied Susan calmly. "You wanted your own life, go on then. Your parents are not bank machines, Sophie."

"I have not asked you for a single thing in eight years," Sophie said angrily. "I am not asking for money for clothes or to go on holiday. This is Maddie's education I am talking about."

"And what of your education?" countered Susan. "We paid a small fortune for that, and look where it got us?"

"Oh, fuck off, Mum," Sophie snapped.

Susan recoiled. "Language!" she cried. "How dare you speak to me in such a way!"

"Don't worry, this was a waste of both of our time." Sophie stood up abruptly from the table. "Do you know, one day you are going to wake up and realise that all the bloody Botox and Dom Perignon in the world won't make up for what you missed out on. I'll find a way to make the money without you. I've managed by myself all this time anyway."

Sophie stormed out of her parents' house and was back out onto the street within moments, inhaling the air that was free from potpourri and prejudice.

She did not feel worse about herself. It was hard to feel less than she already did. The flaws that her mother pointed out, Sophie was already well aware of.

But if anything, it was confirmation that she had done the right thing all those years ago. Getting out of that house was the best thing that she could have ever done for her own sanity.

As Sophie got off the train and climbed the stairs back up onto Charing Cross Road, she decided then and there that she was going to ask Pete to work weekends. If she worked all seven days, she hoped that the extra money would help her to scrape together what she needed to send Maddie to the psychologist.

The poor kid wouldn't get a weekend at home, but at least she would be taken care of academically.

The idea continued to hit her though. Maddie might have autism. It hurt her very soul to think of Maddie having anything that would make her life harder than it had to be. She already missed out on so much and she didn't even know it.

She walked back into Pete's and she was certain that she looked just as devastated as she felt, and she needed to get a handle on her facial expression before anybody asked any questions.

She looked around for Maddie and found her colouring bits laid out on one of the tables, but Maddie was not sitting there. She was sitting up at the piano next to Noah.

Noah was looking at Sophie, questions and concern on his face. Maddie noticed her moments later, and a huge smile filled her face.

That was enough to shake Sophie out of her mood.

Maddie clambered off the stage and immediately ran towards her, weaving in between the tables before reaching her. Maddie crashed right into Sophie, who needed to brace herself on Pete's door to keep herself from toppling over.

"Mummy! Mummy!" she cried excitedly. "Guess what?"

"What?" Sophie asked, putting on just the level of excitement that Maddie needed.

"I can play a song!" she squealed; her face filled with delight.

"You can?" Sophie enthused. Bless Noah. He had probably taught her chopsticks or something.

"She sure can," interjected Pete, who appeared from the back-room. "Quite the little musician is your Miss Maddie."

Maddie twirled confidently as she accepted the compliment. Sophie shot Pete a grateful look for going along with Maddie's story.

Maddie seized Sophie's hand and subsequently dragged her towards the piano. Sophie had to twist awkwardly to stop her hips from bumping into chairs. Maddie stopped just before the stage, before she climbed back up next to Noah.

Sophie smiled at Noah, her heart swelling at the confidence and the joy that she could see in Maddie's face as she settled into the piano stool. She had never seen Maddie look so happy to be applying herself to anything.

Just as she was about to start cheering for Maddie's clumsy rendition of chopsticks, Maddie began to play.

Play.

Sophie's eyes widened in pure shock as Maddie's fingers began to play a tune. Noah joined in on the duet, playing the lower notes as Maddie took responsibility for the higher notes. She knew exactly what to do.

"Have you got this, kid?" Noah asked her.

Maddie nodded, and Noah stood up from the piano, leaving Maddie to play alone. She placed her left hand where Noah's had just been, and she started to play his portion of the duet.

It was a song. A real song. It was the bloody song from "Big" and Maddie was playing it by herself.

Sophie had planned on cheering, but instead she burst into tears for the seventh time that Friday morning, and clapped with pure pride, clasping her hands together and holding them under her chin.

Noah jumped down from the stage and came to stand beside Sophie.

"I had no idea she could do that," whispered Sophie in utter shock, unable to wipe the smile from her face.

"She can do a whole lot more," replied Noah. "I thought you might like to know your daughter is not stupid."

Sophie's head snapped around to look up at him. "I beg your pardon?"

"Kids can't just do what she's doing. She's not stupid. Quite the opposite, in fact. If she's got what I'm pretty sure she has, she's ten times smarter than any kid in her class. Smarter than her teacher, probably. Kid's just bored out of her damn mind."

Sophie's brain shorted out with her second stroke of the day. "How could you possibly know that?" she managed to choke out.

Noah shrugged his shoulders and put his hands in his pockets. "She's like me," he said simply.

CHAPTER 7

"What do you mean she is like you?" Sophie asked, still absolutely overwhelmed after her marathon of a morning. Sophie could not comprehend any sort of explanation that led her to believe that Maddie was exceptionally bright.

However much she would want this for Maddie, she had just been told by three seasoned educators that Maddie needed to see a paediatrician and a psychologist for suspected autism!

"Look, I can't be sure, and I don't want to get your hopes up, but Maddie reminds me so much of myself as a kid," Noah replied.

"How?" pressed Sophie.

"Look at what she's doing," Noah gestured to Maddie at the piano. "Has she ever had a lesson?"

Sophie shook her head. Maddie had never even expressed interest in taking music lessons. She saw that piano every day and had never even asked to have a play with it.

And now she was playing it, knowing exactly which keys to press to complete her song.

"Have you ever heard of an eidetic memory before?"

"Is that sort of like a photographic memory?" Sophie asked.

"Not sort of, exactly," clarified Noah. "I have an eidetic memory. What that means for me is anything I see, anything I read or watch or notice, once I understand it, I never forget it," he explained quietly.

Sophie had heard of people with a memory like that. They were able to pass examinations without studying. What Sophie would have done to get through her GCSE's with an eidetic memory.

But was Noah actually suggesting that Maddie could have a memory like that? Wouldn't Sophie have noticed? Wouldn't that mean that she could know her readers without having to look back at the pages?

"I also have an auditory eidetic memory," Noah continued. "It's helped me a lot in my career as a musician. Anything I hear, any conversation I have, any sound, any tune, any melody, anything I come up with, I'm never at risk of losing it in my short-term memory. I don't forget it."

"Well, that's extraordinary, Noah, but I don't understand how Maddie could have something like this without me knowing," Sophie said, shaking her head.

Noah crossed his arms across his chest and called out to Maddie. "Hey, kid."

Maddie stopped playing and turned to look at Noah.

"Play your mom the song I was working on today. The one that you liked," Noah encouraged.

Maddie nodded excitedly as she turned back to the keys, her little tongue sticking out of her mouth as she concentrated. She found the right notes, and she began to play a proper, professional piece of music.

If Sophie's jaw could hit the ground, it would have. She fumbled getting her phone out of her back pocket so that she could take a video. She needed to show this to Maddie's teacher.

"She doesn't know the notes yet. She can't read the music. But she saw what my hands were doing. She remembered the tune, and she understood the process. That is how she's able to reproduce it now," Noah said proudly. "When you have this ability, it's very easy to become overwhelmed, to lash out, and to definitely check out. You're smarter than a lot of people, and it takes something really interesting to draw you out of your head."

The piece of music was short, and Maddie finished with a delighted grin.

"Take a bow, kid," Noah instructed, demonstrating from next to Sophie how it should look.

Maddie climbed off of the stool and took an excited bow. "Was I good, Mummy?" Maddie asked as she jumped off of the stage.

Sophie voice broke with emotion as she said, "You were excellent, sweetheart. How talented you are! It is about lunch time though, so why don't you sit down and eat your sandwich."

Maddie bounced back to the table where her things were laid out and fished her lunchbox from her backpack.

"I just sat in a meeting where I was told that my daughter might have autism, and that her teachers were going to do everything they could to keep Maddie from falling even further behind than she already is," Sophie told Noah.

It seemed strange really, to have such a sudden rapport with this relative stranger. Sophie did not even know Noah's surname. And yet this man had managed to make Maddie smile bigger than

Sophie had seen in months with something as simple as a music lesson.

After that meeting this morning, and her horrid argument with her mother, Sophie felt just about as run down and defeated as a person could.

Noah was dangling hope in front of Sophie's eyes, like a carrot on a string, and she was desperate to bite down. What she would give for such a simple solution, and to believe Maddie was brilliant.

"I'm not a professional shrink or anything. I'm not a parent. I don't even have a pet," Noah replied. "But I think there's something pretty special about your kid, Sophie. I know it's none of my business, and you'll do what you've got to do." Taking a deep breath, he finished with, "A piano lesson literally drew me out of my head, and it started a lifelong passion in music. I was able to channel my ability, and nobody ever had the balls to call me dumb again."

For the rest of the day, Sophie felt like she had millions of images and memories filling her head as she tried to comprehend what an actual clusterfuckof a day it had been!

She watched Maddie like a hawk, having urges to show her copies of Pete's menus and then quiz her of what the seventeenth word in the first section was to test Noah's theory.

But then, the issue still was that Maddie couldn't read.

Or could she? Could it be true that she was just bored?

As the night shift started, Sophie heated Maddie a chicken and leek pie and set her up in the backroom like usual. She needed to stop thinking about this if she was going to get through the next five hours with her sanity still intact.

Holly and Amy arrived, chatting about their days, and Sophie did her best to sound interested. Tony and Charlie, Pete's bouncers, also arrived, ready for the usual business of a Friday night.

Sophie got on well with the bouncers, and they looked after the girls inside.

"Alright, Sophie?" asked Tony. Both Tony and Charlie played rugby at the weekends, and had the perfect, muscular, stocky builds to be chucking drunks out of the pub of an evening.

"Alright, Tony." Sophie smiled. "Let's get on with it."

Friday nights were always very busy. Even at five o'clock, the tables were filling, the floor was busy, and the barstools were occupied. There were people dressed for the theatre, people dressed in their work attire, and people who just came to Pete's for a good time.

Noah was at the piano, once again with his own bits put away. He was playing the instrumental version of "Memory", and Sophie suddenly remembered that she was supposed to be singing tonight. In all her stress during the day, she'd completely forgotten that she was singing. She hadn't packed anything nice to wear. She had not even brought any makeup with her.

She would look like a tired, frumpy mum in the waitress uniform singing a cover of Elaine Page.

"Pete!" hissed Sophie, as she darted around the bar and ran up to him.

Pete was in the middle of flirting with a tradesman in a paint-stained denim shirt and was none too pleased that Sophie had interrupted him in pouring a Guinness. The head was far too big, and Pete had to abandon it.

"I'm ugly!" Sophie whispered.

"And I'm a flaming homosexual," he replied. "But what's that got to do with the price of tea in China?"

"Don't sass me," snapped Sophie, rolling her eyes. "I didn't bring anything with me to wear. I can't go up there looking like I do. I can't sing tonight. Do you mind very much?"

"Jesus, Sophie, you don't need a nice outfit ... excuse me, darling, would you shag her?"

It took Sophie a second to realise that Pete had turned to the tradesman that he had been flirting with and had asked the man to appraise her.

"Yeah, why not? She's fit," he said casually, and Sophie just about wanted to die of embarrassment.

"There you are, problem solved. Make me proud tonight." Pete grinned smugly as he turned his back on Sophie and started to pour another Guinness.

But as she came around the bar with her pen and notepad, the tradesman appeared in front of her, smiling cheekily.

"So, are we going to do this?" he asked excitedly.

Sophie was going to kill Pete. "Lord, no," she said firmly, before she scurried out of his path, and into her section of the pub.

For next few hours, Sophie took orders, fetched drinks and nibbles and was as charming as she possibly could be.

She had been hit on four times, three of whom were so drunk that they probably only minded that she had breasts and would have taken anyone. Lovely Tony promptly escorted out anyone who could have gotten remotely handsy.

Just after eight o'clock, the door to the pub opened as new customers strolled in, and Sophie had to hide the urge to groan out loud.

"Bleeding haemorrhoid, one o'clock," whispered Holly as she moved past Sophie with a tray of drinks in her hand.

"I saw him," Sophie replied under her breath.

Beck walked with the confidence of a man six and a half feet tall. In reality, he was just over five foot nine, but compensated for his lack of height with daily gym sessions, and weekly rugby matches.

What Sophie had ever seen in him, she would never understand. It was more likely that she had been suffering from a brain tumour between the months of August and November nearly nine years ago.

Beck worked as a plumber, and him and his mates liked to frequent the West End Piano Bar on a Friday night, though not because they enjoyed musical theatre.

Beck strolled over directly to Sophie's section, and plonked himself down at a table that had only just been vacated by a group of girlfriends off to the theatre.

"Do you want me to take care of him?" Holly asked over Sophie's shoulder. "And by take care of him, I mean spit in his drink and drop an ice bucket on his balls?"

Sophie chuckled. "No, it's alright. I've got it."

Sophie walked over to Beck's table and clicked her pen. "What'll it be?" she asked disinterestedly.

"Nah, come on, Soph," complained Beck. He ran a hand back through his blond hair, deliberately flexing his arm as he did. "Aren't you going to ask me about my week?"

"Are you going to ask me about Maddie's week?" Sophie countered.

Beck's face fell and he huffed, Sophie taking the wind out from under him. His mates beside him were whispering under their breath. Sophie honestly wondered what a man's mates thought when a father refused to step up for his daughter.

"She alright?" Beck muttered.

Sophie could have told him about her meeting that morning. She could have told him about the eighty quid a week for a psychologist that she would need, but in knowing Beck, he would cry poor, even though he would easily drop that amount on beers and take aways this weekend.

In a lot of ways, Sophie did seriously resent Beck for his ability to just shut himself off from Maddie. He saw her occasionally, mostly on holidays when his parents asked to see her around Christmas and Easter, and on school holidays. Beck had never gone out of his way to ask Sophie for any visitation. He had never been to Sophie's flat to see Maddie. He had never read a school report. He would not know the name of any of her teachers.

Beck wouldn't even know that Maddie struggled at school.

And in the same respect, Sophie was glad, because it meant that she didn't need to share her daughter, and that, she knew was selfish. Her poor girl really didn't know what it was like to have a dad.

"She had a piano lesson today," Sophie decided to say. "She loved it."

Beck nodded. "How much are those costing?"

Sophie's eyes flashed up to Noah, whose eyes immediately diverted from her. "I don't know," she replied. "I will have to see."

"Music's expensive, alright? Don't go shelling out if she's just going to drop it five minutes later."

Beck would never volunteer to pay, and Sophie knew better than to ask him.

"Three pints, love," demanded one of Beck's mates impatiently. "On you go."

Beck snapped out of his mood just as soon as his mind got back onto their evening activities, and a cheeky smile spread across his face. "You're looking especially fit in that skirt, Soph," he flirted. "You working out?"

"Yes, I run," Sophie replied facetiously, writing down their order, before turning away from them. "After your eight-year-old twenty-four hours a day, seven days a week, you fucking wanker," she added under breath.

Sophie took Beck's order up to Pete, and rested on the bar.

Pete grabbed three pint glasses, before saying, "I hope your pipes are ready, Sophie. You're on."

CHAPTER 8

S ophie nervously tucked her loose hair behind her ears as she approached the stage. She didn't know why she was so nervous. It wasn't as though this was the first time that she was singing in the pub.

Although, this was the first time in a very long while that she was singing with a piano man, and not just as CD playing the music in the background for her.

Noah caught her eye as she climbed up on stage, and he offered her a reassuring smile. Sophie smiled back at him, before she turned her back to him and adjusted the microphone, switching it on.

She cleared her throat, and the attention of all the patrons turned to her. It was very much a full house, and she deliberately avoided looking over to Beck and his mates.

"Good evening, everyone, and thank you so much for joining us here tonight at the West End Piano Bar," Sophie welcomed, her voice surprisingly steady considering how her heart was hammering. "My name is Sophie, and the talented musician behind me

is Noah, our new piano man. We hope that you enjoy the music."
She turned her head and gave Noah the cue, and Elaine Paige's
signature tune began to play.

"Midnight not a sound from the pavement. Has the moon lost
her memory? She is smiling alone. In the lamplight, the withered
leaves collect at my feet. And the wind begins to moan."

Sophie sang as clearly, and as beautifully as she could muster,
and the room was silent as they listened to her. When she started
to sing, the nerves melted away, and she felt the loudest, and the
most powerful that she ever could be.

It was hard to think of a professional actress in a theatre only
a few doors down was performing the same song in Cats and
being lauded for it, while Sophie sang in a pub for minimum wage.
She put in as much passion and effort to the song as any other
Grizabella would.

"Touch me!" she cried. "It's so easy to leave me. All alone with the
memory, of my days in the sun. If you touch me, you'll understand
what happiness is. Look, a new day has begun."

As Noah played the final note, Sophie opened her eyes, and
remerged from her mind as the sounds of applause and cheers
sounded from around the pub.

Sophie looked back to Noah and he was beaming at her, clapping as well while he shook his head, almost in disbelief. Sophie
grinned, laughing, as she bowed.

"Do you know 'Don't Cry for Me Argentina'?" she asked him.

"Yes, ma'am." Noah chuckled and he turned back to the piano.

Sophie sang her favourite from Evita before finishing up, and
making Noah take a bow as well. She then hurried off stage,

thanking the customers for their compliments as she passed them, and quickly claiming her note pad and pen again.

"You sound so good every week, Soph," Beck said slightly slurred as he came up behind her.

Beck placed an arm around her, and Sophie quickly shrugged him off. "Thank you," she said tensely. "Keep your hands to yourself. You're sloshed."

Beck rolled his eyes. "Why can't you be nice to me?" he whined, beer on his breath.

Sophie hatedthe smell of beer on a man's breath. "Letting you touch me is being nice, is it?" she challenged, raising her eyebrows. "Bugger off, or I'll have Tony toss you out."

Sophie honestly had no idea why Beck insisted on trying his luck with her every other week. He had not succeeded since they were a couple for five minutes all those years ago. He had a casual girlfriend every so often, and whenever he mucked things up, he liked to try and get attention from Sophie.

He was a child, really, and he needed ego-stroking attention. Perhaps Sophie had been a child as well when she had been interested in him, but parenthood had made her grow up. It was a shame that it had not done the same for him.

"I like you even more when you're mean, Soph," Beck purred in Sophie's ear, and Sophie pushed him away.

She immediately caught the eye of Tony, who was on the door, and she waved him over. Tony made his way through the crowd and took Beck immediately by the upper arm.

"Hey!" he cried. "Hands off, mate! I'm just talking to her." Beck's thrashing about was no good for Tony's hulking frame, and he was promptly removed from the pub. His mates quickly followed after him, no doubt off to continue their night at another establishment.

Sophie had the sudden need to wash her hands, and she darted around Pete's side of the bar and pumped some liquid soap into her hands.

"Gorgeous, as always, Sophie," Pete complimented as he added tonic and a lemon wedge to a glass of gin. "That painter I was talking to before is not gay unfortunately, so if you still wanted a quick shag, I could definitely arrange that. You probably need it."

"Do you know, Pete? Discussing my sex life in any other work environment would probably be classed as sexual harassment," Sophie informed him casually, quietly praying that nobody had overheard him.

Pete laughed. "I look out for my girls, don't I?" He elbowed her playfully.

"You listen here, Peter," Sophie said firmly. "I do not want a shag, quick or otherwise." She tapped the side of his face in a playful slap, and Pete grinned. "What you can do for me, however, is let me work weekends."

Pete frowned. "Weekends? You want to work seven days a week? You're not struggling are you, Sophie?"

Struggling? Always. "Maddie's got to have some appointments which are going to cost me a bit, so I need some extra hours. Do you think you could manage?" she asked hopefully.

"For you, anything." He nodded. "I can only give you the nights, though. You know Holly and Amy work the extra day shifts on weekends."

"That's perfect," Sophie replied gratefully. "You're an angel, thank you."

At least that was a weight off of her shoulders. Stressing about finding an extra eighty quid a week would hurt a little less now.

Though Sophie usually worked until ten, as it was a Friday night, and they were indeed very busy, Pete begged her to stay. Sophie settled Maddie in the backroom, and she was fast asleep on the sofa, and so Sophie was able to work until midnight.

Although still technically open, the customers had thinned, and those who had been to the theatre had had their after-show drink and had gone home.

There were still a few men at the bar, and Pete was seeing to them as Sophie, Holly and Amy cleaned the floor.

With a cloth and spray in hand, Sophie was wiping down all the tables free from sticky alcohol and food crumbs. Holly was sweeping, and Amy was coming along behind them with the mop.

"I'm going to shoot my shot," Amy decided, her eyes on Noah.

Sophie looked up at Noah, and he was slouched over his phone at the piano, texting someone. She did want to speak to him before she went home, but it seemed Amy was going to get there first.

"What are you going to do?" Holly asked. "If you're bringing him home, can you please be quiet. Babes, I need some sleep."

Amy grinned and winked at her friend. "I'm just going to give him my Snapchat and grab his," she said innocently. Amy began to sashay her way over to Noah, taking her phone out of her back pocket.

Sophie and Holly stood together as they watched the exchange, though they were standing too far away to hear what they were saying.

"Quite cute though, right?" Holly asked Sophie. "An American and an Australian coming together in our city."

Sophie frowned and rolled her eyes with a smirk. "It's Snapchat, Holly, not a marriage proposal."

"But it's modern dating, innit?" Holly continued. "I'll more likely meet my future husband on Tinder than I will at a coffee shop."

"How are you going at meeting husbands on Tinder, Holly?" Sophie asked rhetorically.

Holly poked her tongue out. "Pretty, but dumb, seems to be my type." She laughed.

Amy turned away from Noah, and by the look on her face, she was disappointed. Amy came back over to Sophie and Holly and sighed in an annoyed tone.

"Babes, what happened?" Holly asked, concerned.

"Well, he is really nice, and really good looking, but I think he's a bit of a dinosaur," Amy complained.

"What?" both Sophie and Holly asked at the same time.

"I asked for his Snapchat, and he just looked at me, dumbfounded, and replied, "I'm twenty-nine"," Amy continued.

A snort escaped Sophie as she burst into a fit of giggles. Holly was no far behind as she clutched her sides laughing.

"It's not funny!" hissed Amy as she blushed a deep red.

Sophie and Holly tried their best to contain their amusement, but they still couldn't help but take the mickey our of poor Amy.

As the clock hit half-past twelve, Sophie was well and truly done and exhausted.

Holly and Amy said their goodbyes, and Sophie remained behind to speak to Noah. As soon as he saw her approaching, he smiled. He had such a nice smile, too.

"Thank you for tonight," she said gratefully. "I didn't have a chance to speak to you earlier."

"No need to thank me. You were doing all the heavy lifting," he complimented. "Can I ask you a question, though?"

Sophie nodded.

Shaking his head, Noah asked, "What the hell are you doing in a place like this when you could be singing in a theatre just down the street?"

Sophie bashfully looked away. "That's awfully sweet of you to say," she said tentatively.

"Sophie, trust me when I say that I know what I'm talking about. I work with a lot of talented people, and you are talented."

"Well, I could say the same to you," she countered. "You are equally, if not more talented than me, and are performing here as well."

"My baggage is a whole other story. Seriously though, how are you this good, and singing here? Don't get me wrong, Pete is a nice guy, but ..."

"Well, she's about this tall," Sophie held her hand up to her rib cage, "strawberry blonde hair, brown eyes, answers to 'Maddie'..."

"Oh," realised Noah.

Sophie shrugged her shoulders. "I'm a mum, and that means that some of my once upon a dreams are put up on the shelf. Of course, I wanted to be a stage actress when I was younger. I even studied it for a little while, but Maddie became my priority, and I don't regret it. Besides, thanks to you, I still get to sing my favourite theatre songs."

Noah grinned. "Well, I'll do my best for you. I mean it, though, Sophie. You are very talented."

"So are you."

"You aren't very good at taking compliments, are you?" Noah observed.

Sophie flushed once more. "I suppose not. I'd better get Maddie home, though. Trains are fewer at this time of night."

"Train?" repeated Noah. "You're still taking the train at this time of night?"

"It's fine," promised Sophie. "I only have to change once from the Piccadilly to the District Line. Takes us to Gunnersbury where we live."

Noah blinked. "I'll pretend I know what that means. Will you let me pay for a cab?"

Sophie vehemently shook her head. "Goodnight, Noah. I'll see you tomorrow."

Just as Sophie turned away, Noah stopped her, jumping off of the stage and placing his hand on her shoulder. "

"What about your number?" he asked. "Would you at least text me when you get home? I know we don't really know each other that well, but ... I make my sister do the same thing whenever she goes anywhere," he explained.

Sophie considered it for a moment before she nodded. She could see the genuine concern for her safety, and she did sincerely appreciate it. "Alright," she agreed. "Are you sure you don't want my Snapchat?"

Noah practically choked on the air that he sucked in as he laughed, shaking his head. Sophie grinned as well. "Oh, I felt really bad," he replied. "My sister's a middle school teacher, and all her kids are on Snapchat, so I just think it's weird for a guy my age to be on that sort of thing. Tally thinks I should be on Instagram, but I have never even taken a selfie in my life."

Amy was right. Poor Noah was a dinosaur, and Sophie found that really endearing.

"Give me your phone," Sophie instructed. "We'll take your first one."

Noah pulled his phone out and gave it to Sophie. A split-second look at the photo on his background showed her three similar looking women, all beautiful and smiling.

"Are they your sisters?" Sophie asked.

"Yeah," Noah confirmed. "All older, though Tally is only older by three minutes. She claims it though," he chuckled. "That's Tally," he pointed to the woman in the middle. Tally's hair was short, and bleached, and she had the same sort of smile Noah did; one that reached her eyes. "Casey is the middle child," he pointed to the sister on the left, with long, brown hair. "And Haley is the oldest." He pointed to the sister on the right. Like Tally, her hair was bleached, but she wore it longer, to her collar bones, and styled in beachy waves.

"I'm an only child. I always wanted sisters," Sophie said wistfully.

"Meet mine and you'll change your mind," he said decidedly, though with a humorous smile on his face.

Sophie giggled and tapped on his camera app, switching it to front camera. She almost changed her mind as she got a view of her face, but she was doing it for Noah. "Alright, smile!" she instructed, holding out her arms to the highest she could reach so that Noah could crouch into the photo.

Noah ducked into frame, and they both smiled, Sophie tapping on the screen to capture the picture. Sophie brought the picture back up and frowned as she looked at herself.

Her mother's comments rung in her mind as she looked at her uneven skin, and shadows, and untidy hair.

"Well, you look nice. I look dreadful. Delete it," she instructed.

Noah snatched his phone away. "Nope," he teased. "That's my first selfie. I'll treasure it. Might just make an Instagram now for the specific purpose of posting it."

Sophie's eyes flared. "You do that and I will hurt you!" she exclaimed, reaching for his phone. All Noah had to do was hold his arm up in the air for Sophie to be jumping for it like an idiot.

Noah laughed teasingly. "I won't post it, don't worry. Can I still have your number? I want to make this your contact picture."

CHAPTER 9

The next morning, Sophie sat with her cup of tea while Maddie munched away on her Weetabix watching a cartoon that she liked on the television.

Weekends were usually a time when Sophie liked to unwind from the stress of the week. She liked to hydrate, ready for a week of crying while fighting with Maddie about school and homework. She also liked to plan little fun things that they could do together so that Maddie's only childhood memories wouldn't be of Sophie screaming and crying about bloody school.

Sophie flipped through her phone as she drank and rolled her eyes when she saw that Beck had sent her a succession of suggestive and lewd drunk text messages, followed by a sheepish apology sent this morning. Sophie just deleted the thread. She would have liked to change her number, but she felt as though Beck had some sort of paternal right to be able to contact her.

She then smiled when she saw that Noah had sent through a text message this morning. She had kept to her word and texted him when she had gotten home the night before. She did think it was really sweet that he was concerned about her.

As soon as she opened the message, Sophie burst out laughing. Noah had sent her the picture that they had taken the night before, only he had photoshopped the Snapchat logo over her face.

This better? he had asked.

"What, Mummy?" Maddie asked, her mouth dripping with milk.

"Noah is being silly, sweetheart. Don't get the milk on the carpet, though!"

Sophie sent him back some laughing emojis and set her phone down. "Maddie," she said tenderly. She had been thinking about this all morning, and truly hoped that it would work. "Did you like having a piano lesson with Noah?"

Maddie nodded eagerly. "Yeah!" she cried. "It was so fun, and I was so good at it!"

Sophie beamed with pride. "That you were," she confirmed, with no hint of a lie. "What do you say I have a chat to Noah tonight about organising some piano lessons for you?" she suggested.

The pure joy in Maddie's face as she cried in delight made Sophie's heart swell. Maddie had never been more excited for anything in her life. Children needed to have activities and things that they excelled in. "Yes, please!" she exclaimed.

"Well, good. I'll speak to him when I go into work tonight. But piano lessons are going to cost money, you know. So, you do need to do something for me." Sophie tried to keep her voice positive. This was not meant to sound like a chore. "If you would like to have piano lessons," with Noah or whomever else was available, "then you need to go to school without arguing about it."

Sophie braced herself for a fight. She expected a tantrum. She expected Maddie to flip her cereal bowl over onto the carpet. She expected Maddie to call her names and to lock herself in the bathroom until Sophie gave in pleading and crying.

But Maddie didn't do any of that. She just smiled, and replied, "Okay." She then turned around and focussed her attention back on the television.

Sophie sat, stunned. Bloody hell, if she'd known all it would have taken was a piano lesson, she would have shoved her on the damn thing years ago.

Noah grinned as he received Sophie's laughing emojis in response to his picture, and he rolled over in bed to pull his charger out. It seemed really stupid, but it was nice to have a sort of inside joke with someone.

Noah knew that Sophie didn't like the picture, but he had no idea why. It must have been a girl thing to always crap on pictures of themselves. Tally's girlfriend, Vanessa, always expressed the same dissatisfaction, and spent hours editing and perfecting her pictures before they went up on Instagram.

She would still be torn to shreds by homophobic keyboard warriors, but her loyal fans would stick up for her. Vanessa Marino was a very successful singer, but before her career, she had been one of Noah's first friends at Julliard. When she had learned that his own sister was gay, she had found the courage to come out to him. Noah was honoured that Vanessa had trusted him with something so personal, just as he had felt the same way when Tally had come out to him when they were twelve.

Not long after, he had introduced Vanessa to Tally, and they had been together ever since. Their relationship was made so much more important by the fact that Tally had loved her before Vanessa was famous.

Noah had actually written the song that had launched Vanessa's career.

In return, neither Tally or Vanessa minded that Noah still lived in their guest room.

Noah looked at the original picture and wondered why Sophie didn't think she looked good in it. She was very pretty. She had to know that. He added the picture onto his text, and sent it through to Tally.

Meet my friend, Sophie, he said.

Tally responded promptly with a picture of her flipping the bird. Meet my friend. Her name is "it's fucking one o'clock in the morning, jackass", she replied.

Noah snorted.

Tally did shoot through another message quickly, though, and added, she's cuuuuuuuuuuuute, Noah and Sophie sitting in a tr-reeeeeeeeeee.

Noah rolled his eyes. She's just a friend, you moron.

Tally sent him back a wink emoji. It sounded like she really believed him.

Now leave me alone. I'm tired. PS Mom knows you've left the country byeeeeeeeeee xxxxxx

Noah's eyes flared and he gritted his teeth. Tally must have told their mom that he'd left the country, which had to mean that Tally had been in trouble for something else and had passed the anger firing squad onto him.

At twenty-nine, yes, they could still be in trouble with their mother, even though both of them hadn't lived at home since they were eighteen.

That only begged the question, why the hell hadn't his mom blown his phone up as soon as she found out? Or ... maybe she was going to let him sweat about it.

As soon as the thought crossed his mind, his phone started to ring. He dared to peek down at the caller ID and breathed a sigh of relief when he saw his dad's name.

"Dad," he answered immediately.

"Noah," replied John Bentley in a warning tone.

Crap.

"Dad," Noah said again.

"How's the score coming?"

It wasn't always the case, but music was something that Noah and his father really connected on. John had really made an effort some years ago to understand Noah's interest, and that act had changed their relationship for the better.

"I had a bit of block," he replied truthfully. "You know how small Tally's condo can get sometimes, so I decided to get out of town."

"Santa Barbara is out of town, Noah," John said dryly. "You left the damned country."

Noah noticed that his dad was speaking quietly, albeit firmly, and so he must have been hiding the conversation from his mother.

"I was going to call," he promised weakly. "It was a spur of the moment thing."

"Noah, what you don't get is that without you kids here, I'm the one who cops all the mom yelling," John hissed quietly. "It's been

World War freaking three here today. Tally's just told Mom that she and Vanessa are going to be in New York for Thanksgiving."

There was the explanation for how his parents had found out about him being out of the country. Traitor.

"And now you're a million miles and an ocean away, and I'm the one who gets yelled out for pure darn convenience!" John huffed. "By the way, your mother wants to know what hotel you're staying at, and the nearest four hospitals to your location."

Noah couldn't help but grin as he pictured his mother stalking around their house as she hunted for down his dad for someone to yell at. "I'm at the Savoy," he replied. "It's very nice. British 911 is 999, I already asked. And I've got no idea about the hospitals. By the way, I would like to point out that Casey is out of the country, too."

Casey, Noah's middle sister, worked as a photographer for National Geographic. She was on assignment year-round in some of the most remote, beautiful places in the world.

"Casey is overseas for work, smartass," John quipped. "And she always sends Mom her itinerary. The woman always has Case's hotel information in her cell just in case, and you can be darn sure she has a list of hospitals, too."

Noah sighed. "I'm sorry, Dad," he finally said, sincerely this time. "I hope I didn't worry you. I'm fine, I promise. My head was going to explode, and my score was going to be a piece of shit if I didn't change my environment. I found my way to this little piano bar in the middle of London. It's incredible, Dad. I'm working on a Steinway."

"A Steinway?" John replied enthusiastically.

Noah enjoyed speaking to his dad for the next half hour. He checked in with him about his work and then they talked through Noah's ideas for his score. They were in the middle of Noah's thoughts about the climax when he heard a static noise, before his mom's voice sounded.

"Noah? Is that you?" Joy Bentley desperately asked. "Hah! I've got you. Your father hid my phone, the bastard."

"Hi, Mom," Noah said guiltily.

"Don't you "hi, Mom" me, young man," Joy snapped. "Do you have any idea what you've put me through today?"

Joy Bentley was nothing if not dramatic. Though Noah wouldn't have her any other way.

"Mom, you know, the umbilical cord was cut nearly thirty years ago, right?"

Joy hissed. "Don't you sass me, Noah Bentley. You're never too old for a talking to. You leave Los Angeles damn county then you had better let me know! What if I needed a kidney, huh?" she challenged. "And the only person with my blood type is my beloved son, and I say, "Oh, Doctor, he's at his apartment in Burbank!" and they come back with, "Sorry, Joy, he's two million miles away, guess you're going to die!" Is that alright with you, Noah? Is my death alright with you?"

Noah shoved his face in his pillow to keep from laughing. If he laughed at her, it would beso much worse. His mom was just getting started. He could hear his dad in the background telling her to calm her crazy. He would be in trouble for that later.

"No, Mom. Your death isn't alright with me," Noah managed to say, by some miracle, with a straight face. "Though you do have three other kids to get your organs from, you know."

"If I want your damn kidney then I'll have your damn kidney, Noah John Bentley," Joy snapped. "But what do you care? You could have been lying dead in a ditch and I, your grieving mother, wouldn't have known because you never thought to call. Am I a burden to you? Is your poor mother's love a hassle? Because I am so sorry for bothering you."

Damn, she was laying the guilt on as thick as molasses.

"So, Tally's not going to be home for Thanksgiving, huh?" Noah changed the subject casually. "What a bitch. So selfish."

"And where will you be for Thanksgiving?" Joy countered.

Shoot. "Mom, I'm working!" he protested.

Joy cried out in agony, and any passer-by would think that his mother was suffering a gunshot wound by the sound that she made. Noah could hear his father groaning.

"Oh my God, I have failed as a mother. My children don't want to spend the holidays with me. Where did I go wrong?" Joy cried out rhetorically. "Casey's in Peru. Tally and Vanessa are in New York. You're in London. John!" Joy shouted. "I'm amending the will. It's all going to Haley!"

Noah smirked while rolling his eyes. "Mom, my kidneys and I will all be home by Christmas. My score is due then anyway."

"John, what is this buzzing, it's annoying!" Joy complained, and Noah could head his mom fussing with the phone. "Oh, you've got a message coming through from Tally!" she called out. "Mom and Dad meet your new daughter-in-law, Sophie, love you, see you at Christmas," she read out, before screaming with glee.

Noah nearly choked on his own tongue as he realised that Tally had sent that freaking picture through to their parents. His traitorous sister was really trying to get out of the bad books.

Noah made a mental note to set off their condo alarm every hour for the rest of her night. He had the code and could control it from his phone. Karma's a bitch.

"Who's Sophie?" Joy exclaimed excitedly. "Oh, John, look at how gorgeous she is! What beautiful eyes, and her hair is such a lovely colour. And look at her smile. You can tell she's nice by the way she smiles."

If Noah didn't stop her soon, Joy would have their wedding planned by dawn. "Mom! Sophie's just a friend!" he shouted.

"What?" Joy gasped, disappointment in her voice. "No, I don't think so. She should be your girlfriend. She looks like a pretty girl for you."

Noah groaned. "Check your meds, Mom. I'll see you at Christmas. I know it's in your power, but please don't track down Sophie's phone number and scare her off with your crazy. I love you. Bye." Noah ended the call before Joy could protest, and he rubbed his temples to delay the inevitable headache.

He needed to get dressed anyway and get back to writing. As crazy as that phone call had been, he did only have until Christmas to submit the score. That meant recorded with an orchestra, and he didn't have squat yet.

As he did get dressed, he thought about that picture, and how it had made its way across the Atlantic Ocean. He felt like teasing Sophie, and he opened up their text thread.

My mom thinks you're pretty by the way, he sent.

Sophie replied in an instant. Tell your poor mum she needs to see an eye doctor!

Noah chuckled, before opening up the app that controlled the condo's security system. Casually, he tapped the alarm, and got on with his day.

CHAPTER 10

Luckily for Sophie, her usual babysitter was available, which meant that she was able to go into work sans Maddie for the first time in a long while.

When she opened the door of the West End Piano Bar, she saw Holly and Amy setting up the tables for the night ahead. It seemed so strange to not be the first one in aside from Pete.

"Afternoon, babes," greeted Holly cheerfully. "Nice to see you on a Saturday."

Sophie returned her smile. "Afternoon, girls. I know it's odd. Let me pop my things down and I'll give you a hand." Sophie gestured to her handbag.

"We're right, Sophie," assured Amy. "Nearly done. Sort yourself out and then come and help me figure out a way to seduce the hottie piano man."

Amy looked wistfully at Noah, who was sitting at the piano with AirPods in, blissfully unaware he was being stared at. Noah looked like he was concentrating hard. He wasn't playing, but writing, as he listened to whatever was in his ears.

Sophie darted into the backroom and hung her handbag up on the hook, before returning back into the pub. She gave Pete a quick hug and came back to join Holly and Amy on the floor. Noah had still not looked up from his notes.

"Do you think I should just straight up ask him out?" Amy asked them. "I don't want to seem desperate, but maybe he'd respond to that. It's not like he's going to text me if he's not on Snapchat."

Sophie's cheeks flushed, but neither Holly nor Amy noticed. It wasn't like she was doing anything wrong by texting him, was it? Amy was only twenty, after all. Noah was probably a bit mature for her.

"I don't know, Amy. He looks busy," Sophie said awkwardly. She did wonder what it was that he was working on. He claimed to be a musician, but what exactly did that entail?

"You seem to get on with him, Sophie," Holly observed.

"Oh, Soph, would you go and speak to him for me?" Amy pleaded. "Subtle like, don't drop me in it. Maybe you could ask if he would hang back for a drink after work tonight?"

Sophie was all but given a shove in Noah's direction before she found herself walking over towards him at the piano. As she approached, Noah noticed her, and he smiled, putting down his sheet music and pencil on top of the piano and removing his AirPods.

"Hey," he said with a warm smile.

Sophie did have her own agenda that she needed to speak to Noah about before she asked him out on behalf of Amy. Oh, bloody hell, that felt weird.

"Hi," she replied. "So, your mum thinks I'm pretty, does she? How could she possibly know that when you were told to delete that photograph?" Sophie smirked, deciding to start their conversation with the banter that was forming between them.

Noah grinned, chuckling. "In my defence," he said, holding his hands up, "I never sent my mom that picture."

Sophie frowned. "She summoned it by magic, then?"

Noah turned around on the piano stool and stood up, before jumping off of the stage to stand next to her. "No, my sister was in trouble with my mom. She has the gall to have other Thanksgiving plans." He rolled his eyes with a smile. "She was just trying to dump me in it by claiming that the picture was of my girlfriend that I'd neglected to tell my mom about." He shook his head. "If a crazy woman named Joy suddenly starts blowing up your cell, don't be alarmed. Or do. Probably do be alarmed. I would be and she's my mom."

Sophie couldn't help but laugh, covering her mouth to stifle some of her amusement. She pulled her phone out of her back pocket and showed him her lack of notifications. "Nothing yet, but I will keep an eye out. Thanks for the warning."

Sophie actually really liked hearing something so petty between siblings. She had grown up as an only child, and with parents like hers, it had been a lonely existence. She did worry about the same thing for Maddie, as well, and did want her to have a sibling one day. Noah was very fortunate to have such a relationship with his sister.

And his mother, for that matter.

"Hold on," Sophie said suddenly. "How did you sister get a hold of that picture?"

Noah shrugged his shoulders and put on the most bewildered expression. "I have no idea."

"Haven't the foggiest?" Sophie continued facetiously.

"Not sure what that is, but I'm sure I don't." He winked.

Sophie huffed, but couldn't hide her little grin. "Listen, I did want to ask you something," she said, changing the subject. "Maddie loved her piano lesson with you yesterday. I have never seen her so excited about something, and if you knew ..." she trailed off, not wanting to start spilling her guts and making herself cry. "I wanted to ask if I could pay you to give her a lesson once or twice a week. Just a little one." As soon as the words came out of her mouth, Sophie felt awkward. "But if you are too busy, please do not feel as though I have put you on the spot. You can absolutely say no and I will completely understand!"

"Sophie, chill." Noah placed his hand on her upper arm and Sophie stopped talking. "I would be happy to give Maddie some lessons, that's no trouble," he promised her. "But I can't take your money."

Sophie's heart swelled as soon as he said yes. "But you must," she insisted. "I could not ask you to do it for free. That would be completely taking advantage of you."

"Sophie, I'm a tourist, remember? I can't work for money. Do you want me to get deported?" Noah raised his eyebrows.

"Nobody would notice if I paid you a tenner, or however much you would charge." Sophie suddenly hoped it would not be too much. She was already going to be out eighty quid at the least for the psychologist.

"I love to play the piano. Sharing it should be free. My real job pays the bills. I don't need your money to share something that I love doing." He smiled kindly. "Tomorrow?"

"Damn it," Sophie hissed under her breath as she quickly wiped a tear away. "I told myself I wasn't going to cry." She shook her head and took a breath. "Yes, tomorrow would be lovely. I made a deal with Maddie that she needed to go to school if she was going to have lessons so we shall see how it goes!" Just as Sophie was about to turn away from Noah, she remembered why Holly and Amy had sent her over. "Do you want to have a drink after work tonight?" she asked suddenly.

Noah looked taken aback, but his surprise was quickly replaced with a warm smile. "Sure," he replied, nodding.

"Amy's wetting her knickers to flirt with you, but please don't tell her I said anything!" Sophie added, before smiling at him one last time, and returning to the girls with her thumbs up.

Amy beamed. "Oh, thank you, Sophie!"

"He seemed pretty happy to," Sophie told her.

Amy clapped her hands and ran off to the bathroom to check her makeup.

"What were you talking about for so long?" Holly asked, bumping Sophie with her hip.

"Noah's going to give Maddie piano lessons," replied Sophie. "He's being so kind about it. And between you and me, thank God he is not charging me for them," she whispered.

Holly pouted her bottom lip. "Oh, babes, that is the sweetest!" she cried. "I'm sure Mads will love that. Makes you wonder though, don't it?"

"What?"

"Well, Pete's not paying him. You're not paying him. What sort of coin does he have?" Holly wondered. "Have to be rich, wouldn't he?

Maybe he has rich folks. Not like he's a famous musician or else we'd know him, wouldn't we?"

Sophie scoffed. "That's none of our business," she scolded. But quietly, now that Holly had pointed it out, it was curious.

On Monday morning, Sophie had phoned the paediatrician and the child psychologist and had managed to secure appointments for Thursday morning. Apparently, the school had notified them ahead of time, and Maddie would begin testing for autism.

The thought made Sophie sick to her stomach with nerves, but she was glad that they were on the right track regardless.

Maddie had kept to her word and had gone into school without a fight. Sophie had walked her to her classroom and watched as Maddie went over to her bag hook that was labelled with her name. Several of the other students stared at her and made comments about her being back.

Maddie seemed to be in her own world, though, as she pulled her school things out of her bag and organised them on her desk. She had something to look forward to, and nothing could bother her.

"Sophie," remarked Judy Forster. "No tears today?"

Sophie was unsure if Judy was referring to her or Maddie. Regardless, it was a no. "Nothing," she replied with a smile. "Maddie is starting piano lessons after school today and she is very excited."

"Oh, that's wonderful!" Judy clapped her hands together. "I'm glad to hear that she is excited about learning something. And piano, you know, is so good for coordination and rhythm and discipline. I hope it will really translate here in the classroom."

Sophie pulled out her phone and opened up the video that she had taken the other day of Maddie playing. "A friend of mine is teaching Maddie," she explained. "He is a very talented pianist and has a photographic memory. He seems to think Maddie might have something similar." Or exactly the same. Sophie played the video and turned her phone around to show Judy.

Judy pulled her glasses down off the top of her head and looked at the screen. The shock and utter amazement on her face very evident. "Oh my God," she gasped.

When the video finished, Sophie put her phone away. "Do you think it's possible?" she asked. "Maddie's never had a lesson before, never touched a piano, and she could do that because she was interested. It makes me wonder what else she could be capable of purely if she is interested in what she is doing."

"I can't tell you, as a teacher, how happy it makes me to see Maddie enjoying something," Judy said sincerely. "I never want one of my students to feel like school is a chore. It should be a place where they are inspired to learn. And that is my job now, to find whatever inspires our Miss Maddie."

Sophie felt a warm sensation of comfort in her chest as she heard that from Maddie's teacher. "Thank you," she said gratefully. "I have made the appointments for Thursday morning, as I obviously still want to make sure that if she is autistic that she is supported."

"Of course," nodded Judy, "and that is the right thing to do. As we explained in the meeting, Maddie does have characteristics in her behaviour and personality that warrant testing. But that does not mean that she cannot learn. So please, leave it to me, and I will let you know how she does at the end of the day."

Sophie walked out of Leicester Square Station feeling a real weight lifted off of her shoulders. There was hope, and there was direction, and best of all, she had not spent the morning crying, begging Maddie to come out of the bathroom.

She was so excited for Maddie's lesson, maybe even more so than Maddie was. Even if Noah wouldn't take any money for the lessons, Sophie still wanted to thank him. She found herself walking into one of the tacky tourist shops.

He was a self-proclaimed tourist, after all.

Sophie picked up palace guard soft toys, and Buckingham Palace coasters, and underground t shirts before her eyes settled on a shelf full of snow globes. She loved snow globes, and she found a gorgeous little one of a red double decker bus that looked as though it was driving down Charing Cross Road in a snowstorm.

It was a thank you, and that warranted the exorbitant nine pounds and ninety-nine p for the present.

As she walked into the pub, she heard Noah having a bit of a row on the phone.

"Holy shit, Mom. I'm not asking Sophie what her damn sweater size is. Are you insane?" he exclaimed. "No, I am not sassing you! I'm stopping you from spreading your crazy to another darn country. And yes, I will curse if I want to. I need the emphasis."

Her sweater size? What on earth was his mother wondering about what size jumper she wore?

"I texted you thinking, 'hey, it's two in the morning, I'll just let her know I'm alive and she won't need to call me'," Noah protested.

Sophie clapped her hands over her mouth as she eavesdropped to stop herself from laughing.

Noah sighed, exasperated. "Yes, Mom, of course I care that you get carpel tunnel from knitting. Technically I'm preventing that. Sophie doesn't need a Christmas sweater! Why? Because she's not my freaking girlfriend." Noah smacked his head with palm. "Have you got selective hearing, or do I need to book you in for some hearing aids?" Noah asked impatiently. "Okay, yes, I was sassing you that time, but you deserved it."

Sophie needed to help him. The poor man was getting nowhere. She quickly weaved around the tables and held her hand out for the phone as she approached Noah.

Noah raised his eyebrows. "Your funeral," he declared, as he handed his phone over to Sophie.

Sophie held his phone up to her ear and caught the tail end of his mother's sentence.

"... these days I'm going to be dead, do you hear me? Dead. And who is going to knit your sweaters then?"

"Hello, is this Joy? Noah's mum?" Sophie asked.

Sophie heard a gasp from her end.

"Yes!" she cried. "Oh, are you Sophie?" she begged to know.

Sophie laughed lightly. "Yes, my name is Sophie. It's lovely to talk to you."

"Oh, you just have the sweetest accent!" exclaimed Joy.

"Thank you, Mrs ..." It occurred to Sophie that she did not know Noah's last name.

"Bentley," Noah whispered.

"Mrs Bentley," continued Sophie with a smile.

"Sophie, it is so nice to meet you, even if it's not in person," Joy continued with happiness as big as her name. "Noah is a nice boy, isn't he?"

"When he's not sassing me, he is nice," Sophie teased, but Joy took the bait. Noah just rolled his eyes.

"Oh, doesn't he just? He gets that from his father. Certainly doesn't come from me," Joy promised. "But what's this I hear about you two just being friends?" she pressed, not holding anything back. "He needs a nice girlfriend, and I think English girls are much nicer than the girls in his line of work."

What sort of women were in Noah's line of work? "Well, Mrs Bentley, Noah and I met on Thursday," she said awkwardly. "We are just friends, I promise. I'm sure he deserves a nice girlfriend, though."

"Well, are you single?" Joy demanded to know.

"Yes, but –"

"How old are you?"

"Twenty-six, but –"

"Perfect!" she cried.

"Mrs Bentley, I'm not looking for a relationship at the moment." Not that this conversation with a total stranger wasn't odd enough. "You see, I'm a mum. I have an eight-year-old daughter and –"

"I HAVE A GRANDDAUGHTER?" she all but squealed, and so loudly that Noah could hear it from where he was sitting.

He looked mortified and snatched the phone back. "Oh, shit, sorry Mom, phone's dying. Goodbye!" and he disconnected the call, quickly switching his phone off. "I am so sorry," he apologised. "My mother needs to come with a warning label."

"She seems lovely," Sophie laughed. "She approves of me whole-heartedly. Your last girlfriends must have been horrors if she likes me purely because of my accent."

Noah chuckled bashfully. "You could say that. You meet a lot of people in LA who are just after a bit of clout." He shook off the thought. "I am really sorry about her, though. I hope she didn't embarrass you or make you uncomfortable. That is just her being her."

"No, no," Sophie said sincerely. "Your mum just loves you. It's a beautiful thing."

"Loves me too much, I think."

"No such thing," Sophie countered. "I'm a mum, I know." Sophie fished into her bag and pulled out the little snow globe. "Here," she offered. "I bought this for you as a thank you slash souvenir to remember your time in London."

Noah smiled widely as he accepted the snow globe, and he peered into it curiously. "Wow, thank you," he said gratefully. "This is actually really cool. I want to ride on one of these while I'm here."

"Trust me, public transport isn't exciting, but I do get the appeal." Sophie grinned. "I wanted to ask you yesterday, but you weren't here. How was your date with Amy?"

Noah hadn't been at the pub the night before, and Pete had popped the CDs back on. Amy had seemed optimistic about it though.

"I was working back at my hotel yesterday," Noah explained, before he pursed his lips. "I didn't know it was supposed to be a date with her," he confessed. "How old is she?" he asked quietly, frowning.

"Twenty."

Noah sucked in a breath. "I need to let her down easy. Or ... you could."

"Hey, I asked you out for her. I am not dumping her for you," Sophie said firmly.

"Okay, okay," he accepted. Clutching his snow glob, he said, "Thank you for this. That's really thoughtful of you, Sophie." He placed the snow globe atop the piano and smiled at it. He then shuffled his sheet music before he found the page that he wanted, and he picked his pencil up.

"What is it exactly that you are working on?" Sophie asked curiously.

CHAPTER 11

Noah could see the genuine curiosity in Sophie's wide, brown eyes. He could also see that she was a normal person, with a normal job, normal problems, and without a hankering for Instagram followers or coveted roles.

Noah had been a little naïve, perhaps, in the past. He hadn't always realised just how influential he was in his industry. He never wielded his influence. He never demanded things of anybody. He never called in favours. He never asked favours. He formed good working relationships, and that, and a little bit of talent, had kept him employed for the last ten years.

Noah knew a lot of people. He knew casting agents. He knew talent bookers. He knew producers. And he knew a lot of very talented directors. His phone book alone was the key to a date with any beautiful, wannabe actress in Los Angeles.

What kid in their early twenties, who still had the remnants of teenage acne, wouldn't fall head over heels in love with a Marilyn Monroe look-alike who seemed to be desperately in love with him?

Only that never lasted.

Tally had pointed out that he tended to get dumped just as soon as his dates started to attend the parties that he was invited to and schmooze the people that they needed to. Before this, Noah hadn't realised that his most attractive feature was his job.

It made dating hard and telling the truth even harder. His two best friends, his only friends, really, were his sister, and her girl-friend. Tally was genetically programmed to never ditch him, and he had known Vanessa for over a decade, and since before either she or him had made a name for themselves.

He knew enough of Sophie's character to know that she was nothing like that. But he liked the anonymity he had in this bar. He liked just playing the piano and being a piano man.

There was also the small legal issue of Noah possessing a burnt copy of the unfinished film which was currently playing on his phone and through his AirPods. He had been listening to a scene and writing before Sophie had come in.

"I'm a musician," he replied. It was the truth, technically.

Sophie furrowed her eyebrows. "What exactly does a musician do? Besides play the piano for no money in a London pub."

"I get paid to write music for other people," he elaborated. Also, not a lie. He was writing this score for his director. He also wrote songs for people.

"What kind of people?" Sophie pressed.

"Talented people," he told her.

Sophie looked at him with an exasperated expression. Noah completely got it. And he knew she wasn't going to let it go. He understood how weird it might seem to someone who did rely so heavily on her pay cheques to get by. Noah knew how fortunate he was in that respect.

Noah liked the rapport he had with Sophie. He liked the back and forth between them, and he could see himself getting on really well with her. He hoped the truth wouldn't change anything.

It had changed every other friendship and relationship he had developed over the last decade.

"You can trust me, you know," Sophie said quietly. "You know an awful lot about me and my problems. And you have helped me incredibly."

Trust never even crossed his mind. He knew he could trust her. She was a good person. Noah liked Sophie, and he didn't want to be dishonest with her.

"Promise you won't see me differently," Noah asked firmly. "Please. I like you, Sophie, and I don't want your opinion of me to change. That is, if you have a good opinion of me. If it's bad, then please let it change."

Sophie looked flummoxed. "Of course, I have a good opinion of you, Noah. Unless you're about to tell me you're a serial murderer, or you keep a bag of your toenail clippings in the back of your wardrobe, I am not going to think differently of you."

Noah chuckled. "Nope, never killed anyone, and no bag of nail clippings either," he promised her. "I do write music for other people," he continued. "That is the truth. I compose music for film," he confessed. "I'm a film composer, I suppose would be my official job title. I score movies. I write the music, songs, lyrics, everything, and when I'm finished, I record it with an orchestra, and then hand it over to the editors so they can work their magic and make the movie perfect."

Sophie blinked, and her mouth opened, but no words escaped. She tucked her hair behind her ears and folded her arms across her chest as she figured out what to say.

"That's what I'm doing in London," Noah continued, feeling the need to over-explain to fill the silence. "That's what I'm doing on this piano. I'm scoring a movie. I'm writing the score on the piano, and when I'm finished, I'll go back to LA and I'll record it with an orchestra. The movie's premiering in the summer so my score needs to be completed by Christmas."

Sophie did not know what she had been expecting Noah to come out with. She would have thought that a semi-successful, one hit wonder pub band would seem more likely than a film composer!

But what an incredible job! How did one even get into a job like that? And how on earth did a person who worked in Hollywood end up in Pete's little London pub?

How could he possibly be writing a film score on Pete's old piano? Sophie's eyes flicked over the dozens of sheet music that he had surrounding him, and it was hard to fathom that this would all turn into a piece of music that you would hear in a film.

Noah had asked Sophie not to change her opinion of him, but it was hard not to! Noah was obviously a very successful person, and ... and she had asked a film composer to give her daughter piano lessons!

"You don't have to give Maddie piano lessons!" she managed to choke out. "You obviously have much more important things to do, and I can find someone online to teach her."

Noah shook his head. "Sophie, no," he insisted. "I told you that I love to play the piano, and I love sharing it with other people.

Besides, I'll bet that Maddie is looking forward to it, and I have no intention of letting her down."

Sophie sat down on the edge of the stage, fearing that she might fall over if she continued standing. Noah sat down beside her.

"She is really looking forward to it," Sophie admitted, "but I do feel terribly guilty now."

"Why?" he asked bluntly. "Why would you feel guilty?"

Sophie pursed her lips and looked up at him. He was frowning at her. "Come on now. You're obviously a very important person, aren't you?" It was difficult not to compare herself to Noah. Despite the fact that he hadn't been taking a wage, he had just been another pub worker only moments ago, just the same as her.

Noah chuckled. "No," he said sincerely. "No more than you, or anyone else. I'm just a guy, from Napa, California, who happened to be pretty good on the piano. I'm not better than anyone else. If somebody ever makes you feel like they're better than you, Sophie, they're an asshole, not someone to be intimidated by."

Sophie appreciated what he was saying, and she could see that he was the same kind person from five minutes before he had told her the truth. "I suppose you aren't better than anyone else," Sophie said with a sly smile. "Your mum does still knit your jumpers."

Noah snorted, and his reaction made Sophie laugh. "That's very true."

"How on earth did you manage to get into that sort of career?" Sophie wondered. She had gone on several auditions during her first few weeks at university, before Beck, and before her pregnancy. She had always been in a room with a hundred other girls who were prettier, more talented, and had far more experience than her. She had never managed to get a call back, let alone a role.

"Well, I got into Julliard after high school. It's a speciality music and performing arts college in New York," he explained, and Sophie didn't let on that she knew what it was. "I've always loved music; I've always loved composing and writing and performing. As a kid, I could pick up any instrument and learn it immediately, but the piano has always been my favourite. I was a bit of a nerd, as you can tell."

"I couldn't," replied Sophie assuredly.

Noah grinned. "Well, I was. I didn't play sports or go to games, and so I spent a lot of my time when I wasn't playing watching TV and movies. And in hearing the greats, I'm talking Vangelis, Ennio Morricone, John Williams, I realised that that is what I wanted to do with my life.

"When you're inspired, you can accomplish great things," Noah said determinedly. "I worked my ass off to get into Juilliard. I wrote like crazy, and I sent demo after demo to every movie studio in the country. I think maybe I annoyed them into giving me a shot." Noah laughed at himself.

"I love Chariots of Fire," Sophie whispered.

Noah appreciated the recognition. "Vangelis is a master," Noah remarked admirably. "A producer found me at school when I was nineteen and gave me, a kid, the biggest break of my life. I scored my first movie, and ten years later, I get to wake up every morning with a job that I love. I am grateful."

Sophie could tell that Noah was grateful. He had true respect for the legends that had come before him, and he had worked hard. How lucky he was to have his dreams come true.

"My first job as a teenager was a piano teacher," Noah revealed to Sophie, "at my mom's church. I taught on the piano that I learned to play on. Every Christmas I still play for the congregation. I know what it is to have a head that can go a million miles an hour when inspired, and I truly hope that I can help Maddie find her passion."

"I think it's a dream, really, to love your work, and to share your passions. Thank you for telling me the truth," Sophie said gratefully, before she stood up. "I really ought to go and pop my bag in the backroom. Where is Pete?" she wondered, noticing that he wasn't at the bar like usual.

"Went to get a coffee as soon as my mom started yelling at me over the phone," replied Noah, smirking.

Sophie grinned, before darting across the floor and making her way into the backroom. As soon as she was alone, she could not help her curiosity. She pulled out her phone, and googled Noah's name.

Thousands of results came up, along with pictures, and articles, and videos of Noah performing. Sophie scrolled in awe, before she clicked on Noah's Wikipedia page. Before now, she had only thought that very successful, famous people had a Wikipedia page. She now realised that Noah was one of them.

"Noah John Bentley, born December 28, 1990, is an American composer, conductor, and pianist, and is regarded as one of the great modern composers of the twenty-first century. He first came to prominence when he became the youngest ever recipient of the Academy Award for Best Original Score at age twenty, for his critically acclaimed work in Forces," Sophie read in a hushed voice, needing to read it out loud to properly comprehend the information.

Sophie remembered going to see Forces in the cinema when it came out, and she had thought it was brilliant. To think that

Noah had composed the music for such a film when he was only nineteen? She would have seen his name in the credits, as well!

Sophie scrolled down and continued to read.

"Bentley was born to winemaker, John (born 1954), owner and operator of Bentley Grange, and Joy Bentley (born 1958), a homemaker, in Napa, California, on December 28, 1990. He is three minutes younger than his twin sister, Hallie "Tally" Bentley, a middle school teacher. He has two older sisters, Haley, a winemaker, and the 2017 Pulitzer Prize winning photographer, Casey Bentley.

"Bentley developed an interest in music at a young age, and became proficient in several instruments, most notably the piano. He attended Jefferson High School and graduated from Juilliard School in 2012."

She felt like she was being terribly nosy, but Sophie couldn't help herself but to keep going. She read paragraph after paragraph, detailing his work on seriously brilliant films. He had worked with famous directors, and on movies with proper film stars.

And then she scrolled down to the section where it detailed his personal life.

"Bentley has been a vocal supporter of several musical, charitable organisations, such as Music For Relief, and Inner City Arts, which is a Los Angeles-focussed organisation assisting at-risk elementary and middle school students to participate in arts programs."

Sophie could not tear her eyes away as the page teased her with a section about his romantic relationships.

"Bentley dated fashion model, Alexis Kane, from 2011 – 2012. He was in a relationship with actress, Cara Lovell, from June to

September 2013. Bentley dated actress, Hannah Wu, from August 2014 to February 2015."

And there was nothing after that. But those three names were of very famous, very beautiful people.

Sophie slumped down on the sofa as what she had read, and what she had learned, truly sunk in. It was enough to make even the most accomplished person feel as though they had nothing to show for their effort.

But for someone like Sophie? Sophie never aspired to be someone important, but she did have aspirations as every person did. And she was staring at the evidence of someone who had managed to achieve his.

She knew that envy was wrong, and she would never begrudge Noah his successes; he deserved them. But whatever he said about not being better than her, he still was an intimidating person all of a sudden.

Sophie clicked back to her web search and found herself on YouTube. She selected the video titled:"Youngest winner EVER of Best Original Score!"

Sophie watched the Oscars on television every year. She might have even watched this year, she didn't know. She watched as the presenters listed the nominees for Best Original Score, and the camera went to each composer.

"Noah Bentley, Forces," read the presenter. Sophie knew who she was, but she couldn't quite put her finger on it.

The camera went to Noah, and Sophie's jaw dropped and an "Aw!" escaped her mouth as she saw him. He looked so young! He looked like a skinny teenager, wearing a rented tuxedo for a school formal. He looked so nervous, and a glamourous, older woman was holding his hand. Just looking at how anxious she was for Noah, Sophie could tell she was his mum, Joy.

"And the Oscar goes to ... Noah Bentley, Forces."

The sound of applause rung out through the theatre, and Noah was immediately hugged by his mum. Oh, God, he looked so ecstatic, and in complete disbelief that his name had been read out.

"This is the first nomination and first win for Noah Bentley. This award makes him the youngest winner ever in this category. He is also nominated tonight for Best Original Song," said the voiceover.

Noah made his way down the aisle and he climbed up the stairs to get on stage. He received his statue from the actress presenter, and awkwardly kissed her on the cheek. He then came to stand in front of the microphone with the biggest smile on his face.

"Oh, God, wow," he said breathlessly. "I never thought this would happen in a million years."

Sophie had to cup her hand over her mouth to stop herself from crying out at the sweetness she saw.

"I'd like to thank Adam Wexler, and all the producers on Forces who took a chance on me. I probably annoyed you into giving me the job, but I think the score turned out okay."

There was a rumble of laughter from the audience.

"The director, George Erwin, for taking me seriously, thank you. The editors, the sound editors, the sound mixers, you guys made my work sound amazing. This was seriously the best experience of my life," Noah continued, clutching his Oscar as though it was his life support. "At the end of the day, I'm just a guy who loves to play piano, and to create melodies and songs that make people feel something is honestly a privilege." He grinned, shaking his head.

"My sisters, Haley, Casey, and my twin and best friend, Tally, I adore you. My parents, John, and Joy. Mom, thanks for dragging me to my first piano lesson. Thank you, everyone." He held up his Oscar and then was led off the stage.

The video ended, and Sophie let out a breath.

"I got so drunk that night. Don't tell my mom."

Sophie jumped as she looked up to see Noah standing in the doorway. He didn't look angry, only amused, as well as searching Sophie's face for her thoughts.

"I was only twenty, but at the after party they kept shoving champagne into my hands and my virgin liver went to town." Noah laughed at himself.

"You're just a guy who loves piano?" Sophie repeated, raising her eyebrows.

Noah shrugged his shoulders nonchalantly. "I'm just a guy who loves piano," he confirmed. "Hey, you want to be really impressed, my sister won a Pulitzer for her series of photographs on the catastrophic effects of global warming in the Amazon. Compared to her, I just twinkle my fingers on a damn keyboard."

Noah held up his spirit fingers and Sophie cracked. What the hell was his mother feeding her children to have them turn out so bloody talented?

"Do you still want to be my friend?" Noah asked hopefully. "I'm nice, I promise. I can't do much else besides playing piano. Like, I can't cook, and I'm terrible with directions," he joked. "I can't do laundry. I buy new clothes, or else I'll turn everything pink. My favourite genre of TV is reality, and I've seen every episode of Real Housewives of Beverly Hills, so I know that's a strike against me.

I live with two girls, so I blame that on them. Um, what else do I suck at?"

"Stop, stop!" Sophie cried, giggling. "You're an idiot, but I do appreciate the sentiment. I'm sorry for snooping on you like this. You probably think that's terribly nosy."

Noah grinned. "No, I don't blame you. I'd be curious, too. And embarrassed, let's be honest, that you now know what I looked like in the best part of my awkward stage. Acne, skinny, that freaking Bieber haircut. Jesus, what were we thinking?"

Sophie covered her face as she laughed, and she mightily appreciated his efforts to make her feel better. He was a really nice person. His mum was right. "Yes, of course I'd like to be friends, Noah," replied Sophie. "You are so very talented," she added sincerely. "I really mean it."

"Likewise," he returned the compliment. "I hope you're not forgetting that I had the pleasure of playing back up for you on Friday night. I know you've got some pipes in your back pocket." Noah came and sat down beside her on the sofa and bumped her with his elbow. "Go on then," he urged.

"What?"

"Well, I crapped on myself for you. You now need to tell me all your guilty habits and personal flaws so I can decide if I want to be friends with you," he said bluntly.

"Oh, well," Sophie sucked in a breath as she thought. "I cry," she began. "I cry all the time. And not just when the situation demands it. When I'm reading, or watching a film, or even an emotional television advert, I will break down. Um, the television show I am currently binge watching with Maddie is Hannah Montana. What's sad is that I am enjoying it," Sophie admitted, laughing. "I can't drive, never learned."

"I could teach you," he offered.

"Not likely, you drive on the wrong side of the road, and in the wrong side of the car!" Sophie pointed out.

"I beg to differ."

"Agree to disagree." Sophie smirked. "What else? The only condiment I like is tomato sauce."

"Not even ranch?" gasped Noah in disbelief.

"I really have no idea what that is," Sophie confessed with a shrug.

"Well, that's it then. Can't be friends." Noah slapped his hands on top of his thighs as he stood up.

He was being silly, but he had really helped Sophie to relax. What's more is that she did think that Noah could be a really good friend. Sophie didn't have many friends, really, as Maddie was a full-time job on top of her work at the pub. So, it was nice to have a comfortable rapport with someone.

Noah turned around and pulled Sophie to her feet. "Are we good?" he asked her seriously.

"Yeah." Sophie nodded.

They walked out of the backroom together, and noticed Pete standing behind the bar. Noah continued on back up to the piano, and he promptly put his AirPods back in. Pete was smirking to himself as he unloaded the dishwasher.

"What?" Sophie snapped, feeling a blush on her cheeks.

"Nothing, nothing," Pete so obviously lied.

"What?" Sophie pressed.

"I'm just starting a betting pool with the girls and the bouncers this week. I've got twenty quid on you two shagging before the month is out."

Sophie's eyes widened so fast it hurt, and she thanked God that Noah couldn't hear them. "Oh my God! Shut up!" she hissed. "That is so inappropriate! We are just friends!"

"And I'm the bloody Queen of England." Pete winked.

CHAPTER 12

S ophie always felt very judged by the other mothers at Maddie's school. They all seemed to collect together in cliques, drinking their designer coffees and teas from keep cups while wearing matching activewear sets.

She knew they all thought of her as the mother of the "problem child". They had observed Sophie fighting with Maddie outside school enough to judge them both. It didn't help that Sophie was at least ten years younger than all of them, which only added to her feeling of inferiority.

But she had something to take her mind off of their sideways glances. Today Maddie was having her first proper piano lesson. Maddie was excited about it, and anything that got Maddie excited made Sophie happy.

God, Sophie prayed that Maddie had had a good day at school today. She had been so good this morning. Sophie hadn't received a phone call, so she hoped that meant everything had been okay.

The school bell sounded at half past three, and the students began to spill out of the classrooms. Maddie's classroom door opened, and her classmates began to run to their mothers. Sophie then saw a flash of strawberry blonde hair as Maddie came rushing out alongside them.

"Mummy, Mummy, let's go!" Maddie demanded. "I want to play on the piano now." Maddie grabbed Sophie's hand and attempted to drag her away from the classroom.

"Wait!" cried Sophie. "We'll go in a minute. I just need to speak to Miss Forster."

Maddie let out a frustrated groan as she dragged her feet back towards the classroom with Sophie.

Sophie knocked on the door, and Judy looked up as she was collecting the students' books from their desks. She smiled as she moved her glasses onto the top of her head.

"Do you have a minute?" Sophie asked.

"Of course, I was going to send you an email," replied Judy. "I do have a staff meeting in fifteen minutes."

"Sorry," apologised Sophie immediately. "I won't keep you. I just wanted to ask if she had a good day today?"

Judy held up her finger and began to sift through the books that she had collected. She then found Maddie's book, which Sophie had painstakingly covered in Frozen contact in an attempt to interest her in her schoolwork. Until now, there had been no success.

Judy flipped open to the latest page and began to read. "On Friday, I played piano with Noah. It was fun. I am good at it. Today I am going to learn piano at Mummy's work. Noah is nice," Judy read, before she flipped the book around to show Sophie Maddie's weekend recount.

It was Maddie's work. She had written it. Of course, her handwriting was appalling, but it would be when she had written five words collectively in her entire school education. She had written sentences. And the words were spelled correctly!

Sophie looked down at Maddie, and into her wide, expressive brown eyes. She had so much in her head, Sophie just knew it. "Look at how wonderfully you wrote, Maddie!" Sophie exclaimed.

"I drew a picture of the piano keys," explained Maddie. "This key is middle C," she pointed at the key that she had labelled. Maddie had drawn a picture of a piano, and it was as accurate as Sophie could imagine. "If you know your ABC's, then you know which key is which, Noah says. I know my ABC's," Maddie boasted.

Sophie had only told Noah this morning that she cried at the drop of a hat, and goddammit, here she went again. She quickly caught her tears with her fingers.

"I read with Maddie today," Judy added quietly. "I tested her on a levelled reader."

Sophie's breath caught in her throat. Maddie had only ever been on the easiest level of readers. She had never moved up. "And?" she prompted.

"Flying colours," Judy reported proudly. "Read at ninety-nine percent accuracy, and full comprehension. I think her only mistake was because she was reading so quickly that she missed a word. I will be really curious to hear the outcome of her appointments this week. But I had a different child in my classroom today." She smiled warmly. "I did switch out her reader. Let me know how she goes, but I know she is reluctant to read at home. I wouldn't force it."

"Mummy! We need to go!" urged Maddie as she tugged on Sophie's jacket.

"Maddie, manners!" Sophie replied in a huff. "We are going to go in a minute. Hold your horses."

"I don't have any horses," Maddie retorted. "We have to get on the train or else we'll be late!"

"Thank you," Sophie said to Judy gratefully. "Really."

"Not at all," replied Judy. "I can't wait to hear all about your piano lesson tomorrow, Maddie. Perhaps you would like to have Show and Tell and teach the class something that you learned. Would you like that?"

"Yes!" Maddie responded eagerly. "Mummy, you have to take my picture so I can show it tomorrow! Please?" she begged, grabbing hold of Sophie's hands as she dropped to her knees.

"Oh, because you found your manners, I suppose I can," allowed Sophie, desperately trying to hide her glee at Maddie agreeing to attend school two days in a row. "Alright, let's get going then so Miss Forster can get to her meeting. Say you'll see her tomorrow."

"See you tomorrow," Maddie repeated with a wave.

The second Sophie and Maddie walked into the West End Piano Bar, Maddie was sprinting up to Noah, and bounding up onto the stage beside him. Sophie raced after her, feeling awful that she hadn't even uttered excuse me. She wanted Maddie to be extrapolite, which was asking a lot of an eight-year-old who was not the best at social cues, especially considering what she now knew about Noah.

But Noah didn't seem to mind. He greeted Maddie with a warm smile and shuffled over on the stool to allow her room. Sophie didn't say anything. She didn't want to interrupt.

Sophie went back behind the bar and stood next to Pete, just watching.

"He's good with your kid," Pete observed. "I'm sure he'll be good at making more with you."

"Oh, piss off!" hissed Sophie with a stupid smile on her face as she whacked Pete in the arm. "I'm in a good mood, leave me alone." Sophie pulled out her phone and snapped a few pictures of Maddie playing with Noah, before quickly emailing them to her teacher for Show and Tell the next day.

The music that sounded out through the bar was not beginner music. It was not chopsticks or Mary Had a Little Lamb. It was proper compositions, and Maddie was playing alone with Noah. God, she was special.

"Can we play the song from the other day?" Maddie asked Noah. "The one I liked?"

Noah positioned his hand to start playing the piece, but stopped himself, deciding to continue testing his theory. "Do you remember how it goes?" he asked her.

Maddie frowned. "Of course." She nodded. "We played it and then I played it." Maddie placed her fingers on the correct keys and began to play the tune that Noah had come up with the other day. She didn't need sheet music. She didn't need Noah's help. She simply remembered what she had seen, she had comprehended it, and she could now repeat it.

But then it changed. Noah's attention immediately focussed as Maddie changed his song. She was concentrating now, blending in additional notes, and changing the melody. Goddamn, it actually sounded very good.

"What are you doing?" Noah asked her.

"I'm making it better," replied Maddie. "I like the way the high notes sound. When I play them at the same time as your song, it makes it prettier. The high notes are the pretty ones," she stated, as though it was a fact.

But damn if she wasn't right. It did sound pretty. It sounded angelic, actually.

Noah quickly scrambled to find his sheet music for that piece, finding it in his pile off mess on top of the piano. Grabbing his pencil, he recalled each note that Maddie had played on top of his composition and added it into his melody.

"You did make my song something really beautiful then, Maddie," Noah agreed. "You're a talented kid, you know that?"

Maddie smiled up at him, and Noah wondered if Maddie had ever been given a compliment like that. He certainly hadn't before he'd found music.

"Let's play it together," Noah decided. "See if we can make it any better than it already is. You take the pretty notes, okay? Do whatever you think sounds good."

Noah could play his composition from memory, his muscle memory alone allowing him to watch Maddie as he played, instead of focussing on what his own hands were doing. Maddie concentrated as she played around in the high register, adding sweet flourishes to what she had already come up with.

When the piece finished, Maddie seemed very pleased with herself, and Noah added in Maddie's additions to the sheet music.

"Can I let you in on a secret?" he asked as he wrote.

"What secret?" asked Maddie.

"I'm writing these songs for a movie that's going to come out in the theatre next summer," he uttered quietly. "Do you know what you just did?"

Maddie shook her head, looking thoroughly confused. "What did I do?"

"You just scored your first movie scene." Noah grinned. "What you did just then is called composing," he explained. "It's what I do for a job. What you came up with is going to be in a movie next year."

"Composing," Maddie repeated, testing the word. "Composing is making songs?"

Noah nodded. "Yes, at the moment, we're writing melodies. When I'm finished with the melodies, I'll arrange them using an orchestra. Do you know what that is?"

Maddie shook her head.

"Well, an orchestra is a big band of instruments. Like violins and cellos and flutes," Noah explained. "The melody will then become a musical score. The score, in my humble opinion, is the best part of a movie." Noah moved his pencil to the top of the page, where he had written his own name. He wasn't about taking other people's ideas, no matter how old they were. Maddie had made his work better with her own ideas. Credit was due. "How do you spell your full name, Maddie?" he asked.

"M-A-D-E-L-E-I-N-E C-A-R-T-W-R-I-G-H-T," Maddie spelled slowly.

Noah wrote down her name beside his at the top of the page. He would need to figure out a way to compensate Sophie for Maddie's idea. That would mean a phone call to his producer, and that was a tomorrow problem. Producers meant questions about deadlines.

"Do you want to know what I always do when I come up with something I think is pretty cool?" he then asked Maddie, putting the sheet music down.

"What?" Maddie asked curiously.

"I FaceTime my sister, Tally," replied Noah. "Tally always gives me honest advice if she thinks my melody is any good. What time is it in LA, I wonder?" Noah checked his cell phone. It was five o'clock, which meant it was ten o'clock in LA. "Great, Tally's on her recess break at school."

After setting off their apartment alarm four times, Tally finally called Noah and apologised for dropping him in it with their mom. Tally, however, still found the whole situation hilarious.

Noah quickly selected Tally's phone number and positioned his phone so that both he and Maddie were in the frame.

The call connected, and he was greeted by Tally's face as she stuffed a mouthful of leafy salad into her mouth. "What?" Tally asked, her mouth full. "I'm eating."

Behind her, Noah could see that she was in her classroom. She had colourful posters and artwork hanging. "We've got something new. You want to hear it?" Noah asked her.

"Duh," replied Tally, shoving another forkful into her mouth, before she stopped. "Wait, we?" she mumbled, peering closer at the phone. "Hey, you've got a kid!" she exclaimed.

"Maddie, this is my sister, Tally. Tally, this is Maddie," Noah introduced. "I've been giving her a piano lesson, but she's managed to help me write something pretty great."

"Hey, Maddie!" Tally exclaimed, waving through the phone with a huge smile on her face. "I'm Noah's big sister. Oh my God, you're so cute!"

"Twin," corrected Noah, rolling his eyes. "She's only older than me by three minutes."

"Still older," Tally retorted.

"Hi!" chirped Maddie, and she waved back to Tally. "Your hair is cool."

"Oh my God, listen to her accent. You're just the sweetest, thank you, girl." Tally ran her hand over the shaved part of her head. She kept part of one side shaved nowadays, and the other side bleached, cropped and curly. No matter what Tally tried with her hair, it always looked cool. "Anyway, you've got to hurry up. Kids are back inside from recess in like five minutes," Tally urged. "I want to hear the new piece."

"You ready?" Noah asked Maddie.

Maddie nodded, and got her hands into position.

Together, they played their new piece, and Noah could really hear it. He could hear how this would sound with strings, brass, woodwind and percussion, with him accompanying on piano. He could see the scene in his head, and he could envisage what it would sound like properly edited.

The melody ended, and Tally's mouth was hanging open. "How old are you, Maddie?" Tally managed to say, her voice filled with shock.

"Eight," replied Maddie.

"Only one other kid I knew who could do what you just did when he was eight," Tally said with a growing smile. "Damn, Noah, that was it. That was the one. Best one you've played for me by far. You've got the sound. That's the one to go with." Tally nodded with finality.

In the background of the call, Noah heard Tally's school bell ring, and she looked up.

"Oh, I've got to go," she said regretfully. "God," she said emotionally, and Noah could see her tearing up, "that was it. I love you as big as the world." Tally leaned forward and kissed her screen. "Bye, Maddie! Well done, sweetheart!" Tally then disconnected the call.

Well, he had something. Tally didn't cry unless he had something.

Chapter 13

Maddie had made it to school without a tantrum on Tuesday and Wednesday and was now only out of school because Sophie needed to take her to the paediatrician.

No matter how hopeful Sophie had felt this week, she was absolutely shitting herself with anxiety about what the doctor and the psychologist would have to say once they assessed Maddie.

Maddie hadn't seen her paediatrician since she was five, when she had her injections before starting school. Perhaps they wouldn't have tested for autism then when she wasn't throwing tanties left, right, and centre. If ever Maddie was ill, Sophie took her to the GP.

The paediatrician's office hadn't changed. It was still decorated in offensively bright yellow and orange and littered with toys that looked about three generations old.

Sophie, holding Maddie's hand, walked up to the receptionist's desk.

The receptionist was still the same, too. Sophie remembered her bringing in Maddie's a lollipop when she'd been grizzling about getting her needles.

"Good morning," she welcomed.

"Hi, good morning," replied Sophie. "I've got an appointment at nine for Madeleine Cartwright."

The receptionist clicked her acrylic nails on the keyboard and smiled when she found the booking. "Yes, you're right here. Have a seat, why don't you? The doctor will be with you in a moment."

Sophie sat down on one of the tired, fraying armchairs, and pulled Maddie onto her lap. Maddie could have sat in one of the other chairs, but Sophie didn't want her to. She wanted to hold her. Sophie smoothed Maddie's ponytail, and retied her maroon scrunchie. She was wearing her winter school uniform for the first time since March. She looked ever so smart in her shirt, tie, and tartan skirt, finished off with a pair of white tights. She looked like a normal little girl, and it was going to break Sophie's heart if a doctor told Sophie that Maddie was going to have something to make her life harder.

"Mummy, can I have another piano lesson after school today, please?" Maddie asked politely as she leaned back into Sophie's chest.

Maddie had already had two lessons this week. Her arranged lesson on Monday, as well as one that Maddie managed to sweet talk Noah into yesterday afternoon.

"Noah's got to work, sweetheart. He can't be giving you lessons every night," Sophie replied softly.

"Please?" Maddie whined, wriggling in Sophie's lap. "Please, I really want to. It's my favourite!"

Sophie sighed, and pulled out her phone from her back pocket, adjusting Maddie as she did. She then saw that she had missed two text messages while they were on the train.

Holly had sent through, "Mads has got this!" alongside a thumbs up emoji.

Noah had sent her a message, too. "Maddie is amazing. Nothing anyone can say is going to change that."

As she was about to reply to them both, the door to the office opened, and Maddie's paediatrician, Dr Lisa Edgeley, stepped out into the waiting room. Dr Edgeley was dressed casually in a floral blouse and a pair of black trousers. Sophie was quietly glad that she wasn't wearing a doctor's coat or anything intimidating.

"If she gives me a needle, I will scream," Maddie whispered in Sophie's ear.

"You're not getting a needle," Sophie hushed, gently pushing her off of Sophie's lap.

"Maddie!" said Dr Edgeley cheerfully. "It's been a while; look how you've grown!" she observed.

Maddie eyed the doctor suspiciously. "I'm older, that's why," she replied cautiously. "You aren't allowed to give me a needle, Mummy said so," she added, embellishing the truth.

Dr Edgeley and Sophie exchanged a glance, and the doctor looked at Sophie reassuringly. "No, no, no needles today," she promised. "You're just here for a visit."

As they got into the office, Sophie saw that Dr Edgeley and laid out several activities on her floor area. There was colouring, blocks, Legos, and dolls. Her anxiety started to pick up again as she wondered which one meant Maddie had autism. Did her choice determine it?

Sophie already knew that Maddie would choose colouring. Was that bad?

Dr Edgeley walked over to her scale, and waved Maddie over. "Jump up on here, Maddie," she instructed. "Let's see how much you've grown." She recorded Maddie's updated weight, and then measured her height, before adding them into Maddie's file. She then told Maddie that she could choose one of the activities laid out for her.

Maddie, of course, went for the colouring immediately. She organised the crayons in rainbow order, like she enjoyed, and proceeded to colour the picture of a butterfly.

"Is that bad?" Sophie asked Dr Edgeley fearfully. "Should she have picked dolls?"

Dr Edgeley frowned and shook her head. "Dear God, Sophie no," she said calmly. "There is nothing bad, and nothing wrong, about any of this," she promised. "The activities are there to keep the children occupied so that I can speak to the parents. Autism Spectrum Disorder screening starts with me asking you some questions."

Dr Edgeley could still sense Sophie's immense anxiety, and she went over to the water cooler and poured her a cup. Sophie accepted it gratefully.

"Autism awareness and support is so much better now than it was ten years ago, even five years ago," Dr Edgeley promised. "It's not a disease, it's not a disability, it is a spectrum, on which people struggle on varying levels with social interaction, communication and behaviour. Can I make an observation without you panicking?" she asked.

"No," Sophie blubbered.

Dr Edgeley smiled reassuringly. "Sophie, I have seen hundreds of children who presenting with symptoms far more troubling. Now, Maddie's behaviour with the crayons, ordering them as she did. Is that something she always does?"

How desperately Sophie wanted to say "no". "Yes," she nodded.

"Okay, well, that is one of many, many ASD characteristics. Lining up objects, ordering objects, is very common in ASD children." Dr Edgeley collected her clipboard and a pen from her desk, and clicked it, no doubt making a note about Maddie's ordering behaviour. "Now, does Maddie have any other behaviours that you would classify as unusual or repetitive?"

"She's had trouble with school refusal," replied Sophie honestly. "She would throw tantrums, scream, lock herself in the bathroom, all to keep herself from going to school. When she gets her way, she is happy. I've only been getting her to school this week without a fight because she has started piano lessons. She likes them, is obsessed with them really, and it's been good motivation."

Dr Edgeley recorded Sophie's answers.

"I think she is really bright, though," Sophie added, a hopeful tone in her voice. "I think her memory is excellent. A friend of mine, her piano teacher, actually, thinks that Maddie has an eidetic memory. She's learned to play the piano professionally with only a handful of lessons. What child can do that? That has to go in her favour, doesn't it?"

Dr Edgeley put her clipboard down. "Sophie, there is nothing wrong with an autism diagnosis. I can completely understand how scary it might be, not knowing how your child might cope. I haven't even begun to properly assess Maddie, but should she be diagnosed, if you let autism be her label, then that is how far

Maddie will go. But if you help Maddie to see her autism as an asset, to use and develop what makes her special,then she will reach for the stars."

Sophie did her best to answer every one of Dr Edgeley's questions as detailed as possible. Maddie didn't fit a lot of the criteria. She didn't struggle keeping eye contact, she did respond when someone tried to get her attention, her voice had expression, and she didn't have sensory sensitivities.

But she did struggle in developing social relationships. She did have trouble interacting with people who did not share an interest with her. She did have trouble understanding how other people felt, or how her actions affected others, and she did get annoyed and angry as a first response.

Maddie's obsessive behaviour was another characteristic of ASD, according to Dr Edgeley. Children with ASD tended to have limited interests and did tend become obsessed over them.

"Have you heard of Mozart, Sophie?" Dr Edgeley asked Sophie as the appointment came to an end.

"Yes, of course," replied Sophie.

"He was a child prodigy. Unparalleled musical ability. God-given, some said," she explained. "Would you agree that he was a brilliant success?"

Sophie nodded, unsure of what she was getting at.

"Maddie seems to love music. You seem to have uncovered a passion, and something that she is terribly good at. Mozart, modern psychologists believe, was on the autism spectrum." She smiled calmly, reassuringly. "He had an eidetic memory, incredible musical gifts ... and possible Tourette's, ASD, Asperger's, ADHD, OCD ... the list goes on." She put a comforting hand on Sophie's forearm.

"Maddie's got a superpower. It's your job to make her feel that way, and it's my job to make sure that whatever the screening concludes with, Maddie goes on to develop just as she should."

Sophie wasn't allowed in the psychologist's office. The paediatrician had called on ahead and had passed on whatever notes she had taken to the psychologist. Sophie was forced to wait outside.

Maddie wasn't diagnosed yet, but Sophie could feel in her bones that Maddie would be. Call it mother's intuition. And she had taken what Dr Edgeley had said to heart. If Sophie let autism be a label for Maddie, then that is all she would be.

Maddie needed to feel as though autism was her superpower, and Sophie needed to be her number one champion.

Sophie replied to Holly, but Holly didn't message back. On a Thursday morning, Sophie knew that Holly would be in one of her uni classes. Sophie decided to call Noah.

He picked up almost immediately.

"Hey," he answered, his voice sounding concerned. "How are you? How's Maddie doing?"

"Did you know that Mozart was autistic?" Sophie asked suddenly.

"No, I didn't," Noah replied, sounding surprised. "Really? Wow."

In the background, Sophie heard Noah begin to play, and if she was a betting woman, she would have said it was Mozart.

"Piano Sonata Number 11 in A Major," Noah uttered quietly as he played. "Composed by a freaking genius."

Sophie didn't reply. She merely listened and closed her eyes.

Noah finished his piece, and Sophie heard him sigh.

"I don't want her life to be any harder than it already is," Sophie whispered. "She's got a moron for a dad, and he's not remotely interested in her. She's got me, and I'm useless most of the time –"

"Sophie, cut the crap," Noah interrupted firmly. "You useless?" he repeated challengingly. "I know I haven't known you that long, but I've never seen someone try harder for her kid. "Maddie is lucky to have you. You're an amazing mom, and no matter what the docs say about her, I know Maddie's going to be fine because she has you."

Sophie's eyes welled with tears. Jesus, she needed to hear that.

"Are you crying right now?" he asked.

"No," Sophie whimpered, her voice giving it away. "I told you I always cry."

Noah chuckled. "I know."

"She's in with the psychologist now," Sophie managed to stammer. "The paediatrician says she has quite a few of the social traits."

"Well, no matter what they say, you know what a kid like her is capable of. Look at Mozart. Is he remembered as the autistic guy, or one of the greatest composers to ever live who happened to be autistic?"

"Thank you, I appreciate this," Sophie said sincerely.

"You're a wonderful mom, Sophie. I really admire that about you," Noah said kindly.

Noah had never seen Sophie screaming through the bathroom door while holding onto the door handle for dear life, but she did really appreciate the sentiment.

At that moment, the door opened, and Maddie came out escorted by the psychologist. Maddie still looked so sweet in her winter school uniform, and Sophie forgot for a millisecond as to why they were there.

Elaine Woodley beckoned Sophie over with a kind smile. Sophie immediately grabbed her handbag and crossed the waiting room over to them both.

"How did it go?" Sophie asked, half in hope, half in anxiety.

"Well, I do think Maddie possesses quite an extraordinary memory," she reported. "It's possible a lot of Maddie's … outbursts could possibly be attributed to cognitive overload. However, I do also see several characteristics that are consistent with ASD. I'd like to continue to see and observe her for a few more sessions before I give you a confirmed diagnosis."

Sophie nodded. "Yes, or course," she agreed.

"Maddie's been telling me all about these piano lessons," Elaine continued.

"Mummy is going to ask Noah if I can have another one after school today," Maddie said excitedly.

"She's a clever cookie, this one," Elaine nodded down to Maddie. "I look forward to seeing you next week, Maddie." She grinned down at her. "If you'll see my receptionist, she will sort you out with an appointment." She pointed over to the reception desk.

Sophie took a staggered breath. Okay. What had she just learned? Maddie's tantrums and outbursts could be caused by cognitive overload. She could just be overwhelmed. Okay. But there were still behaviours that were consistent with ASD. Okay, Sophie could deal with that, too. It wasn't bad. It wasn't a label.

Mozart, Sophie said to herself. Maddie's potential would not be limited.

"Sophie," called Elaine.

Sophie snapped out of her own thoughts. "Yes?"

"You have a wonderful daughter," she complimented, "and I would be letting you know if I was worried about her."

Sophie managed a small smile, and she and Maddie made their way over to the reception desk. The receptionist flipped over her large diary to the following week.

"What day were you thinking?" she asked. "We have the same time available next Thursday."

"That's fine," agreed Sophie.

She watched as the receptionist wrote down Maddie's name next to the appointment time. She then wrote it down on a reminder card for Sophie to keep.

"Now, do you have private health insurance?" she asked, clicking onto the computer and getting out the credit card machine.

"No," confessed Sophie. This was why she was working the extra shifts.

"Okay, not to worry. I'll just set you up as a new client. There is a five pound new client fee on top of your session cost."

Sophie sucked in a breath. "Okay," she agreed.

"I'll need your name, date of birth, and mailing address as guardian, and then Maddie's name and date of birth."

"Sophie Cartwright, fourth of April, ninety-four. We live in Unit 4, 5 Carrington Lane, Gunnersbury, London W4 5PT. Maddie's full name is Madeleine Cartwright. Her birthday is fifth of June 2012."

The receptionist typed their information into the system. "And just a contact number and an email address?" she then asked.

Sophie gave her that information as well.

"Okay, lovely. That'll be eighty-five pounds for today then," She pushed the buttons on the credit card machine and then turned it around for Sophie.

It physically hurt Sophie to put in her PIN number. She did not think she had spent eighty-five pounds on anything before, except for of course rent and utilities. But this was necessary, and she was willing to do whatever was needed.

And what she needed to do right now was to get Maddie back to school so that she could get back to work to earn enough to pay for her session next week.

Chapter 14

It would be two weeks on Monday since Noah had begun giving Maddie piano lessons, although, she seemed to be teaching him more than he did her. Noah's own mind had helped him to understand every possible combination of sounds a piano could make at a young age, but Maddie was proving him wrong.

Maddie definitely got her creative talent from her mom. Not only did she have a brilliant memory for music; Noah could teach her a piece and Maddie could repeat it immediately, but she had a real knack for coming up with brilliant twists to his melodies.

Maddie simply claimed that she was making them sound better, and that was exactly what she was doing. She understood the instrument, how it sounded, how it worked, and she knew what she could make it do.

Since starting to play with Maddie, Noah's score had begun to explode out of him. He had his sound, as Tally had told him, and he could now hear the entire movie. He was writing page after page of music, and then was putting it to the rough scenes that he had on his laptop. During their lessons, Noah would play what he had come up with for Maddie, and she would make it better, quite literally.

This kid was brilliant, and Noah often sat in awe of her.

Watching Maddie play had relaxed Sophie quite dramatically, Noah observed. She had been a wreck after her first appointment, and she was, of course, still anxious about Maddie's pending diagnosis.

But no matter what the doctors said, it couldn't take away Maddie's talent, and Noah believed that Sophie knew that, too.

Sophie had always looked like she was carrying around such a huge burden, like she was walking with a hundred-pound bar-bell over her shoulders that she couldn't seem to shift. She now seemed to be carrying herself a little differently.

She was standing taller, and she was smiling. Smiling at her co-workers, and she was smiling at him. Sophie actually had a really beautiful smile. When she smiled, her whole face warmed, and you couldn't help but feel the same way.

Sophie's energy was incredibly warm anyway. He'd never seen someone so wholly care for another before, without any concern for themselves. He understood that she was a mom, and her daughter came first, but Sophie really didn't think about herself at all.

He'd caught himself staring at her several times in the last week. He hadn't meant to; it was just hard not to notice the change in her as she cheerfully went about preparing the bar floor for a night of customers.

She was wearing her hair down tonight. Sophie had such beau-tiful hair that was a really interesting light shade of red. Maddie had the same colour. She had a slight olive-y undertone to her skin, which was smooth and clear. Her eyes, Noah thought, were perhaps the warmest part about her. It didn't hurt that the shade of brown reminded him of his favourite kind of chocolate.

Any.

She had a cute little nose that was ever so slightly upturned at the end, and her lips were soft, full, and pink. She didn't seem to wear much makeup. Or perhaps she did, he wouldn't know. His only experience, really, was the Sephora store that was set up in his bathroom as Vanessa liked his vanity more than the one in hers and Tally's bathroom.

Well, whatever she did or didn't use, she was pretty. God, she was really pretty.

Sophie made her way across the floor, laughing along with something that Holly had said, as she carried a tray of salt and pepper shakers. Holly was refilling the napkins.

As Sophie moved, her hair swished behind her, and Noah found that he couldn't take his eyes off of her. He wanted to know what she was laughing about. He wanted to be the one making her laugh.

Shit, Noah realised. He was crushing on Sophie. Oh, good God, was he in middle school? A freaking crush?

Noah managed to snap himself out of his thoughts and to concentrate on Maddie's playing in time for Sophie to join them.

"How is the lesson going?" she asked them both, setting her tray down on the closest table as she folded her arms across her chest.

"Good, Mummy," chirped Maddie happily as she played. Maddie was playing the overture that Noah had composed for the opening credits of the film. Of course, she was tweaking it and making it better, as she had done with every piece of music that he had produced.

If he wasn't so in awe, his ego would have been a little wounded.

"Are you ready for tonight?" Noah asked, managing to find a coherent question in his brain to ask her.

Sophie took a shaky breath but nodded. "Les Mis and Phantom are always crowd favourites, even if I Dreamed a Dream is an incredibly difficult song to sing well."

"Sophie, do you not realise just how talented you are?" Noah asked in disbelief. "You know now the kind of people that I work with, that I listen to. Trust me when I saw you're special. I really mean it." In more ways than one, Noah was learning.

His heart seemed to stir as a flush of red came into Sophie's cheeks. Yep, this was definitely a real crush alright.

"Alright, well, when this song is finished, you need to come and have your dinner, Maddie," Sophie reminded. She offered Noah a smile as she turned away, returning her tray to the bar.

God, if Sophie's life had gone another way, she really could have been incredible. Not that she wasn't already. She had a beautiful, crystal clear theatre voice. But had she had the time to commit to theatre, Noah had no doubt that she would have been a star.

The customers were silent as Noah played the final notes of the Les Mis ballad, and Sophie sung, "Now life has killed the dream I dreamed." Her last ethereal note finished, and the bar erupted into applause.

Noah, too, stood up and clapped for Sophie, and she looked back at him with a bewildered, yet energised smile, as though she stillcouldn't believe that these people were clapping for her.

She reached back for him, taking his hand, and pulling him forward so that they could bow together. There was a second wave of applause for him, too, and Noah was wholly unused to receiving accolades from a live crowd. After all, he usually worked in a shoe-box sized studio.

Both of them jumped off the stage, and Sophie beamed up at him. Noah could have easily gotten lost in the moment. He could have kissed her right then and there. Could he do that?

But before he could even finish the thought, they were interrupted by a booming, possessive voice.

"Babe! Soph!" he called. An average sized blond man was pushing his way rudely through the crowd. Though not tall in stature, he was absolutely thickwith muscle. His arms alone looked like tree trunks in his tight, black shirt,

Noah watched as Sophie's excited demeanour immediately disappeared as she dreaded the approach of this man. Noah had seen him the last few Fridays. He tended to sit with friends in Sophie's section. He hadn't asked Sophie who he was, but it was not hard to guess that Sophie had a history with him.

Was this her type? Noah certainly didn't get biceps like thatplaying the damn piano.

"Beck, I was in a really good mood a moment ago. Must you ruin it?" Sophie asked facetiously as the man, Beck reached them.

Beck's blue eyes looked over Noah is an egotistical way. Dismissing Noah, he edged him out of the conversation before it had even begun by turning his back on him. "You look hot tonight, Soph."

Sophie rolled her eyes. "You're arriving later than usual."

"Had a late call out," replied Beck. "Went home, got changed, and came out with the lads. Caught the end of your song though, babe. You sounded alright. Looked even better."

Noah hated him. It felt strange to so viciously hate someone after thirty seconds of being in their presence, and yet here he was.

Beck threw a glance back over his shoulder as he asked, "How's ourdaughter?"

Holy crap, this asshole was Maddie's father. Of course, she had history with this guy. She'd had a kid with him. And Noah suddenly felt more jealousy in that moment then had since he was in the eighth grade crushing on Missy Janowitz.

Noah immediately left them, not wanting to overhear their conversation. He didn't like feeling jealous at all. He wasn't a teenager, and it simply felt ridiculous. Noah weaved around the customer's and passed Pete at the bar.

"Just getting some air. I'll be back to play in a few minutes," he called as he walked out onto the street.

Jesus, the London wind had bite. He wasn't used the cold as a California native. He didn't really own anything thicker than a sweater and to be in a place like London as they headed into winter, he would need to invest in a coat.

Shaftesbury Avenue was heaving with people on a Friday night. There were cars and busses on the road, and people crossing every which way as they entered the theatres, restaurants and bars.

Noah pulled out his cell phone and FaceTimed Tally, but she didn't answer. He then realised that with the time difference, she would be teaching her afternoon classes. Crap, just when he really needed her.

He decided to call Vanessa instead, and he leaned against the wall of the bar as the phone rang.

"Hey!" cried Vanessa as she answered the phone.

"Hey," replied Noah. "Are you busy?"

"I'm just doing a yoga class at home, but I can finish it later. What's up?" Vanessa asked.

Whereas Tally was blunt, honest, and funny, Vanessa was romantic, creative, and passionate. Perhaps she was the right person to talk to about this sort of thing.

"How would you want to be asked out on a first date?" he asked. "Hypothetically, imagine you have a daughter, say eight years old, who is incredible, but has a lotgoing on. Oh, and your giant dick of a baby daddy is hanging around your place of work. How would you want to be asked out?" he repeated. "And would you even say yes given all that?"

"Well ... I haven't exactly been on a first date in nine years," Vanessa replied coyly, "but if I swung that way, I'd totally say yes to you, no matter my baggage, Noah. You're a good guy. A really good guy, and Sophie would be lucky to have you."

"Tally's a big, fat tattle tale, isn't she?" muttered Noah.

Vanessa laughed. "It's sort of my fault. I've got a charity thing in New York over Thanksgiving weekend and I didn't want your mom to hate me or Tally for missing dinner in Napa."

"You know you are her favourite child most of the time, you realise," Noah reminded her. It was true. Joy loved on Vanessa twice as hard sometimes because Vanessa's own parents couldn't ... or simply didn't want to. "I'm serious though. Sophie's got a lot going on. And I've just realised that this asshole that hangs around the bar every Friday night is Maddie's dad. She's probably not going to be interested ... and what would we even do? I'm going back to LA to record in December anyway."

"Excuse, excuse, excuse, excuse," Vanessa scolded. "Don't let your own worries stop you from going after what you want."

And she was right. Noah had just gone from confessing that he had a big ol' crush on Sophie, to then creating half a dozen reasons in his head as to why he shouldn't do anything about it.

Noah hadn't dated anyone in a long time. Once he had finally wised up to the beautiful models and actresses who only seemed interested in him for as long as they needed him to get some relevancy, he had become very reluctant to get back into the dating sphere.

Sophie wasn't like that.

And he didn't think of her baggage as ... well ... baggage. Maddie was incredible, in every sense of the word.

And really, jealousy was for teenagers. He was an adult. If he had feelings for a woman, he needed to grow some balls and do something about them. What's the worst that could happen?

"Maybe I'd get a great heartbreak song out of it?" Vanessa suggested teasingly, and Noah could hear the smile in her voice.

Noah hadn't realised he'd asked that question out loud. "Jesus, Vanessa, I could get you a whole album," uttered Noah.

At that moment, the door of the bar opened, and Sophie stuck her head out. When she spotted him, she stepped out into the street and rubbed her arms as the wind chilled her immediately.

"I've got to go," Noah said quickly.

"Call me later!" cried Vanessa. "I'm invested now. I need to know what happens."

Noah ended the call and shoved his cell in his back pocket. "Hey," he greeted.

"I'd wondered where you'd got to," Sophie said as she approached him. "What are you doing out here?"

"Just needed some air," replied Noah.

"Me, too. Though it's bloody freezing." Sophie laughed at herself. Noah then wished he was wearing a coat that he could wrap around her like in a cheesy movie. "I'm really sorry about Beck," she apologised, her face falling, and her mouth pressing together in a distasteful expression. "Holly calls him a walking haemorrhoid."

Noah couldn't help but burst out laughing as such an accurate insult. "He did seem like a total dick," he replied honestly. "But you don't need to apologise for him, Sophie." Taking a breath, he asked, "How long ago did you guys break up?"

Sophie exhaled, and shook her head. "Um, about seventeen seconds after I told him I was pregnant," she said bluntly.

Noah nearly choked on his tongue as he took in what Sophie said. What the actual fuck? And the guy still had the balls to walk around like he had some sort of right to impose upon Sophie?

"What an asshole!" hissed Noah.

Sophie nodded. "I know, don't you worry. We aren't together. He doesn't even have a relationship with Maddie, really. I think he only asked about her tonight because you were standing there, and he's a possessive prick. I'm the one who usually reminds him that he has a child." Sophie then added shakily, "I'm honestly embarrassed that you had to see that. I don't want you to think badly of me for being with a man like that. All I can say is that I was a lot dumber at seventeen when I met him."

Noah's finger was underneath Sophie's chin, lifting it up, before he had a chance to realise what he was doing. "Sophie, it's impossible for me to think badly of you. I think you are wonderful," he said honestly.

And here went nothing. Worst case scenario, he was old enough to accept it if she did say no, and he would understand her reasons for it. But God he hoped she said yes.

"Sophie ..."

"Yes?"

For want of a better word, he continued, "I've got a huge crush on you." The words came out surprisingly smoothly.

Sophie's eyes widened, and her jaw dropped in shock.

"Would you like to go and grab a coffee with me sometime?"

Chapter 15

The last time Sophie had accepted a date, she had been seventeen, and Beck had said, "You're bangin', Soph. Let's go out." She had giddily agreed to that. She was not even sure if sitting in a living room of a flat that Beck shared with three of his mates while they all watched football even counted as a date.

She had been asked out on several occasions over the years. Her line of work meant that she was often in the eye of socially lubricated men. But she had never accepted. She had always put Maddie first. Before her career, and certainly before her love life. There had never been room for a relationship before.

She had not expected Noah to ask her out on a date. She had not even realised that he had feelings for her. But perhaps she was just terribly inexperienced at this sort of thing that she wouldn't notice.

Noah wasn't a tosser who got drunk with his mates. He definitely wasn't the sort of man to try to cop a feel while she walked past his table.

Oh, dear, why was she even thinking about Beck and every other loser that she had encountered at a time like this? Noah was standing in front of her, losing heart and confidence with every passing second that Sophie stayed silent, staring at him with her mouth agape like a bloody flytrap.

She knew the man that Noah was. She knew that he was different. Good different. He was ever so kind. The way he had connected with Maddie over the last few weeks had made her heart grow three bloody sizes to the point that sometimes it didn't feel like it could fit in her chest. He was not only good to Maddie, but he was so sweet to her. He had quickly become a very good friend to Sophie, and were it not for him, she would surely have gone mad in the wait to hear of Maddie's diagnosis.

Noah listened to her. She could unload her problems and stressors and he would come back with genuine, kind advice and reassurances.

He was gifted at what he did. Sophie didn't think she'd ever met a more talented person in her life. He liked to call her talented, but she indeed needed to hold up a mirror to him.

And he was dreadfully adorable. She would be lying if she hadn't caught herself smiling as his shaggy, dark hair, fell into his eyes when he concentrated too hard on a piece he was writing throughout the day.

Sophie realised that she liked Noah, too. Perhaps it had started the first time he had played the piano with Maddie. No, Sophie realised. It had definitely begun when she had first watched him connect with her daughter at the piano.

"You know what? Don't even worry about it," Noah said finally, his cheeks flushing as he held up his hands. "I'm really sorry if I've just made you feel really awkward. Forget I said anything. Don't even mention it. It's cool. I don't mind at all. Like, I completely get it –"

"Aren't you going to let me answer then?" Sophie asked suddenly, interrupting him.

Noah shut his mouth.

A smile spread across Sophie's face as a terribly excited feeling begun to swell in her stomach. Was she going to do this? Too bloody right, she was. "I'd love to go out with you," she accepted, "but I must tell you, I don't drink coffee."

Noah let out a staggered breath as he smiled with relief. "Coffee, tea, soda, water, I don't care," he said breathlessly. "Yeah?" he furrowed his eyebrows. "Are you sure?"

Sophie laughed. "Are you trying to talk me out of it?"

Noah shook his head. "God, no, I just … I'm really glad you said 'yes', Sophie. I think you're something special, and I really like you."

Sophie wondered if it was her erratic anxiety or her moaning that had attracted him, but either was, she was suddenly so bloody excited to be doing something like this for the first time in so many years.

"I really like you, too," reciprocated Sophie. "But if I'm going to have all ten of my fingers on this date, then I had better go back inside."

As Sophie rubbed her hands together, Noah suddenly enveloped them in his own large hands. Sophie gasped, and immediately felt an immediate electric shock of warmth. He was looking down at her with his focussed, blue eyes, and a smile on his mouth.

"Are you free on Sunday?" he asked quietly.

"Y-yes, during the day," stammered Sophie. "I'm working at night."

"Perfect. Can I pick you up at say, ten? The hotel I'm staying at does this amazing looking breakfast brunch set up. I think they do tea. You're a tea drinker, right?"

Sophie frowned. "You want to pick me up at my flat, and then travel all the way back into the city to your hotel?" she clarified. "I could just take the train ..."

"Do you think my mother would ever let me sit at her table again if I didn't pick a lady up on the first date?" Noah admonished comically.

Sophie giggled. "No, I suppose not." She immediately thought back to her conversation a couple of weeks ago with Noah's mum. Lord, she would be having conniptions if she knew about these events, Sophie theorised.

"Can you text me your address, and I'll be there on Sunday?" Noah asked.

"Oh, sure." Sophie nodded, managing to hide her sudden panic at needing to manically tidy her flat. It was even more of a pigsty now that she was working weekends. That was when she usually caught up on tidying, dishes and washing. So long as Maddie's school uniform and her work uniform were clean, she counted that as a win. "I ought to get back inside. Pete will be wondering where I've disappeared to." Sophie pulled her hands from Noah's and skipped back inside to pub. Noah followed her, passing her at the bar as he went back up on stage to resume his normal playing.

Just as Sophie was about to pick up a tray of drinks, her phone vibrated in her back pocket.

Pulling it out, she saw that she had a text from Noah.

Can't wait.

He wasn't looking at her, but he was grinning as he began to play again for the customers. Sophie couldn't help but sheepishly smile herself as she lifted her tray into her arms. Not even Beck and his mates sitting in her section could spoil her mood.

Sophie checked her appearance right before she went into Pete's the next evening. She felt really silly for wearing makeup. She hoped it wouldn't appear as though she was trying too hard, but she wanted to make an effort to look nicer. Sophie didn't own much in the way of expensive makeup. She did have some products from way back in her teenage years, but they were all so horribly expired that she was certain she might contract a yeast infection from using them.

Sophie was wearing a tinted moisturiser, some mascara, and lip gloss, the latter of which had immediately fascinated Maddie. As she had strawberry blonde hair, her eyelashes were naturally fair, and so she liked the look of them with mascara. Perhaps she might continue to use it.

As soon as Pete saw Sophie, he noticed her appearance, and a sly grin spread across his face. "Oh, now, don't we look gorgeous this evening," he remarked.

"Shut it," Sophie whispered.

Noah looked up from the piano as soon as he heard Pete's comment. His eyebrows rose when he saw her, and he smiled, too.

And now Sophie felt ridiculous. It probably did look as though she was trying too hard. She just didn't want to look like a tired mum for once.

Sophie dashed into the backroom, where she found both Holly and Amy sitting on their break before the evening shift.

"Oh, Sophie!" cried Holly. "Look at this fittie I matched with on Tinder today." Holly leapt off the sofa with her phone, quickly shoving it in front of her face.

Sophie was not greeted with the face of a good-looking man, but a Tinder profile featuring his eight-pack abdomen. "You could grate cheese on those things!"

"I know right," Holly bragged. "His name is Eamon. He's a swimmer. I didn't even know you could be a swimmer outside of the Olympics but apparently you can. We're hooking up after work tonight." Holly suddenly noticed Sophie's face, and she gasped excitedly. "Well, don't you look pretty, Mummy dearest!" she cried.

"The whole point was to not look like a mummy dearest," mumbled Sophie as she hung up her bag and her coat.

"I love it, Sophie," complimented Amy. "You look really nice. And what even are you wearing anyway? A dash of concealer and some mascara? Me? I've still got my puberty acne and I'm twenty."

"I still get acne and I'm twenty-six, but thanks, Amy." Sophie smiled at her, and then felt a pang of guilt considering that Amy had liked Noah initially. She hadn't tried anything with him since her failed attempt at a date a few weeks ago. She hadn't even mentioned him. "Hey, I hope this doesn't upset you, but I've sort of agreed to go out with Noah tomorrow."

"WHAT?" Holly all but screamed. She practically tackled Sophie onto the Sophie, holding her down, before she exclaimed, "Tell me everything!"

Amy quickly followed. "No, it's alright!" she promised. "Nothing happened there. I've sort of started seeing someone else anyway."

"She's shagging Tony," Holly translated. "Haven't you noticed them making gooey eyes at each other? It's so cute." Holly was finished with that story and had moved back to Sophie, not giving Sophie any opportunity to ask Amy about bouncer Tony. "So?" she pressed. "When did this happen?"

"Last night," Sophie admitted. "He's taking me out for break-fast/brunch type thing tomorrow." She felt her cheeks warm. "He's just been so sweet to Maddie, and he's such a nice guy. He's a good person, and he's close with his family, and he's ever so talented –"

Holly suddenly gasped as she jumped up from the sofa and ran over to her hanging handbag. She pulled out her purse and rifled through it, coming back out with a business card. She held it out to Sophie. "This is my salon. As for Olga. She does a Brazilian that you can't even feel. Incredible!" she promised.

"Oh my God, Holly, we're going out for breakfast. You're about twenty-seven steps ahead of me!" Sophie hissed. She couldn't even think that far ahead, let alone plan for it.

Holly leaned around Sophie and slipped the business card into her back pocked. "Well, for when you need it then!" she insisted.

"Get your head out of the gutter, Holly," Amy playfully scolded.

Holly poked her tongue out. "Whatever, you loved Olga. Now, what time am I coming over to babysit Mads?"

Sophie softened. "Thank you," she said gratefully. "He's picking me up at ten."

"I'll be there at nine to make sure you're looking to die for, babes."

"Are you three done gossiping, or can I join?" Pete asked as he entered the backroom. "What's this I hear about our Sophie dusting out the cobwebs?"

"You're terrible," Sophie accused, blushing.

"The piano man has asked Sophie out for breakfast tomorrow," Holly reported flirtatiously. "Pete, I need the day shift off so I can babysit Maddie!"

"Are we meant to be surprised by this?" Pete asked. "Every straight man knows the way to a mum is through the kid. Boy's got game," he praised. "Sure, Holly," he added. "Sophie needs a man."

"Oh, hush!" hissed Sophie, slapping Pete lightly. "Noah's not like that at all and you know it. Now if you lot don't mind, perhaps we ought to start getting ready for tonight."

Sophie stepped out into the pub and found that Noah had left the stage and was walking over to her. She couldn't help but smile at him, and she sucked in an excited breath as he reached for her. Sophie hugged him, wrapping her arms around his waist as she rested her head against his chest. She felt him rest his chin on the top of her head. Holy hell, this felt really nice.

But she ended it, pulling away so as not to be caught and teased by her gossipy colleagues.

"Thanks for sending me your address," he uttered quietly.

"Do you know which train to take?" Sophie asked.

"I was just going to get a cab," he replied.

"A taxi all the way out to Gunnersbury?" Sophie frowned. "That's an expensive fare."

"I'd probably need a local to teach me the subway," he murmured slyly. "Maybe for our second date, you could show me the ropes."

Sophie's heart flip-flopped. Her phone suddenly started to vibrate, indicating a phone call. Sophie immediately started to panic, thinking that there was something wrong with Maddie. But as soon as she looked at who was calling, she saw that it was Elaine Woodley calling.

"It's Maddie's psychologist," Sophie whispered. And she was calling on a Saturday. Sophie immediately knew she was about to hear news that would change everything.

CHAPTER 16

"Hello?" Sophie answered, honestly shocked that her voice sounded as steady as it was. She couldn't even feel her individual heartbeats as the poor muscle moved at a hum.

"Hi, Sophie," said Elaine. "I am so sorry to call at such an odd time, but I thought that you would want to hear this just as soon as I had come to a diagnosis."

Diagnosis. Sophie's heart all but fell out of her chest and onto the floor. She could see that Noah was reading her face exactly. Sophie braced herself for the words.

"Upon thorough screening, I am confident in my diagnosis of Maddie having Autism Spectrum Disorder," she said calmly, but not apologetically.

Sophie's eyes filled with tears as she looked up at Noah, willing herself not to drop her phone. All feelings of preparedness for this day had fully gone out the window. As much as she didn't want to be, Sophie felt devastated.

Noah rested his hands on Sophie's shoulders, but there was not much that he could do to stop her from losing it.

"Sophie, I completely understand that even though we have been discussing the possibility for weeks, that this can come at a shock, and that such a diagnosis can be very disappointing for most parents." She took a steady breath. "Maddie is what many would classify as high-functioning. She is highly intelligent and articulate. Her limitations lie in how she is able to socially function. Her ability to form social relationships, and how to properly manage her emotions is something that I can help with, and her school can assist with now that we have this diagnosis. I would like to continue to see Maddie once a week, and we shall see how we go from there."

"Okay," whispered Sophie.

"Are you alright, Sophie?" asked Elaine.

"No," replied Sophie honestly.

"Are you alone?"

Looking up at Noah's concerned face, Sophie repeated, "No."

"I promise that this isn't the end of the world," Elaine assured her. "You know more than anyone what a special girl you have. I will do my best to make her life, and yours, a little easier."

"Thank you," Sophie managed to say.

"You have a good evening, now, Sophie. Please don't hesitate to ring my office with any questions." Elaine then hung up the phone.

Sophie's knees suddenly gave way and she fell to the floor. Noah quickly dropped to his knees as well, looking a little lost at what to do.

"She's autistic," Sophie murmured, shaking her head. "I mean, I already knew it, really ... but ..."

"It's not the same as a shrink confirming it," surmised Noah.

Sophie's lip trembled as she felt like grizzling. She felt like such a terrible person for wishing Maddie was different. Of course, she loved her regardless, ridiculously so, but how she wished Maddie's life would not be so hard. She already had it tough with Sophie as a mum.

"I wish she didn't have it," Sophie confessed, her voice so soft she could barely be heard.

"Of course, you do," replied Noah quietly. "No mom wants her kid's life to be any harder than it already is."

Sophie honestly felt like grieving, as though she was mourning the loss of the future that she had once pictured for Maddie. Her future was now foggy; Sophie couldn't see it clearly, as they were both about to step into an unknown. "I ... I don't think I can go tomorrow," she decided vulnerably.

Noah frowned. "Oh ... okay." He nodded. "That's fine, I get that. We can make it for another day."

"No." Sophie shook her head. "No, I can't. Not like this. Maddie needs me to be there for her, and I can't be ..."

"Yes, you can," Noah interrupted firmly. "Maddie is going to be finebecause she is an incredible kid. You start smothering her and fussing over her now that she has a label and you're going to make her feel different."

Sophie blinked and fell back off her knees and onto her backside. She had not been expecting such a harsh truth, but bloody hell if that's not what it was. Truth.

"I'd planned on giving you this tomorrow. I sort of hoped it might have made you like me more, but I think you need to see it now." Noah climbed to his feet and jogged across the bar, back to the stage. She jumped up on the stage and began sifting through his sheet music before he found the piece he wanted.

How was a piece of sheet music supposed to make Sophie like him more? Was he going to play for her? That idea was quickly quashed when he left the stage and walked back over to her with conviction.

Noah held out the music to her, and Sophie took it, confused. She couldn't read music, and so all the notes, flourishes and treble clefs were lost on her. But the title she could read.

Mother & Daughter, she read.

Music by Noah Bentley and Madeleine Cartwright.

Sophie's mouth opened, but she could not think of what to say as she comprehended what she was reading. This piece of music was written by Noah and her baby.

"You gave her credit?"

"A diagnosis doesn't mean there is anything wrong with her. Some thingsaregoing to be a little harder. And that's where you can help. But you celebrate the good, Sophie. And there is a lot of good in that kid's future." Noah smiled. "And of course, I gave her credit. I couldn't have written that piece without her."

Sophie clutched the music to her chest as happy tears began to fall. "I did tell you that I cry all the time," she reminded him. "Do you still want to go out with blubbering me tomorrow?"

"Ow, bleeding hell!" Sophie swore as she stubbed her toe on the foot of her sofa as she folded the bed away. She nearly spat her toothbrush out of her mouth as she raced to brush her teeth and arrange the cushions on the sofa at the same time.

She had barely slept. She had been up late after work tidying and had woken up early to tidy some more. She had scrubbed and dusted every surface of her tiny flat ... and had shoved washing into wardrobes and dirty dishes into the oven and Maddie's toys underneath her bed.

Sophie arranged a throw rug on the sofa to look casually strewn and placed a teacup just so on her little side table, in an effort for the cleanliness to look lived in, and not so obvious that she had tidied because there was a guest coming.

Maddie was happily eating her Weetabix in front of the television. Sophie quickly raced into the bathroom to spit out her toothpaste and to pull the rollers out of her hair. She teased and combed her hair, and sprayed it when the casual, no-effort-but-took-hours curls fell just so.

Sophie checked the time on her phone and saw it was nearly half past nine. Oh God, he would be here soon, and she hadn't even decided on something to wear. She didn't really have any outfits nice enough for a date.

Most of her clothes were either work things or pyjamas.

There was a sudden knock at the door, and Sophie swore again under her breath. That had to be Holly. She knew the door code to her block of flats. She ran from the bathroom and pulled the door open.

"Babes, you look gorgeous!" Holly exclaimed.

It didn't escape Sophie's notice that Holly was in her work outfit from last night. She must have spent the night with the swimmer. But Sophie was still grateful she had made it on time. She was, however, holding a dry-cleaning bag over her shoulder.

"I haven't started my makeup, and all of my clothes are pyjamas," Sophie complained.

Holly held up the dry-cleaning bag. "My date outfit from last night. I thought you would need it, so I didn't wear it. Not that I needed an outfit for long anyway." Holly winked and strutted confidently into Sophie's flat. She laid the bag out on Sophie's sofa and unzipped it, pulling out a gorgeous, black figure-hugging minidress. It was plain, but it didn't need embellishment to know that it would look amazing on Holly.

"Are you mad?" Sophie hissed. "I don't want all of London to see the skin folds I have left over from having her." She motioned to Maddie who was blissfully unaware of their conversation.

"You exaggerate," Holly said dismissively. "Pop on a cute cardigan and this is absolutely a banging day dress. This little number has never failed me," she said wistfully. "She's gotten me two football players from Leeds United, one b-list reality star, and a guy who could have been Zac Efron's long lost twin brother."

Sophie rolled her eyes but couldn't help smirking. She loved how confident Holly was. "Will you zip me up?" she asked.

Holly grinned.

Sophie had to suck it in, but Holly did manage to get the zip up. It was tight, really tight, but it did hold in any unsightly features and make Sophie look a lot more like she had an hourglass shape. She added a cream coloured cardigan and a pair of plain ballet flats and was satisfied that she was ready to go.

Ready to go on her first date in nine or so years.

But before she had time to start panicking, her phone rang. Sophie saw that it was Noah calling. Holly squealed in excited delight as Sophie answered.

"Hi," she said breathlessly.

"Hey, I wanted to be a gentleman and knock on your door and everything, except I have no idea which doorbell is your apartment as the numbers seem to have rubbed off and your building is serviced by a combination lock." He laughed at himself.

"Why don't I come down?" Sophie suggested. That way Noah wouldn't have to walk through the halls of her block of flats and see the awful graffiti and the cigarette butts and every other charming addition that made it such a nice place to live. Not giving him a chance to respond, Sophie added, "I'll be there in a minute."

As soon as she hung up the phone, she gasped. "Oh, God, we spent so much time forcing the bloody zip up on this dress that I forgot to put on makeup!" she cried.

"I have lip balm," Holly offered. "You might need it." She made a kiss face.

"Oh, sod it. He's used to me looking like a tired mum." Sophie went over behind Maddie and kissed her on the top of her head. "Will you be good for Holly?" she asked.

"Yes, Mummy," replied Maddie with a smile.

"We're going to have loads of fun, aren't we, Mads?" Holly urged Sophie out the door. "Babes, seriously, have fun. You deserve it."

"Thank you," Sophie said gratefully. She grabbed her handbag and keys and locked the door behind her. She flew down the flight of stairs and reached the entrance door in a matter of minutes.

Noah was waiting out on the footpath looking ever so dapper. He was wearing dark trousers and a button-down blue shirt, with a smart navy blazer. His dark hair was combed out of his face, and he looked a little nervous.

Sophie pushed open the door and stepped out onto the path, and Noah turned at the sound of the squeaking hinges. The moment he saw her, he grinned, looking terribly pleased, and Sophie was suddenly very glad that Holly had talked her into wearing this dress, and that she had been able to suck her stomach in enough to be zipped into it.

"Wow, you look beautiful," he remarked tenderly.

"You look very handsome yourself," she returned the compliment, tucking one leg behind the other as she stood before him.

Noah produced a single pink rose from behind his back and met her with it. "I didn't know what kinds of flowers you like, but my dad always buys pink roses for my mom and they make her smile, so I thought I'd see if it worked on you."

Sophie grinned as she accepted the rose, bring it to her nose as she smelled the beautiful perfume.

"Ah, it works," he observed, satisfied.

Sophie laughed lightly. "I've never been given a flower before," she commented. "I don't really know what sort I like. This is very beautiful though, so maybe pink roses will be my favourite."

"Got it," he replied, as though he was committing it to memory. "How are you?" he asked, his tone changing.

Sophie knew exactly what he was asking. "Okay," she said truthfully. "I am okay. I needed to be shocked, and I needed to have a little grizzle about it. I haven't told her yet, but ... no label is going to change how brilliant she is, is it?"

"Not at all." Noah offered Sophie his hand, and she placed hers in his, lacing their fingers together effortlessly.

CHAPTER 17

"Did you take a taxi out here?" Sophie asked as she turned her head down the street, looking out for a black cab.

"I did, but I was nearly late with how long it took to drive out," mused Noah. "Thought I'd ask for those subway lessons early."

Sophie grinned. The tube was so much easier. They walked together, chatting, to Gunnersbury Station. Sophie enjoyed the ease of their conversation, liking that they could chat about something as menial as movie genre tastes when only yesterday she had been blubbering in front of him.

"You like romantic comedies?" Sophie asked in disbelief.

"Don't you?" Noah countered.

"Well, yes, of course. But I've never met a man brave enough to admit to liking them."

"Well, perhaps I'm more secure in my masculinity then," Noah joked. "Some of my favourite film scores are from romantic comedies."

"The music makes you feel warm and fuzzy, does it?" Sophie smirked.

"Yep," Noah replied confidently as they walked inside the station.

Sophie led Noah over to the tube map and watched in amusement as Noah's eyes widened in shock. She could understand how the tube might seem overwhelming to tourists.

"What the hell?" he gasped. "Correct me if I'm wrong, but this is supposed to be easy, right?"

Sophie laughed. "It is. Look, see here," she pointed to Gunnersbury. "We are here. And where are we going?" she asked. It occurred to her that she didn't actually know which hotel Noah was staying at.

"The Savoy," he replied.

Sophie sucked in a breath that got stuck in the back of her throat, forcing her to cough. Oh dear, what luck. Not only was the Savoy one of the most expensive hotels in the city, it was also where her parents used to take her for High Tea when she was a child. Her memories of that place were filled with lectures about table manners and posture.

"Alright, well, I suppose we would get off at Covent Garden." Sophie pointed to Covent Garden Station. "The train lines are all colour coded. We are on this line here." Sophie ran her finger along the green line. "This is the District Line. Covent Garden is on the Piccadilly Line."

"Do we need to go to a different station?" Noah asked.

"No, you see these little white bridges?" Sophie showed him the symbol. "That means it's an interchange station. We can switch trains at South Kensington, and we'll be taken to Covent Garden."

Sophie could see that Noah really had no idea what she was talking about, but she loved that he was listening. "Come on, I'll have you travelling like a true Londoner in no time."

Sophie helped Noah to buy an Oyster card and then took him onto the train for the first time. It was quite busy for a Sunday, and so they both had to stand, but it only made for several opportunities to spontaneously grab hold of the other as the train jolted and moved. Every tough made Sophie blush, and smile like a teenager with a big crush.

They passed the time by continuing to get to know each other's random little interests.

"Last song you listened to?" Noah asked curiously.

Sophie smirked, thinking that he would like her answer. She pulled out her phone and tapped her music library. She was halfway through a song. She spun her phone around to show him the screen, and a wide grin spread across his face.

"My song?" he remarked, raising his eyebrows. "Well, I can't criticise your taste. That is an excellent choice." He winked.

It was part of his score from his Oscar win. "I actually went to the pictures to see Forces when it came out," she revealed. "I thought it was very good."

"Made only better by my exceptional prowess on the piano," he boasted comically. He laughed at himself. "No, I joke, but I am very proud of what I achieved with that film. I wrote it while I was in college. Took my first trip to LA to conduct an orchestra as a kid who was half the age of every other musician there." He smiled again. "I've got the same feeling about this score now, the one I'm working on."

Sophie's eyes widened. "You think you'll win for this one?"

Noah shrugged. "I don't know. I can hope, and I know when something I've written is good."

Goodness, Sophie wondered what that must be like.

Sophie showed Noah how to switch train lines, and they arrived at Covent Garden Station within the hour. He seemed to recognise his surroundings a bit more from there, and they walked together towards Noah's hotel.

"Does your mum know you are going out with me today?" Sophie asked curiously.

"God, no," he chuckled. "If she did, she'd be on FaceTime trying to watch us or something, sticking her nose in and screaming at me to pull out your chair."

"Oh, dear, I shall have to dob you in if you do not pull out my chair then," Sophie teased.

Sophie felt a little tense as they approached the hotel. Visions of her parents hissing at her, criticising her, threatening her with punishment filled her head. They would never reprimand her in public. They would never be anything other than perfect in public, but their harsh discipline was enough to quieten Sophie into never making a peep while dining in such a place.

"Sophie, are you okay?" Noah suddenly asked, rounding on her.

They were only about fifty feet from the hotel's entrance. Perhaps Sophie's hand had become too sweaty and he'd noticed.

"Yes, of course," Sophie said flippantly.

Noah arched an eyebrow.

Sophie sighed. "I'm sorry," she said sincerely. "I just used to come here with my mum and dad when I was younger."

Noah seemed to read between the lines, and he nodded. "There's a Costa Coffee around the corner. Come on," he urged.

"My dad was never around, never home, and when he was, he was viciously unpleasant and cold," Sophie explained as she sipped her tea.

They were seated within the little Costa on a wooden table in the corner. Noah was drinking an overly complicated coffee, while Sophie had been brought a little teapot. They had ordered one of every pastry and cake in the display and were quite content eating their weights in sugar.

"I grew up in a beautiful home in perhaps the richest suburb in London. I went to the most prestigious private schools and had every door there was opened for me if I ... if I did and said whatever my mum and dad wanted," Sophie continued. "My mum is obsessed with image. Hers, my fathers, and mine, once upon a time. You can imagine, I'm sure, their reactions when I told them my idiot boyfriend of five minutes had gotten me pregnant."

Noah listened. He kept eye contact with Sophie, his brow deepening with every poor rich girl detail she revealed.

"I left home, I got myself the only flat that I could afford, and I found a job at Pete's. He took me under his wing, fudged the paperwork a little seeing as I was still a few months shy of turning eighteen. It's been hard. God knows it's been hard," Sophie voice cracked. "But there have been so many more highs when I've had four pounds to my name, than when I seemingly had everything." Sophie felt her eyes water. "Oh, Jesus. I need to get my tear ducts glued shut or something." She fanned her face with her hands and looked up, trying to dry her eyes.

"Your eyes get a little lighter when you well up," Noah observed. "Almost a gold tinge to the normal brown. It's really beautiful."

"Stop it," Sophie demanded. "You can't make me start as well!" She quickly fished one of the napkins out of the dispenser and dried her eyes.

Noah chuckled. "Okay, you want to laugh?" he asked, raising his eyebrows. "My mom asked out and paid my prom date in senior year." He held up his hands. "No word of a lie."

Sophie didn't mean to, but she snorted as she tried to stifle a giggle. "What?" she asked in disbelief.

"I hadn't asked anyone because I really wasn't planning on going. But my mom had it in her head that she wanted a picture of Tally and me going to our prom. It's a twin thing. Apparently, we can't be photographed by ourselves." He shook his head. "So, she went up to a girl that she deemed good enough after school one day, asked her out, and paid her twenty bucks to go out with me."

"All for a picture?" Sophie smirked.

"All for that picture. It's still hanging up in my parent's house next to Haley and Casey's prom pictures."

"Your mum really does sound like bundles of fun," promised Sophie.

Noah exhaled. "I know I'm lucky. As much as she kills me sometimes, she has the best heart, and she would do anything for anybody." He smiled at her. "You ought to be really proud of yourself, Sophie. Really proud. I've thought you were a good mom from pretty soon after I met you, but you really have become an even better one despite the crappy hand you were dealt when it came to the lottery of moms and dads."

That really did mean a lot to Sophie coming from someone else. "I often feel like I'm a shit mum," she said honestly. "It's hard to feel like you're doing anything positive sometimes." Especially when a child struggled like Maddie did.

"Have you ever given up on Maddie?" Noah asked bluntly.

"No," Sophie said vehemently.

"Then you're not a shit mom," he promised her.

"You've honestly made me feel less shit in these last few weeks than I have in months," Sophie said croakily. "What you've done for Maddie I will forever be grateful for."

"It's been my pleasure." Noah smiled warmly at Sophie, and reached across the table for her hand, which had been resting on the side of her teacup.

Sophie linked her fingers with him and breathed easily at the calm that spread over her. "Tell me more about your family. I don't want you to see me cry for the seventeenth time this week. I liked that prom story," she teased.

"Oh, trust me, there's plenty more of Joy where that came from," he assured her knowingly. "Well, where to start? I grew up in Napa, that's northern California. Wine country. My dad's family have owned Bentley Grange for four generations. That's what my dad does, and my oldest sister now. My dad is a winemaker, and my sister, Haley, runs the business side of things. She's got an MBA and is smarter than everyone.

"Haley was definitely our second mom at times, but I do look up to her. She's sensible and responsible, and she is the person I would go to if ever something was really wrong. She has been dating a guy named Mark for about seven years or so. He's in the Marines. They're waiting for him to retire before they settle down.

"My middle sister, Casey, is hardly ever in the same place between phone calls. She's a photographer, and her job takes her all over the world. She words for National Geographic. She's very good at her job, and always has the best stories. She's in Peru at the moment and her assignment is finishing before Christmas so I'm looking forward to seeing her then. Casey is married to her job, and I can't see her ever settling down or having a family. She's very passionate and creative, and she loves travelling and adventure more than anything.

"And Tally, well, Tally is the reason why my mom knows about you." He rolled his eyes. "Tally is my twin, as you know. But she's also my best friend. I adore her, I trust her. She's got my back with the real things, and I probably wouldn't have gotten through my childhood without her kicking the ass of several bullies. I talk to Tally every day and it does feel really strange to be so far away from her.

"I live with Tally and her girlfriend, Vanessa. Vanessa, as well, is a very close friend of mine. She'd have to be to put up with me as a roommate." He chuckled. "I hope you get to meet Tally one day, because I know she'd love you. She'd probably help you to gang up on me." Noah winked.

Sophie smiled. "I hope I do." She really loved how affectionately Noah spoke about his sisters. She had always wanted siblings as a child and had envied several of her friends who had them. "I've never actually heard the name "Tally" before."

"It's a nickname," Noah explained. "She was Hallie for about a week when we were newborns, before Casey started calling her Tally and it stuck."

Sophie could just imagine a little toddler babbling as she attempted to say a new word. It reminded her of when Maddie was first learning to talk.

"Are you close with your dad?"

"I am." Noah nodded. "We weren't always. Not for a long time, actually. Uh ... you could say I wasn't exactly the son that he envisioned." He grimaced a little, and Sophie could see that this was a sore spot for him. "Only son with three girls, he was looking forward to ball games, me going out for varsity sports, bragging to his friends about however many touchdowns I was going to make. He even put a basketball court in our backyard the minute he found out that he was going to be having a son." Noah sighed. "Obviously that never happened. He took me down for peewee football when I was a kid, and I lasted ten minutes. He tried me in basketball, and in baseball. I hated everything, and ... well, for a long time my dad did give up on me."

Sophie's face fell as she took in that awful statement.

"I was into music. He wasn't. He didn't really have anything to say to me. He didn't know how to connect with me, and he stopped trying. Some of that's on me, too. I didn't try with him either." Noah's voice began to sound very raw, and Sophie wondered if he'd ever told anyone this before. "We could go weeks, really, with barely more than a passing greeting."

Sophie, who was still holding his hand, squeezed it in comfort.

His eyes had dropped, but he lifted them back up to her. He smiled reassuringly. "I definitely can empathise with you, Sophie. I know what it's like to feel like a complete disappointment to a parent. I wasn't what my dad wanted, and for about fifteen years, if there was a return to sender option, I honestly thought my dad would take it, and order a new son who wanted to go outside and throw a damn ball."

"How did you fix it?" Sophie wondered.

Noah smiled at the memory, and a lot of the sadness left his shoulders. "I came home from school one day. I think I was about sixteen or seventeen. I went into my bedroom, and on my bed was a brand-new acoustic guitar," he recalled. "There was a note on top telling me to bring the guitar out to the basketball court. So, I did. And I found my dad outside with a guitar of his own." His smile grew. "He'd been taking lessons. And we played together for the first time on that basketball court. Not the game my dad envisioned for us, but we played together. And we've been playing ever since."

Sophie gasped as her heart swelled in her chest. Just like that, Noah had gained a relationship with his dad. "Oh, for God's sake," she squeaked, seizing another napkin. "I thought you were going to make me laugh." Sophie wiped her eyes.

Noah chuckled. "Alright then, let's circle back to Joy." He thought for a moment. "When I was five, she dressed me up as her fourth daughter Noeline, to win a Mommy and Me, Mother Daughter beauty pageant as I was the only one of her kids who had a showcase-able talent. We won."

Sophie all but snorted tea from her nose as she burst into a fit of laughter.

"Yes, I know," Noah said dryly. "I should really bill her for all the therapy I need," he joked. "Um, what else? When I was twelve, she tested her new box dye peroxide on me, and paid me ten bucks for it, and I spent the next month being called "Slim Shady" before it finally grew out enough for me to cut it off."

Sophie continued to try to stop herself from laughing uncontrollably.

His face softened, before continuing softly, "She put a band-aid on every little scratch I asked her to. I never went to school without my favourite lunch. She was front row at every single performance I ever gave. She never made me feel weird or different, but special and talented. We tease her and make fun of her, but Goddamn am I grateful for her."

Sophie and Noah spent the rest of the morning exchanging stories, and simply getting to know what events had led them being exactly where they were on that day.

Sophie found the way that Noah spoke about the people who were important to him one of the most attractive things about him. His people were his grounding force, and he loved and adored them.

The second thing that she found really attractive about him was, aside from Sophie bringing up his music on the train, he didn't at all feel the need to talk about his success or his fame for want of a better word.

They were discussing what parts of their lives had shaped themselves, and Noah's thoughts went solely to his family.

It was really decent of him, Sophie thought.

The third thing was, perhaps, that the more he spoke of his love for his family, the more handsome he became to her. He already looked terribly good looking in his smart attire, but he had a certain smile, and a certain look in his eyes, when he spoke about his family.

They ate as much as they possibly could as they talked, and Sophie knew she was in for a crash after so much sugar. They both ordered another hot drink and were all but rolling out of the Costa around lunch time.

"Do you want to do something really cliché and tourist-y?" Noah asked her as they stood out on the street.

"Absolutely," Sophie agreed.

"How do you feel about the London Eye?" Noah shielded his eyes from the spontaneous sunshine as he looked to wonder which was to go.

Sophie took Noah's unsuspecting moment and stood up on her toes, gently pressing her lips to his. She pulled away after only a few seconds, and said breathlessly, "The London Eye it is."

Chapter 18

The rain had begun to sprinkle down as Noah and Sophie looked out over London from one of the pods.

Sophie had pointed out St James' Park that led toward Buckingham Palace. Noah was a right tourist as he stood up as close as he could get to the glass. As much as Sophie could have got lost in this moment, the slow spin of the wheel allowed her mind to wander, and of course it went to Maddie.

"I don't know how I'm going to tell her," Sophie admitted quietly.

Noah's head turned immediately, frowning. His expression told her that he knew exactly what she was talking about. "You tell her the truth," he advised. "She's smart, Sophie. She'll know if you're bullshitting her."

"But how can I tell her the truth? How can I tell her that something as simple as making a friend will be monumentally difficult for her?" Sophie's voice was so quiet that Noah had to lean in to hear her.

"She'll learn," Noah insisted. "Anything she can't do now, she'll learn. Besides, she does know how to connect with people ...

people who are on her wavelength. I'd wager she hasn't been able to make friends in her class because all those other kids are ten times too dumb to hold Maddie's interest."

Sophie playfully slapped Noah's arm. "Stop it, that's cruel," she scolded, though she couldn't hide a burgeoning smile. As much as she wanted to believe that what Noah said was all true, Sophie knew it wasn't. Maddie needed to be taught to connect with her peers and continuing to see her psychologist would help her build skills to do that.

She did wonder, though, that if she met other children who were as intellectual as she was, would she have the same issue? She had managed to form a connection with Noah simply because they were both as bright as each other.

"You've got to keep seeing beyond the immediate future, though, Sophie. This next conversation that you have with Maddie won't be life defining. The kid's got a lot to do and being autistic is not going to hinder her."

Sophie's head went to seeing Maddie's name atop Noah's sheet music, written as one of the composers of the piece. God, she knew Noah was right. Maddie did have a lot to do in her life. It killed her that doubt kept creeping in.

"If I tell her today, would you be there?" Sophie asked, looking up at Noah, before immediately wishing that she had bitten her tongue. Oh dear, that was far too heavy. "Please do not feel put on the spot. I don't mean to pressure you or to make you feel uncomfortable."

Noah frowned again, this time with a curious grin on his face. "Should I be offended that the offer was all but rescinded as soon as it was made?" he asked. He snaked an arm around Sophie's waist, and he pulled her against him as they leant against the rail. "Of course, I want to be there," he told her sincerely.

Sophie was internally cringing as she entered the code to her block of flats and let Noah through the door. Every so often, the teenagers in one of the other flats would through a party and their friends would graffiti the walls with profanity and lewd pictures.

They were often cleaned, but when the light hit just so through the windows, you could see exactly what was there. Sophie walked Noah up the stairs to her flat and pulled out her key to unlock her door.

"It's not much," she said bashfully. "I rented this place when I first got a job at Pete's and it was all I could afford." It was all she could still barely afford.

"I think you're forgetting I live in my sister's guestroom," Noah calmed her. "You don't need to be embarrassed."

Sophie sucked in a breath as she pushed open the door that opened up right into her living room, stroke bedroom of a night time. She thanked God silently that it was still as clean as she had left it this morning.

Sophie could hear Holly and Maddie's voices coming from the bedroom. "Please, have a seat," she offered, gesturing to her sofa. She took the few steps to her little hall that contained doors to Maddie's bedroom and the bathroom. She opened Maddie's door quietly to find she and Holly sitting on the bed reading a picture book.

Maddie was reading the picture book.

"Mummy!" cheered Maddie when she looked up from the pages. She smiled brightly. Sophie returned the warm greeting and noticed Maddie's strawberry blonde hair was fixed perfectly in two Dutch braids.

Holly's dark hair was fixed the same. "Hiya, babes," Holly winked.

"Hi," said Sophie, grinning. "What book are you reading?"

"The Day the Crayons Quit," Maddie cheered. "It was the deal."

"The deal?" repeated Sophie.

"Me and Mads was watching Hannah Montana, weren't we? I started doing my hair like, and she demanded hers be done the same way. But what was the deal we made, Mads?" Holly asked.

"I had to read Holly a book that had more than ten pages," Maddie informed Sophie. "Look, Mummy!" Maddie wriggled off of the bed to hold up her braids proudly.

"She was doing so well with the reading, too, weren't you, Mads?" prompted Holly, as she wriggled off the bed as well.

"I was," boasted Maddie. "I know all the words already."

"Well, aren't you clever?" Sophie said proudly. "Noah is in the living room, though, Maddie. Would you like to go and say hello?"

Maddie gasped excitedly and sprinted from her bedroom.

Sophie turned back to her friend and pouted her bottom lip. "You're amazing," she gushed.

"Babes, aren't I?" Holly teased. She bumped Sophie with her hip. "So," she urged. "How was it?"

"Really good," Sophie said sincerely. "He was going to take me to High Tea at the Savoy, but as soon as I said I used to go there with my mum and dad when I was younger, he changed the plans immediately and we went to Costa."

"Costa?" repeated Holly sneering. "You went from bloody schmoozing at the Savoy to flipping Costa? Babes, do I need to give you a lesson in dating. Always choose the most expensive option. If men at work learn all they need to win you over is a two quid cup of tea at Costa then I'm blooming done for."

Sophie couldn't help but laugh. "Stop it, it wasn't like that. It was sweet of him! We had a really good chat, got to know each other even better, and it was really nice. He even took me on the London Eye. If it makes you feel better, he paid for the express ticket."

"He paid, what, eighty pounds to skip the line?" cried Holly.

"I told him I was okay waiting, but I think he was excited to ride," chuckled Sophie.

"Oh, babes, that's the dream, to have a man with enough cash to skip lines," Holly sighed wistfully.

"You need a new dream," Sophie rolled her eyes, smirking. "Anyway, I had better go out there and save him. Thank you for today, Holly. It means a lot to me."

"Sophie, don't be silly!" exclaimed Holly. "You know I'm happy to help you get a shag."

"Oh, for fuck's sake," hissed Sophie.

"Exactly." Holly winked. "Alright," she kissed Sophie's cheek. "I'll see you at work tonight." Holly sashayed confidently out of Maddie's bedroom and Sophie followed her, watching as Holly said her goodbyes before leaving out the front door.

Maddie was sitting beside Noah on the sofa. Noah's sheet music was in his hand, and he was pointing at a particular line as he explained something to Maddie. Maddie was focussing intently, her rigid stare almost startling as she listened.

"Hey," greeted Noah with a smile. "I was just teaching Maddie how to read her sheet music. Once she's got it, she'll be able to play anything."

He said it like he was teaching Maddie to tie her shoelaces, but really, he was meaning Maddie could suddenly pick up a bloody Mozart symphony and she would be able to play it. The idea seemed too incredible.

"Do you drink tea?" Sophie asked Noah, leaning against the wall of her little hall. "I'm afraid it's all I've got." Next time she was at Tesco's she would need to pick up some coffee.

Noah shook his head. "No, that's okay, thanks." Noah motioned for Sophie to come over and join them on the sofa.

Sophie came and sat down beside Maddie, leaving her in the middle of Sophie and Noah. She was still studying the sheet music intently. "Maddie," Sophie said quietly, but Maddie didn't stir. "Maddie," Sophie said again. "Maddie!"

Maddie's head snapped up. "What?"

"Pardon," Sophie corrected.

"Pardon," repeated Maddie.

Sophie met Noah's eye, and he nodded encouragingly. Taking a deep breath, Sophie began. "Maddie, I had a phone call from Elaine yesterday. You know how you have been visiting with her every week for a little while."

"Yes," replied Maddie.

Sophie turned her body, tucking one of her legs underneath herself so that she could properly face Maddie. "Sweetheart, you have something called autism," Sophie explained tenderly. She would not call it a disorder in front of Maddie.

"What's that?" asked Maddie.

Breathe, Sophie, she willed herself. "It means that some things are a little tricky for you, Maddie. It's a little tricky for you to make friends, and to understand other people. Do you find that?"

Maddie frowned. "They just call me dumb," she retorted. "They're not my friends."

If some of those kids at that school were anything like their activewear clad mothers, then Sophie was not surprised that they were all little snots. Now that she was no so worried about Maddie's academics, she would be onto the school more about the name calling.

"No, kid. You're right, kids who call you names aren't your friends. They don't deserve to be your friends. They're ass ... asking ... they should ask your forgiveness." Noah managed to skate around his swearing not-so gracefully.

Sophie smiled at him slyly. "But if you ever met someone that you would like to be friends with," Sophie continued, "then it might be little difficult for you."

"Why?" wondered Maddie.

"People with autism struggle to understand how other people feel, Maddie," clarified Sophie gently. "But Elaine is going to help you with that. She's going to teach you, and you know how clever you are when you want to learn." Of course, Maddie had to want to learn. "But," Sophie emphasised. "Autism makes you special, too. Amazingly so. You have incredible focus on things that you are passionate about, Maddie. Like piano. It's helped you to realise your talent, sweetheart. It's like a superpower." Sophie nodded. "It isa superpower, and do not let anybody tell you any different."

Maddie's face contorted a little as she thought, before she looked up at Sophie with a decisive expression. "Sometimes when people have powers, it means they can fly. But my superpower is autism because it means I am super good at the piano." She then nodded, as if she had made a decision and that was that, before she picked up the sheet music and held it up to Noah. "I want to read this now," she urged him.

Sophie blinked, before managing to utter, "Manners, Maddie."

"Pleasel want to read this now," she said impatiently.

"She can learn anything," Noah assured Sophie. "Even how to make a friend." He placed his arm over the back of the sofa, his hand reaching Sophie's shoulder.

Sophie knew that wasn't the last conversation that she would have with Maddie about this. She certainly knew it wasn't the worst. But Maddie knew, and Sophie prayed that she continued to feel the way that she did now. Sophie brought her knees up to her chest and rested her head against Noah's arm as he continued his lesson in musical theory.

CHAPTER 19

Nearly a week had passed since Noah had taken Sophie on their first date. It was now Friday, and they hadn't managed to go out again, but that hadn't stopped Noah from staring at her every chance he got.

How on earth had he not noticed how pretty she was before? He didn't wear glasses, but maybe he needed to. The way she smiled was so natural. The way she moved was so graceful. Noah had honestly never met anyone like her before.

But then, maybe it was a good thing that it had taken him a good minute to notice her outside, because it was her good inside that had drawn him in in the first place. She was so sweet, and so kind, and so fiercely protective as only a mother could be.

Noah hadn't been the only one obviously staring. He had caught Sophie looking his way plenty of times, and her fair cheeks blushed every time. It was so goddamn adorable.

God, he liked her. He liked her a lot.

When Noah wasn't spending his time daydreaming like a teenager, he did manage to work. And thank God for that, as in little over a month, he was due back in LA to start recording his score. He hadn't stopped writing. He had spent most of his nights this week staying up into the early hours of the morning watching The Last Hope and planning music, before spending the days composing on Pete's Steinway.

He had continued Maddie's music lessons, which seemed to occur most days after school at Noah's request, where she would do something that Noah hadn't thought of, which would make his piece even better.

Noah had taken to letting his phone record his writing sessions with Maddie. He almost felt like he needed to document this kid. He needed to prove that she really was writing, changing, and playing herself.

Maybe one day she could use this footage to bolster a college application. He saw a lot of himself in Maddie, and if she wanted to, nothing could stop her.

Noah checked his phone and saw that it was nearing five. Sophie would be returning soon from picking Maddie up from school ready for the night shift. Holly and Amy had both arrived for work, and Pete was behind the bar organising himself like normal.

As it was Friday, Sophie would be singing, and it was also the night that Maddie's biological father liked to frequent the bar. The asshole liked to harass Sophie. He liked to make her uncomfortable, to put Sophie in her place, and to try to weasel his way back in with her.

Noah knew he wasn't Sophie's official boyfriend or anything. They'd been on one date, technically, but if Beck thought for one second that he was going to get away with his usual behaviour he had another thing coming.

Noah's phone suddenly rang. Expecting it to be Tally, or even Sophie, he picked it up without registering the caller ID.

"Hey," he answered casually.

"Noah, it's Rick Walsh, how are you?"

Noah suddenly sat up straight as he realised, he had his director on the phone. "Great, thanks, Rick," he replied. "How's things?"

"Fine. Getting along with post," he replied. "Looking forward to hearing the score," he hinted.

"Yes, I'm sure. Not due till Christmas, though, remember?" prompted Noah.

"I remember the contract, don't you worry," Rick assured him. "Listen, the score is not why I've called. I know the score is in good hands. I wouldn't have insisted that we hired you if I thought otherwise."

Vote of confidence. "Thanks."

"It's the song."

Noah felt himself physically pale. Shit. He hadn't even thought about the song yet. He was so focussed on getting the score right that the end credits song was a complete after thought at this point. "What about it?" Noah tried to ask nonchalantly.

"I need a copy of it," requested Rick.

A copy of a song that didn't exist. "Why now?"

"Because the studio is shopping for singers, Noah, and we need the song to get a deal done," Rick urged.

Noah clenched his teeth, knowing Rick was right. "Can't you sign someone using my reputation?" he asked. He hadn't meant to sound like a dick, but he hadn't written a flop yet.

"Is there a problem with the song?" Rick demanded to know.

"No," assured Noah. "It just needs a little ... tweaking."

The door to the bar then opened, and Maddie bounced inside, closely followed by Sophie. The minute she crossed the threshold, she looked up at him and smiled.

"What if I told you that I had a singer?" he asked Rick. "An amazing one."

"You've got a singer? Who?"

"She's an unknown. Her name is Sophie Cartwright. She has one of the most beautiful voices I've ever heard, and I'll bet I can get her a deal for royalties only. Upfront costs will be a steal."

Rick groaned. "Come on, Noah. You know all the money is in royalties."

Noah did know that. That was why he had suggested it. "Only if the song is successful," he replied casually.

"And is the song going to be successful?"

Noah scoffed. "Of course, it is. I'mthe one who's written it."

Sophie was setting Maddie up at one of the tables, pulling a container of strawberries out of her lunchbox before giving it to her.

"The studio wants a name, Noah," Rick replied firmly.

"She'll be a name," Noah said confidently.

"Who the hell is this girl then?" Rick demanded to know. "How did you discover her?"

"Look, I'm in London," he admitted. "I'm working in a piano bar, and she works here. She sings every Friday night, and I'm telling you, she's amazing." Noah took a breath. "Sophie, could you come over here?"

"She's there?" exclaimed Rick.

Sophie frowned as she made her way over to the stage. "Is everything alright?" she asked.

Noah put his phone on speaker, and then said, "Sing something for me."

Sophie looked like a rabbit caught in the headlights, but she managed to open her mouth. It was almost like instinct as she sang the first verse of I dreamed a dream.

Her voice was clear and beautiful, and if she was nervous it didn't show.

Noah grinned at her and nodded when she needed to stop. He took Rick off of speaker and said, "Well?" Sophie continued to look at him with utter confusion.

"Well, maybe I could swing it with the studios," he admitted begrudgingly, as though he didn't want to let Noah know that he was right. "Probably be happy not having to pay an exorbitant fee for a name."

"Of course, you can swing it," Noah assured him.

"You're telling me royalties will get it done?" Rick checked.

"Yes," confirmed Noah. The last song that he had written for the mainstream market had spent three weeks at number one, and a year in the top one hundred. He could most definitely make royalties work.

Now all he had to do was write the goddamn song that he had just hyped up. Simple.

"While I've got you on the phone, Rick, I do need to speak to you about something else."

"Mummy!" whined Maddie from her table. Maddie's voice distracted Sophie from her confusion, and she left Noah to see to whatever the problem was. Sophie quickly ushered Maddie out of her chair, and they headed back towards the backroom.

"Why do I have the feeling this is about to affect my budget?" groaned Rick.

"It's not going to affect your budget at all, just your editing department, specifically those responsible for typing up the end credits," Noah said calmly. "And I want to halve my salary."

"Done," Rick agreed.

"Not so fast," Noah said dryly. "I want to give a co-credit. I've had help composing this score. A lot of help, really, and I want to give credit. Her name is already on everything I've written, and I want it in the credits. I also want half my salary put in a trust of something for when she's eighteen."

"Eighteen?" repeated Rick. "How old is this kid?"

"Eight," replied Noah.

"Eight?" cried Rick. "What kind of composer is eight?"

"A damn talented one," he retorted. "Can you make it happen?"

Noah heard Rick sigh on the other end of the phone. "A credit I can do. Salary, contracts, all that bullshit is not my problem. I'll pass this on to the producers and I'm sure they'll be in contact with you about the money. So long as this isn't costing me anything out of my budget, I don't give a shit. When can I expect the song?"

"On the due date with everything else. You won't be disappointed, Rick," promised Noah.

"You're a cocky son of a bitch, you know that?"

"Thanks, Rick," said Noah gratefully, and he ended the call. Noah placed his phone down next to the snow globe that Sophie had bought him, and he stood up from the piano stool.

Sophie walked out of the backroom alone this time, and she noticed she immediately that he was no longer on the phone. She quickly darted across the room to him. "What was all that about?"

she demanded to know. "Who was that on the phone? Why did you want me to sing?"

"That was my director, Richard Walsh," explained Noah. "He was asking for a song I haven't even begun to write yet because they wanted to lure in a huge singer to perform it for the movie, but you just auditioned and got the job instead," Noah said in one breath. "How as the train? Crowded today?"

Noah didn't think it was humanly possible for human eyes to widen as far as Sophie's did as every manner of shock expression filled her face.

"What on earth are you talking about?" Sophie gasped, cupped her hand over her mouth.

The door to the bar started to open with customers making their way inside, dressed in business attire on their way home from work. They immediately made their way up to the bar to get a drink.

God, she deserved this. She worked so hard. She worked seven days a week and did everything she possibly could to support Maddie with no help from anyone, least of all the sperm donor who'd fathered her.

"You don't have to do it if you don't want to," promised Noah. "But you just auditioned to sing the end credit track on the movie I'm composing. I'm going to be writing the song, and it will be professionally recorded and distributed as part of the marketing campaign for the film."

"You want me to record a song?" she gasped in disbelief. "Surely there is someone better, someone more qualified –"

Noah smiled, and wrapped his arms around her. He loved the feeling of Sophie immediately relaxing against him. God, it felt natural. "Wrap your head around it," he encouraged. "But I believe in you, Sophie. I wouldn't have suggested it if I didn't think you could do it and do it beautifully." He kissed the top of Sophie's head.

"Oi, Soph. What the fuck is this?"

Both Sophie and Noah were startled at the sudden abrasive, aggressive tone coming from behind their embrace. They broke apart to turn around to see Beck standing before them, a furious, possessive expression on his face, and his hand clenched in a fist.

Chapter 20

Sophie glared at Beck, not believing his audacity. She then had to mock herself because she knew that Beck was capable of being this giant of a prick.

"Go and sit down," Sophie encouraged firmly. "I'll take your order. But if you continue to take that tone with me, then I will have Tony throw you out," she threatened.

"Who the fuck do you think you are putting your hands all over her?" Beck snarled, poking Noah in the chest so hard that he knocked him off balance for a moment.

Noah quickly righted himself, and took a step forward, purposefully positioning himself between Sophie and Beck. "You heard Sophie," Noah said coolly, "take a seat."

Peering around, Sophie could see the hard stare in Noah's eyes. He stood about five inches taller than Beck, but that only made her moronic ex puff his chest out more and flex his tree trunk arms.

"Are you fucking him?" Beck demanded to know, his filthy glare moving to Sophie. He looked upon her like she was a dirty, worthless slut.

"That is none of your business," snapped Sophie. "You have no right to be sticking your nose into my life, Beck. Bugger off back to your mates and leave me alone," she hissed. Sophie placed her hands on Noah's arms, attempting to drag him away from Beck. Even though he was shorted, the man was stupid enough to punch Noah for the hell of it, and there was no way Sophie was going to allow that to happen.

But Noah stood his ground, not wanting to be the one to walk away and concede. Stupid male pride.

"Who the fuck is this guy? What the fuck do you think you're doing going around fucking people with my kid in the picture?" Beck seethed.

Sophie scoffed, nearly laughing. "Your kid?" she repeated. "That's rich considering you don't want anything to do with her. If it weren't for your mum and dad, you wouldn't even know Maddie's name." Sophie stepped around Noah, bypassing the arm he out-stretched to keep her behind him. She stood up to Beck, glaring up at him. "You haven't bothered concerning yourself with Maddie in eight years. Don't start now," she growled. "My life, and who I choose to spend time with, is my own affair."

Beck's eyes narrowed as a smirk teased at his lips. "Say what you want, but that kid is half mine, legally, biologically, and anything in between. If I don't like who you're exposing her to, then I might just have to do something to change our arrangement. Who's going to look better to a judge? A dad with a stable, full time job, owns his own flat, has a car, didn't drop out of school. Or a university drop out teenage mother, who's achieved nothing more than waitressing?"

All of the blood left Sophie's face as she saw crimson red. She screamed as she threw her hand up, it colliding with Beck's face, her nails digging into his cheek and drawing blood.

Noah immediately wrapped his arms around Sophie and pulled her away. "Don't you fucking threaten her," he snarled. "Don't you dare threaten her. You can't control her, and you have no right to Sophie's daughter. If you even think about coming near her, or this bar, again, then you'll be leaving with much worse than a scratch on your cheek."

Beck pulled out his phone, and quickly snapped a picture, positioning his cheek in the frame. "For my lawyer," he said snidely. "Evidence. Poor Maddie's got an abusive mum who shags anything that moves. Particularly yanks who can't do much better than playing a fucking piano for five quid an hour."

Tony, the bouncer, had pushed his way through the crowd upon hearing Sophie's scream. He had arrived then, and grabbed Beck's upper arm, and began dragging him to the door. Beck shrugged him off, laughing, and pocketed his phone, leaving willingly. He waved his mates over and they all left the bar together.

Sophie's heart was thundering in her chest, and her breaths quickly became short and shallow as she struggled to fill her lungs with air. An overwhelming feeling of doom filled her as she felt the terror set in. Noah rounded on her when he realised what was happening.

"I can't breathe!" she rasped.

"Sophie, it's going to be okay. You're having a panic attack. Come on, I'll take you to the backroom and you can calm down."

"No!" cried Sophie, her voice strained and staggered. "Maddie's in there! She can't see me like this."

Noah nodded, and pulled Sophie back up onto the stage. He pulled her behind the piano and sat her down. He knelt down beside her and helped Sophie to put her head between her knees.

"Okay, in a second, I want you to breathe in as I count to four, keep breathing until I get to four, and then hold it. And when I say, breathe out on a count of four."

Sophie nodded as she trembled, struggling to suck in enough air. She felt like she was suffocating.

"Breathe in, two, three, four."

Sophie did her very best to try to inhale one, continuous breath. It was shaky, but she did it.

"Hold."

Sophie closed her mouth and blocked her nose, closing her eyes to try to focus.

"Out, two, three, four."

Noah kept repeating, kept counting, until Sophie was breathing normally. Sophie didn't know how long she was sitting behind the piano with her head between her knees, but it could have been a while.

When she finally felt her pulse return to normal, and she could fill her lungs properly, she looked up. Noah looked so calm, his blue eyes so assuring.

"He's right about me, though," Sophie whispered. "All I am is this. What judge would look at me and think that I'm good enough?"

Noah frowned, a deep line forming between his brows. "All you are? Sophie, a person's job in not what defines them, is not what makes them a good or a bad person. It's the choices you make, and I don't think you've ever made a choice that does not put Maddie first. A judge would look at you and see a mom doing her best, and raising a healthy, happy kid, who is loved beyond measure."

Sophie whimpered. "It means a lot to me that you see that in me," she breathed. "I don't want you to ever see what he sees."

"That's impossible," Noah said vehemently. "Sophie, that guy is a loser. I get that you have a history, and that there's obviously a lot of hurt, and a lot of pain. But he's not a threat to you, or to Maddie. He's not calling a lawyer. If he was going to seek any kind of custody, he would have done it years ago. Right now, he's just a kid in the sandbox who sees his favourite toy being played with by someone else. It's a horrible analogy, I know, but that's probably the guy's mental capacity."

Sophie let out a pained chuckle.

"Guys like that take pleasure in getting a rise out of you. He's won. He's made you upset. He's affected you. That's what he wants. You can't let him get to you. You can't let him win."

Sophie knew that Noah was right. But that didn't change the fact that Beck had just managed to shake her to her very soul with one little threat. As much as she wanted to be free of him, she relied on the two hundred pounds he deposited into her account each month. If she didn't need that then she would have washed her hands of him a long time ago.

"You sang beautifully tonight," Noah added tenderly. "You always sing beautifully. That's why you've got this shot."

Oh God, how had she forgotten about that? How had Beck reduced her to feeling like she was some lowly little scrubber when she did have ambition and promise? If Sophie could make something of this singing opportunity, then she could finally be able to tell Beck to go and fuck himself. She wouldn't need his two hundred pounds.

"Thank you," Sophie uttered as Noah placed his hands on top of her knees. She covered them with her own. "How did you know what to do? How did you know I was having a panic attack?" she asked quietly.

Noah's eyes softened at the memory. "Do you remember me telling you about my sister's girlfriend, Vanessa?" he prompted, and Sophie nodded. "Before she was out, back when we were in college, she used to have them all the time because of the stress and anxiety, and they became even worse when she told her parents she was gay. I did some research, and this used to always help her calm down."

"Is Vanessa okay now?" Sophie asked.

"Yeah," Noah smiled. "She's okay now."

Sophie exhaled a long breath. God, she never wanted to feel like that again. It was almost as though she was having a heart attack, drowning, and suffocating under a pillow all at once.

"I'm really sorry for Beck," she apologised. "I'm really sorry for how he spoke to you, spoke about you. I'm embarrassed, ashamed really, that I ever went out with him."

Noah rubbed her legs reassuringly. "You've got nothing to be sorry for. We've all got exes who really don't look great upon reflection." Noah's expression seemed as though he had some stories.

Sophie sighed. "As bad as him?" she asked. "God, the idea now that I ever ..." Sophie shuddered. "It feels as though I have insects crawling up me now whenever I think about it. I'm honestly not convinced I ever liked him. I just went out with him because I knew my parents would hate him. My seventeen-year-old idea of rebellion."

Noah smiled and shook his head. "You got something amazing out of it. That's your takeaway."

Sophie smiled back, knowing he was right. "I know I did," she agreed. Her mind began to drift to Maddie's upcoming Christmas visit with her grandparents. Keith and Maureen Becker saw Maddie twice annually. Around her birthday and around Christmas. Sophie had kept up this relationship so that Maddie could have some familial connection beyond her. Beck always made an appearance at these visits, too. "I know I'm going to hear all about this at Maddie's Christmas visit with Beck's mum and dad."

"Is he a tattle tale?" mocked Noah.

Sophie snorted. "You could say that. Basically, Beck tells them whatever he wants about me. Paints me as the evil bitch who denies him everything. I'm sure he'll invent something fanciful to explain why I slapped him."

"Don't go," Noah said simply.

Sophie frowned at him. "They're Maddie's grandparents. She hasn't got anyone else. It's not like my mum and dad are champing at the bit to get to know her. She deserves grandparents. It doesn't matter what they do to me."

Noah didn't say anything, but Sophie could see that he had something on his mind.

"What is it?" she pressed.

Noah shook his head, pushing away whatever the thought was. "No, it's not important right now. Don't worry about it. Look, can I take you home?" he asked. "I think you deserve a night, or half a night, off." Noah stood up on his knees and looked over the piano.

"Pete's looking over here. He seems very concerned. I'll go ask him
to let you off, and I'll get Maddie."

"No!" exclaimed Sophie, grabbing Noah's arm.

"What?"

Just because Noah was able to work in the piano bar for free,
it didn't mean that Sophie could. There was a reason she was
working seven days a week and taking a night off and forgoing any
generous cash tips was simply not an option. As it was, poor Holly
and Amy were probably covering her section and Sophie needed
to get back on the floor.

"I'm okay now, I promise," Sophie insisted as she climbed to her
feet. "Beck's gone and I can get on with my shift." She could see
the concern and conflict on Noah's face, and her heart physically
swelled in knowing that she was cared about by this man. "Have
you ever had a proper Sunday lunch before?" she asked. "Yorkshire
puddings and everything?"

Noah simply shook his head. "Can't say I know what those are.
But I'd be willing to try."

Chapter 21

Noah wasn't sure if English people usually ate their hot meal at lunchtime, or if Sophie was preparing this special meal for him during the day as she would be working that night.

He wanted her to take the night off, especially after having a panic attack on Friday, but he knew she wouldn't, and he knew why. She needed the money. Noah knew broaching the topic of him helping her out was a bad idea.

In the long run, he knew that Sophie singing his original song would earn her more from royalties, but he quietly wished there could be a sort of signing bonus or something.

As he approached the front door of Sophie's block of flats, he wondered if he could get away with writing her a cheque and passing it off as some sort of bonus. Would that be right?

She was bound to find out, and would that only make things worse? He wanted Sophie to be able to trust him.

Sighing, Noah knew it was best to not bring up the subject of money. Sophie was managing as best she could. Her finances were her own business.

He texted Sophie to let her know that he was outside, and moments later he heard the lock on the door click, and he was able to pull it open freely. Noah then made his way up to Sophie's flat. Her door was open, and Sophie was standing in the doorway waiting for him.

She wore her hair down; it looked redder today, and it had a natural wave to it. She was dressed casually, wearing a light blue sweater over a pair of leggings, and her feet were bare. God, she was pretty.

Sophie's smile only grew as he approached, and it filled him with an odd sort of satisfaction knowing that it was his coming that was making her this happy. As soon as he reached her, Sophie stood up on her toes and placed a light kiss on his lips, and God, didn't he feel like a teenager again with a giant, old crush on the hottest girl in school.

"Hello," she chirped. "I hope you are hungry."

Noah could smell something delicious wafting through the air. "Famished," he replied.

Sophie led him inside her flat, and he could see that it had been compulsively cleaned. Even the pillows on her sofa had those catalogue home chops in them. If only she saw his own bedroom slash studio at Tally's place would she understand that he really didn't care if a space looked lived in.

Maddie was lying on her stomach in front of the television watching Frozen. She was so absorbed that she hadn't noticed Noah arriving.

"Maddie, aren't you going to say hi?" prompted Sophie.

Maddie looked up when she heard her name, and her face lit up as her brown eyes settled on Noah. She leapt to her feet and bounded across the living room, jumping into Noah's arms.

Noah staggered a little, not expecting that Maddie would come to him like that. But the moment she did, he lifted her up and gave her that attention. It wasn't like she was ever going to get it from her real dad.

"Do you want to watch Frozen?" Maddie asked eagerly.

"Oh, I would, but you've already started it," Noah said regretfully. "I've missed the beginning so that's too bad."

"Oh, don't worry," Sophie assured him, "Maddie knows how to work the DVD player. She can restart it for you, so you don't miss a thing." Sophie winked at him, and he gave her a very unimpressed look.

Maddie nodded. "I can!" she exclaimed. "I'll go start it again. Sit!" she demanded, pointing to the sofa.

Sophie laughed. "Go on then. I'll have dinner ready before you have to hear "Let It Go". I'll make that a challenge for myself, so I don't have to hear it again."

Noah did as he was told, and Maddie restarted the movie. While he wasn't remotely interested in the film itself, watching Maddie was fascinating. She sat beside him on the sofa, her eyes glued to the screen. He wasn't sure if Maddie even realised, she was doing it, but she was reciting every line. She knew the script by heart and was uttering each line under her breath.

That kid had an incredible memory, and completely untapped potential. God, she could go far. Noah hoped that having her name attached to this film would open doors for her. Opportunities for schools, scholarships, connections, and jobs in the future.

He knew there was obviously a huge chance that Maddie would have an entirely different career dream, but nobody could deny that the kid was talented in this avenue.

Noah's arm was resting over the back of the sofa, his forearm leaning against the wall behind him. Scene by scene, Maddie edged closer to him, to the point where she was almost sitting in his lap by the time that Elsa was running away into the forest.

It was normal to feel a bit of apprehension when a kid was involved. Maddie was clearly attached. For a child like her, making connections with people was very difficult.

Noah could completely empathise. He had grown up very similarly. He was smarter than everyone else when he was a kid. Finding commonalities with people was virtually impossible. If it weren't for Tally, he probably could have gone whole school years without talking to anybody.

Factor that in with Maddie's autism as well, forging relationships was going to be something that she would struggle with. But Maddie felt a connection to Noah. She felt comfortable with him, and Noah knew the privilege that it was to be someone that a child like Maddie could connect with.

He also knew that he was in for a world of confusion when it came time for him to go home.

A noise from the kitchen pulled his attention away from his thoughts as he watched Sophie carry a steaming dish of something over to her little dining table. She was focussing, her long hair pulled back and fixed with a white scrunchie.

She looked up at him, and her mouth immediately opened as she whispered, "Aw," under her breath at the sight of Noah and Maddie.

She pouted her lower lip as she pulled out her phone to take a photo of the two of them together.

The first bar of "Let It Go" caught both of their attention and Sophie clapped her hands quickly. "Alright, Maddie, go and wash your hands!" she instructed.

Maddie climbed off of Noah's lap and trotted off to the bathroom.

"You know, I could teach her to play that on the piano," Noah said with a wicked smile as he got up from the sofa.

Sophie gasped. "Don't you dare!" she hissed, and Noah laughed.

Noah followed Sophie toward her little kitchen and inhaled the delicious smell. It smelled like Thanksgiving, only better. Sophie had prepared a glorious looking roast, with crispy roasted potatoes, steaming vegetables, gravy, and some ... were they hollow muffins?

"Might take a picture of this and send it to my mom ... tell her she's got some competition," Noah teased. He would think twice about that seeing as Joy did not yet know that Noah was dating Sophie. Keeping his mother in the dark was the best of everyone's sanity.

"You're terrible," admonished Sophie. "I'm sure your mum can do much better than some beef and roasties."

Maddie flitted back into the room, taking a seat at the table and hungrily looking at the food before her. "Mummy, we never have food like this!" she cried.

"It's a special occasion," replied Sophie. "Noah needed to try a proper British Sunday lunch once."

Sophie set to carving the meat. She did her best, but her knives were rather blunt. Noah didn't mind at all. It would still taste the same.

"Oh, bloody hell, I've overcooked it," Sophie said, frustrated as she peered at the inside of her meat. "There's a pub around the corner that does a beautiful carvery," she suggested.

Noah frowned. "Sophie, I've been eating dry Thanksgiving turkey for thirty years. I can handle some well-done beef. Gimme," he encouraged.

Sophie rolled her eyes and obliged him, popping meat onto all three plates. "Well, at least we know the poor cow is dead and is not still mooing." She then spooned carrots and Brussel's sprouts onto Maddie's plate, and a handful of roast potatoes, before giving Maddie one of the hollow muffin things. She poured a splash of gravy over the whole thing, and Maddie tucked in eagerly.

"Please help yourself, I hope you like it," Sophie willed.

"Ladies first," Noah said vehemently. "But you do need to tell me what those things are. I can identify everything else." Noah pointed to the muffins.

Sophie grinned proudly. "They turned out pretty good if I do say so myself! They're Yorkshire puddings, and a roast is not the same without one. Or in my case, three." Sophie helped herself to three puddings.

"A pudding is dessert, right?" Noah clarified, furrowing his brows.

"Yes, but it can be savoury or sweet, just depends on what you serve it with."

Noah wondered if they were anything like popovers. His mom made them whenever they watched Royal weddings and served them with jam and cream. It made Joy feel very fabulous. Noah was summoned home each time much to his delight.

Noah helped himself to the puddings, the vegetables, and the roast potatoes, following Sophie's lead by pouring gravy over the top of everything. He eyed the Brussel's sprouts with a subtle look of disdain, but he was determined that he would do whatever he needed to in order to get a Brussel's sprout down his throat. Reese's. Imagine it's a Reese's peanut butter cup.

Noah loved every delicious bit of Sophie's cooking ... even the sprouts. Sophie had roasted them with the meat juices, and it made them edible. His own mom just boiled them until they were grey and flavourless.

The Yorkshire puddings were very similar to popovers, but he was a convert to eating them with a roast.

He could see how proud Sophie was, and how excited she was to be eating a meal together like this. It could have been strange how normal it seemed to be having a meal together on a Sunday like they were, but it wasn't. It didn't feel weird, and Noah found himself really enjoying it. A sense of belonging was quickly beginning to creep up on him, and it was one that he had not really felt before.

As much as he adored Tally and Vanessa, he lived in their guest room, and had done since he had graduated college. All of his things, his life fitted into that room. He didn't really have a life beyond work. His longest relationship was with a piano.

But Sophie had a life. It was different, and it was hard; God knew it was hard, but she had a life. Noah found himself quickly feeling like he could fit right in if he wanted to.

His director wanted to end his movie with a message of hope, of triumph over adversity, with the promise that good things do come. That was what Noah's song needed to represent.

And he now had an idea of where he wanted to start.

Chapter 22

Before leaving on that Sunday, Noah had asked Sophie to be his girlfriend, and Sophie had accepted without hesitation. It was perhaps one of the only decisions she had made in that last decade without hesitation.

She didn't know what it was with Noah, but it was something. It was special, and comfortable, and it felt real and genuine.

Sophie and Noah dated happily for the entirety of November. They fell into a sort of routine, in which Noah would spend every spare moment he had that he was not working on his score with Sophie, either at the bar, or at her flat. When they could, they went out, and Sophie took him on cliché tourist expeditions, taking photos of Noah posing in telephone boxes and riding atop a double decker bus.

Sophie enjoyed every minute that she spent with Noah. She loved his company, and his intelligence, and the way he spoke about his passions was so bloody attractive. He was caring and compassionate, and he never made her feel inferior despite the huge differences in their situations.

Maddie continued to take lessons from Noah, but they really became writing sessions. They worked on Noah's score together, and come the twenty-fifth of November, he was certain that he had finished it, and it was ready for recording.

Maddie had made massive changes over that month. She had not refused school once.She was now a top reader and speller and had joined the school band on piano. The latter had taken some convincing as Maddie had no interest in playing with children her own age, but Noah had been the one to convince her.

Noah had played piano in his school band, and Maddie simply had to do the same. Maddie had stars in her eyes when it came to Noah, and Sophie was quickly realising it was like mother like daughter.

Maddie had continued to see her psychologist weekly in an effort to build her social skills, the expense of which stretched Sophie to her last ten pounds every payday. While Maddie hadn't made any friends, the fact that she was interacting with others was a huge step forward.

She had even asked Sophie how she was feeling the other day, something that she had neverdone before. As expensive as it was, Sophie would keep paying for it.

Everything had really been wonderful. But when one's life had as many roller coaster loops as Sophie's did, she was only waiting for the dip. A whole month of sweet company, with no Beck stalking her at work, and Maddie thriving. She was bound for a fall.

And she knew what it would be.

Noah would need to return to America soon. Sophie knew that his score was due by Christmas, and that it needed to be his completed score, recorded with an orchestra. Sophie had yet to record her song, or even hear what it would be, but she assumed that would happen before he flew home.

It had been so easy to feel as though he lived in London. She saw him every day. But this wasn't his home. His home and his lovely, large, nosy but good intentioned family lived thousands of miles away, and that was where he belonged.

No new relationship could survive that distance, could it? Noah hadn't told Sophie that he loved her, and Sophie hadn't told him either. It seemed inevitable, really, as December rapidly approached.

But Sophie tried to push it out of her mind on this special Thursday. In America, it was Thanksgiving, and Noah wasn't with his family. Sophie hadn't found a proper turkey as Christmas was a month away, not that she could really afford it anyway, so she had bought some turkey breast from the delicatessen and prepared some Thanksgiving inspired rolls.

She had even taken the night off work. Her first shift off ... well, probably since she had given birth to Maddie. As much as she needed the money, she really didn't want to let an important day in Noah's life pass by without acknowledging it.

Noah smiled at a pregnant woman as he stood up on the tube, allowing her to have his seat as he listened to the dial tone. He held onto the pole and waited for his mom to pick up the phone.

It would be one o'clock at home, and he knew his mom would be cooking up a storm, shouting at his dad to turn the game down, and complaining that no one was helping her.

No one could help her. Apparently, there was a right and wrong way to peel a potato and if you aren't going to do it right then Joy might as well do it herself, be off with you.

"For God's sake, John, turn that game down, I'm on the phone!" shouted Joy as the call connected. "Noah?" she said excitedly.

"Hi, Mom," Noah greeted. "Happy Thanksgiving."

"Happy Thanksgiving, sweetheart!" she cried excitedly. In the background Noah could hear the sound of the exhaust fan going, and the noise of spoon hitting the sides of a stainless-steel mixing bowl.

"How are you? Are you good?" Noah asked.

"I'd be better if someone around here would bother to give me a hand cooking," Joy uttered bitterly.

Noah smirked, enjoying the familiarity of how predictable his mother was. "Darn selfish of them," he teased. "I'm sorry I'm not there," he apologised, his voice turning sincere. As overbearing as she was, he really did miss his family today.

The sound of the mixing stopped, and Joy sighed. "I'm sorry, too, honey," she said softly. "I miss you and your squishy face."

Noah needed to blink his eyes tightly. "Jesus, Mom, I'm nearly thirty."

"You're the youngest and you're my baby," Joy replied unabashedly. "I'm allowed to think you're squishy if I want to. What're you doing today? I hope you don't have to work."

"No, I actually finished my score yesterday." At two in the morning, actually, as he watched the movie for about the hundred and fourth time, putting every single note that he and Maddie had written to it perfectly. God, it was going to be good. He knew when something was good, and he was itching to take control of that orchestra and make it as beautiful as it sounded in his head.

"Oh!" cried Joy. "That's wonderful! I can't wait to hear it. Does that mean you're coming home sooner than you thought?"

That was a complicated question, and it was also part of the reason as to why he'd called his mom. He hadn't told her about Sophie. He had only told Tally, and by some miracle she had managed to not open her big mouth.

Noah knew his return date was fast approaching. He had to go home. There was no way around it. But he had no intention of that being the last that he saw of Sophie.

He had felt more at home with her, more himself with her than he had ever felt before. It was natural, as easy as breathing with Sophie, and there was no way he was letting her go because of something as trivial as geography.

He wanted to bring Sophie and Maddie out to LA to record his original song. He wanted Sophie to have the experience of being a professional singer, and he wanted Maddie to play with the orchestra.

His plan was to bring them over on Maddie's school Christmas break. It would be a narrow window, but he could make it work. But that would mean Christmas at his parents' house.

It was highly possibly that the holidays with Joy Bentley might push Sophie over the edge. The woman needed a good month to calm her crazy for Sophie and Maddie got there.

"I'll be home for Christmas, I promised you that," Noah reiterated. Taking a breath, he added, "And I might be bringing someone." Noah shut his eyes and winced as he heard a clatter of dishes and the absolute scream of joy erupting from his phone's speaker.

Even the people around him on the train could hear the noise and were looking at him like he was insane. He wanted to let them know that it was his mother who was the crazy one.

"What the hell is wrong with you, Joy?" cried John. "Oh my God, you dropped the yams!"

Oh God, not Dad's yams.

"Oh, Noah, this is so exciting!" Joy squealed. "Is it Sophie? I just know it's her. I could tell from the minute I spoke with her that she was a good girl," Joy gushed, before gasping. "DOES THIS MEAN MY GRANDDAUGHTER IS COMING, TOO?" she screamed with delight.

"I've changed my mind. I'm not asking them," Noah decided, shielding his face from the embarrassment.

"What?" cried Joy. "No, no!" she protested. "They have to come. How do I spell Maddie's name? I need to start knitting. You make them come or I'm only baking Tally a birthday cake!" she threatened, before there was a staticky noise. "John, talk to your son. I need to find my knitting needles!"

"Noah," grumbled John.

"Dad," replied Noah.

"She dropped my yams," he moaned.

"She's holding my birthday cake for ransom," Noah shot back.

"But you finally got a nice girlfriend?"

Noah smiled. "Yeah," he said, nodding.

"She worth holding onto?"

"Absolutely."

"Worth setting Mom on her?"

"Regretfully, yes."

John chuckled. "She'd better be. She's the reason my Thanksgiving yams are soaking into the damn hardwood."

The train stopped at Gunnersbury station, and Noah stepped off onto the platform. "Dad, she really is important. Can you ...?"

"I'll take care of it," John assured him. "Hey, kid?"

"Yeah?"

"I miss you."

Noah sucked in a breath, and just paused for a second, remembering that it wasn't long ago that he and his dad really didn't have a lot to say to each other. John Bentley was not the type of man who could easily express how he felt. It took nearly seventeen years for him to find the words to connect with Noah. But the small things meant a lot coming from him, and Noah knew he meant them.

"I miss you, too, Dad," he murmured sincerely.

"You do what you need to, and I'll see you when I'm looking at you." Noah could hear how John's voice had thickened softly, and he thought that his father was thinking the same thoughts.

They said goodbye and Noah hung up the phone, shooting off a quick text to Tally as he walked out of the station.

Mom knows. She's knitting. Happy Thanksgiving x

He then texted Haley and Casey, before receiving Tally's reply.

It was a video file.

He smirked, opening it up as he walked.

It was Tally and Vanessa in frame teasingly singing. "You're still the one I run to. The one that I belong to. You're still the one I want for life.You're still the one that I love. The only one I dream of. You're still the one I kiss goodnight!"

"Happy Thanksgiving!" they cheered in unison, before Tally pointed the camera at Vanessa. She did a cute little twirl in her hand knitted sweater that Joy had made for her all those years ago.

Noah rolled his eyes. Leave the singing to the professionals, Tally, he texted back, but he knew exactly where they were going, and God knew he was heading there, too.

Chapter 23

"Now, you aren't going to worry about a thing, right?" Noah asked Sophie for the fortieth time that day.

They stood in the international departures section of Terminal 4 at Heathrow Airport. Sophie had always loved airports ever since she was a child. There was something fascinating about watching the flights come in and go out, seeing the flight information change on the screen, and watching the people rush about with their large suitcases as they jetted off on holiday. She had been one of those people once. Her parents preferred to summer in Spain or Italy or Greece.

But she didn't love the airport today. It was December. It had come too quickly. Christmas lights and decorations were up, and tacky ornaments were being sold in the airport shops. And Noah was flying home.

The previous night had been his last at the West End Piano Bar. Pete had shut the pub early and they had all sat around for several hours drinking and laughing. Sophie laughed to keep herself from crying.

Well, Pete didcry at the realisation that he would have to actually pay his next piano man.

What was silly was that she knew it was not goodbye forever. Noah had invited both Sophie and Maddie to Los Angeles at Christmastime. Sophie was going to go to a real recording studio to sing the song that Noah had written for his film, and then they were going to fly up to Napa to spend Christmas at his parents' house.

Sophie didn't think that she had fully wrapped her head around that idea. It was sodifferent from the Spam sandwiches she had served Maddie for Christmas dinner last year as that was all she had been able to afford.

All she could think about was the fact that when she went into work later, that Noah wouldn't be there at the piano. She had only just found him, and he was going.

"Sophie, everything is going to be fine," Noah assured her. "I'll send you the flight information when I get back, and I'll call you when I land. It's not even a full three weeks."

"Two weeks and six days," murmured Sophie. They would be arriving in Los Angeles on the twenty-first of December.

"I'm going to miss you, too," Noah uttered, cupping her face. "I'm soglad I met you, you know. To think I could have missed out on it ..." Noah trailed off and sucked in a breath. His eyes flicked over her face, as if to commit to memory those minor little details that made up a whole person. "You'll tell Maddie I'm sorry?" he asked.

Noah had already apologised to Maddie profusely the night before in Sophie's flat, but she had slammed her bedroom door and thrown a whale of a tantrum. Sophie had not heard one like it for a long time. She did not take the change well, and it had not hit her that Noah would be leaving, albeit temporarily, until he was saying goodbye to her.

Holly was kindly looking after Maddie as she refused to come to the airport. She refused to come out of her bedroom to speak to Noah after that.

Maddie had wept her little heart out that night, sobbing until she had no tears left. She had cuddled with Sophie all night, and her eyes had still been swollen this morning. Maddie was how Sophie felt.

"Yes, I will," Sophie whispered.

"Do you think she'll forgive me?"

Sophie could hear the genuine fear in Noah's voice. It really hurt him that Maddie was upset, and he really did care about their relationship. As if she needed another reason to think him a good man.

"Of course, she will forgive you," Sophie promised. "She loves you." Her tongue nearly tripped over the word, and they both realised that it was the first time that either one of them had uttered the word.

It had not even been six weeks really, and it did seem a little soon, but they both stared at each other, watching for what the other would do.

Noah broke first, sighing, and then smiling. "It's not goodbye," he said decidedly. "It's see you soon. See you real soon. Think of all the Joy you've got to look forward to."

Sophie knew he meant his mother, and not the emotion. She laughed, and Noah grinned, tapping her chin in triumph. He then leaned down, and placed a very soft kiss on her lips, lingering there for a moment.

"Go on then," Sophie said, her voice thickening. "British customs will want to know what your ex-girlfriend's cousin's uncle did for a living twenty years ago, so you had better get going."

Noah chuckled. "You're right about that. Okay, I'll see you on my side of town real soon."

"I can't wait," Sophie replied, fall back on her heels as she watched him pick up his carry-on bag.

With one last kiss, he turned away from her, and walked through the departures gate.

On her way home from the airport, Sophie had stopped by a pound shop and had bought a calendar that was going out for ten p. The clerk had looked at her like she was foolish to purchase a calendar when there was only a month left of the year, but Sophie had another plan for it.

With Maddie, she circled the day that they would be arriving in LA to see Noah, and every morning it was Maddie's job to cross off a day. Having a visual helped Maddie to focus, to gain back the control that she had lost with the change in her routine.

Noah had called Sophie the minute he had landed in LA, and it seemed so weird to be talking to him when he was now on the other side of the world. Maddie had promptly forgiven him and demanded that she be given the phone each time Noah called.

Noah now called during the day to talk to Maddie, and he spoke to Sophie again in the evening once Maddie had gone to bed.

Maddie had been working on reciprocal conversation with her psychologist in an effort to help her make friends with her classmates. As much as it hadn't helped her to connect with her peers yet, it made Sophie's heart swell every time she heard Maddie has Noah a question that flowed in their conversation.

Work was strange without Noah, but she was glad at least that Beck had not resurfaced after his altercation with Noah. She still had Maddie's annual Christmas visit to her grandparents to look forward to, but he hadn't bothered her at Pete's.

Sophie was working all the hours she could to cover the two weeks that she would be away. The afternoon that she had taken off to pick Maddie up from school on the day that broke for the Christmas holidays was the first time off she had had in weeks. And unfortunately, she had to spend that afternoon with Maddie at Beck's parent's house.

Sophie supposed she was lucky that they did want a relationship with Maddie, as without them, Maddie would not have a passport. They had taken her on a holiday to Fuerteventura last summer which had been a disaster on two parts.

Sophie had been a nervous wreck without Maddie, and Maddie had been a tantrum throwing terror according to Keith and Maureen.

"Now, what must you say to Grannie and Grandpa when they give you your gifts?" Sophie asked Maddie as they walked through the little gate into the Becker's' front garden. Keith and Maureen lived in a little semi-detached cottage in Watford.

"Thank you," said Maddie with a sigh. "How many minutes is it now until we see Noah?" she asked for the zillionth time.

"You marked the calendar this morning. You tell me," Sophie countered. She couldn't do the maths in her head, and if Maddie could then, Sophie would be impressed.

Sophie rang the doorbell, and the door was promptly opened by Maureen Becker.

Maureen was a short, plump woman, who was always made up beautifully with her blonde hair freshly styled at the hairdressers. Her fingernails were the same bright pink as her lips, which promptly curled into a warm smile as she looked upon Maddie.

"Maddie!" she cried. "Look how big you are in your school uniform! Halfway through Year 3 already, my goodness!"

Maddie had grown this year. Sophie would have to let down her winter skirt before school went back after the holidays.

Maureen scooped Maddie into a tight hug, and Sophie watched as Maddie stiffened as she came face to face with the giant Rudolph on her grannie's jumper.

Maureen released her and ran her hand down one of her strawberry blonde plaits. That was when she finally lifted her blue eyes to Sophie, and she managed a cordial smile.

"How are you, Sophie?" she asked.

"I'm well, thanks, Maureen," replied Sophie. "How are you and Keith?"

"Happy to be seeing our Maddie," Maureen said as she took hold of Maddie's hand and led her inside. She left the door ajar but didn't invite Sophie to follow.

Nonetheless, Sophie sighed and let herself into the house, shutting the door behind her. It was warm in the house thankfully, and she could smell baking. Carols were playing, but Sophie could also hear the sound of football.

Beck's dad was a staunch Crystal Palace supporter and could be found in front of the television watching his team play or watching recordings of old matches when they weren't playing.

Maureen's decorating was a tribute to the eighties. She loved salmon floral wallpaper, lace doilies, and potpourri. Keith was in the sitting room, beer in hand, watching the television in a Christmas jumper that Maureen had no doubt insisted that he wear. As Sophie rounded the corner to stand fully in the sitting room, she saw that the pink patterned armchair was occupied by Beck.

Sophie had known that he would be here, but it hadn't really hit her until now. Seeing Maddie and Beck in the same room just felt wrong, almost as if she was cheating on Noah in a way. Beck just had no place in Maddie's life, and Noah actually wantedone.

Beck wasn't wearing Christmas attire, but he was dressed smartly in a button-down shirt and some dark jeans. He, too, had a beer in hand. Keith looked away from the television momentarily to greet Maddie, and to offer a polite salutation to Sophie, before his focus returned to the screen.

"Alright, Soph?" Beck asked her casually.

The scratch that Sophie had inflicted had fully healed, but she hadn't forgotten the threat that had followed it.

Sophie managed a polite smile, for all of their sakes. "Yes," she murmured. "You?"

"Alright," he replied, nodding.

Maddie didn't interact with Beck. It was honestly terribly sad watching them. She knew that he was her father, but Maddie had no idea what to do with that information. She didn't really understand what a father was beyond the name.

Beck never asked for a cuddle. He never asked for anything period. He simply watched, and waited for the visit to be over.

Maureen had left the sitting room and returned with a tray of exquisitely decorated gingerbread biscuits. She took the remote from Keith and switched off the television, shooting him a warning look when he opened his mouth to complain.

Maureen tried her hardest to quiz Maddie on school, but having a conversation with Maddie on a topic that she was not remotely interested in was virtually impossible, and Sophie was bitter enough not to render assistance.

"Who are your friends?" Maureen prodded, her impatience growing after Maddie couldn't name a favourite subject at school, or what she liked about her teacher.

"Noah and Elaine," chirped Maddie as she helped herself to a second biscuit.

"Oh, Elaine is an old-fashioned name," commented Maureen. "Is she in your class?"

"No!" exclaimed Maddie. "She teaches talking and feeling."

Oh, dear. Dread filled Sophie as she realised that she might just have to explain Maddie's diagnosis. Noah had repeatedly told her that Beck wouldn't do anything, and deep down she knew that, but if they knew that Maddie had additional needs, it would be something that they could use against her.

"Talking and feeling?" repeated Maureen, confused. She then looked to Sophie for clarification.

Beck had a frown on his face as he, too, had no idea what Maddie was talking about.

"Elaine is Maddie's psychologist," Sophie explained reluctantly. "She has only lately been diagnosed with autism, haven't you, sweetheart?"

Sophie could have cried when she saw Maddie smile at the word. "Yep!" Maddie said enthusiastically. "I have a superpower!" she said proudly. "I can concentrate the best, and I am the smartest at the piano."

Sophie watched as Maureen, Keith and Beck's jaws all dropped. Sophie thanks God for the blessing of Maddie's obliviousness.

"She is seeing a psychologist to help her with her socialisation, and she is doing really well," Sophie concluded. "There is nothing, nothing wrong with her."

Maureen was the first to recover. She composed her facial expression, and said, "Well, of course there's not! I'm sure Elaine is a nice lady. Is Noah a friend from school then, Maddie?"

"Nope," sniggered Beck.

Sophie's eyes narrowed.

"He's a low rent piano player at the pub," Beck mocked. "Sophie's been shagging him. And letting Maddie around him, it seems."

Keith merely looked surprised, while Maureen looked down on Sophie like she always did when Beck spouted some lie about her. She had mum goggles on when it come to her son, and Beck could do no wrong. She couldn't even see that he wanted nothing to do with his daughter.

But Sophie wasn't concerned for herself. She just wouldn't have Noah spoken of like that.

"Noah Bentley is my boyfriend," Sophie told Keith and Maureen. "He had been working at the West End Piano Bar for free while he worked on his film score." Sophie's eyes flicked to Beck. "He is American, and he works in Hollywood as a film composer. He's had a little success, I suppose, if you would call being the youngest ever recipient of an Academy Award for Best Original Score successful," she said sarcastically. "Noah is kind, and he is decent, and he has taken more of an interest in Maddie these last two months than Beck has in Maddie's eight and a half years."

Once again, all three of their jaws dropped, and Sophie felt a sweet sense of comeuppance. Beck would not shit on her this afternoon. She did not deserve it and she would not put up with it.

"Noah is my favourite," Maddie piped up, hearing Noah's name but not absorbing the context whatsoever. "He taught me how to play the piano and now I play it the best… he says so!" she boasted. "Mummy and me are seeing him in … sixty hours I think."

Sixty hours, was it? The time couldn't pass quickly enough.

"Oh, is Noah spending Christmas in London?" Maureen asked casually.

"No!" cried Maddie. "Mummy and me are going on an airplane to America!"

Three weeks of discussions at home and with Elaine to get Maddie used to the idea of travel had made her excited about the journey, and not only the destination. So excited that she had managed to blurt out their business to the Beckers.

"You're going to America?" Beck asked in disbelief.

"You're taking Maddie out of the country?" Maureen said next, equally in shock.

"Noah has invited us to his mum and dad's for Christmas in California," Sophie said through gritted teeth. "But I made sure our travel plans would not interfere with our Christmas visit here." She didn't like to divulge her plans as it really wasn't their business.

The horrible voice in the back of her head had her once again wondering if international travel was another thing that Beck could use against her, but Sophie shook it away.

Oh, God, the sooner those sixty hours passed, the better.

Chapter 24

To the other passengers sitting in first class, Sophie was sure that she looked like a terrified flyer. They were sipping their two hundred quid a glass champagne and looking upon her like she was a maniac.

The lovely flight attendant had brought Maddie some apple juice in a champagne glass and has asked her how she was feeling.

Maddie had replied, "Good, thank you. How are you?"

And that was when Sophie had burst into hysterical sobs. Maddie had been working on reciprocal conversation with Elaine, and she had just engaged in a two-way conversation with a stranger that did not hold an interest for her. Sophie had never seen Maddie do that before.

"Ma'am, can I get you anything at all?" the flight attendant asked, her voice concerned.

Sophie grabbed the linen napkin that had been put before her along with her champagne and dabbed her eyes. "Oh, please don't mind me," she excused. "We'll be alright."

The flight attendant smiled and left to check in with the couple travelling in the seat behind them.

"Mummy, this is such a big chair!" Maddie exclaimed, wriggling her little bottom into the seat.

"I know," remarked Sophie, dabbing her eyes again. No one could have been more surprised than her when she and Maddie had arrived at the desk for their flight to receive their boarding passes, only to learn that they were travelling first class. Sophie and Maddie were promptly escorted to a lounge that was posher than anything she'd seen before.

Maddie had helped herself to the masses of gourmet fruit arrangements, cut and placed to look like bunches of flowers. No sooner had they been touched, an attendant quickly replenished them so that they looked just as perfect.

They had waited in the lounge on two of the comfiest leather armchairs for several hours, watching the planes come and go, from the best window in Heathrow. They were never without any-thing, as waiters roamed with tea and coffee and trays of delicious canapés and vol-au-vents.

When it came time to board, Sophie felt really awkward at being escorted onto the plane, and given priority boarding over the other passengers. But she couldn't deny that sitting with Maddie in their own little cocoon would make the journey that much easier.

They sat in two wide, comfortable chairs with a wide armrest in between them. In front of them was a table filled with complimen-tary snacks and lotions, as well as sets of pyjamas and blankets.

The television came stocked with more films than she could count, and Maddie had already discovered the remote, though nothing would play just yet, as there was a message on screen about the upcoming safety demonstration.

Sophie hated to think how much these tickets were costing Noah. She could not afford to fly to Ireland in economy, let alone Los Angeles in first class. She had texted Noah, admonishing him for the expense, but he had merely told her to have a safe flight and that he would see them both when they landed.

It had been a long three weeks, and Sophie was so excited to see Noah. Sophie had never experienced missing someone before.

Aside from, of course, Maddie's fateful trip with her grandparents to Fuerteventura which ended very prematurely due to Keith and Maureen not knowing how to communicate properly with Maddie when she was having a meltdown.

But Sophie had been more worried, really, and too terribly anxious to think about missing Maddie.

Sophie had never been attached enough to another person to miss them. She did not have that sort of relationship with her parents, and the only boyfriend that she had ever had was Beck.

She missed laughing with him and feeling a sense of ease in a day that might have been filled with tears. She missed talking to him, and feeling like she could tell him anything, confess to any guilty thought that had crossed her mind and receiving nought but a supportive ear. She missed the way he talked about his family. She liked hearing about his sisters and listening to the admiration in his voice as he spoke of them. Sophie adored how he complained about his mum, but in a way that told her that Noah would walk through fire for her if she asked.

And gosh, Sophie missed seeing him. She missed turning her head to the right as she walked through the door of Pete's and seeing Noah at the piano. Even more, she missed seeing Maddie sit right up there beside him.

Sophie had received Maddie's half year school report a few days earlier, a day which she had only a few months ago been dreading. Every report that she had ever received had said the same thing in the nicest possible way.

With support, Madeleine is developing her knowledge of phonemes to decode unknown words.

With encouragement, Madeleine is beginning to write her letters with correct directionality.

With assistance, Madeleine can identify two-digit numbers and is working towards counting by 10s.

Sophie knew how to read between the lines.

But this report ... Sophie wanted to print it out and frame it! Maddie had progressed. She was now at a Year 3 level in maths. Her reading had moved forward by eighteen months.

Madeleine demonstrates outstanding phonemic awareness and is working towards reading for meaning in more challenging texts.

Sophie had needed to Google what phonemic awareness was! Never in her wildest dreams could she had imagined that in only a few short months she would be reading such things about Maddie!

Her pride needed to spill out, and she had emailed her report to Noah, wanting to share it with someone. Really, she wouldn't have blamed him if he hadn't taken much notice.

But he had sent back a video of himself telling Maddie that he was so proud of her.

And the tears shed on that night were probably the reason that Sophie was feeling dehydrated now.

She couldn't wait to see him.

Once the flight attendants had done their safety demonstration, Sophie pulled Maddie's new noise cancelling headphones out of their carry-on bag and gave her a sweet to suck on for the take off to pop her ears. The headphones had been advised by Elaine, to limit sensory overload. While Maddie didn't seem to have any sensory sensitivities, a long-haul flight was new, and it was best to travel on the safe side.

Sophie held Maddie's hand, but Maddie's eyes were fixed out the window as she watched the plane take off. She was amazed.

While she never imagined herself to be a snob, not even when she lived in Kensington with her parents, being able to lie down flat on a twelve-hour flight was a dream.Both she and Maddie had managed to get some decent hours of sleep while on the flight and had filled the remaining hours with some really nice food, and a succession of Disney princess movies.

The flight attendants came around and prepared the cabin for landing and Sophie filled out her customs form. She and Maddie both sucked on another sweet for the landing before she checked that her phone had automatically changed time zones.

She decided not to take her phone off of airplane mode. She couldn't risk being charged by the phone company an exorbitant fee for an international text message. It would mean that nobody back home would be able to contact her, but after saying her goodbyes to everyone at Pete's, they shouldn't have needed to.

US Immigration took a long time, and keeping Maddie entertained was an effort in itself. There was only so much I Spy that Sophie could take. Just like UK Immigration was incredibly strict for foreign visitors, the US was no different.

"Where are you from, ma'am?" asked a gruff inspector, seated behind a clear, Perspex screen.

"We're from London," replied Sophie shakily.

"What's the purpose of your visit?"

"We are on holiday," continued Sophie. She did not need to be nervous, but it was hard not to think you were going to be carted off to airport jail when these officers were scrutinising your passport. "Visiting my boyfriend for Christmas."

The immigration officer slipped Sophie's and Maddie's passports back under the screen and waved them on, calling for the next family in line.

"Happy Christmas," she wished, before moving on.

Sophie and Maddie collected their luggage and made their way through customs before they could finally walk out into the airport arrival hall. Sophie had a vice grip on Maddie's hand as she they walked. She had never seen an airport so busy before, but it was only a few days to Christmas. Maddie trotted alongside Sophie as she looked through the crowd for a familiar face.

Sophie finally spotted Noah leaning against the wall of a souvenir shop, waiting with a shorter blonde woman. The moment he saw Sophie, a huge smile spread across his face and he launched off of the wall, weaving through the crowd and running towards her.

The moment he reached her, Sophie released her suitcase and wrapped the arm that was not holding onto Maddie around his neck. Noah leaned down and kissed Sophie deeply and she could have melted into him in that moment.

"God, I missed you," he whispered as they parted.

"I missed you terribly," Sophie whispered back, uttering the understatement of the century.

Noah beamed down at Maddie, his blue eyes lighting up. "Hey, kid!" he exclaimed.

Maddie pulled her hand from Sophie's so that she could jump up to Noah. Noah received her enthusiastically and hugged Maddie against his chest.

"You got taller!" he cried. "I missed you, too!"

Sophie wasn't going to cry, she willed herself.

"Mummy only let me play on the piano sometimes," Maddie cried, as though three weeks hadn't passed, and she was continuing a conversation. "So can we play on the piano again?"

Noah chuckled. "I'm afraid my piano isn't a Steinway, not even close. But you can play on it all you want."

"She watched a video on YouTube of someone playing Frozen on the piano and picked it up ... there's only so much I can take," Sophie explained with a grimace.

"Maybe my piano is broken?" Noah winked.

Sophie laughed as Noah took the handle of their suitcase in one hand, and Maddie's in the other, and led them over to the blonde woman that he had been waiting with.

Sophie had seen her picture on Noah's phone, and so she recognised her as Tally, his twin sister. Sophie's first impression of Tally was that she was so cool. Her hair, the way she dressed, her jewellery ... everything completed her look. Her hair was bleached, and shaved on one side, with the other side curled and tousled to perfection. Her ear was visible on the shaved side, and Sophie could see about seven small lobe and helix studs sparkling. Her face was thin and angular, but in a way that made her look elegant and distinctive. She had achieved the sort of winged eyeliner that Sophie could only dream of, and her full lips were painted a nude pink.

She wore tight black jeans, cut off at the ankles with a pair of white, platform trainers, and a cropped sweatshirt with an expensive looking logo printed across her chest.

But her big smile that touched her eyes made Sophie feel less intimidated. It still wasn't lost on Sophie that Tally was his sister and his best friend rolled into one. If they didn't get on, it would be game over.

"Sophie, this is my sister, Tally," Noah introduced proudly. "Tally, this is my girlfriend, Sophie."

"It's so nice to meet you," Sophie started, trying to sound confident. "Noah has told me so much about you."

Tally grinned. "I'm so glad go meet you!" She hugged Sophie in greeting, and Sophie relaxed a little more. "And thankful that you're here. It means Noah can stop crooning and whining so much after he gets off the phone with you."

Noah rolled his eyes. "Did I mention that Tally's adopted?" he bit back.

Sophie laughed. "I've probably been the same way, don't worry."

"Oh my God, I'm obsessed with your accent," she gushed. "You sound just like Hermione from Harry Potter."

Sophie thought it such a random comparison, and it made her laugh again.

"But I know you!" Tally exclaimed knowingly at Maddie, grinning down at her. "We've met before. Do you remember me, Maddie? I was about this big on Noah's cell phone." Tally made a rectangle phone shape with her fingers.

"Yes, I like your hair," replied Maddie nodding. "What are your interests?"

Sophie beamed proudly. "It's the reciprocal conversation she's been practising," she explained to Noah and Tally.

Tally took a breath and thought, "Well, I'm interested in school, my sixth graders, my family, my friends, new," she smiled at Sophie, "and old. And I love Disney movies, and listening to beautiful piano playing. What are you interested in, Maddie?"

Maddie beamed. "I like Disney and piano, too!" she cried. She had been learning to identify common interests in hopes that she could connect with children her own age.

"What a coincidence!" cried Tally. "Come on, let's get out of here. We've got Disney plus at home."

Noah and Maddie walked ahead with Sophie's bags while Tally and Sophie walked together as they all made their way out into the carpark.

"I feel like I should give you a heads up about Joy. I know Noah probably already has warned you, but you really need it twice," Tally murmured comically.

"He might have said something," replied Sophie.

"Mom only had one out of four kids home for Thanksgiving. Christmas is going to be nuts. And Noah has a girlfriend ... Joy will be having conniptions. You will probably be able to sue Noah for your therapy. You'll also go home having gained five pounds in sugar cookies and a hideous Christmas sweater."

Sophie would take an overenthusiastic mum over her own any day. "I'm really excited to meet her," she confessed. "Nervous as anything, but excited."

"Were you nervous to meet me?" Tally asked curiously.

"Yes," admitted Sophie. "Noah adores you. If you hate me, I have no chance."

Tally smiled slyly. "I feel oddly powerful," she joked. She then bumped Sophie with her hip. "The adoration goes both ways. I love my brother, and it means everything to me to see him happy," she said sincerely.

CHAPTER 25

Tally drove a white Range Rover, which was as nice inside as it was on the outside. Sophie prayed that Maddie hadn't touched anything sticky recently.

When she opened the door to the car, she was greeted by a child's car seat, and a coy smile from Noah confirmed that he had organised it.

They drove for about half an hour, and Sophie couldn't get over how the sky was blue in the middle of winter. When they left London, it had been raining, and washing away the snowy sludge on the roads.

Noah and Tally lived in Burbank in a private, gated group of condos. They all faced onto a shared, beautiful courtyard, which had a feature fountain in the centre.

"Our neighbours are mostly retired couples," Tally informed Sophie. "Which is good because they leave Vanessa alone."

Sophie frowned in confusion as they all crossed the pebbled courtyard towards the front door of one of the condos. Tally unlocked their front door and welcomed them all into entrance hall.

Their ambience of the house was very warm. Sophie was standing on an orange, terracotta floor, and right in front of her was a staircase that was decorated in a beautiful, floral talavera tile. They had immediately caught Maddie's eye, and she had gone over to inspect the patterns.

A large, ornate wooden mirror hung on the wall by the door, and a narrow hall table stood in front of it, holding a dish filled with keys. Tally tossed hers inside.

"Vanessa!" called out Tally. "We're back!"

A blue painted archway led into the main living area of the house. There was a cosy lounge room with a comfy sectional sofa and a television, an eclectic dining room with mismatching chairs around a green, circular table, and a modern kitchen with a large, midnight blue tiled island.

Sophie was really unsure of what she had expected, but she found that she adored what she had found. She loved the colours and the warmth of the furniture and the décor.

Sophie heard the sounds of footsteps coming down the stairs before they were promptly joined by another person, a woman who was wearing leggings and a grey singlet top.

She was about the same height as Sophie, with long, straight brown hair. She had an olive complexion, and brown eyes, and beautiful natural bone structure. She wasn't wearing a speck of makeup, but her skin was clear and radiant.

The type of skin a celebrity boasted.

Sophie knew exactly who she was, and with every fibre of her being, she willed herself not the freak out.

How many times had Noah mentioned Vanessa, Tally's girlfriend, Vanessa, whom he lived with? And yet Sophie now knew that Noah had never told her Vanessa's last name.

The famous, incredible singer Vanessa Marino was standing in front of Sophie in house clothes, arms extended to hug her in greeting.

"I'm so glad to finally meet you!" Vanessa cried.

"You, too!" coughed Sophie, utterly ungracefully.

"Noah tells me you're a singer?" she added excitedly. "Oh, I can't wait to hear you. I'm sure you're going to be so amazing on this track. Noah wrote my first song, too, did you know?"

Sing in front of Vanessa Marino? Sophie couldn't think of anything more daunting. "N – no," she stammered. "I mean, yes, but no."

"Might have left out a few minor details about one of my roommates," Noah told the room sheepishly.

"Might?" repeated Sophie. Out of the corner of her eye, Sophie spotted a display shelf near the kitchen. On it were several golden trophies, and God a lot of them looked like Grammys.

Vanessa laughed awkwardly and went to stand beside Tally.

"She's kind of a dork, really," Tally told Sophie with an amused grin. "Her Instagram is mainly pictures of breakfast food."

Vanessa nudged Tally. "I went to the store and specifically got English Breakfast tea bags. Noah told me those are the ones you like," she said, changing the subject, and trying to appear as casual as possible. She motioned for them to follow her through the living and dining rooms toward the kitchen.

"Yes, they are," Sophie nodded, forcing herself to take a deep breath. She was not going to make a fool of herself. She looked up at Noah discreetly waiting for an explanation.

"I told you we've been friends since college," he said quietly under his breath.

"A little warning would have been nice," Sophie whispered back. "That way I could have practised my facial expressions, so I didn't look like a deer in the headlights."

"Vanessa doesn't care, I promise," Noah assured her. "They're just so excited to meet you."

"Crap, I don't know how to make tea!" Vanessa exclaimed as she got the teabag out of the box. "I should have looked to see if they made tea pods for the Keurig."

"Are you serious?" Tally frowned. "We've been together for nearly ten years and in that time you didn't know you had to dunk a teabag in some water?"

"See, Tally told you that she was a dork," laughed Noah, before looking back into the entrance way to Maddie. "Maddie, you should see the snacks that Tally and Vanessa have bought you," he called out to Maddie, who had gone back to tracing the talavera tiles on the stairs. "Maddie, come on," he said again, and this time Maddie looked up and she listened.

Maddie wandered into the room and followed Noah towards the kitchen. Noah opened up a double doorway which led into an enormous walk-in-pantry. On the bottom shelves were a dozen packets of all sorts of terrible things that Sophie knew Maddie would enjoy.

Sophie turned her attention to Tally and Vanessa as they continued to make tea. She frowned in confusion when she saw Tally putting a cup of water into the microwave.

"What are you doing?" she wondered.

"Heating the water," explained Tally.

"Why don't you use a kettle?" asked Sophie.

"We have one, but I'm too impatient to wait for the stove to boil water," Vanessa replied.

"Don't you have one that plugs in? My kettle at home boils water in about thirty seconds."

But Noah piped up as he and Maddie emerged from the pantry with a packet of chocolate sweets. "Oh, we need to get one off of Amazon," he urged. "Sophie just presses a button on her kettle, and it's done in no time."

Perhaps it was because she was British, but heating water in a microwave almost seemed personally offensive. Vanessa did end up fishing their stainless-steel kettle out of one of the drawers and she placed it on the stove to boil. Sophie thought it the oddest thing but found that she enjoyed having that simple interaction as it helped her to relax a bit more around these two women who were the closest people to Noah.

Vanessa served Sophie her tea in a mug that was shaped like an apple, on the side of which read "World's Greatest Teacher". Tally made coffee for herself, Vanessa and Noah using a fancy looking coffee machine. Tally also fetched Maddie some juice from the fridge.

As the others carried the drinks over to the dining table, Sophie rummaged through her carry-on bag for a colouring book and a box of pencils to keep Maddie entertained. Maddie accepted them immediately and settled down on one of the dining chairs. She immediately arranged her pencils in the order that she liked, before beginning to colour the picture she had chosen.

Tally stacked some papers and placed a laptop on top of them, moving them out of the way, giving them room. "I've got tests coming out of my ears this time of year," she complained with a roll of her eyes.

"What year do you teach?" asked Sophie.

"Sixth grade English," replied Tally. Tapping the stack of papers, she added jokingly, "I get to do homework, too."

"Tally's awonderful teacher," Vanessa chimed in.

"And I've got a cabinet full of mugs to prove it," Tally teased

Sophie shoulders relaxed as she laughed, and she enjoyed her cup of tea and their company for the next hour. Noah had soon stretched his arm out, resting it on the back of Sophie's chair. She could feel him absentmindedly playing with the hair in her ponytail as they talked and laughed. Every time there was a soft pull of her hair, she felt a tingle down her spine.

Tally and Vanessa both asked Sophie lots of questions, never leaving a silence for long. They were curious about her, naturally, but they never asked her the normal sorts of questions that one would usually get. They didn't ask about her family, or her past relationships, or even Maddie's anti-social behaviour, which was already very evident. Noah had very obviously coached them, and while she was grateful for not being put on the spot, she couldn't help but worry about the negative thoughts that might have been crossing their minds. It was a horrible insecurity.

"I really love your house," Sophie complimented Tally as she helped her carry the mugs to the sink, leaving Vanessa, Noah and Maddie at the table. "I've never seen this sort of decorating before."

Tally smiled. "Thanks. Vanessa's the designer, really. She's a col-lector, and that's why nothing in this house matches. But it works." Tally put the mugs into the sink and turned on the tap, muffling their voices. "This place is where we can be ourselves. Their lives are crazy," she said softly, nodding towards Noah and Vanessa. "Noah's been in the studio for weeks. Vanessa's going on tour in the new year. There are always events and parties and people to meet. It's not my world, and I never want it to be. My world is considerably smaller, but it's a place that I keep safe for them to come back to." Tally's voice had become suddenly very raw and emotional, and Sophie knew that she was really being included by her.

"I've had a lot of practice in creating a safe world for someone I love very much," Sophie replied quietly.

"Noah cares about you so much, Sophie. You can't know how much I've wanted a normal person to enter his life. It's important for you to have a safe place, too. Especially as you dip your toe into his world."

Sophie glanced back at Noah, and he met her eye the minute she looked at him. With how she'd been feeling without him this last few weeks, she was fairly certain that wherever Noah was, she was safe.

"It literally is a studio with a sofa bed, isn't it?" Sophie gasped as Noah led her and Maddie into his bedroom.

Bedroom really was a poor word. It was the one room in the whole house that wasn't eclectically decorated. It was large, definitely a very generous size, except three quarters of the room were sealed with glass, soundproof panels. On the inside of the studio was an upright piano, and drum kit, a microphone, and three different guitars. There were wires everywhere, and an intense looking control panel on the outside with about four dozen different dials. The remainder of the room consisted of a plain, cream-coloured sofa bed, and timber bedside table, and a white lamp.

Noah grinned. "This is where I work. I could rent studio space, and I do book studios in the city, but I don't want to drive downtown when an idea hits me at three in the morning."

Sophie had never seen proper musical equipment in real life before, and she wondered if this was where she would be recording Noah's song. She hadn't even heard it yet. Noah wanted it recorded raw.

"The bathroom is in there." Noah pointed to a white panelled door next to the soundproof glass. "Vanessa likes my vanity more than hers, so her makeup and products are everywhere, but feel free to shove whatever in the cabinet to make space for your things."

It was then that Maddie looked up from her colouring book, which she had been flipping through as Sophie and Noah had been talking. She saw the musical equipment and gasped, a bright smile spreading across her face.

"There is a piano in your bedroom!" she squealed with delight. Maddie dropped her colouring book on the floor at her feet and ran over to the glass, pressing her face up against it.

"Maddie, stop!" cried Sophie. "You'll get fingerprints everywhere!"

Noah chuckled. "She's okay. Watch this." Noah opened the door to his studio and let Maddie inside. "Do you think you could play Frozen for us, kid?" he asked as he went over to the piano and lifted the lid.

Maddie quickly climbed up onto the stool and Noah adjusted the height for her. Noah then swiftly left the studio and closed the door behind him, just as Maddie started to play.

And Sophie couldn't hear a thing.

Noah looked very proud of himself. "Genius, right?"

Sophie laughed. "Absolutely!"

"You have the prettiest smile," Noah said softly, suddenly changing the tone of their conversation. "You get these little nose crinkles. They're so cute."

Sophie's hand instinctively went to her nose, but Noah captured it, and held it against his chest.

"I'm so glad you're here. I have been going out of my mind missing you. Going from seeing you every day to nothing has been horrible."

Sophie sucked in a breath. "I know what you mean. Every day I walk into the pub and turn to look at you at the piano and you're not there, and it hits me right in the stomach."

"I know two weeks isn't going to be long enough, but God am I going to enjoy them." Noah kissed Sophie softly. "So, game plan. We're recording the song tomorrow. The final score is due in four days. Postproduction is wrapping up in the early new year. I've been recording the score since I got back, but I saved Maddie's first piece so that she could record it with the orchestra."

Sophie's jaw dropped at the thought. Maddie was going to play with a proper orchestra!

"I want to record the song tomorrow. We'll do it here as I'm producing it. I do want to warn you though, like most artists, I'm a perfectionist, so please tell me to back the fuck off if I'm becoming an asshole."

Sophie had a hard time believing that Noah could be an arsehole. She was more concerned with getting her head around the fact that she was going to be professionally recording a song she'd never heard tomorrow for a proper film.

"We're booked on an eight o'clock AM flight up to Napa on the twenty-third. We've got a lot to do, but just think, in two days ... it gets a whole lot worse." He grinned.

"Stop talking about your mum like that," Sophie playfully scolded. "Seriously, I am so happy to be here." Thinking about the foul visit with Beck and his parents only a few days earlier made her stomach churn. "I'm certain that I'm going to love your mum. I already like your sister and Vanessa. They are really nice people ... and I forgive you for not giving me a heads up beforehand."

Noah laughed. "I am sorry. And I know you'll love my mom. It's hard not to." He leaned over and pressed a button on his control panel. "Way to go, kid! You sound great!"

CHAPTER 26

"Nope, I didn't like that run. Do it again," Noah ordered, his voice coming through the headphones that she was wearing.

Sophie was standing before a microphone that she had turned around to face the wall as she couldn't look at him as she sang the song. The first time has been wonderful. But Noah hadn't liked it.

Sophie had never received any sort of criticism before, constructive or otherwise. She had a terrible habit of taking things personally, and she tried her best to make her mind understand that this was Noah's song.

On the handful of auditions, she had been on before she had fallen pregnant with Maddie, she had been one of five hundred other girls, and the casting directors had barely said anything to her before waving in the next actress.

Noah had turned on his perfectionist mode. He reminded her of the first time she had ever seen him at the piano in Pete's at the beginning of October when he was blocked, and nothing was working for him. He was frustrated.

And Sophie was the cause of that.

It didn't help that she couldn't read music or minds.

This song was to be played at the end of the film, when the main characters were boarding a ship to emigrate to America. It was a song of hope, a song of seeing something just out of reach, and taking that final leap to grab a hold of it.

Sophie took a deep breath and nodded for him to start the music again. The opening piano melody began, and Sophie started to sing.

She had barely made it through the first verse before Noah interrupted her again.

"Softer, Sophie," he instructed curtly.

Sophie clenched her teeth together and pulled her headphones off, hanging them up on the stand. She turned around to look at Noah through the glass and said, "I don't know how else to sing!" she exclaimed. "I'm a theatre singer. Maybe you need someone more versatile." Really, she was more like a pub singer.

He did have Vanessa bloody Marino living down the hall from him.

Noah's facial expression softened, and he held up his finger, indicating for her to wait a minute. He then got up from his chair and ducked out of his bedroom. He returned a few moments later with Vanessa.

Oh God, that had been a sarcastic thought. Was he really going to replace her? Not that she'd blame him as she obviously wasn't understanding how he wanted this bloody song to sound.

Noah opened the door to the studio and he and Vanessa entered. She was wearing a matching spandex yoga outfit, with a crop top that showed off a perfectly toned stomach. Sophie had never felt frumpier or more untalented.

"I'm going to play the piano live," Noah told her, "just like I did at Pete's when we performed together. Vanessa's going to handle the recording for us."

Vanessa looked between them, and no doubt could see the intimidated expression on Sophie's face as she tried pathetically to mask it. She fished her phone out of her bra and flicked through it until she found what she wanted. "I send this video to every new cell phone I get," she explained, "to remind me of the nicest producer I ever worked with." She flipped her phone around to show Sophie a video of what looked like some grainy security footage of a studio.

Vanessa was at the microphone, and Noah at the controls. Vanessa was singing, and Sophie recognised the song immediately. It had been on the radio while Sophie was doing her GCSEs. It had put Vanessa Marino on the map.

"What do you think?" Vanessa asked Noah as she finished the song.

Sophie saw Noah's face drop as he realised what was coming.

"Jesus, Vanessa, did you gargle razors or something this morning? Do it again, and do it better," Noah demanded in the video.

"You're being an asshole, Noah!" Vanessa retorted into her microphone, before she flicked Noah the finger.

Vanessa laughed as she put her phone away. "Six months later I won Best New Artist at the Grammys, and Noah won Song of the Year."

"In my defence, I knew you could sound better," Noah protested.

Vanessa grinned. "Our dear Noah is just a moody artist at the end of the day, but he knows what he's doing, and we love him despite his flaws. Didn't he tell you to call him out if he was being an asshole?"

Thankfully, Sophie felt a few of the butterflies in her stomach flutter away. "You're being an arsehole," Sophie told him. "You didn't include perfectionism in your list of character flaws that you told me, remember?" Sophie prompted back to the day when he had told her his real purpose for being in London.

Noah smirked and rolled his eyes. "You know how talented I think you are. I want you to sing like it. I feel like I can hear your doubts in your own ability when you really go for it on a run. Cut that out," he instructed, and Sophie made herself take that advice on board. "Alright, let's do this. Vanessa, get out."

Vanessa saluted playfully before she exited the studio to sit down at the control board. Noah went to his piano and adjusted the stool from where Maddie had been playing it.

"I know I told you that this song is about the characters in the movie, their hopes for the future," he murmured, "but it's not. It's about you and Maddie, and what I want for us."

And then he began to play, and Sophie began to sing, her voice catching on every word with such emotion.

As she got to the chorus, Sophie truly felt every word. Noah had written this song about her, and about her daughter.

"It's been a long time searching

and now I see,

It's been a long time waiting

and you've found me.

Yes, I can finally see it

It's within my grasp

It's the life I've been waiting for

And by God I'm taking this chance."

Sophie finished singing, and she hadn't realised that several tears had fallen down her face. She quickly wiped them away as Noah suddenly wrapped his arms around her, squeezing her impossibly tightly and kissing her neck.

"That was perfect!" he whispered.

"Noah, would you kill me if I told you I'd forgotten to press record?" Vanessa asked through the main speaker.

Noah went stiff as he looked up at Vanessa. "What?" he cried.

Vanessa burst out laughing. "Wow, you're so easy!" she exclaimed. "Put that forehead vein away. Gosh, Sophie, that was so beautiful! You nearly had me in tears!"

Noah swore under his breath, but he reiterated Vanessa's praise. "That was how I wanted it to sound. That was how I knew you could sound."

"I felt like I was going to cry the whole time," Sophie confessed, worrying about her voice hitches.

"It sounded raw," insisted Noah.

"I can't believe you wrote that for us. For me," Sophie said vulnerably.

Noah brushed her cheek with the back of his knuckles, wiping away any stray tears. "I was inspired." Smiling, he added, "Come on. The recording is saved on my hard drive, so I'll finish it off on the plane. We've got one last thing to do."

Sophie had experienced a lot of pride in her daughter over the last part of the year as she had learned to deal with her autism diagnosis and make her way into the world.

But this was quite possibly the proudest moment of Sophie's life. She watched Maddie play at a piano that was quite possibly thirty times bigger than her, dressed in a jumper decorated with butterflies, while being accompanied by two dozen professional musicians possessing instruments that probably cost more than a car.

Maddie knew the piece. She had learned it at Pete's, written it alongside Noah, and could recall it perfectly. She played beyond her years; with no notion of the astronomical feat she was per-forming. Sophie could see it on the faces of the other musicians. They played, but their eyes went to Maddie in awe.

Sophie cried, as she always did, from outside the studio, and snapped photos and took videos of Maddie doing one of many things in her life that would truly be amazing.

As each capture saved, Sophie's mind momentarily went to Beck, back in London, and missing out on the ten thousand things in Maddie's life that he hadn't seen. It was not him that she felt for, but for Maddie lacking her dad.

But the feeling was fleeting, because Noah was right there, leaning against the wall of the studio watching, listening to her play. His eyes never left her, and the prideful expression on his face was everything to Sophie.

Thinking back to the lyrics of the song that he had written for them; Sophie knew that Noah was the one. The elusive one that was meant to be out in the universe. Somehow, she had managed to find hers, discovering in the process that she was capable of such deep feeling that she hadn't known was possible.

When the piece finished, Noah clapped his hands, before con-versing with the producers and dismissing his musicians. He then jogged over to Maddie, scooping her up into his arms before swinging her around proudly.

Maddie squealed with delight and she held onto Noah, her long plait spinning around after her.

Sophie entered the studio and joined them, hurriedly drying her eyes with the sleeve of her jumper.

"Maddie, you are so good!" cried Sophie.

"Mummy, do you think Santa could still bring me a piano for Christmas?" Maddie exclaimed as Noah placed her on the ground.

The instrument before them was a behemoth, and there was no way Sophie could ever afford something like that ... not that it would have fit in their little flat anyway.

"I don't think a piano will fit on Santa's sleigh, sweetheart."

Maddie frowned, but seemed to accept the logic. "I'm hungry," she announced, moving on from their discussion with no real feeling at all for the occasion.

Maybe when she was older, or when she saw the film, she would understand what she had just been a part of.

"It's Vanessa's annual cheat week so she's asked for McDonald's for dinner. Sound good?" Noah offered.

Maddie beamed, as though the idea of a takeaway was more exciting than what she had just done. Maddie skipped off out of the studio, anxiously waiting near the exit.

Sophie looked up at Noah and shook her head. "I'm honestly at a loss ... I cannot really fathom what we've done today," she said breathlessly.

"I won't deny that I really do love what I do. It's a privilege to get paid for doing this ... but today was really special, I agree." Noah reached for Sophie, and she met him, wrapping her arms around his waist and settling her head against his chest. "Thank you for singing for me. Thank you for not dumping me, too."

Sophie laughed. "It was close there for a while," she teased.

Noah chuckled and squeezed her.

"Mummy, Noah!" shouted Maddie. "Hurry up! I want a McDonald's now!"

"And I want a jet ski, kid!" retorted Noah over his shoulder. "What do you want me to do about it?"

"Manners!" scolded Sophie.

Maddie pouted, before conceding. "I want a McDonald's now, please!" she emphasised.

Noah's hand slipped to hers, and he pulled her from the studio and towards Maddie.

After ordering a meal each, and then half the menu for Vanessa on her cheat week, they all ate together back at the condo, before getting an early night ready to catch their early flight the next morning.

Sophie and Maddie were sharing Noah's bed, while he was sleeping downstairs on the couch. Sophie did feel bad for taking his bedroom, and it did make her wonder as to the sleeping arrangements at his parents' house.

Noah hadn't said anything, nor had he rushed Sophie into something that she was not ready for, and she did sincerely appreciate that. She hoped that she would be roomed with Maddie, purely because Maddie had only slept away from Sophie once on her holiday to Fuerteventura and that had been a royal disaster. If Maddie was going to throw a wobbly then Sophie needed to be on hand to calm her.

Their alarms all went off at half past five, and they and their bags were all piled into the car service by six. It was then that Sophie began to feel that fluttering in her stomach at the upcoming meeting with Noah's parents.

She knew that Joy Bentley was excited about her, but if anyone loved their child more than Sophie, it was Joy. Once the initial excitement wore off, she hoped, she prayed, that she would meet Joy's expectations.

Their flight to Napa was on a smaller plane without a first-class cabin, so they were all together in economy. This meant that Vanessa was recognised by several passengers despite her large sunglasses, but she happily took pictures with whomever asked.

Sophie sat next to Maddie, while Tally and Vanessa were in front of her, and Noah was by himself across the aisle, sitting beside a man in a business suit. Sophie gave Maddie sweets to suck on for the take-off and landing and tossed a wrapped barley sugar to Noah to suck on as well.

The flight wasn't long, and they landed in Napa in the midmorning. As the plane was small, they descended down onto the tarmac before following the crowd into the airport. It was colder in Napa than in Los Angeles, and Sophie pulled her cardigan tightly around herself, wishing that she could fish an extra coat out of her bag for Maddie.

The airport was so much smaller than LAX, but Sophie immediately liked the feeling of being somewhere a little secluded. After twenty-six years of living in one of the busiest cities in the world, this was a nice change.

There was a small crowd gathered inside to greet the travellers, and Noah, Tally and Vanessa immediately started looking at the faces. Sophie hadn't thought to ask about who would be picking them up.

Two women suddenly emerged from the group, excitedly waving at them. One had layered blond hair that fell to her shoulders. She looked to be in her mid-thirties and was wearing jeans and a comfortable hooded sweatshirt. The other had long brown hair, fixed in two Dutch braids. She seemed to be a similar age to the blond, though perhaps a little younger. She was very tanned and was wearing black leggings and a light wash denim jacket.

The brunette flew into Noah's arms, while the blonde hugged Tally. After a few moments, they switched, before greeting Vanessa warmly as well. Sophie remembered seeing their faces in the picture that was set as the background on Noah's phone. These women were his older sisters.

All four siblings spoke at the same time, asking each other rapid questions without actually answering them. It seemed it had been a long time since they had all been together, and Sophie watched them, honestly feeling a little envy at being an only child.

When they broke apart, Noah quickly wrapped his arm around Sophie's waist, bringing her forward. "Sophie, Maddie, these are our big sisters. Haley," he pointed to the blonde, "and Casey." He gestured to the brunette.

"We've been so excited to meet you, Sophie," Haley spoke first, coming forward and greeting her with a hug and a kiss on the cheek. "And Maddie, you have no idea how excited our mom is to meet you."

"It's lovely to meet you both," said Sophie nervously as she greeted Casey with a hug next. "Noah only has such nice things to say about all his family."

"Oh, so he hasn't warned you about Joy?" Casey asked in disbelief.

No, he had, and Casey was now fourth person to mention it.

"Of course, I have," retorted Noah. "What am I, an animal? I'm not sending her in there blind. I won't be able to afford my own therapy, let alone hers."

Sophie playfully slapped Noah on the arm. "Stop being so horrible about your mum!" she scolded.

"Mom would have been here to pick you up except the banner arrived late and she didn't trust Dad to put it up without her there to supervise," Casey tsked.

"Banner?" repeated Sophie, raising her eyebrows.

Casey and Haley exchanged an amused smile, while Noah rolled his eyes.

Chapter 27

Sophie couldn't believe her eyes as they drove through impossibly large wooden gates that were emblazoned with "Bentley Grange". The car seemed to continue down a long and winding road that was bordered on both sides by acres and acres of dormant grape vines.

The vines were planted in perfect rows for as far as the eye could see. Sophie didn't think she'd ever really seen a vineyard before, let alone known anyone to have owned one.

Noah was sitting beside her in the back seat of the large four-wheel drive, and was chatting animatedly to his elder sisters, Haley driving, while Casey was in the front seat. He was catching up with them and did not notice Sophie's astonishment.

The sheer size did make Sophie wonder if Noah's privilege was similar to hers growing up. Though it was clear in the man that he was, and in his relationship with his sisters, all of whom seemed to be the salt of the earth, that a proper family was not made with money.

The road finally ended when a great sandstone house came into view. It looked positively enormousand was covered by thick walls of ivy. There was a large, circular driveway before the house, with several expensive range rovers parked sporadically around a cherub fountain fixed in the centre. Beyond the driveway was a huge wrap-around porch that was decorated with Christmas lights and comfortable outdoor furniture.

"Look at the lights, Maddie. Can you see them?" Sophie pointed to the columns supporting the upper storey that were adored with colourful twinkle lights. Even though it was still daylight, they were on and flashing. Sophie was sure they would look ever so pretty at night.

Maddie pressed her face against the glass of the window as Haley parked the car. Her wide, brown eyes taking in all the new all at once. "Is it a castle?" she whispered.

The large stone that cladded the wall did make it look like a castle, but the huge windows and the light filled balconies and porches were a giveaway that this would indeed be a beautiful home.

No sooner had the engine shut off, a small woman shot out of the house like a bolt of lightning. She stood before the car, practically bouncing as they all climbed out.

Joy Bentley was a very short woman, probably no more than five foot one. Her hair, like two of her daughters, was coloured blonde, and she wore it in a short, tousled bob that suited her round face. Her eyes were blue, just like Noah's, but smaller, perhaps made so by her larger than life smile that was impossibly radiating off of her face.

She was wearing a red and white striped candy cane jumper and some acid wash jeans, which clung to her trim figure well.

Her smiles were directed at Sophie the minute Joy saw her, and an odd sense of calm filled her considering the seriousness of such a meeting.

Tally was the first to greet Joy, though. "Mommy!" she cried, dramatically throwing herself into Joy's arms.

Joy laughed and hugged Tally tightly. "I've missed you, baby!" She ran her hands up and down Tally's ribs and then immediately tutted, pulling away. "You're too thin!" she scolded. "Just imagine how I'm going to feel if you drop dead because you didn't eat a darn cheeseburger!"

Tally immediately craned her neck to look at her three siblings and Sophie. "Who had Mom lays on the guilt within thirty seconds?"

"I had two minutes. Rookie mistake," hissed Noah.

Casey laughed. "I had under a minute. You all can Venmo me." She winked.

Joy scoffed and rolled her eyes, before turning her attention back to Sophie. "Sophie," she said sweetly, her smile returning, "I'm assuming you're Sophie, as not one of my dear children has had the manners to introduce me. What am I? Oh, only the woman who endured a hundred and twenty hours of excruciating unmedicated labour collectively to bring them into the world." Joy eyed all four of them.

Noah rolled his eyes, in a way that showed Sophie he had inherited the trait from his mum. "Mom, please allow me to introduce you to Sophie. Sophie, this is my beloved birth giver, Joy."

Sophie felt Maddie hide behind her nervously, but Joy didn't bring attention to it if she noticed. Sophie held her arms behind her, holding onto Maddie's head as comfortingly as she could.

"Sophie, welcome," greeted Joy. "It is so wonderful to have you here with us."

"Thank you so much for letting us come," replied Sophie. "I sincerely hope we will not be an inconvenience. I'm sorry about ..." Sophie nodded behind her. "She's met a lot of people this week and I'm not sure if Noah's told you but ..."

Joy nodded understandingly, and winked, letting Sophie know that she knew exactly what was going on. "Not at all," Joy promised. "You can't imagine how long we've all waited for Noah to find someone nice to bring home. Although why you'd want to be with my son is beyond me. Did you know that he left the country without telling me?" she admonished, shaking her head.

Noah rolled his eyes again. "I'm here, and so are my kidneys," he groaned.

Sophie furrowed her eyebrows wondering what that meant.

"I'll get you when little miss is feeling a little more settled," Joy promised Sophie as she moved right past Noah and ran over to Vanessa with open arms. Joy cuddled her as tight as could be, and Vanessa smiled brilliantly. "Oh, how are you, beautiful girl?" asked Joy. "It's been far too long."

"I'm doing really good," replied Vanessa cheerfully. "We're doing really good. I'm so sorry about Thanksgiving," she apologised. "We won't miss next year, I promise."

Joy scoffed. "Oh, don't give that a second thought. At least you had the decency to call," she said passive aggressively. "Now, I've been using that skin cream you sent me, but I have absolutely no idea what to do with the serum so you're going to have to teach me."

"Of course, I will," Vanessa assured her, before nodding to Noah. "Noah is really sorry, Joy," she urged.

Joy dramatically sighed before conceding and walking over to her son before standing up on her toes to pull him down to her level for a hug. Noah chuckled and returned his mum's gesture. Joy cupped Noah's face and kissed his cheek. "Oh, you're too handsome to stay mad at," she decided, before she tapped his tummy.

"Thanks, Mom," said Noah, shaking his head. He went over to the boot of the car and pulled out Sophie's suitcase, before saying, "Maddie, do you want to come inside and see my piano from when I was your age?"

Maddie's ears pricked up at the mention, and she nodded. She let go of Sophie and flitted over to Noah's side, walking inside the house with him.

Joy watched them walk together, and Sophie watched as she brushed a tear aside. She was not the only one who loved the sight.

The moment they were inside, Joy turned back to Sophie for the third time. "I told you, I'd get you!" Sophie was soon enveloped in one of the oddest hugs that she had ever experienced.

And not odd in an uncomfortable way, but quite the opposite. She had never felt this sort of security from another woman before. It was ... maternal.

"I am so thankful that Noah managed to find you," Joy whispered in Sophie's ear.

"I could be an axe murderer or something," murmured Sophie thoughtlessly, wondering why she had come out with something so weird in return of something so kind.

But thankfully, Joy chuckled. "But you're not," she said confidently. "I think I have a special sort of ESP when it comes to the partners my kids bring home. Tally in high school, yikes!" she shuddered.

"Hey!" cried Tally.

"Was I, or was a I not, lovely the minute you brought Vanessa to meet us?" challenged Joy, and Tally reluctantly nodded. "See, I know when you four have got a good one."

Haley, Casey, Vanessa and Tally all began to move the luggage into the house, and Sophie lingered behind with Joy. She felt bad that she wasn't helping, but she could tell that Joy still wanted to chat. And she had some things to say as well.

"Noah is so good with Maddie," Sophie told Joy. "He was honestly a saving grace when he came into our lives. Maddie was still undiagnosed, and I was honestly at my wit's end. And then we found Noah, and she found the piano."

Joy smiled. "I can't know what it's like to have a child with autism, but I do know what it's like to raise a child who is incredibly different. I don't know what Noah's told you, but his life wasn't always very easy. And I'm ashamed to say that his life at home was much the same. We're moms, we're born to worry, born to bleed for our kids if it saves them from pain."

"I was worried you might think differently of me for having a child out of wedlock," Sophie felt terribly old fashioned for even saying the term. "You would judge me for being so irresponsible."

Joy frowned. "Oh, Sophie. Guilt, you'll get, passive aggression, nagging, yelling, shouting … but never judgement."

Sophie shakily nodded at hearing those blessed words.

"Oh, sweetheart," Joy said softly, her blue eyes scanning Sophie's face. "I can see you've had a hard run, too. Come on," she urged. "Let me show you around, show you where you'll be staying, and then I'll guilt you for something. It's my special talent. You'll feel right at home."

Joy led Sophie inside the house and her jaw unwittingly dropped. She was standing in anenormous foyer, which was completely open to the floor above. Light filled the space, streaming in from the huge skylights above them. The walls were white, accented with dark, timber beams framing each doorway, ceiling and skirting board.

There was a huge banner that hung from the landing above that read: Welcome to the family, Sophie & Maddie!

Every available surface was draped in Christmas garlands and lights, and there was a beautiful scent of baking in the air. A Christmas tree stood perfectly decorated by the dark, timber staircase, with not an ornament out of place.

A formal sitting room was off to Sophie's right, while a formal dining room was situated in the opposite direction. Everything was pristine and decorated to perfection.

Another thing that Sophie noticed as there was not an empty wall in sight. Framed pictures of Noah and his sisters hung everywhere. Starting from when they were babies, and right up to adulthood. It also did not escape her attention that pictures of Vanessa were among the group, too, as well as a man in military uniform.

"You didn't have to make a banner," said Sophie bashfully.

Joy laughed. "I just wish I'd seen Noah's face when he walked in. That's the reward. But the sentiment is sincere. You are so welcome."

Joy led Sophie upstairs to the open landing. Up and out of sight was a less formal lounge, with a television set, and a coffee table, which held a vase filled with pinecones and Christmas baubles.

There were several doors off of the this room, and Joy selected the room closest to the stairs.

Inside was a neat and cosy bedroom. A large, white bed with matching bedside tables rested against the far wall. A huge window let in the afternoon sun, and a trundle bed was set up on the floor.

"I'm not old fashioned or anything," clarified Joy, "but I just assumed that you would prefer to sleep in with Maddie. If I'm wrong, then please don't hesitate –"

"No, this is wonderful, thank you," interjected Sophie. "I don't know if Maddie would cope by herself in a new place."

Joy smiled. "Well, there's a bathroom in there." She pointed to a panelled door off the bedroom. "I've been shopping and put in a load of toiletries but if there's anything I've forgotten, please let me know."

Joy showed Sophie around the rest of the floor, before leading her back downstairs to the main part of the house. She was brought into a huge open space, which featured an enormous chef's kitchen with a granite island, a comfortable dining room, and a sunken lounge with a plush sectional sofa.

The rest of the family were gathered in here, and Sophie quickly realised why.

Noah was playing the guitar with Maddie sitting beside him, watching intently. She was studying his fingers, learning, and committing what he was doing to memory. On Noah's other side was an older man, with grey, curly hair. He wore a flannel shirt and jeans, and his tanned skin was a little weathered from the sun, but he was grinning at Noah from ear to ear. He, too, strummed his guitar with ease and experience, jamming along with his son.

Sophie heard a yelp get stuck in Joy's throat as she clapped her hands together over her mouth. Sophie knew how special Noah's father was to him. He had told her about it. She wondered if those thoughts were passing through Joy's mind at that moment.

She didn't have to wonder for long.

"That's my husband, John," Joy said quietly. "He's the strong, masculine type, you know. He doesn't say much, but what he does means something. I talk enough for the both of us. Well, anyway, you can imagine that after two girls, when he found out that one of our twins was going to be a boy he was just over the darn moon. He was so excited to have a son, and oh, good God, did John love on Noah when he was little. Parents aren't supposed to have favourites, but John was so darn smitten with Noah when he was a baby," Joy recalled. "But when Noah started to get bigger, started to show his personality, and his interests, John realised that Noah wasn't the boy he wanted. John got him into football and baseball. He even built a basketball court in the backyard to play with him. But Noah wasn't interested. He hated everything, and John was just heartbroken.

"What broke my heart was seeing Noah not understand why his daddy pulled away from him. At some point, John just gave up on him," Joy admitted. "You bet John and I have some vicious fights about that, but John really had no idea what to do with Noah. They had nothing in common." Joy nodded toward Noah. "You can see what finding music did for Noah. He found his passion, and he never looked back. John still couldn't see it. He'd see kids in letterman jackets and think that Noah was missing out on something. I could count on one hand the number of conversations that John and Noah had up until Noah was sixteen. I nearly divorced him when he asked if we could try for another son. I told him right then and there that if he didn't make an effort, that Noah was going to leave this house and never come back.

"Something clicked. I don't know what, but something did. And John did try. He bought himself a guitar, and he took lessons from the music teacher at the high school. When he was ready, he bought a guitar for Noah as well, and he changed.They changed. They've been close ever since, and John loves his boy."

Sophie had heard the story from Noah but hearing it from Joy hit her a little differently. Just hearing the change in a father, the effort in changing to meet the needs of a child, made her heart ache for Maddie.

But then all she had to do was look at who she was sitting beside to have hope.

Noah's sisters and Vanessa were all seated on the sofa listening, tapping their feet and nodding their heads along to the tune.

When John and Noah strummed the final note, John laughed and wrapped his arm affectionately around Noah, pulling him to his side, and placing a kiss on the top of his head.

"Just you wait to see what I bought you for Christmas, son," John said excitedly.

"Oh, God, John is itching to give the damn thing to Noah," uttered Joy. "Honey, didn't you see who'd joined us?" asked Joy to the room.

All eyes went to Joy and Sophie, with Sophie nervously smiling at John. Noah jumped off of the sofa, settling his guitar with Maddie, as he came over to take Sophie's hand. He squeezed it reassuringly.

"Dad, this is Sophie," he introduced. "Sophie, this is my dad, John Bentley."

John, too, climbed off of the sofa, and came over to shake Sophie hand. "It's a pleasure to finally meet you, Sophie," John said kindly.

"Noah has told me so much about all of you," replied Sophie. "So, it is lovely to meet you as well."

"God, the British have a way of making the simplest words sound fancy," commented John.

But no sooner had he said the words, the sound of the guitar sounded again, only this time it was coming from Maddie. She had the guitar laying flat on her lap. Her hands were too small to fit around the neck of the instrument, and her arm was too short to fit over the top of the body, so she played by pressing down on the frets and plucking at the strings over the sound hole.

It was slow, but it was a tune, and Sophie's mouth once again fell agape.

"Only one kid I've ever known to be able to do that," murmured John.

CHAPTER 28

"Okay, eat up everybody," instructed Joy as she dolloped a huge lump of macaroni and cheese on Noah's plate. "We've got a big day tomorrow. Tree trimming, volunteering, church!"

Joy had prepared a smorgasbord of food for dinner, and Noah was in heaven. He couldn't really fend for himself, and with Vanessa on a diet fifty-one weeks out of the year, his pantry at home was never really inspiring.

In the centre of the long, oak table were dishes of crispy bacon, scrambled eggs, biscuits, pancakes, waffles, sausage, as well as macaroni and cheese. Breakfast food was Joy's tradition on December twenty-third. Christmas Eve was always Chinese takeout before Church, and then Joy really put on a show for Christmas dinner on the day.

Noah was actually very proud of his mom. He could see that she was making a huge effort to control herself. If it were just Sophie, he knew she would have been ten times worse, but Noah had pre-warned her to control herself around Maddie. And she was.

She was being the perfect hostess, even though Noah knew she itching to grill Sophie within an inch of her life.

"Do you like macaroni and cheese, Maddie?" Joy asked softly. She was making her way around the table with her large serving bowl and a spoon normally used for salad. She had just scooped an extra-large helping onto Vanessa's plate and she was now going to town.

Maddie had been very quiet. Noah had seen a glimpse of her normally when she had got her hands on his guitar, but he could still see that she was very unsure of these new people. Noah could subsequently see that Maddie's reservedness had Sophie on edge, as though she was waiting for Maddie to throw an epic tantrum before she bolted.

Noah honestly didn't know how to make it better. He wished he knew more about autism, wished he'd done more to research what it would be like for Maddie to come into a new environment like this. Feeling useless in that respect was awful, as all he wanted to do was to make this stay a stress free one for Sophie.

He hoped that she could see that his family adored her already. Noah knew that his sisters would welcome her with open arms. Joy, he could tell, wanted so desperately to love on her. She had a big mouth, but an even bigger heart, and loved to collect baby birds with broken wings.

His dad was much simpler. If Noah was happy, John was happy, and that was that. It had taken a long time for it to be that way, but Noah wouldn't have it any different.

"Yes, thank you, Mrs Bentley," said Sophie gratefully as she picked up Maddie's plate to hold it up to her.

"Just Joy, sweetheart," corrected Joy as she spooned a helping onto Maddie's plate. "And for you?"

"Yes, thank you, Joy." Sophie smiled and Joy dished some up for her as well.

Noah was seated opposite Sophie. He would have sat next to her had Joy not practically pulled the chair out from under him to sit their herself. He managed to catch Sophie's eye, and he mouthed, "Relax," when she saw him.

Sophie took a dramatic deep breath, before she smiled at him. She picked up her fork and began to eat her dinner.

Noah helped himself to eggs and bacon, loading his plate up with enough grease to take down a horse.

"So, Sophie, don't your parents mind us stealing you away for the holidays?" Joy asked nonchalantly as she took her seat, starting her questioning as casually as she could muster.

Noah paled as Sophie stiffened. Shit! Noah quickly went through the list of subjects he had told his mom to avoid and honestly couldn't remember if Sophie's parents were one of them.

"Um, no," Sophie replied quietly. "I ... er ... don't really have that sort of relationship with my parents actually."

The murmurs of conversation around the table stopped as his family tuned in to what Sophie was saying.

Joy's face softened. "Oh, no, why?"

"Mom!" snapped Noah.

Both Sophie and Joy turned their heads to look at Noah. Joy knew that she had struck a nerve, but Sophie said, "No, it's alright. It's not exactly hard to imagine why, is it?" She gestured beside. "My mum and dad had an idea of what my life would be, and they didn't like that I went another direction. I've seen them once in the last nine years." Sighing, she added, "But, I think I got the better end of the deal."

"Amen!" cried Vanessa, toasting her glass of wine. "Parents suck, Sophie. Sometimes you get lucky second time around." She winked at Joy and drank from her glass.

"I hate this!" Maddie announced to the table, spitting out the mouthful of macaroni cheese that she had eaten. Her sudden speech drew all the attention, and Sophie looked completely mortified.

"Oh my God, Maddie do not spit out your food. That is so terribly rude!" cried Sophie hysterically. "You eat it now!" she demanded.

The raised tone, and her mother's order put Maddie over the edge. Noah could see it happen before it did and leapt out of his chair as Maddie started to scream.

Maddie turned red as she screamed, and the entire table went into a state of shock. All except for Noah who was racing around to them, and Sophie who was vociferously apologising while trying to calm Maddie down.

Maddie's meltdowns were not bad behaviour. It was her reaction to being overwhelmed and feeling a loss of control. His research had told him this much. He needed to get her to a place where she could calm down and regain that control.

Noah scooped her up into his arms, still screaming her little lungs out. He raced down the hallway which held doors to the powder room, the garage, and his father's den. Noah took Maddie into the den and shut the door behind him. He placed her down on the ground and she threw herself onto her front, screaming so loudly that her vocal cords had to hurt.

Noah prayed that it was still in the closet. He opened the closet doors and thanked his lucky stars that his old electric piano was still on one of the shelves in and amongst all the junk. He pushed some things aside to pull the heavy instrument down, carrying it over to the nearest power outlet. Noah was some ten feet from Maddie, who was still throwing a fit on the floor. He plugged in the piano and was pleased when it lit up for the first time in years.

He began to play the first tune that popped into his head, being the first one that they had composed together at Pete's. Maddie's screams stopped almost instantly as she recognised the melody, and her head popped up.

Maddie's brown eyes were already red with tears, but she stared at him as he played. Noah watched her physically calm, her breathing slowing as her attention went from his face to his hands. She scooted across the carpet before sitting up in front of him, the piano in between them. Like Noah, Maddie crossed her legs.

"Would you like to play, Maddie?" Noah asked softly.

Maddie nodded and she crawled around to sit beside him at the piano. Her small hands immediately took over the playing, continuing the tune seamlessly.

Joy kept shelves of photographs in every room of the house, and he wondered if it would make things easier if Noah showed Maddie pictures rather than her having to enter back into a room full of strangers again. Noah got up and went over to the timber shelves above the mantle and he collected framed pictures of his family.

He brought them back over to Maddie and he sat down beside her. Noah held his parent's anniversary picture in front of Maddie, taken a couple of years back. "This is my mom and dad," Noah said gently. "Mom," he pointed to Joy, and "Dad," he pointed to John. "Just like you have your mommy, this is mine."

Maddie kept playing, and Noah hoped she was listening.

"This is Haley." Noah chose a picture of Haley at her grad school graduation. "She is my oldest sister. She is very nice, I promise." Joy had framed a picture of Casey in a desert somewhere, beaming from ear to ear. "And this is my middle sister, Casey. She takes pictures all around the world. I'm sure she'll take a nice picture of you with your presents from Santa in a couple of days."

Maddie kept playing.

Last was a picture of Vanessa and Tally at an event. Joy kept it framed because it was the one-time Tally let her pick out a dress for her. Tally preferred edgy, fitted clothing.

"And you met Tally and Vanessa at my house. Tally is my twin sister, and Vanessa is her girlfriend. Tally is my best friend, and Vanessa is a musician like me, and like you."

Noah laid the frames out in a line in front of the piano, and just waited as Maddie finished the piece. She had completely calmed down, and her hands came to rest on her knees.

"I want pancakes," Maddie then said decidedly.

Noah was taken aback, before he nodded and smiled. "You got it, kid."

They both climbed to their feet before leaving the den. Maddie trotted back out to the dining room with Noah following her.

His family kept their eyes on each other purposefully, but Sophie leapt to her feet. She looked in anguish, and Noah immediately went to her side, wrapping his arms around her securely.

"It's okay," he uttered. "She just wants pancakes."

"Oh, God, I'm so embarrassed," Sophie whispered, only for him. "What must they think of me? Of her? I don't want them thinking badly of her."

Noah looked over Sophie head at his mom, who was watching them with concern. "Maddie wants pancakes, Mom."

Joy immediately jumped to her feet and rushed to grab the dish of pancakes for Maddie. "How many do you want, sweetheart?" she asked tenderly.

Maddie peered up at Joy and cocked her head. "You're Noah's mummy," she observed bluntly. "I think you are pretty."

"Oh," Joy remarked, chuffed. "I think you're pretty, too, Maddie." She speared a pancake with a fork and popped it onto Maddie's plate, which was now free from any macaroni and cheese. "Would you like ice cream? Chocolate syrup?"

"Mom definitely likes her," Noah whispered to Sophie. "We were never allowed sugary shit on our pancakes. Her words, not mine. She likes to think she doesn't curse but she does."

"Yes, please," replied Maddie, and she sat patiently as a joyful Joy went to the refrigerator to get what she needed.

It was like nothing had happened. Maddie hadn't been upset. She was just overwhelmed, and now that she had regained control, she was okay. She was excited when Joy scooped ice cream onto her plate and drizzled chocolate syrup overtop, and she hungrily tucked in.

"These people are my people, and they want to be yours too," Noah murmured. "I want you to get out of your head and to start believing that you have something to offer. I know you do. I wouldn't have fallen in love with you otherwise."

Sophie's head snapped up at him, and she stared at him with wide, disbelieving brown eyes. Noah merely smile and placed a quick kiss on her forehead.

The remainder of the meal was fairly uneventful, and the details for the following day were finalised. Their family Christmas tree was always decorated on Christmas Eve. Joy had a dozen other fake ones perfectly decorated around the house, but she always had a perfect blue spruce on reserve at the Boy Scout lot to be decorated by the whole family.

The rest of the day was spent volunteering and varying community organisations. Noah had dressed up as Santa one year at the children's hospital, they worked at homeless shelters, the church toy drive, delivering meals ... there was always something that needed to be done, and Joy's big heart couldn't give enough.

After their takeout dinner, the family attended Joy's church, and Noah always played for the congregation.

And then, of course, Santa came.

After the dishes had been cleared and leftovers put in the refrigerator, Tally put on It's a Wonderful Life in the living room. To Noah's surprise, Sophie had never seen it.

Maddie was sitting on the floor, entirely engaged in the movie. His family were all on the sectional sofa, with him and Sophie cuddled up together on one end. Sophie was more relaxed now, and Noah secretly hoped it was because of his little confession. It seemed weird for her not to know. He honestly hoped that this trip out here showed her how serious he was about her, and about Maddie.

He didn't need to hear it back right away. He wasn't so insecure. But it would be nice, and he looked forward to it, if and when it happened.

About halfway through the movie, Sophie suddenly gasped quietly under her breath.

"What?" he whispered.

"I just saw your mantle," replied Sophie quietly.

Noah followed Sophie's line of sight and realised she was talking about his mom's bragging mantle. Nothing shoved her kids and their achievements in the faces of her friends more than that damn mantle.

On the wall in the centre hung Haley's MBA. She was the most educated out of all the Bentley siblings. Either side hung Noah's diploma from Julliard and Tally's from USC. On the oak mantle rested a collection of different trophies and awards gathered by them all over the years.

Joy kept Casey's Pulitzer, along with her award-winning photograph on the mantle. "The plaque is Casey's Pulitzer," Noah murmured. "She takes some real nice photos, apparently," he joked. "Haley's high school chess trophy, Tally's state track medal."

"I love that she keeps them all," Sophie whispered back. "She must be really proud of you."

"Exceptionally," chuckled Noah quietly.

"Is that your Grammy?" she wondered, looking at the Gramophone award beside Haley's chess trophy.

"No, that's Vanessa's. Her first one for Best New Artist. I told you a bit of what her parents are like. But basically, when she came out, they disowned her. They didn't want anything to do with her. I honestly don't get how a parent could reject their child over anything, let alone for loving someone. But she sees my parents as her own, and they feel the same way about her. My mom, of course, celebrates her on her brag mantle."

"I'm glad that Vanessa found a second chance," Sophie almost said soundlessly.

God, before this vacation was out, Noah just knew his mom was going to give Sophie everything she didn't know she needed, while being terribly over the top in the process.

"And I suppose we're just going to pretend I don't see the Oscar on the end there." Sophie subtly motioned to Noah's statuette that was kept on the end of the mantle.

Noah grinned sheepishly. "That's pretty cool," he admitted.

"Only?" she teased. "I do love that you keep it with your parents, though."

The back of Noah's head was suddenly pelted with popcorn.

"Will you two shut up?" groaned Tally. "We're getting to the best part!"

"Don't curse, Tally!" scolded Joy.

"Shut up is not a curse word, Mom. If I wanted to curse, I would say fu –" but Tally stopped herself before she swore in front of Maddie. "Fungi," she finished. "Shut the fungi up, Noah, or I will choke you with fungi popcorn." Tally smiled sweetly. "I fungi love you."

"Fungi is now a banned word in this house," Joy declared. "Really, Tally? What must poor Sophie be thinking of us? She'll be thinking that I raised a bunch of bad-mouthed hooligans."

"Well, that is pretty fungi accurate," chimed in Casey.

"I can't be the only one jonesing for a mushroom omelette right now, can I?" asked Haley.

Maddie suddenly turned around and asked, "Mummy, what is fungi?"

To which she was met with a sudden burst of laughter from everyone. Noah was pleased to see Sophie laughing, too.

Chapter 29

After spending a Christmas Eve with Noah's family, Sophie felt terribly guilty for how she had spent it every other year, even when she still lived with her parents.

She usually spent it lying on the couch, gorging herself on sweets and watching awful Christmas romantic comedies. She liked watching carols and looking out the window for any glimpse of snow.

Her parents usually attended a formal Christmas party, and she had usually been forced to go. But even then, the evening was vapid and superficial.

She had spent the majority of her day at Joy Bentley's church, in a great room filled with boxes of toys. Volunteers from the congregation, including Joy's own family, were boxing food hampers for families in need, wrapping presents for under-privileged children, and coordinating donations from local businesses to go to those who needed it most.

Joy was in her element, and Sophie respected her deeply for it. She didn't need to be fearful of Joy. Sophie finally got it, understanding now that she would never be judged by Noah's mum.

Maddie coloured in the corner of the room, perfectly content by herself. She had been much calmer today, and there was no repeat of her meltdown from the night before. Sophie, in hindsight, should have seen it coming. Maddie had been so terribly quiet that she knew everything would eventually get to her.

It didn't stop the guilt though. Maddie couldn't communicate her emotions properly. She couldn't tell Sophie what she needed and that was why she had thrown a fit. Elaine had explained this to Sophie in an attempt to stop her from feeling guilty, but it worked quite the opposite.

Mothers, Sophie believed, always had something to feel guilty about.

Noah and his dad spent the day ferrying the hampers and gifts out into the community, so Sophie saw him sporadically throughout the day. It didn't stop him from smiling brilliantly at her every time he entered the church. It made her heart flutter over and over again.

He had told her that he loved her the night before. In so many words; Sophie had heard it. Nobody had ever said that to her before. Nobody had ever felt that way about Sophie. And Sophie had certainly never felt like this about anyone before.

God, how had she gotten so lucky? Surely nothing could stop this, ruin this.

Sophie wanted to tell Noah that she loved him, too. But having never said those words to anyone, the idea of them spilling out was quite daunting. It was as though she was taking her heart out of her chest and saying, "Here you go. Do with it what you will."

John and Noah were going for Chinese take away before the family would be heading to church in the evening. Sophie learned from last night's mistake to read through the menu with Maddie on Noah's phone, allowing her to make her choice beforehand.

Maddie was easy to please with fried rice and satay chicken. Sophie decided on the same.

They waited in the living room for the John and Noah to arrive with the food, and Sophie discovered that an enormous Christmas tree had been delivered during the day. Joy and her daughters fetched boxes of Christmas decorations from a cupboard and started unloading them, simultaneously playing Michael Bublé's Christmas album.

The decorations for this tree were much more sentimental than the other perfectly decorated ones around the house. Joy had glittery pasta garlands and clay handprints and photographs in sloppily painted frames.

She smiled and gushed over every piece and shared a unique story of how she came to possess it. Sophie enjoyed watching her interact with her daughters, Vanessa included.

An outside could see her as silly and sentimental to be getting teary over a hand painted Rudolph, but she would then hug Casey or Tally or whomever had made it for her, and she would tell them how happy she was that they were home.

She wished her own mother could see Joy, and then she might know how she ought to have been.

As Tally wrapped Vanessa in a garland of macaroni, and Casey and Haley sprinkled glittery snowflakes over the tree, captivating Maddie, Joy came to sit beside Sophie on the sofa.

"It's terribly tacky, I know, but these decorations are my favourite because they're attached to a memory of one of my kids thinking that their decoration was just the best thing ever, and they were so excited to give it to me." Joy grinned, shaking her head.

"Not at all, I think it's wonderful. I hope my tree is filled with these sorts of things one day," replied Sophie. She had her own little box of Maddie's crafts in her flat back home.

Joy leant her arm up against the back of the sectional and rested her head on her hand. "How are you coping, Sophie?" she asked, furrowing her brow. "Are you okay?"

Sophie had answered that question dozens of times, it felt, and she had always replied, "yes", but it felt like a lie, and she couldn't lie to this woman. "I think some days I'm really good at handling it, and others I ... well, I feel like a completely awful and terrible mum who does nothing but shout and cry."

Joy's gaze softened. "I know exactly what that feels like," she murmured.

"Really?" Sophie had a hard time believing that.

But Joy nodded. "Of course. If a mom ever claims to have it together every minute of the day, she's a fucking liar." Joy's eyes widened. "Oh, pardon my language.

Sophie chuckled.

"Good moms win and laugh and ... trim trees with tacky ornaments," Joy began, "but great moms never give up on their kids even when it feels like they're drowning. We just keep treading water, knowing the land will come. We shout and we cry, and we curse a whole lot, but your kid will remember the fact that you were there, caring. Kids never see their parents as failures when they show up."

Sophie's eyes flicked over to Maddie. She was still so captivated by the glittery snowflakes. Sophie hoped that Maddie, with her wonderful memory, would feel that way about her.

"My mum gave up on me a long time ago," confessed Sophie, really understanding Joy's point. If her mum had been there, no matter what she had said, or how she had scolded Sophie, their relationship could have been entirely different. "The minute she found out I was pregnant. Probably before then, really." Looking up, she added sincerely, "I think your family are really lucky to have you, Joy."

Joy's face warmed as she smiled. "Everyone deserves a mom, Sophie." Subtly gesturing to Vanessa, she continued. "She might not be the one who gave birth to you, but she'll love you as big as the world anyway."

The sound of plastic bags rustling and the front door slamming drew all of their attention. Joy tapped Sophie on the nose playfully before climbing off of the couch.

"About time!" she cried out. "What, did you want me to die of starvation?" Winking at Sophie, she added quietly, "And you get the guilt for free, of course."

Noah and John carried all the food into the room and set it down on the coffee table. The aromas immediately filled the vicinity and Sophie's mouth began to water. She hadn't realised how hungry she was until that moment. A full day's work took it out of her.

Noah helped to divvy out the food to everyone, finally grabbing a box of fortune cookies, and handing one by itself to Tally.

Sophie separated half of the chicken and the rice onto a plate for Maddie, and she settled down on the floor in front of the sofa happily eating this time. Sophie ate from the box and found that the hot food satiated her quickly.

Noah had a noddle dish and was eating expertly with chopsticks. In fact, she and Maddie were the only ones using forks, and Sophie felt envious of such a nifty talent.

"Eat up everybody, the service starts at eight," Joy urged.

There was a hum of conversation in the room as everyone chatted amongst themselves. Sophie turned to Noah and decided to confess something that had been on her mind today.

"Noah, do you mind that I'm not religious?" she asked.

Noah frowned. "Of course not," he said emphatically. "I'm not religious either. I haven't been for a very long time. It's just not something that makes a lot of sense to me. But it does to my mom, and church at Christmas is important to her, so I go. We all go for her."

"Your mum is so nice," Sophie told him with a sigh, resting her head on his shoulders.

With the take away containers empty, everyone was tossed a fortune cookie.

"Vanessa, this one is yours," Tally said, handing one to her.

Sophie broke open her cookie and read the fortune.

A handsome, smart, loving person will be coming into your life.

"Look," Sophie held it up to Noah, "I'm getting a new boyfriend."

Noah laughed sarcastically, but his eyes were on Tally and Vanessa. He pulled out his phone and began recording. It took Sophie a moment to realise what was happening.

Vanessa happily broke into her cookie and smoothed out the message with her fingers. She read it casually before freezing. "Vanessa, will you marry me?" She slapped her hand over her mouth as her head snapped around to Tally, who had produced a shiny, little ring.

In the short time that Sophie had known Tally, she had thought that Tally was a very cool, confident person. But now she looked a nervous wreck.

"I love you," Tally said to Vanessa, a little shakily. "I have loved everything about you for ten years, and I want to spend the rest of my life with you. Will you mar –"

Tally had not managed to get the rest of her question out before Vanessa launched at her, kissing Tally all over her face, crying "yes!" between each one. Vanessa had burst into happy tears as she allowed Tally to slip the ring on her finger.

Vanessa was not the only one crying. Joy had promptly burst into tears as she raced around the coffee table to hug them both, and John went to the kitchen to fetch glasses and champagne.

"You knew about this?" Sophie asked Noah.

Noah grinned and nodded. "Tally can't keep a secret from me." He went over to kiss his sister's cheek and to hug them both.

The champagne was poured, and Sophie sat down on the floor beside Maddie, wrapping her arms around her as such a feeling of joy filled her stomach.

They all charged their glasses, and John began to toast.

"Congratulations, Tally and Vanessa. I'm so proud of you, kiddo," he said to Tally.

"Thank you, John," Vanessa cried as she clutched her ring hand to her chest.

Tally climbed to her feet to hug her dad emotionally. John kissed the top of Tally's head.

Joy couldn't stop wiping her eyes as she joined in. "Well, we've got to start planning, obviously," she began. "I mean, really we're behind already if we're thinking about June. How perfect would that be? Pride month! I have a binder of a few magazine clippings I put away just in case one of your four decided to let me be mother of the bride or groom once. We could do it here in the summer and you wouldn't even need to pay for a venue. That would be beautiful."

"Oh my God! Can we do up the old barn?" asked Vanessa excitedly. "How amazing would it look with fairly lights and flowers?"

"Yes!" cried Joy, before she looked at her watch. "We have time, I think. Come on, my binder is in my closet."

John placed a calming hand on his wife's shoulder. "You have all Christmas vacation for that damn binder. Come on, we've got to get going."

"Oh!" Joy suddenly realised, before she raced over to the Christmas tree. There were already parcels underneath it, and she began to hand them out to everyone. Saving the final two, she brought one over to Maddie, and then gave one to Sophie. "To Sophie, from Santa," Joy whispered, a twinkle in her eye.

The present was beautiful wrapped in brown paper with red ribbon and a sprig of holly. Sophie almost hated to ruin it, but she was excited to see what was inside. Everyone began to unwrap their gifts as they pulled out a knitted Christmas jumper.

It was navy, with a snowy pattern decorating the front, with a snowman in a red scarf featured in the centre. On the snowman's belly was a large "S", knitted in his buttons.

Maddie's was the same, only with an "M".

It was soft and warm, and just about the most personal gift she had ever received. Joy suddenly was slipping her own jumper on and was urging everyone to do the same.

Noah grinned at her as he slipped his "N" jumper over his head. "You're officially inducted now."

CHAPTER 30

R egardless of the fact that she was not religious, Sophie really enjoyed attending Joy's church. She got a wonderful feeling of community and spirit, as well as overwhelming excitement for the holiday.

The Bentley family occupied an entire pew, and Joy seemed to be stopped by every second person to be kissed and wished a merry Christmas.

The church itself was modern with a large stage area for the preacher and the band, with several microphones on stands. There was seating enough for five hundred, and on Christmas Eve, it was standing room only.

Sophie sat in between Noah and Maddie for the sermon, but Noah disappeared as soon as the hymns were to start. Sophie could remember Noah telling her once that he had learned to play the piano in his mother's church, and she wondered if the piano in the corner beside the stage was that very instrument.

Sophie chose this moment to quickly fetch the noise cancelling headphones that she had brought for Maddie to use on the plane from her bag. She didn't really know the extent of Maddie's sensory sensitivities, or if it was just a reaction to her new environment, but she didn't want the sudden music to be overwhelming for her.

Noah made his way down the right-hand aisle to sit down at the piano and Vanessa jogged up onto the stage.

Sophie gasped as she hadn't even noticed Vanessa leave her seat with Noah. There was very brief applause and a murmur of excitement within the congregation when they saw her, but Vanessa held up her hand to stop them.

"When I sing in this church, I don't do it for praise, but I do it so He can hear me," Vanessa said into the microphone, holding her hand over her heart. "I asked our pastor before the service if I could sing this song to you all. It's my favourite song to sing at Christmas, and it's especially important to me and my family right now." Vanessa smiled knowingly. "Can you please turn to page twenty-three, "Song of Joy"?"

Sophie grinned as she fetched the book of Christmas hymns from the pew in front of her and flipped to the carol.

The orchestra made up of high school aged musicians, as well as Noah on the piano, began to play a tune that Sophie immediately recognised as Beethoven's Ode to Joy.

Vanessa pulled her microphone off the stand and began to sing.

"Come, sing a song of joyFor peace shall come, my brotherSing, sing a song of joyFor men shall love each other

That day will dawn just as sureAs hearts that are pureAre hearts set freeNo man must stand alongWith outstretched hands before him

Reach out and take them in yoursWith love that enduresForever moreThen sing a song of joyFor love and understanding."

Sophie had heard Vanessa sing hundreds of times on television, on the radio, on YouTube, but she'd never heard her live before. She was floored at the crystal-clear power she projected with ease right up into the church rafters. She walked across the stage like a seasoned pro, smiling and engaging with every audience member as though she was speaking directly to them.

People stood in the pews, singing along with her, and Sophie happily joined in. Joy had shuffled along the pew to be standing beside her in Noah's absence, and she sang loudly and cheerfully, too, taking Sophie's hand and swaying with her as they did.

Sophie could have quite easily spilled happy tears in that moment.

When Song of Joy finished, the congregation didn't clap, which Sophie thought was oddly respectful. It wasn't a concert, and as Vanessa had said, she wasn't singing for praise.

"The next song is my very favourite Christmas hymn. I used to sing this song in my church as a child at Christmas, so can you please turn to page twelve, "The Holy City"?"

Sophie flipped backward to find The Holy City. Funnily enough, it was one of her favourites, too. The chorus was rousing, and she often found herself singing along on television at Christmastime.

"But before I start, I want to invite my new friend up here to sing this song with me," Vanessa said into the microphone. "Miss Sophie Cartwright is here visiting us all the way from London, England, and she has the most beautiful singing voice."

The only thing stopping Sophie from shitting her pants right in that moment was the very fact that she was in a church. She completely paled and her eyes widened. Vanessa had found her face in the crowd and was motioning for her to come up on stage.

What? If they wanted a rendition of Memoryor I Dreamed a Dream then Sophie was your girl, but a Christmas hymn where the lyrics honestly blended into themselves that she made a lot of them up as she went? Oh dear.

"Oh, my goodness!" cried Joy. "Yes, go on. I've been desperate to hear you sing. Go on then," she urged.

Sophie gulped and moved past Maddie into the aisle and walked up towards the stage. She felt hundreds of curious eyes on her as she climbed up the carpeted steps onto the stage towards Vanessa. Sophie caught Noah's eye at the piano, and he winked at her. She wondered if he was in on this.

"Vanessa, I don't know the words properly," hissed Sophie quietly.

Vanessa blocked her microphone with her hand before she smiled reassuringly. "So long as you've got the Hosanna's, you're fine," she promised. "If you just want to jump in on the chorus, that's fine, too. That's what everyone does. I just wanted to sing with you." She motioned to one of the other microphone stands.

Sophie went and collected another microphone and she came back to stand beside Vanessa. Looking out over the congregation, she could see a sea of uplifted people. They were happy and spirited and wouldn't care if she mucked up some lyrics. Sophie decided to get out of her head.

The music started and Vanessa held Sophie's eye as she began.

"Last night I lay asleepingThere came a dream so fairI stood in old JerusalemBeside the temple thereI heard the children singingAnd ever as they sangMethought the voice of AngelsFrom Heaven in answer rang."

As she sang the last lyric and the music lifted, Vanessa nodded and Sophie knew the next two words at least. She lifted her microphone to her mouth and sang. To her relief, the people began to join in, too.

"Jerusalem, Jerusalem! Lift up your gates and sing, Hosanna in the highest. Hosanna to your King!"

The hymn continued to build and build and build, and Sophie found something extra in her lung capacity to find the power.

When they got to the final chorus, Sophie took one final deep breath.

"Jerusalem! Jerusalem

Sing for the night is o'er

Hosanna in the highest

Hosanna for evermore!"

As the musicians finished, Vanessa hugged Sophie, and Sophie exhaled a delighted cry. They both bowed to the musicians and descended the steps to return to their pew.

Joy received them both, kissing their cheeks. "Oh, you two were spectacular!" she cried. "You are doing that again tonight when we get home because that cannot be the last time, I hear that song sung by you both. But what am I talking about? You'll definitely be singing that song again at church next year. I'll insist on it."

The certainty in which she spoke comforted Sophie, who was still feeling a wave of exuberance over what she had just done. Would she and Maddie be here next Christmas with them all? She bloody hoped so.

"Mummy, does Santa know where we are?" Maddie asked Sophie in a concerned tone as she tucked her in.

Sophie sat on the edge of Maddie's trundle and stroked her forehead comfortingly. "Of course, he does, sweetheart," assured Sophie. "Santa is magic. He knows where all the good boys and girls are." Leaning down, Sophie kissed her hair. "Come on now, it's time to sleep. When you wake up, Santa will have been."

"I took my headphones off when you were singing, Mummy," Maddie told her, seemingly very proud of herself. Smiling, she said, "You were loud and good."

Any sort of compliment from Maddie made Sophie feel very chuffed. "Thank you, my sweetheart," she said gratefully.

Sophie kissed her one final time and left the bedroom, closing the door quietly. She had purposefully removed the suitcase with Maddie's presents from Santa earlier that morning so that she wouldn't be sneaking into the bedroom when Maddie was sleeping. She had stashed the suitcase in Noah's bedroom, which was an homage to everything early 2000s.

Downstairs, Joy had made coffee and a tea for Sophie, and there was a tin of fudge being passed around. There was a Christmas film muted on the television, and everyone was sitting on the sectional in their pyjamas.

Sophie spotted Tally sitting with the plate of Christmas shortbread that Maddie had left out for Santa, and Vanessa was munching on the carrot that had been left for Rudolph.

"It's been so long since we've had the illusion of Santa in this house," said Joy excitedly as she darted over to the hall cupboard. "Noah, get over here. I need your height!" Joy demanded.

Noah placed his mug down on the coffee table and jogged over to reach up onto the top shelf of the cupboard. He began to lift down parcel after parcel. There were at least two dozen perfectly wrapped gifts of all shapes and sizes that had quickly formed into a pile that any child would be delighted to see on Christmas morning.

"Oh, Joy," Sophie gasped. "Really, I hope these are not all for Maddie."

Joy frowned. "Well, of course they are!" she exclaimed. "I've finally got a grandchild to spoil! I'm so excited! I might have gone a little overboard but it's not like any of those four have done anything before now to give me a grandbaby."

"Ma!" shouted Tally defensively, her mouth full of biscuit. "I just got engaged!"

"Yes, Tally, one less thing I can nag you about," Joy shot back. "But do I hear the pitter patter of my grandchild's angelic feet? No!"

Vanessa giggled.

Sophie lowered her voice. "No, it's not that," she said, regaining Joy's attention. "It's just that I would worry Maddie will think that Santa doesn't like her as much next year than he does this year if she doesn't have the same pile. She's the sort of child who would notice that sort of thing and bluntly announce it."

"Sophie is Maddie's mom," Noah added, standing by Sophie's side.

"Oh, God, please do not think I am ungrateful," Sophie pleaded, realising how this all probably sounded.

Joy scoffed. "Oh, honey, no," she said, shaking her head. "I thought this might be a problem, so I did use different wrapping paper just in case. Can I add the candy cane gifts to Maddie's Santa pile, and the snowman ones will be from John and I?"

Despite Joy's graciousness, Sophie did feel terribly bad for not accepting the presents as they were meant. Joy was excited and wanted to make Maddie's Christmas magical. Sophie just wanted to keep all of Maddie's Santa Christmases magical. She would never forgive herself if Maddie worked out that her pile was smaller next year because she was Santa.

As they arranged the Santa pile together, Joy asked Sophie, "How old were you when you had Maddie if you don't mind my asking?"

"Eighteen," Sophie replied tentatively.

"So young," remarked Joy, though she, of course, did not sound judgemental.

"My parents thought so," confessed Sophie. "Everyone thought so."

"People and their opinions." Joy rolled her eyes. "Do you know, I was twelve weeks pregnant when I married John. Wedding was planned in a month. My parents couldn't stomach the idea of a baby born out of wedlock. Haley was the first ten-pound preemie in Northern California." She laughed lightly.

God, Sophie was glad that she hadn't married Beck. Not that he'd asked, or her parents had insisted, but she couldn't even beginto imagine the shitshow her life would have been had she actually stayed with him.

"And can I ask about Maddie's father?"

"Um," Sophie said hesitantly. "Well, he was my first boyfriend, and I picked him as an act of rebellion, I think. He was someone that my parents would have hated." And they did hate in the end. "We were together for all of five minutes before I was pregnant, and he didn't hang around for long. His parents are involved in Maddie's life on holidays and that is when Maddie sees Beck. Maddie's aware of him but she has no interest in a relationship with him. And vice versa really."

"Jerk," decided Joy.

"Absolutely," agreed Sophie. "But he did a number on my self-esteem. He honestly has been doing so for years. I think I spend far too long worrying about what other people think of me," confessed Sophie.

"But you know what they say, opinions are like assholes, everyone has one and most of them stink," Joy added poignantly.

Sophie nearly choked on an unexpected laugh.

"Worry about the important people, Sophie," encouraged Joy. "You've got a great kid, and a wonderful man, even if I do say so myself."

"I would have to say I agree with you." Sophie smiled.

"Noah is a very special person, and I'm not just saying that because I'm his mom. He's never really been understood or appreciated by anyone outside of this room. He's had horrible girlfriends who have just used him." Joy stopped herself and took a breath, calming herself down before she got agitated. "But he's different around you, and you him. I can see it's just the beginning of something very real, and very lasting. And it honestly warms my heart to see him understand and relate to Maddie. I only wish that there had been someone like that to help Noah when he was Maddie's age."

"You can't know how grateful I am for Noah," insisted Sophie. "He honestly saved me, saved us both. I am so relieved that Maddie knows what it's like to have a male figure in her life that cares and takes an interest in her." Adding quietly, "And I can honestly say the same for myself."

CHAPTER 31

"Another Frozen dolly, Mummy!" screamed Maddie in pure and utter delight as she tore the wrapping paper off of one of Joy's Santa gifts. She threw the paper behind her without care and held up the Elsa doll gleefully.

Joy was positively beaming from the sofa as she watched Maddie unwrap her presents. In fact, most of the family were completely mesmerised as Maddie excitedly devoured her pile of gifts from Santa.

Maddie was in her element and was absolutely delighted with everything that she opened. Sophie was really pleased that Maddie was able to get a few toys that she would never have been able to afford herself. Sophie had bought Maddie new colouring books and pencils and a few piano books, as well as a few new films for her to watch. Of course, Maddie had been just as excited to receive them as well.

Joy had indeed gone mad, but so long as Maddie was happy, Sophie didn't mind.

Sophie absently bobbed her teabag in her mug as she watched Maddie. Noah sat beside her, his arm over the back of the sofa, allowing her to lean on his shoulder.

Tally was on the floor beside Maddie, seemingly as excited as she was, helping her to choose which present she wanted to open next. Sophie liked that she was able to hang back and allow Maddie to bond with the other members of the family. Tally had been wonderful that morning in running with Maddie between the empty cookie plate and the munched on carrots and exclaiming with her that Santa had been.

Vanessa, Haley, John and Joy were all sat on the sofa as well, but Casey had out her professional camera and was snapping pictures of them all. Sophie honestly couldn't wait to see them as she was certain they would look better than anything her phone could take.

The living room was a sea of Christmas paper when Maddie was finished. It was John, then, who found himself on the floor with Tally and Maddie as he helped her to cut some of her new toys out of their packaging. Sophie and Noah fetched a bin liner to tidy away the paper, and Joy, Haley, and Vanessa got started on making something for breakfast. Only light, of course, as Joy wouldn't have their appetites spoiled.

Sophie held open the bin liner as Noah set to work at clearing away the paper. John was lying on his side, his legs outstretched, just about underneath the tree as he listened to Maddie jabber on excitedly about how wonderful Elsa was.

Oh, dear, she could have died from this family's sweetness ten times over this trip already.

Noah began to turn the chore into a game, screwing up the paper and shooting it at Sophie as though it was a basketball hoop.

Sophie laughed as he purposefully missed, getting her in the face almost every time.

A flash went off as they mucked around and Casey snapped a photo of them.

They ate a simple breakfast of cereals and toast before the rest of the gifts were to be opened. Tally resumed her spot on the floor with Maddie and popped a Santa hat on her head.

Maddie didn't complain, and Sophie was silently thankful that this sweet, little gesture was not a sensory issue.

"Okay, are you going to be my present hander-outer-er?" Tally asked Maddie.

Maddie nodded.

Tally pulled the first gift out from under the tree and read the label. "To Casey, from Mom and Dad." Tally handed the present to Maddie and she immediately got up and walked over to Casey.

"Thank you, Maddie," said Casey gratefully as she put her camera down on the coffee table. Casey unwrapped the present and held up book. From the looks of it, it looked like a travel book. Casey frowned as she read the cover. "A hundred and one things to do in Napa, California," she read. She looked at her mother deadpan. "Funny," she said dryly.

Joy shrugged her shoulders nonchalantly. "I just saw it at the mall and thought it looked like an interesting read."

"I'd like to state for the record that even though my name is on the tag, I've got nothing to do with whatever stunts Mama's pulling under that tree," John said with his hands up defensively.

Casey opened the front cover of the book and a folded document fell out. She unfolded it, and snorted. "Real estate listings!" she cried with a laugh. "For where? Oh, what do you know? Napa, California!"

"Well, there's some absolutely beautiful places on the market right now, and really, now is a great time to buy," Joy said, again, as innocently as ever.

Casey shook her head and rolled her eyes. "Nice try, Mom. I might need some listings for Australia because that's where I'm spending the next six months. I'll be back for fourth of July, though."

Joy sighed. "It was worth a shot."

Noah, Tally, and Vanessa all received a copy of the same book, and a printout of real estate listings in the area, too. Joy Bentley was about as subtle as a gun.

Tally fetched the next present and read the tag. "To Sophie, love Noah. Aw. Go and give that one to Mommy."

Maddie obediently brought the present over to Sophie.

"Thank you, darling," Sophie said gratefully. "You're doing such a good job!" The gift itself was an envelope with a ribbon tied around it. "You really didn't need to get me anything," she told him as the rest of the family looked on in anticipation.

"Yes, I really did," Noah said assuredly.

Sophie furrowed her eyebrows in curiosity as she removed the ribbon and opened the envelope. It took a moment for her to realise what it was. It was a gift voucher. "Good for one free driving lesson with Noah." Sophie burst out laughing, as did the rest of the family.

"Can you not drive, Sophie?" exclaimed Haley in surprise.

"No," replied Sophie with a laugh. "I grew up in Kensington, right in the heart of London. I had no need to with the Tube."

"Well, you don't want Noah teaching you. Teaching him to drive was the reason I had to start colouring my hair," Joy shuddered in recollection as she ran her fingers through her bleached blonde hair.

Sophie continued to laugh. "I don't think I want him teaching me either considering the fact that he drives on the wrong side of the car, and the wrong side of the road," she reminded him of the last time they spoke about driving. She lifted her head up and kissed his jawline. "Thank you for the thought."

Noah nudged her playfully. "Hey, you might get used to this side of the road, you never know."

Tally grabbed the next gift, and Sophie recognised it as her present for Noah. "To Noah, love Maddie and Sophie."

"Oh, I know what this is!" cried Maddie. "I picked the colour!" She all but snatched the present off of Tally and bounded over to Noah to present it to him.

"Thanks, kid," Noah said gratefully, winking at Maddie as he unwrapped the present. It was an A4 leather bound book, teal in colour thanks to Maddie, and monogrammed with Noah's initials, NJB. It had cost a little, but Sophie had made it work.

Noah let out a soft, pleased, "Wow," as he opened the book, and found an inscription:

"And those who were seen dancing were thought to be insane by those who could not hear the music."— Friedrich Nietzsche

To Our Piano Man,

Thank you for sharing the music with us.

Love Maddie and Sophie xx

The book was filled with hundreds of blank sheet music. Noah often wrote on loose paper, as evidenced by the chaos that often surrounded him at Pete's. Sophie thought it would be a nice idea to have his works all in one place.

"This is perfect," Noah decided, his voice a little thicker than usual. "Thank you." Noah leaned down and pressed his lips to her softly, before kissing her forehead as well. "You helped pick this out, kid?" he asked Maddie, his voice louder now.

Maddie nodded proudly.

"Get over here then," Noah beckoned, waving Maddie towards him.

Maddie skipped into Noah's arms, wrapping her arms around him tightly as she hugged him, and thankfully, a flash went off, and Sophie knew that she would have a picture clearer than her blurry, tear-filled eyes.

Gifts continued to be exchanged, with Joy managing to give some that did not come with a side of guilt. Sophie finally received Noah's actual present, which was honestly a little confusing at first.

It was a picture frame, but instead of a photo, it was a document. Sophie read the letter head before she gasped. It was from Richard Walsh, Noah's director.

From: Richard Walsh

To: Noah Bentley

Date: December 24, 2020 00:13

Subject: RE: "The Dream of Life" original song performed by Sophie Cartwright

Never heard of Sophie Cartwright, but I think that'll change. Goddamn what a voice.

The song's perfect. She's perfect.

Sophie read the email three times over to be sure that her eyes hadn't deceived her. "He liked it?" she asked excitedly, grinning up at Noah.

Noah chuckled. "Yes, he did." He nodded. Noah then produced a CD and gave it to Sophie. "Your first single with the crappy print out cover every junior high mix tape had."

Sophie laughed as she accepted the CD. Oh God, it suddenly felt very real. Her singing was on this disc, and it would be playing at the end of an actual film. People would hear her ... people that were not piss drunk in Pete's pub were going to hear her!

"Damn it, Noah. Who the hell owns a CD player anymore? How the hell are we supposed to hear it?" Tally moaned.

"I wanted something tangible!" retorted Noah. "It's not the same feeling as receiving your first single as an mp3 recording over email."

"Well, some of us are not millennials," Joy said melodramatically, "and still own a CD player relic. My boom box even has a cassette player!"

"Ooh, I forgot Mom is old!" cried Tally. "Goodie, we get to hear it." She clapped her hands together.

Joy playfully slapped the back of Tally's head. "Watch who you're calling old, kiddo," she snapped, rolling her eyes. "You're about to turn thirty."

"Ouch, Mama claps back," Tally sucked in a breath as she flinched.

"Was that the last present?" Vanessa asked, spying the now empty space under the tree. "Should we start cooking?"

"No, no, not the last one," John said suddenly, perking up and climbing to his feet. "I've got one more gift out in the garage. It's for you, kid," John said to Noah, motioning for Noah to follow him.

Everyone followed John out to the garage curiously. Sophie saw the look of intrigue and excitement on Noah's face as he tried to work out what it could be.

They all walked down the hallway and through the garage door, descending down a flight of stairs and stepping onto a cool, concrete floor. The garage was huge, big enough for eight cars at least, and did house a few pick-up trucks and an enormous workstation with dozens of professional tools having on stainless steel hooks.

But in the middle of the garage was a piano. It was old, and terribly weathered, with wood missing and chipped. The legs were beaten, and upon closer inspection, there were several keys missing off the keyboard. It looked in very poor condition.

But Noah looked the very picture of a kid on Christmas as his blue eyes went over his new toy. He had the biggest smile on his face as his jaw dropped.

"Are you joking?" he asked in disbelief.

John looked really proud of himself, and it was honestly adorable. He stood beside the piano with a chuffed look on his face. "You like it, kid?"

Noah left Sophie's side and hugged his father tightly. John chuckled as he reciprocated the action and Casey was there to capture the moment. Sophie could see that John wasn't the type to show this sort of affection, but underneath the exterior it meant a lot to him to have Noah react this way.

"I can't believe you got me a Steinway," Noah kept an arm around his dad as he looked back over the piano.

"I know you always wanted one, and I've been hunting for one that I could afford for months. She's not much to look at now, but

I thought it could be a little project for us, you know. We'll fix her up when you're home. Might bring you back home more often."

Sophie's heart swelled at the sentiment, and the clear idea behind the gift. John just wanted to spend time with his son.

"Dad ... this is ... this is perfect," Noah said, nodding his head. He then began to run his hands over the back of the grand piano, inspecting the wood.

"It's a 1911 antique Steinway," John explained. "That's all original rosewood ..."

As John and Noah began to discuss the mechanics of the piano, Joy shuffled everyone back upstairs. Everyone except Maddie, who was, of course, fascinated by all things piano, and was listening eagerly.

When they returned to the living room, the women realised that they were not alone. A man stood in the doorway, dressed in a crisp, formal military uniform. He wore a navy buttoned coat adored with colourful service decorations, and white trousers. He held his hat in one hand and a bag in the other.

He was a handsome man, looking to be in his mid-thirties, which short, black hair and dark brown eyes. And he seemed to belong to Haley judging by the ecstatic scream she let out upon seeing him standing there.

He dropped his bag and placed his hat on an armchair just in time to catch Haley as she launched at him, wrapping her legs around his waist and kissing her passionately.

"Surprise," he chuckled as they pulled apart. "Merry Christmas, babe."

Tears were streaming down Haley's face as she slapped his chest. "Oh my God, why didn't you tell me you were coming? I would have gotten so much prettier! Definitely would have tried to ditch the five pounds I've gained in fudge." Haley was still wearing her pyjamas, as were they all.

"What're you talking about? You're perfect," he admonished. He kissed her again before looking to the rest of the room.

The minute Haley was on the ground, Joy was racing over for a hug. She stood up on her toes to reach the tall military man so that she could kiss his cheek. "It's so good to have you home safe, Mark," she gushed. "Now, I don't want to give you any ideas or anything, but I will just let you know that Tally and Vanessa have just got engaged. So, if you were thinking about popping the question, no rush, but I could totally plan a double wedding for the summer."

Mark looked up to the girls and frowned. "Was there a pool going for how long it would take Joy to drop a hint or lay on the guilt?" he asked.

"Yep, you missed it. I won," Casey boasted. "I had under a minute."

Mark laughed as Joy huffed. "Congrats though, girls," he said to Tally and Vanessa.

"Mom, Tally and I are not forty-seven-year-old twin sisters. There will be no double wedding," Haley added, embarrassed.

Sophie saw the idea cross Joy's mind just as it did hers, and Sophie paled.

"Twins, huh?" Joy pondered.

Sophie laughed awkwardly. "And in the grand scheme of all these relationships, Noah and I have been together for three minutes, so a double wedding is not on the cards, I'm sorry."

Sophie had drawn attention to herself, and Mark suddenly realised that there was someone in the room that he didn't know.

"Mark, this is Noah's girlfriend, Sophie Cartwright. Sophie, this is my partner, Mark Reynolds," Haley introduced.

"Master Sergeant Mark Reynolds," added Joy boastfully.

Mark grinned. "Pleasure to meet you, ma'am," he greeted.

"You too, I am glad you are returned home safely," replied Sophie.

Joy clapped her hands. "Alright. Haley, you take Mark's things up to your room. I need to start cooking."

After one of the most delicious meals that Sophie had ever eaten, Christmas Day had ended with a hilarious game of charades and a hot drink by the fire.

After putting Maddie to bed, Noah had invited Sophie out onto his balcony. It was one of several balconies on this side of the house, and Sophie could see the faint shadows of the rows and rows of vines in the moonlight. She was sure that it would be a most spectacular sight during the day, and even more so when the vines were full of life.

They sat together on a wooden bench, Noah stretching his legs out to rest his feet on the balcony railing, crossing his ankles over. It was cold, and Sophie was wrapped in Noah's dressing gown.

"You survived your first Bentley Christmas," he murmured quietly.

"I wouldn't say that," she replied with a laugh. "I enjoyed my first Bentley Christmas. Immensely," she insisted. "Honestly, I've never experienced anything like that before. Your family, these lovely, wonderful, kind people just love each other endlessly. It's so beautiful to be around. Christmas growing up just wasn't like that for me. My parents weren't sentimental, and they were nearly always hungover from a Christmas party the night before. I often ate by myself, or with my nanny when I was young enough to have one.

"Even now, when it has just been Maddie and I, I could only ever dream of filling a home with people like this. I'm so thankful that she was able to experience this." Sophie nuzzled into Noah's chest.

"I love them," Noah said simply, "and they love you."

Sophie smiled. "I know things aren't going to be straight forward, and there are going to be challenges and ... and I'm just making things bloody complicated by ... I've just never said this before and it's like my brain is trying to make it ..." Sophie exhaled, before sitting up straight and looking at Noah. "Nobody has ever loved me before." That confession in itself was like poking an open wound within her. "Ever. It wasn't until I met you that I knew what it felt like to have someone care about me. I heard what you said the other night. You told me that you had fallen in love with me. I want to tell you that I have fallen in love with you, too."

A smile, even bigger than the one on his face when he had seen the antique Steinway in the garage, spread across Noah's face as he heard her words.

Noah kissed Sophie deeply, tangling his fingers in her hair. Sophie was the one to break the kiss, wanting to be brave. "Can I stay in here tonight?"

"Are you sure?" Noah whispered, his voice suddenly husky.

Sophie nodded. "Yes, I'm sure," she replied, as she brought his lips back to hers.

CHAPTER 32

Noah had wanted a Steinway piano for as long as he could remember. They were the best of the best, and up until Pete's piano in London, he had only played on one a handful of times.

He could never justify buying one himself. A top tier Steinway could cost upwards of two hundred thousand dollars. Noah had no idea what his father had paid for this piano, but because of its condition, he hoped that John had got a great price.

The bones of the piano were good. The bridges and soundboards on the interior were still good, and the frame was as strong as when it had been carved in 1911. There were bass and treble strings broken, and tuning pins missing, as well as keys that were missing their ivory. But all of that could be replaced. This piano could be brought back to life, and Noah was eternally grateful that his dad had honestly cared enough to find this for him.

Joy had taken the girls off shopping as it was the day after Christmas, and Haley and Mark had gone off on their own to catch up. John and Noah remained behind in the garage with Maddie as they started on the piano with a gentle sandpaper.

"Do you see these lines here, kid?" John asked Maddie as he ran his finger along the wood. "This is called a grain. You always sand with the grain. You start going all side to side, you tear the fibres of the wood and you'll ruin it. Go on and show me what you've got," he urged.

Maddie was wearing an Elsa costume, one of her present from Santa yesterday, and she just looked absolutely priceless as she diligently followed John's instructions dressed as an ice princess.

Noah started gently sanding the wood on the cover, going with the grain as his father had instructed. "Did you know that Maddie is a great pianist as well as a guitar player, Dad?" Noah asked purposefully to prick Maddie's ears. "She helped compose my score."

"Really?" replied John, impressed. "Are you better than Noah, Maddie?"

Maddie thought for a minute. "Well, I am only eight years old and Noah is a man so I can't be better than him yet," she replied bluntly.

John laughed but Maddie missed the humour.

"But, did you know I have a special superpower which makes me concentrate on piano really good?" she continued.

"A superpower?" repeated John, raising his eyebrows. "What's your superpower, kid?"

Maddie's back straightened proudly as she looked up at Noah's father. "I have autism," she told him. "I can do lots of things good, and some things are hard, but I am smart so I will get better."

John's blue eyes flashed to Noah as he raised his eyebrows with a smile. Noah had honestly been impressed with his dad's behaviour towards Maddie so far. He had certainly been a lot more tolerant and interested in her than he had been when Noah was a kid. Times had changed, and kids didn't fit into perfect boxes anymore.

"Well, that does sound fine now, doesn't it?" John played along. "Go on now, get sanding. You're slacking off like Noah is."

Noah chuckled as he returned his focus to the cover. Maddie's laser focus quickly zoned her out of what was going on around her as she concentrated on her task.

"Dad, it seriously means a lot to me that you would find this, buy this for me," Noah told him again, for quite possibly the twelfth time that morning.

John just shook his head, not one to get mushy or sentimental, even though he might have been feeling it inside. "When I think of all the damn prom dresses and spring break trips and cars I bought for your sisters, it was only fair. Damn Tally totalled at least three cars." He shook his head as he cursed under his breath.

"Dad," Noah said insistently. "Seriously, I know the thought, the time, and the effort that went into this, and I promise I'll make it home more to work on it with you."

John looked away from Noah, but he did have a small smile on his face. "Well, it wouldn't kill you to make it back here a little more often," he said stiffly. "We know you kids have all got your fancy lives down there in LA, but you know we'd have you any other weekend. Doesn't just have to be a holiday."

Noah did often get caught up in his work. He could work for weeks straight without taking a day off. Tally often had to drag him from his room to take a break. As much as his mom was over the top, this was his favourite place in the world.

"You've got it, Dad," promised Noah.

They continued to work for the next half an hour, John stopping every two minutes to check Noah's work, to correct it, and to tell him what he was doing wrong, before demonstrating how to do it right. Noah wished he could say that he was doing it on purpose, but he was not at all handy.

He could tell, though, that John enjoyed teaching him. This was what John had wanted out of buying this piano, and Noah was indeed learning something. He might not have been able to learn how to throw a football from his dad, but he could treat some timber just fine.

"So, what are you going to do about Sophie?" John asked, in a tone that suggested he had been building the courage to finally bring it up.

Noah frowned. "Don't you like her?" he asked, eyeing Maddie who was not at all aware of the conversation that was going on around her. She was humming to herself, a tune from their score.

John huffed. "I like her just fine. Mom is planning your wedding already, don't you know? But what are you going to do about her? It's not like she lives in Downtown LA."

Noah sighed, resting against the piano as he abandoned the sandpaper momentarily. "I know," he said, resigned. "We haven't talked about it. I suppose that will be a conversation that is coming soon." One that Noah had absolutely no idea of how it would turn out.

"You can't move there, kid," John said emphatically. "It would break your mother's heart. She stresses enough that Casey is here, there, and everywhere year-round."

"Dad, I don't need second-hand Mom guilt from you," Noah groaned. Although, he knew his dad was right. Joy would absolutely lose it if she thought that Noah was going to move to London.

Logistically, it was difficult. His work, his studio, his connections, his colleagues, his favourite orchestra were all here in California. So were his family.

He struggled to make it home to see them living in the same state. He'd never get home living in another country.

He thought about Tally and being that far away from her permanently. God, they were about to turn thirty, but the idea of not seeing her every day was just unthinkable.

But Sophie was in London, and so was Maddie. Would she consider moving? For either of them, it was so much change, so much to give up for the other person. The end result was worth it, but who was going to make that sacrifice?

"I'm going to make it work, Dad," Noah said firmly. "And I'm going to do what I have to do to make it work. I'm not letting her go, I'm not losing her if distance is going to be the problem."

John nodded once as he listened to what Noah had to say. "Is she the one?" he asked simply.

Noah nodded this time. "Yes," he said confidently.

"And the kid?" John motioned to Maddie. "You're ready for that?"

Noah nodded again. "I'm learning to be what I need to be for her," he replied. "But the point is I want to be there for her."

John clapped Noah on the back, a gesture of approval. "I'm not going to pretend I don't want you all to end up here, because that would be a lie. If you moved there ... I'd miss you, kid," John admitted. "But I'll be proud of you whatever happens."

Noah felt a tug in his chest. "Thank you, Dad."

Sophie was suddenly blinded by a bright light and deafened by an excited cheer on the morning of the twenty-eighth.

Squinting and looking at the digital clock on Noah's bedside table, she could see that it had only just gone five in the morning.

Tally had leapt onto Noah's bed, landing directly on her brother as she cried, "Happy birthday to us!"

Noah groaned as her knee got him right in the stomach. "Jesus, Tally!" he exclaimed as he sucked in a breath and sat in a tight breath.

Tally wriggled into the bed between them and clapped her hands. "Mom, we're ready!"

It was like a parade, and Sophie felt like she was a teenager being caught in her boyfriend's bed as Noah's parents, sisters, partners and Maddie came prancing into the bedroom singing Happy Birthday at the top of their lungs. Joy was front and centre carrying a plate with two gourmet cupcakes, decorated with sparklers and candles.

Sophie quickly hopped out of the bed and stood with Maddie as she joined in the singing, self-consciously wishing she was wearing more than a thin singlet and short shorts.

Noah looked a little bashful as well, but the kind you experienced when people were all singing Happy Birthday to you. Tally was enjoying every second as Joy placed the cupcakes down on the bed between them.

"Okay, okay!" shouted Joy over the top of the noise. "It's 5:04! Thirty years ago, right now, Tally was born! Happy birthday, Hallie Elizabeth!"

They all cried, "Happy birthday!"

Tally clapped her hand again as she closed her eyes and blew out her candle. The moment she had made her wish, Noah tapped his ear, and Tally whispered something to him.

Did they share their birthday wishes? Sophie's heart melted.

Moments later, Joy shouted out again. "Okay, and at 5:06, thirty years ago, right now, my baby Noah John was born! Happy birthday, honey!"

Noah grinned as he received the well wishes, before he closed his eyes and blew out his candle. Just as Tally had done, he then whispered his wish to her.

Noah looked to his sister and held up his fist, saying, "Came into this world together ..."

"... got your back now until forever," finished Tally, completing their adorable fist bump explosion.

It seemed like a ritual; one they completed every year on their birthday. Sophie wondered if they'd ever had a birthday apart. What must it be like, she wondered, to be bonded with a twin?

"Maddie!" Noah called, beckoning Maddie to come over to his side of the bed. "Come and help with this, would you?" he urged, holding up his cupcake.

Maddie didn't need to be asked twice as she raced over to Noah's bed, climbing atop the covers to inspect the treats. Tally wasn't sharing as she swiped her comically.

And then Joy started to cry. It was refreshing for Sophie to be the one not crying for once. John wrapped an arm around her and rubbed her arm comfortingly.

"My babies are thirty!" she stressed. "When did that happen?"

"Well," said John, "they turned one in 1991 and have been getting older every year since."

Joy slapped John's chest. "Oh, stop!" she scolded as they all laughed. "Okay, I've got a new poem for this year." Joy cleared her throat, pulled out her phone and her glasses as she found whatever she was looking for.

"Mom likes finding twin poems in Facebook groups," Casey uttered to Sophie.

"So many good things come in pairs,

Like ears and socks and panda bears.

But best of all are sets of twins,

With extra laughter, double grins.

There's so much fun in having two,

With twice as many points of view.

So much alike, forever linked,

And yet they're also quite distinct.

They share a birthday and a name,

But moods and tempers aren't the same.

Although at times they may dispute,

Their loyalty is absolute.

From days of youth till life is done,

It's one for both and both for one.

We're all quite novel and precise,

But these special twins God made them twice."

Joy managed to hold it together as she pushed her glasses up on top of her head. "You might think your mom is cheesy and silly but that doesn't change how much I love you two, and how much I love the way you love each other."

"Naw, Mom, you're hitting me right in the feels." Tally jumped up on the bed, stepping over Noah and Maddie before bouncing down onto the floor to give Joy a hug. Noah was quick to follow, kissing Joy on the cheek.

"We love you, cheese and all," added Noah.

"Okay, we sang, we heard the poem, are we all allowed to go back to sleep now, it's five in the freaking morning," Haley urged.

Tally laughed. "Are you saying you don't want me to wake you up at 2:13am on the fourth of July to sing to you?"

Haley pinched Tally's nose. "You're so cheeky. You're thirty now. Happy birthday, baby sister and baby brother." She took Mark's hand and led him out of the bedroom.

Birthday wishes were exchanged before everyone dispersed, with Joy taking Maddie last, promising to put her back to bed. Noah shut the door behind them and exhaled, before turning back to face Sophie.

"I mean, just when you were starting thing these people were normal, once of us has a birthday," he laughed, shaking his head.

Sophie laughed, too. "I don't know why you feel the need to dismiss or make fun of any of this. Really, I think everything, every little tradition and ritual you have with your family is precious. People like this are not a dime a dozen or whatever the saying is."

Noah grinned. "Don't I know it." They sat back down together on the bed and Noah placed the empty plate on his bedside table.

"Happy birthday," she said, leaning over and kissing him softly, careful of the fact that she hadn't cleaned her teeth. "I have a little gift for you, but it's in the other room. I'll fetch it later."

"Thanks," he replied cheerfully.

"Did you tell Tally your birthday wish?" Sophie asked curiously.

Noah grinned sheepishly. "Yes," he admitted. "We've always shared everything, including birthday wishes. I can't tell you what it is, though, or else it won't come true. Sharing with your twin doesn't affect the bad juju." Noah winked. "And I really want this one to come true, so I'm not risking it."

Sophie smiled coyly.

Noah suddenly frowned. "When is your birthday? I feel like I should know what. And Maddie's, too."

Truthfully, Sophie only knew when Noah's birthday was because she had stalked his Wikipedia page back in London. They hadn't talked about birthdays.

"The fourth of April," replied Sophie. "And Maddie is the fifth of June. It would have been quite funny if they'd already been and you'd missed them," she teased.

Noah laughed. "Okay, and do you know what time you were born exactly? I have to organise flights, cupcakes, and inappropriate entourage of Bentleys bursting into your bedroom ..."

"Oh, yes, I see your dilemma," Sophie joked. And as funny as she found the jesting, just the mention of flights caught her off guard a little. The distance was looming in the background, and was determined to be addressed very soon.

CHAPTER 33

The two weeks that Sophie and Maddie had spent in America had flown, much faster than any other fortnight that Sophie had ever experienced. They spent another week with Noah's family, exploring beautiful Napa, before flying back to LA for their last few days in the States.

Sophie and Noah had decided to leave their distance conversation until the end of the trip, choosing to both think on things before coming up with solutions when it was time for Sophie and Maddie to go home.

The day before they were due to fly back to London, Noah surprised Maddie with a day that she would never forget. Sophie didn't think that she had ever seen Maddie as happy as she was walking down Main Street USA in Disneyland.

Maddie loved every minute of that day and had been absolutely ecstatic when she had managed to meet Elsa and Anna. Sophie honestly wanted to hug the ladies wearing the costumes. They were in complete character and made Maddie's year.

Spending that time together, just the three of them, for Sophie it felt like they were a real family. She loved driving with Noah. Just that simple thing of sitting in the front seat beside him with Maddie in the back felt like such a normal activity.

They had agreed to think about the distance and Sophie had been.

Sophie lovedLondon. She loved the atmosphere, the culture, the sounds, the rhythm. But it was a city. It wasn't people. And she could always fly back and visit.

Sophie had found people in coming to America. Family it felt like. Joy was ready to smother her with love when Sophie was ready for it. Sophie had never had that before, and to think that she could be taking Noah away from that hurt.

She didn't want to take Noah away from his family, the same as she didn't want to be away from them either. The idea of moving was terrifying. It wasn't like she was moving from London to Cambridge, she was moving from London across the bloody world. And she wasn't moving alone.

How would Maddie handle such a change? There was so much to consider! Her school had only just started to make things work for her and she had a lovely psychologist.

The upside was that Maddie didn't have many personal connections at home. That was terrible, really, but she wouldn't miss anyone if they moved to America. She would have aunts and grandparents ... and a dad, too.

Sophie knew that it would be quite possible for her brain to talk herself out of this decision, but she knew it in her gut that this was the right one. It would be frightening and challenging, but it was the right move.

She and Maddie belonged with Noah.

It was Sophie and Maddie's last night in America. They were flying home in the morning. Maddie was upstairs asleep in Noah's bed, and Sophie and Noah were staying in Vanessa and Tally's bedroom while they stayed on in Napa.

Sophie sat on the sofa with her legs crossed facing Noah. They had been watching a film absently, but Sophie had switched it off, gaining his attention.

"This is it, then?" Noah asked her.

Sophie nodded. "Yes ..." she said softly.

Noah took a deep breath. "I don't want you to feel pressured or anything. But I do want you to know that I want to make this work," he said determinedly.

"So do I," replied Sophie. "I've been thinking about it really carefully, and I know it won't be easy, and I know that there is obviously a lot that we will need to sort out. But I think that ..." she took a breath, "... I know that the right decision is for Maddie and me to move here."

Noah looked genuinely surprised. So much so that he recoiled a little as she revealed her decision. "Really?" He sounded relieved, and Sophie didn't blame him. She couldn't imagine how she would feel if she were facing the prospect of leaving those wonderful people behind. "I'm not going to lie, I didn't want to leave here. I'd miss them. Tally is my best friend ... but I would, you know," he insisted. "My choice was going to be you. I was going to move. I still can." Noah grabbed hold of Sophie's hands and squeezed them. "You're the most important person in my life now, Sophie, and I want you to know that if there's a choice, when there's a choice, it's you."

Sophie shuffled over onto his lap, wrapped her arms around his neck and kissing his cheek. "I know you would, and you can't know what it means to know that you would pick me. But it's not the right decision for the three of us. I want to be a part of what you have here. And I want Maddie to have the experience of growing up with people who only want to lift her up." The more she spoke, the more confident she became in her own decision. This was the right thing to do.

Noah kissed Sophie softly. "Guess I've finally got to move out of my sister's guest room," he joked quietly, though by the look in his blue eyes, Sophie could see he was thrilled with her choice.

Sophie laughed. "Yes!" she exclaimed. "And you must invest in a bed that is not a pull-out couch!" She smiled happily. "I don't think it can be before the summer six weeks holidays. Maddie ought to finish off Year 3 with her teacher."

"No, that's probably a good thing. Gives us time to organise all your documentation, and I'll start looking for some places to live that will suit the three of us," Noah said excitedly, before he kissed her again. "God, I wish you didn't have to go. I'll fly over as soon as I get the all clear about the score. I'm sure Pete's missed me."

Sophie and Maddie both fell into their flat what felt like an eternity later. The shut up smell of the flat immediately hit her nose as soon as they walked in, and Sophie immediately went to open the windows in the kitchen and the lounge.

Maddie attacked the suitcase with all of her Christmas presents first. She was practically in the doorway pulling her dolls out as Sophie pulled her phone out of her back pocket.

She switched it off of airplane mode for the first time in weeks, ready to call Noah to let him know that they had landed safely.

"I'd better check what time it is, actually," Sophie said to herself quietly. But the minute she had put her phone back to normal, it began to light up like a bloody Christmas tree.

Texts, phone calls, emails, dozens and dozens of them, began to flood her phone. No sooner had Sophie read the first word of one, another appeared on screen. And the majority of them were from Beck.

When her phone finally stopped throwing a fit, Sophie opened Beck's text message thread and she couldn't believe her eyes.

Bring her back, please!

Don't take her from me!

You're kidnapping her!

Please, I'll do anything!!!

Sophie answer me!!!!

The messages went on like that for weeks. What the actual fuck was this man on? Had he been drunk for the past month? In what universe was Sophie kidnapping Maddie? Was he insane?

Sophie then went to her emails, and found she had several from an address called Bryan, Burnbaum & Tate. Fuck. That sounded like a law firm. It couldn't be, could it? Beck wasn't that fucked in the head, was he?

Sophie scrolled down to the first email that they had sent her, and she opened it.

Dear Ms. Cartwright,

We are writing behalf of our client, Kyle Becker, to notify you of the filing of form C100 in the Family Court as of December 20, 2020.

Mr. Becker is seeking full residential custody of the minor, Madeline Cartwright.

As there is no legal custody agreement between your two par-ties, and Mr. Becker is the first party to seek legal residential custody, as of the aforementioned date it is unlawful for you to remove the minor from the United Kingdom without her father's written consent under the Child Abduction Act 1984.

Removal of the child from the United Kingdom without consent will result in a warrant being issued for your arrest and an emer-gency custody order being sought by my client.

Please see attached a copy of the C100 form for your records.

Kind regards,

Genevieve Warren

Family Solicitor

Bryan, Burnbaum & Tate

Sophie could barely finished reading, she was shaking so much with rage. WHAT THE ACTUAL FUCK HAD BECK DONE?

She immediately dialled his number, and Beck answered straight away.

"Soph?"

"Don't you "Soph" me, you fucking insane prick!" seethed Sophie. "What the fuck have you done? What in the flying fuck did I just read?"

Sophie didn't think she'd sworn so much in her entire life, but she needed to. It was cathartic.

"You're fucking lawyer didn't even spell my daughter's name correctly!" Sophie continued yelling. "Or was that you who doesn't know? In what parallel universe would you ever want custody?"

"Look, Soph, I think you need to calm down. It's probably not good for Maddie to hear you use language like that," Beck said, so sickeningly cool that it made Sophie want to vomit. "You've got to own up to what you've done. That order was filed before you left the country, and you went anyway. You broke the law, and I've been worried sick."

"I didn't break any fucking laws, you moron!" hissed Sophie. "You don't have custody. I do!"

"Soph, we don't have anything in writing. I want custody, and Mum and Dad are supporting that. We filed the motion, and it prevents you from taking Maddie out of the country without my permission. Last time I checked, you never asked." His tone was so condescending that Sophie was about to throw her phone.

She was shaking so hard that she thought she was going to explode. "Is this some sort of sick way at getting back at me for having the gall to move on with my life?" Sophie demanded to know. "Are you that jealous of Noah that you would really stoop this low? Beck, you don't want custody. Honestly, I would bet everything I have that you couldn't even tell me what colour Maddie's eyes are! You don't give a rat's arse about her!"

"You're wrong, Soph," Beck snapped. "The only thing I care about is Maddie, and what's best for her. She needs her father."

Sophie laughed mockingly. "Are you actually joking?" she exclaimed. "She needs her father? Well, you know what? She's got one now! Noah shits all over you, Beck. I don't give a flying fuck if you're jealous, because this is absolutely bullshit and you know it."

She heard Beck suck in a tight breath. "Oh yeah? Well, Golden Boy can bail you out of jail then. You took her out of the country without my permission, Soph. That's illegal," he said mockingly. "I'll be calling my lawyer now, and she'll call the cops. She's had the emergency custody order ready to go for when you got home. Maddie's coming home with me tonight."

All the blood rushed out of Sophie's face as she fully realised what Beck was threatening her with. He was seriously going to take Maddie away from her. Sophie rushed around the corner, out of the kitchen and into the living room. Maddie was none the wiser that Sophie was upset. She was playing with her toys near the front door, fully immersed in her own world.

Sophie burst into violent sobs at the idea of Maddie being more than five feet from her. How was this actually possible?

"Bye, Soph," sang Beck, before he disconnected the call.

Sophie immediately fumbled with her phone and found Noah's number. Noah picked up on the second ring with a cheerful greeting.

"Miss me already?" he asked teasingly. But then he heard Sophie crying, and his voice immediately changed. "Sophie? What is it? What's wrong?"

"I don't know how it happened," Sophie whimpered. "I didn't know it was a thing, it was possible."

"What?" pressed Noah. "Jesus, Sophie, you're scaring me."

"I think I need a lawyer," she whispered. Sophie's legs became like jelly and she fell to her knees. "Noah, will you help me? Please, I need you," Sophie begged. "Beck's filed for custody. There's a law where I needed to ask him permission to take Maddie out of the country and because I didn't, they're going to arrest me, and Beck is going to get emergency custody!" A loud, painful sob escaped her chest. "Oh my God, he's going to take my baby!"

CHAPTER 34

"What in the actual ...?" Sophie heard Noah exclaim on the other end of the phone. "What do you mean you're going to be arrested? What the fuck happened?"

"Because I fucking kidnapped my daughter!" Sophie shouted at him irrationally before she hiccoughed another sob. "I didn't know. Oh my God, I didn't know. I took Maddie out of the country without fucking Beck's consent and now he's going to get custody and I'm going to prison! Noah, I don't know what to do."

Sophie had made enough noise now to bother Maddie. She was looking up from her game, and looked properly concerned at the state in which her mother was in. Maddie immediately abandoned her dolls and came to stand before Sophie.

She wanted to smile, but all Sophie could do was snatch at Maddie, knocking her off of her feet and cuddling her to her chest.

"Mummy, what's wrong?" Maddie asked, concerned. "Why are you crying?"

Ordinarily, Sophie would have been so terribly proud to hear her asking sympathetic questions. But that fact barely entered into her psyche.

"Alright," Noah said firmly, seemingly grabbing a hold of the situation. "You need to pull yourself together, Sophie. I say this out of love, you know I do, but cut it out and get it together. If police are coming, then you need to prepare Maddie for that. If she's going to be sleeping away from you, you need to prepare her for that. I don't know what sort of fucking law they're talking about you breaking, but you and I both know Beck doesn't have any sort of claim, and any case he has is wafer thin. Don't be stupid, though, okay? Don't admit to anything, don't say anything until you have a lawyer beside you. I'm getting on the next flight."

Sophie whimpered.

"Do you understand me, Sophie?" Noah demanded to know. "Tell me you understand."

"I understand," she managed to croak out.

Calmer now, he said, "Sophie, it's going to be okay," Noah promised. "You're a good mom, and I know two dozen people who can attest to that. The same amount can attest that Beck is no more than a fucking sperm donor."

A sperm donor with a C100 form and a lawyer and a Child Abduction Act to hide behind. Oh, God.

"I'm going to call my attorney and get them to contact someone good in London. Don't say anything until they get there, okay? I'm going to hang up now. I'm going to throw some shit in a bag and get to the airport. I'll be there as soon as I can," Noah assured her.

"Sooner than that, please," Sophie whispered as she hung up the phone. She abandoned it on the floor beside her. Pull yourself together, Sophie willed herself. She took a deep breath and looked down into Maddie's trusting brown eyes. Most people who saw Maddie didn't see her eyes, didn't know her true personality, or get to experience her pure, innocent nature.

They saw the tantrums, the rituals, whatever could be perceived as odd or unusual behaviour. But Sophie was Maddie's mum, and the person she trusted most in the universe, and she had the privilege of knowing every gorgeous facet there was to the child that was Maddie.

Beck couldn't tell a judge three things about Maddie. Sophie could list a thousand.

"Okay," Sophie began. "So, we're going to go on a little adventure, it seems." God, she hoped her voice sounded convincing. "In a police car!" Sophie forced a smile. "How exciting is that?"

Maddie didn't look convinced.

"Some officers are going to need to talk to Mummy, and you might need to sleepover with Dad, or at Grannie and Grandpa's house," Sophie continued, as spirited as she could manage.

Maddie pursed her lips and cocked her head as she thought about this. "No," she decided emphatically. "I don't want to. It's not Christmas or my birthday so we don't see Grannie and Grandpa," Maddie reminded Sophie of their usual plan. "I want to play with my Frozen dolls." Maddie was a stubborn as a mule and shifting her mind and interfering with routine was virtually impossible.

"You can take your dolls with you," Sophie promised. "I'm sure Grannie and Grandpa wouldlove to see them. Mummy might need to stay and talk to the police officers, but they will be so excited to see you."

Sophie was dying inside. Each lie was a knife to her heart.

But Maddie caught that piece of information and her eyes flared. She was too clever to misunderstand. "Why aren't you coming to Grannie and Grandpa's house?" she demanded to know, her temper boiling, her shoulders rising and falling quickly as her breathing rapidly increased.

Fuck Beck. Fuck him to hell.

"I told you, sweetheart," Sophie said as calmly as she could manage. "I might need to speak to some people, so while I'm doing that, you might get to have a sleepover. And then we will see each other when I'm finished." That could be the biggest lie she would ever tell. And Sophie didn't even know what the truth would be. How the fuck couldn't she know the answer to that? How could Beck be holding her fate like this?

And Maddie screamed. She screamed bloody murder as everything overwhelmed her and Sophie utterly failed to make her feel any sort of calm over what was going to happen. But Sophie didn't blame her one bit, as she wanted to scream, too.

Sophie managed to calm Maddie by holding her, sitting with her on her lap on the sofa. Maddie was cuddled against Sophie's chest, her legs wrapped around Sophie's waist in a vice grip.

Sophie did the same, just stroking her hair calmly. God, this had to be okay. A little over half an hour later, there was a knock at her front door and Sophie's guts fell out of her stomach and onto the floor.

Maddie wasn't letting go, so Sophie stood up with her and carried her to the front door. When she opened it, she was met with two police officers wearing their dark navy uniform.

"Sophie Cartwright?" the female officer asked. She looked to be Sophie's age, maybe a little older, and she looked upon Maddie with a sympathetic eye.

"Yes," Sophie confirmed, unable to shake the terrified tone.

"Ms Cartwright, I am Constable Dan Holding," said the male officer, who appeared to be in his mid to late thirties. "This is Constable Anna Plenty. We are here to place you under arrest. You are being charged with the wrongful removal of a child from the United Kingdom and you must now accompany us down to the station."

Sophie didn't hear any of that over the sound of her own hammering heartbeat. "What is going to happen to my daughter?" she asked. "She can't be separated from me. She never has been. I am her mum, I'm her primary caregiver, and she has special needs."

Sophie watched as the officers exchanged a confused glance. Were they unaware? Had Beck even remembered that Maddie had been diagnosed with autism? Was he too fucking stupid to know what autism was?

"She will be placed temporarily with a social worker down at the station while we wait for a court order. A judge will determine which parent to place the child with for now." Constable Plenty did look genuinely sympathetic. "Please be assured, Ms Cartwright, an emergency custody order is only granted in extreme cases."

Sophie believed that this was supposed to make her feel better, but the idea of anyone deciding what was best for Maddie other than herself was unthinkable.

"Ms Cartwright, you will need to fetch your passports so that they may be surrendered, and then you will need to leave the premises," urged Constable Holding.

Jesus, did they really think she was that stupid? Sophie tried to put Maddie down, but she wouldn't budge, instead she tightened her grip on Sophie, not even lifting her head to look at the police officers.

Sophie looked down at the bags in the doorway. "Our passports are in my handbag, there," she nodded down at the bag.

Constable Plenty immediately retrieved them, and Sophie was led out of her flat by the officers. She thanked God they hadn't handcuffed her, not that they could have pried Maddie off of her. Had they been able to, they probably would have, which would have been traumatising in itself.

Maddie was screaming. Sophie was sitting in an interview room listening to her, a camera facing her, and a surly looking officer on the other side of the table. She was handcuffed now, and the arresting officers were cautioned in the middle of the station for not handcuffing her in the first place.

Maddie was pulled from Sophie, which had immediately started her meltdown. Beck and his parents, Keith and Maureen, were at the police station, looking every bit the concerned family, only they were not allowed near Maddie without the court order. The social worker was responsible for her until then.

"For God's sake, will you let me see her?" she asked the officer. "Can't you hear her?"

"Kids throw tanties all the time. She'll get over it in a minute," grunted the officer.

"She's not throwing a bloody tantrum; she is having a meltdown because she has autism. She cannot process her emotions and she doesn't know how to calm herself down!" exclaimed Sophie. "Go out there now and tell the social worker first that she is autistic.

I'm not sure her father, the claimant," Sophie said sarcastically, "is even aware of what that word means. Then will you please tell her to take Maddie to a quiet room. She needs to turn the lights off and give her a distraction, a toy of some sort, some colouring, anything."

Sophie had been informed of her rights in the interview room, and she was following Noah's advice of not saying anything until an attorney arrived. The interviewing officer was just sitting there, listening to Maddie cry.

After another five minutes, he got up in a huff and left the room. Maddie's crying became fainter, as though she was taking further away, and Sophie prayed that her advice had been followed.

The officer returned, but he was not alone. He was accompanied by a woman wearing a fitted, white, knee length dress and matching coat, as well as carrying a black leather Chanel briefcase. Her raven hair was slicked back into a bun with not a hair out of place, and she wore a serious, determined expression on her face.

God, Sophie hoped this was her lawyer. She looked like a damn shark. The officer turned the camera off.

"And remove her damn handcuffs. She's a mother, not a murderer," the woman demanded.

He begrudgingly acquiesced, using a key on his belt to unlock and take away the handcuffs. Sophie instinctively rubbed her wrists as he left them alone.

The woman sat down in the officer's chair and laid her briefcase down on the table to her left.

"Sophie, my name is Olivia Hayes. I am a solicitor specialising in Family Law. I have been briefed on your charges, but first I want to inquire about your treatment?"

Oh, she didn't care about that! "Can you go and see if the social worker has calmed Maddie down?" Sophie insisted.

Olivia pursed her lips. "Maddie is fine, Sophie. I was given explicit instructions to check on her. The social worker is aware of her special needs, as is the judge."

"The judge?"

Olivia opened her briefcase and removed an official looking document. "This is the C100 form that was filed on behalf of Kyle Becker, Maddie's father. He has applied for residential custody. Can you confirm that you have no formal agreement specifying Maddie's current custody arrangement?"

"No, we don't," admitted Sophie. "There was no need," she continued, frustrated. "Beck dropped with me the minute he found out I was pregnant. Maddie has been mine always. Beck's never been interested. It's his mum and dad that insist on seeing her twice a year. Please, I do everything. Beck is just jealous of my boyfriend and he's doing this to spite me."

Olivia placed her perfectly manicured fingers on the table and exhaled calmly. "Sophie, I want to assure you that I am on your side. I kill people like Beck for sport, okay?" she said confidently, and damn, Sophie believed her.

"Okay." Sophie nodded.

"Good, now," Olivia continued. "What's going to happen is we are going to go over your statement, then you are going to give it to the police. You will then be bailed and allowed to go home. I have already spoken to the judge about the emergency custody order that has been filed by Beck's solicitor. I want to assure you that this will not be granted. An order such as that is only granted in cases of serious abuse or neglect. Maddie will remain with you until your court date."

Relief filled Sophie and her shoulders relaxed, filling her back with pain from the tension. "But what's going to happen then? Have I broken the law?"

"Did you tell Beck that you were going overseas?" Olivia asked, pulling a notepad and fountain pen from her briefcase.

Sophie's eyes widened. "Yes!" she cried. "Yes, I did. I took Maddie to visit Beck and his parents for a Christmas visit before we left. It was her last day of school, December 18th."

Olivia scrawled down these details. "And did Beck consent?"

"Well ... no, he didn't really say anything. He was shitty with me because we were going to visit my boyfriend in America for Christmas."

"He was shitty with you?" Olivia repeated. "Do you believe his mood on the day could have resulted in him unreasonably refusing to give consent to Maddie travelling abroad?"

"Absolutely," Sophie said emphatically. "But I didn't exactly ask rather than tell him that we were going. Maddie sort of dropped me in it. I wasn't actually going to tell them we were leaving."

Olivia looked up at Sophie. "And that is not a detail that you include in your statement," she said sharply. "The point is that you informed him of your travel plans, and you did not know that you would be breaking the law."

"I didn't, I swear," promised Sophie.

"There are three defences that we can use here, Sophie. One: where you believed Beck consented or would have consented had he been aware of all the circumstances. Two: where you had taken all reasonable steps to communicate your intentions to remove your child, but you had been unable to do so. Three: where the other parent whose consent is require unreasonably refused to give their consent." Olivia put down her pen and knitted her fingers together. "We are going to use number three, and we can use this because Beck does not have a residence order, or any formal arrangement where he has a preordained legal right to Maddie."

Ordinarily, Sophie would have been able to follow along, but she couldn't. "Am I going to get into trouble?" she asked fearfully.

"This is a criminal charge, do not mistake that, so yes, you are in trouble. But I'm not paid to let my clients go to jail for bullshit offenses. You are going to tell the police that you didn't know you were not allowed to remove Maddie from the UK. You will tell them that you did inform Beck of your travel plans, and that his personal feelings towards your relationship meant that he was uncivil and narky … or however he was behaving. That is it. That is the truth. I will refer back to your statement to support your defence in court. Your statement will then conclude, you will be given a court date and allowed to leave. The order from the judge to allow Maddie to remain with you should be coming through soon." Olivia tapped her phone to see if anything had come through.

Sophie let that settle in. She could say that, and it wouldn't be a lie. She had told him, no matter the circumstances, and he had been an arsehole about Noah. "And what about the custody filing?" Sophie then asked.

"The criminal charge is what we need to handle first," Olivia said firmly. "I try and get custody disputes settled in mediation. You can negotiate visitation or whatever he wants, and I will fight tooth and nail for what you want."

"But Maddie and I were planning on moving to America in the summer holidays." Sophie bit her lip nervously.

It looked like information that Olivia didn't want to deal with. "As I said, criminal charge first. I'm going to go and get Officer Handcuffs and then we'll see about getting you out of here."

Chapter 35

Sophie was made to be fingerprinted, photographed, forced to surrender her and Maddie's passports, processed and bailed before she was allowed to leave the police station.

Even then, until her court date, she was required to check in at the police station once a week like a paroled criminal all because her dropkick of an ex-boyfriend had a jealousy complex.

What was worse was that this all happened in front of Beck, Keith and Maureen, as they still had not left the police station. Sophie could have sworn that she saw Beck filming her, as though he was getting the biggest kick out of seeing her humiliated.

As Sophie was collecting her personal belongings from behind the counter, Beck approached the bench, standing next to her.

"So, uh, when do I get my kid?" he asked the officer, though clearly trying to elicit a reaction from Sophie.

As if fate was listening, Olivia's phone pinged, and she smiled a smug smile of satisfaction.

"Not today, Mr Becker," Olivia replied bluntly. "I have an order from the judge ruling that Sophie's daughter will remain with her."

Sophie saw Beck's blue eyes flare. "What?" he exclaimed. This reaction drew in his parents, as they rose from their seats. "My lawyer filed an emergency custody order!"

"I don't abuse my child, you absolute moron!" hissed Sophie, but Olivia placed her hand in Sophie's shoulder to stop her.

"An emergency custody order is only granted in extreme cases of abuse or neglect. As Sophie's daughter has so clearly suffered neither, she will remain with her mother." Olivia spoke so condescendingly, but in a way that she was sure it would go over Beck's meaty head.

"I can't believe you're pushing him into this!" Sophie accused Keith and Maureen. "You knowhe's got no interest in being a dad. You practically have to force him to be around when Maddie comes over."

"Sophie," uttered Olivia.

"We're not forcing him into anything!" Maureen exclaimed defensively. "Kyle is Maddie's father, and nothing is going to change that."

Beck grinned. "Not even your boyfriend's going to change that, Soph," he taunted.

"Mr Becker, you will kindly refrain from speaking directly to my client. Should you struggle with this, I will have no qualms in taking you to court, wasting your time and money, and getting a restraining order for harassment."

Beck chuckled and shook his head. "Money, huh? Guess we know who's bankrolling you now, Soph. Shallow bitch."

Olivia sighed with a smile, before she turned around to the officer at the front desk. "May I speak with the lovely Constable Hendricks?" Turning back to Beck, she grinned and let him know, "she adores me," before she turned back to the police officer. "I need to make a report about harassment."

"Fuck me, fine!" hissed Beck. "Let's go."

Olivia fished into her briefcase and produced a business card. "For your solicitor."

Beck snatched it out of her hand before motioning for his parents to leave. They promptly left the police station.

"Um, ma'am, there is no Constable Hendricks," the police officer informed Olivia.

Olivia winked at Sophie. "Oh, drat," she uttered facetiously before she returned to her phone. "Now, I have just received a court order telling me that my client is to retain custody of her daughter until her court date. You will have received the same document. Can you please see to it that Maddie is returned immediately? My client has been inconvenienced enough as it is."

Sophie hadno idea what Noah was paying for Olivia, but she was worth every penny.

"I have it here," murmured the police officer in reply as he scanned the computer at the desk. "I'll be right back."

"Alright, Sophie," said Olivia. "Your court date is on February first. Three and a half weeks. You were very lucky to get a date so soon. I'll do everything in my power to get rid of the criminal charges. I am confident that they will be dismissed. I will contact Beck's lawyer to arrange mediation for after the court date. I sincerely hope that the custody case will not need to be heard before a judge. Your best bet to achieve the outcome that you want is through mediation, okay? I don't want any contact between you and Beck. Everything is to go through me. You want to call him a prick, you let me know first, understand?"

Sophie nodded. Okay, what had she absorbed from that? Criminal charges … Jesus, criminal charges … Olivia was confident she could get them dismissed. She needed to play nice. Mediation was her best bet. God, if she could get in a room with Beck …

Well, she hoped by the time they were due for mediation, he will have lost interest in seeking any custody rights. Over her dead body was Beck and his short attention span and moronic rugby mates having anything to do with Maddie permanently.

She and Maddie were going to start a new life with Noah in America, and he couldn't stop them.

The police officer returned shortly with the social worker, with Maddie trailing along behind them. She was gripping a stuffed animal that Sophie didn't recognise but assumed was instrumental in calming her down earlier.

"Maddie!" cried Sophie. God, it had been a few hours since she'd seen her, but it felt like years. It was enough to scare her for life.

Maddie looked up when she heard her name and beamed when she saw Sophie with her arms outstretch. Maddie bounded into Sophie's arms, exclaiming, "Mummy!"

Oh, Sophie could listen to Maddie calling her name all day.

"I'll be in touch, it's time for you to go home," Olivia said, as she straightened her coat and left the police station.

Sophie took Maddie's hand and left the police station, too, only to be greeted by Pete and Holly who were both waiting against a lamppost on the corner. The moment they saw her, they cried out in delight and ran over to meet her.

Holly flung her arms around Sophie and squeezed her tightly. "Oh my God!" she cried. "Thank God you're okay. We went in to bail you out but apparently that's only a thing on television," Holly exclaimed. "Then we saw Tweedle Dumbfuck and his parents and thought it best to wait outside for you to leave." Holly then slapped a hand over her mouth when she saw Maddie. "Oops."

"Noah called me," Pete explained. "He told us what happened, and he wanted someone to be here for you while he was trying to get a flight." He leaned down and kissed Sophie's cheek. "But, of course, we're going to be here for you."

Sophie's eyes welled up. "Thank you," she said gratefully.

As much as she wasn't in the headspace, Sophie needed to work the next day. Two weeks without pay was difficult, and if she and Maddie wanted to keep the lights on, she needed to go back to working her double shifts each day.

Maddie was thankfully okay, and happily went back to school without a fight.

Working ended up being a good distraction, though. Interacting with Pete and the customers during the day and getting back into her normal routine was the best thing to keep her mind off of fucking Beck.

She had called Noah the night before, but his phone had gone directly to voicemail, so she assumed that he was in the air. God, she was grateful that he was coming. She didn't know if it was entirely necessary, but selfishly, she wanted him with her, telling her that everything was going to be okay.

And she got her wish at half past two that afternoon. Noah burst in the door at Pete's, and his head snapped left to right, searching the pub for Sophie. She was carrying a tray of glasses out of the backroom, and thankfully managed to put them down on the bar before she ran to hug him.

"Oh, God, I've been worried sick," he said into her neck. "I've aged ten years in twenty-four hours."

"I'm so glad you're here," whispered Sophie, tearing up as everything that she had experienced in the last day bubbled to the surface.

"Sophie!"

Sophie's head jerked up as she recognised the voice, and over Noah's shoulder she could see Joy, Tally and Vanessa coming into the pub, luggage in tow, after Noah. Her eyes widened in complete surprise as she gasped.

"Oh, sweet baby!" cried Joy, practically shoving Noah aside so that she could hug Sophie tightly. It was a suffocating, motherly hug, and Sophie loved every second. When Joy released her, she hugged Tally and Vanessa as well.

"I have a hundred and three million Instagram followers, Sophie. Say the word and my fans will hunt him down," Vanessa offered seriously. "He won't be able to make a tweet, Snapchat, Insta, Tumblr, Facebook post, or fucking Tik Tok without being cancelled."

"Oh, they can come for whomever you want, Sophie," Tally attested. "Some homophobic bastard was trolling our engagement post and they got his account suspended."

"God, as much as I want to take you up on that," Sophie said regretfully, "I have to play the long game. The custody needs to be settled in mediation and not in court, and if it gets nasty, Beck's unlikely to do what I want." Taking a breath, she suddenly said, "Gosh, I can't believe you all came. You didn't have to, really!"

"That's what Noah said when I asked him to wait at LAX for us," replied Joy with an arched brow.

"And then what did you say, Mom?" huffed Noah.

Joy pursed her lips. "If I'm such an inconvenience, don't worry about having a funeral for me when I die as I don't want to be a burden."

And Sophie laughed. It was like lifting a weight off of her diaphragm. "I'm sure he meant it like I do. You came all this way for me?" She chewed on her lip anxiously. "And I feel bloody awful now seeing as I thought I was going to be locked up right now." Even associating herself with prison was frightening. Sophie had never bloody jaywalked.

"Sophie, sweet girl, you've got a family behind you. And when something terrible, awful ... wonderful, or just plain average happens, you've got people who will rally behind you," Joy promised. "I want you to contact that fancy lawyer, Noah, because I want to be in that witness stand," she decided. "I also want to speak to this Beck character's mother. My God, does he need an attitude adjustment."

Noah rolled his eyes. "Mom, why don't you all go to the bar and get a drink. I'm going to speak with Sophie for a second, and then it's nearly three o'clock, so we can all go and pick up Maddie from school if that's okay with her."

Joy liked that idea, and Tally and Vanessa led Joy over to Pete at the bar, while Noah and Sophie stepped outside into the street.

They hugged again, and Noah kissed Sophie's forehead.

"How are you?" he asked softly.

Looking up into his blue eyes, Sophie blubbered, "Terrified," in a voice barely above a whisper.

Noah cupped Sophie's face. "You're going to get through this, okay? And you and Maddie are going to come out the other side just fine. I will do whatever it takes to make that happen."

CHAPTER 36

Noah had never been more afraid in his life than when Sophie had called him in tears. Never could he have imagined what she was to say, and in that moment, and the days after, Noah could have killed Beck with his bare hands.

Who the hell did he think he was to put an innocent woman through something so cruel? What the hell was he getting out of it? He certainly didn't want Maddie, so what was the reward?

Noah had asked his attorney for the best family lawyer in the UK. He had recommended Olivia Hayes. She was a cutthroat shark, apparently, and often represented celebrities in their divorces and custody battles. She charged five hundred pounds and hour, and Noah was happy to pay whatever to ensure that Sophie went through this experience entirely unscathed.

Despite being frustrated that his mom, Tally and Vanessa coming had held him up at LAX, he was glad that the noise they created was a distraction for Sophie. Tally was even taking vacation days to be there for Sophie, not that Noah expected anything less of his sister.

Joy had wanted to take Sophie out for dinner the following evening, to treat her after her ordeal, but Sophie had to work. It came as a shock to Joy just how much Sophie did indeed work.

"Double shifts five days a week, and night shifts on weekends," Noah told his mom in their suite at The Savoy.

Vanessa had been papped at Maddie's school the day before, so instead of babysitting at Sophie's flat, Maddie was hanging out in their hotel room. The three were in Tally and Vanessa's bedroom watching a movie. Maddie's choice, of course. She was the first kid either of them had cared for together, even if it was only babysitting. While Tally taught all day, she'd never been responsible for a kid properly before.

They were enjoying it, and Noah was confident they would be good moms one day.

Joy's eyes went from the closed bedroom door back to Noah. "What about the song from the movie?" she asked. "Isn't she getting paid for that?"

"Of course," confirmed Noah. "But I negotiated a contract based on box office royalties, streaming and downloads. She'll get a much more lucrative cut that way."

Joy nodded in understanding. "Well, can't you help her out in the meantime?" she asked. "The poor thing shouldn't have to be working herself to the bone."

Noah stared at his mother, honestly annoyed that she thought he honestly didn't care enough to help. "Jesus, Mom, your faith in me is heart-warming," he said sarcastically. "Sophie's been on her own since she was nearly eighteen. She's taken care of Maddie by herself all these years, finding a way to pay for her therapy and everything. She's proud, and not at all in a bad way. I respect her work ethic, her integrity ... honestly, it's part of what made me fall in love with her."

Joy conceded. "Fair enough," she granted. "It just hurts me to think that she's having to work all these hours with this on her mind ... meanwhile that rat bastard is probably getting drunk on lite beer with his loser friends, laughing about this whole thing. Honestly, how his mother could let her son disrespect a woman in this way is beyond me. I'll tell you something, Noah, if this were you, you wouldn't survive a goddamn walloping from me."

Noah gritted his teeth. "He is a fucking asshole," he seethed. "What he's put Sophie through all these years ... to do this now?"

"Ordinarily I'd be asking you to mind your language, honey, but in these circumstances, I think it's necessary," Joy allowed, shaking her head.

"What kills me is that this is all my fault." There was a huge pile of guilt in the pit of Noah's stomach, knowing that Sophie was going through all of this because he was in her life. The look in her brown eyes as she told him she was terrified was enough to slowly bleed him to death. She was terrified, because at the end of the day, she'd been charged with a fucking crime.

One that A: she wouldn't have committed had he not flown her to the States.

And B: she wouldn't have committed had they not been together.

But the guilt didn't take away his logic. He knew that he and Sophie had a right to be together. They were free adults who could do whatever they wanted. Sophie hadn't had a boyfriend since Beck, and he saw it as a privilege to be in hers and Maddie's lives.

"Oh, sweetheart, it's Beck's fault ... what else would a moron with a name like that do with his time except for try to ruin his ex-girlfriend's life with her wonderful, handsome new man?"

Noah scoffed, feeling like he did on prom night when his mom tried to give him a self-esteem pep talk. "Mom, I'm not feeling insecure," he retorted. "But fucked if I'm going to sit here and bitch when I could be going out there and fixing this." He got to his feet abruptly, and Joy followed suit with a shocked look on her face.

"What do you mean?" she demanded to know.

"I mean I'm going to go and talk to Beck and find out what the fuck he wants from Sophie and find the most painful way to give it to him," snapped Noah.

"Are you insane?" Joy demanded to know, latching onto Noah's forearm. "I thank God I came with you, because I think I was meant to stop you from doing anything so royally stupid!"

Noah sneered angrily. "The guy's problem is with me, Mom. I'm going to go and fix it." He shook her off of his arm and started towards the door.

"And what if this hurts Sophie's case, huh?" challenged Joy as she darted after him.

"Sure as hell can't make it any worse." Noah grabbed his wallet and the hotel key from the hall table and left the suite, slamming the door behind him.

Noah had a copy of the custody form thanks to the fact that he was the one being billed for Olivia's time. This meant that he had a copy of Beck's address. He was sure that he looked like an absolute nutcase on the train, but he didn't care.

Beck lived in a grotty looking flat in South London on the lower level in a terraced house, on a street where they all looked the same. Noah marched straight up to the door as soon as he saw the right number and he pounded on it three times with his fist.

Noah could hear the faint sound of a soccer game on the TV inside the apartment, and the faint noise of squeaking floorboards as someone crossed a floor.

The front door to Beck's place opened, but it wasn't Beck who stood at the door, but one of his friends. Noah recognised him as someone who used to frequent Pete's with Beck.

He was wearing a stained t-shirt and a stupid look on his face. "What do you want?" he asked, his words slurring a little, evidently drunk by the beer he held in his hand.

"I want to speak with Beck," Noah said firmly. "Is he here?" he demanded to know.

His friend nodded and turned his head. "Oi, Beck!" he shouted over his shoulder, before he left the entry, leaving the door wide open. Noah didn't enter, though.

Beck emerged from somewhere within the apartment, probably also watching the game as he wore casual, dirty clothes, and was carrying a beer. He rested it on the front window ledge as he folded his arms across his chest, a smug smile teasing at his lips.

Noah wanted to punch it right off of him.

"Came running, did you?" he taunted.

Noah wouldn't be goaded. "Why do you want custody of Maddie so badly?" he demanded to know. "All of a sudden, why?"

"She's my kid," retorted Beck. "Not yours. Whether you like it or not, Maddie is mine, made by me and Soph."

"Yes, I took middle school sex-ed," you fucking moron, Noah neglected to add, "I'm well aware how a kid is conceived." Even though he'd never admit it, he really didn't want to picture Sophie and this dick for brains together. "My question is why now? Why do you want to be involved?"

Beck scoffed. "You just don't like that Soph is always going to be tied to me. No matter what you do, you'll know I got there first."

Oh, now Noah was really going to punch him. What the fuck did he want to do, piss on Sophie? Did he really want to mark his territory that badly?

"Do you not understand that this is Sophie's life that you're screwing with?" Noah asked in disbelief. "This isn't a game. This isn't something to do to get back at her, or me. Do you get that?"

Beck rolled his eyes and stepped down onto the front path, puffing up his chest to mask the fact that Noah was a head taller than him. "I have rights," he sneered. "Rights to my kid, and rights to her mum."

It took every ounce of self-restraint that Noah had to keep his fist balled at his side. "You don't have rights to Sophie," he said sharply. "You never did. You can't have a right to a woman, and if you think that way, you're never going to find someone to fucking tolerate you. Furthermore, if you wanted to have rights to Maddie, then you would have made an effort to be in her life from the day she was born, not from when I became involved in her life.

"There's no such thing as a part time dad. A real dad shows up to the point where his reliability is boring and predictable."

Noah was still angry, but he honestly felt like he was the first man to have this discussion with Beck. His own father certainly hadn't, and he honestly couldn't fathom why this guy didn't see it.

But Beck was either too stubborn, or too damn dense to see Noah's point. Instead, he laughed. "You ride your white horse all you want, mate. Doesn't change the fact that Maddie is my blood, and not yours. I'll get what I'm owed, and you can't do a thing to stop it. Soph will see me all the time ... and you know what's going to happen when she's coming round here ..." he taunted again.

Noah's eyes narrowed. "Okay, you want to talk rights, what's owed?" he clapped back. "How much do you make a year? About thirty-five grand?"

He'd gotten Beck's attention instantly the moment he'd started to talk about money. "How the fuck do you know that?" he growled.

"My lawyer is more expensive than yours," Noah snapped. "You've been paying Sophie two hundred pounds a month since Maddie was born ... but based on your annual salary, and the fact that Sophie has retained one hundred percent residential custody of Maddie since the day she was brought home from the hospital, you owe her ... oh, about three hundred and fifty-eight pounds and seventy-two pence a month."

And Beck took a step back as his eyes widened with shock. "What?" he gasped. "Three hundred and fifty-eight quid?"

"And seventy-two pence, don't forget that," said Noah curtly. "But that's not all, if my math is correct, and I'm fairly certain it is, Maddie is a hundred and two months old. A hundred and two times by two hundred is twenty-thousand, four hundred pounds. Not too bad." Noah nodded. "But considering you were grossly underpaying Sophie for Maddie's maintenance all these years, if you were paying the correct amount, you would have paid So- phie thirty-six thousand, five hundred and eight-nine pounds and forty-four pence."

Sophie had shown Noah the little dossier that the lawyer had prepared last night. Noah thanked God that this shark lawyer had been so thorough so quickly. She really was worth every cent.

"If I'm not mistaken, that's a difference of sixteen thousand, one hundred and eighty-nine pounds and forty-four pence. Will that be cash or credit?"

"Are you fucking mad?" Beck yelled, almost panting as such a colossal sum filled his head with panic.

"But ... she'syours, isn't she?" Noah said innocently, honestly being a teasing little shit in that moment. "You have rights ... obligations to pay for her maintenance ... and you can bet your ass that if you do anything other than be a fuckingangel to Sophie throughout these proceedings that I will sue you for every damn dime."

Beck owned his flat, but it was mortgaged to the hilt. He couldn't afford the additional maintenance, let alone a lump sum payment like that. He again could thank Olivia for her thorough work.

Beck was backed into a corner, and Noah could see the panic in his eyes as he tried to figure a way out. And Noah could hand it to him.

"Look, you and I both know that you don't want custody. You never wanted a kid, and I'm going to give you a way out. First, you need to accept that you and Sophie are never going to happen again. She's moved on, and you damned well need to have enough respect to let her. Second, Sophie's criminal charges," Noah clenched his teeth, visually knocking this guy's two front teeth out, "will be dismissed by the judge. So, when you both are in mediation, you are going to sign a document that excuses you from all parental responsibility, giving Sophie total authority, and you no financial obligation. No future maintenance, and you're off the hook for the sixteen grand."

Beck's face became neutral as he listened.

Could Noah push his luck? "If you contact your lawyer tomorrow and withdraw the C100 form and sign that agreement then and there ... I will pay your legal bills." Was it bribery? Probably. Was Beck greedy enough to take it? Fucking hopefully.

CHAPTER 37

Sophie's phone vibrated in her back pocket for the third time in a row, and she was finally able to answer it as she didn't have her hands full. It was after eleven on a Thursday, so it was quietening down.

Sophie pulled her phone from her back pocket, and she saw it was Beck calling her. She rolled her eyes so hard they might as well have been looking at her brain. Obviously, her lawyer's threat had gone in one ear and out the other.

"What?" she snapped, bringing her phone to her ear, before Olivia's reminder to play nice echoed in her ear.

"You sent him over to bribe me so that's equally bad!" Beck cried, the panic in his voice evident. She could also hear the alcohol in the way he slurred some of his words.

Sophie's blood immediately ran cold. She had never heard Beck sound frightened before. Cocky, smug, belligerent, definitely. But scared? What the hell was scaring him? And why the hell was he talking about bribery?

"Beck, what are you talking about?" Sophie demanded to know, her tone forceful and stern as she frowned deeply with worry.

"I called 999, okay? I did the right thing ... but you can't tell me that bribing is not worse because it is!" Beck didn't sound like he was convincing himself, but Sophie still had no idea what he was talking about. All she knew was that something terrible had happened and Beck was freaked out beyond anything.

"What did you do?" Sophie growled. "Why did you call 999?"

"Your boyfriend!" Beck cried in anguish. "He tried to bribe me, okay? That's bad, you know. If the judge knew, that's bad! But you know what I'm like, Soph," he stressed, "I mouthed off, wanted a bit of sparring, and he wouldn't come back at me, so I hit him."

Sophie fell into the bar, using the counter to support herself as she gasped. Pete immediately noticed Sophie's sudden reaction, and he raced over to her, placing a hand on her back.

"What's wrong?" he whispered.

"I didn't mean to, Soph!" Beck promised. "I didn't think he'd go down like that!

Visions of Noah's lifeless body filled her head as she imagined the worst. She had seen enough security vision of brawls on the news to know what happened when a man threw a fist at another's head. Hell, she worked in a damn bar! Skull fractures, brain bleeds, concussions, and even death. Oh God, it couldn't happen to him!

Bribery or not, he had obviously gone to try and help her! And fucking Beck had thrown his fist at him!

"Where did they take him?" Sophie demanded to know.

"They said St Thomas' A&E," replied Beck, panting with panic. "I'm sorry, Soph! I didn't mean to! You've got to tell him that! When he wakes up, tell him that! You don't have to call the bobbies!"

And there was confirmation that Noah was unconscious. Sophie couldn't even comprehend what Beck was asking her to do. Sophie ended the call and looked at Pete with pure fear. "Beck's punched him!" she exclaimed. "He's unconscious, taken to A&E. I've got to go!"

"Oh, Jesus! Let me give you money for a cab!" Pete insisted. "Please." Pete ran to the till and pulled open the drawer, grabbing out two fifty-pound notes.

Sophie didn't have the clarity of mind to argue. All she could do was to grab the cash and run out the door into the street, not even bothering to grab her coat or her bag. She ran along Shaftsbury Avenue until she found a black cab, luckily only a few minutes later, wrenching open the door and throwing herself into the back.

"Where to, love?" asked the driver.

"St Thomas' A&E!" cried Sophie as she fumbled with her seatbelt. As soon as she was belted in, she pulled up her phone and growled with fury as a dozen messages began to pop up of Beck begging her forgiveness and mercy. Sophie ignored them, finding Joy's contact details in her phone that she had thankfully gotten before she'd left Napa.

Joy answered virtually immediately. She sounded fearful, as though she already knew something was wrong. "Sophie! Have you heard from Noah? Tally thinks something's wrong."

Sophie knew there would probably have been a better way to break the news to Joy other than shouting, "Beck's assaulted him!" but in that moment her brain couldn't think of it. "He's been taken to St Thomas' A&E. Go down to reception and ask for a taxi to take you there! Please can you ask Tally and Vanessa to mind Maddie for me a while longer?"

Joy immediately started to panic cry, and Sophie couldn't blame her. Her own heart was beating so fast it was more of a consistent hum than a pulse. She watched out the window anxiously, willing the driver to go faster.

Sophie heard Joy shout at Tally to watch Maddie, while Tally anxiously demanded to know what was wrong with her brother. Sophie wished she had answers.

Fate, traffic, and the universe were on her side as the taxi trip only took just over ten minutes. Sophie barely heard what the driver charged for the ride, throwing both bills at him as she tore out of the cab and raced into the A&E ward through the patient entrance.

The smell of bleach, stainless steel, and the sick that would not go away immediately filled her nostrils as she ran over to the reception desk. The waiting room was filled with patients awaiting being seen by a doctor. There were mothers with children, elderly citizens, and teenagers supported by their friends.

An overworked nurse was on the desk, currently on the phone to someone, and she eyed Sophie with a frown. "Let me call you back," she said into the receiver as she hung up her end. "Fill out his form and bring it back," she instructed, grabbing a clipboard and a pen and holding it out to Sophie.

"No!" Sophie stressed, holding up her hands. "I'm not a patient. My boyfriend has just been brought in by ambulance. He was ... well, I don't even know what happened! He was hit! His name is Noah Bentley. I believe he was unconscious, but he would have had his driver's licence on him."

She did appear sympathetic, but regretful. "Look, I'm afraid I can't disclose any information if you're not family."

Sophie eyes flared. "Can't you bend the rules? Please?" she begged. "I need to know if he's okay!"

"I'm sorry, but I can't. Please, have a seat, and we will contact the next of kin."

"Sophie!"

Sophie's head snapped around as she saw Joy and Tally racing into A&E, both wearing expressions of pure dread. Both were in varying states of loungewear and pyjamas.

"Thank God!" cried Sophie. "She isn't allowed to tell me anything because I'm not family."

Tally raced into Sophie's arms, gripping her tightly, while Joy slammed her hands on the counter like a complete Karen.

"My son, Noah Bentley, was just brought into your ER!" exclaimed Joy hysterically. "I need someone to tell me what happened immediately!"

The nurse looked back to Sophie again with a sympathetic expression, as though she didn't like the policy, but she brought up Noah's file on her computer screen.

"He was brought in a half an hour ago," read the nurse. "Presented with a suspected compound skull fracture, and possible fractures to the ribs and his right hand. He's currently getting a CT, but I will have the doctor come out and speak with you as soon as he can. Take a seat. I promise your son is in good hands."

Sophie's fears were confirmed when she heard that. Skull fracture ... brain damage ... oh, God!

"Compound fracture?" stammered Joy fearfully. "What exactly does that mean?"

"It means that he presented with an open wound to the head. The skin and tissue have been broken and his brain has been exposed. He's gone straight up for treatment. You'll have more information as soon as it's available."

"Mom, come on," urged Tally, as she led both of them over to the waiting area. They chose three seats together that were facing the glass sliding door that was emblazoned with "authorised personnel only".

"I told him not to go," Joy hissed as she sat in between Tally and Sophie, holding onto both their hands. "But he couldn't be reasoned with. Stupid, stubborn ass!"

Silent tears spilled down Sophie's cheeks as she thought of Noah's mindset. He would have only been trying to help her, trying to stop Beck from ruining her life. And Beck had gone and put him in the hospital for his trouble. Oh, God he had to be okay! This wasn't right!

Sophie kept her eyes on the door, willing someone to come through to tell them that Noah was going to be alright.

"Tally, what's happening?" Joy whispered to her daughter.

"He's not dead." Tally spoke coolly with certainty, and Sophie broke her eye contact with the door to look back at her with furrowed brows.

"How do you know?"

Tally's eyes were swollen and filled with anxiety for her brother. "I can feel it," she said simply. "I could sense something was wrong, and Noah wouldn't answer his phone. And then you called. I can still feel that same feeling. He's hurt, but he's not dead." Her conviction sounded like a prayer.

Joy accepted it, believing in the connection between her children. Right then, Sophie wanted to whole-heartedly believe in it, too.

They waited for what felt like hours. Patients came into A&E. People in the waiting room were seen. Patients went home. Sophie, Joy and Tally didn't leave their place as they willed Noah's doctor to come out and speak to them.

Joy prayed. Sophie listened in earnest as Joy begged God to keep Noah safe, to heal him, and to protect him from any more harm.

At just after four o'clock in the morning, the sliding door opened and a middle-aged doctor wearing navy hospital scrubs entered the waiting room. He spotted them waiting, and all of their postures suddenly straightened.

"Noah Bentley's family?" he asked.

"Yes," confirmed Joy desperately.

"My name is Doctor Sanders. I took Mr Bentley's case when he came in through A&E."

Joy didn't have the patience for introductions. Neither did Sophie or Tally. "Please, tell me my son is okay?" Joy pleaded.

"Your son is okay, Mrs Bentley," confirmed the doctor.

Relief washed through Sophie as she closed her eyes, exhaling a deep breath.

"Oh, thank you, God!" cried Joy. "Because I'm going to kill him myself!"

Doctor Sanders was confused momentarily, but he continued, choosing to sit down in the empty seat beside Sophie as he spoke to the three women. "Noah presented with several injuries, the most serious being a compound skull fracture to his frontal bone. Noah's initial CT scan showed signs of brain swelling so I inserted an intracranial pressure monitor in between his skull and brain. An ICP alerts us to any changes to the pressure inside a skull."

Sophie gasped. "Didn't you just tell us that he was going to be okay?" she exclaimed.

"Whatever you just said was in goddamn Japanese and it certainly didn't tell me that my beautiful boy is healthy," Joy snapped, panicked.

Noah's doctor nodded and took a breath, before repeating his treatment. "Noah has a head injury, and we use a CT scan to check for brain bleeding or swelling," he explained. "Noah's scan showed signs of swelling, but it wasn't enough for me to send him into surgery. I inserted the ICP to monitor the swelling. He has been monitored for a few hours while I tended to his other injuries and the good news is that the swelling was very mild and is nothing to be concerned about. There is no bleeding on the brain, and the swelling will go down by itself."

Okay. Thankfully the doctor knew more about brains as any sort of trauma or swelling sounded catastrophic to Sophie.

"Noah's x-ray showed that his skull fracture is not depressed. This is good news. It means that there are no bone fragments pressing on his brain. As the fracture was open and his brain was exposed, Noah was immediately placed on antibiotics to prevent infection. He has been sewn up and bandaged and I will remove the ICP in a few days."

All three women nodded as they absorbed what the doctor was saying. Sophie was understanding that Noah was bloody lucky indeed, and so was Beck.

"You mentioned other injuries?" prompted Tally.

"The paramedics reported that after sustaining the head injury, Noah had fallen on some concrete steps, the force of which had resulted in two rib fractures, and a fracture in his right wrist, index and middle fingers."

"Are those very difficult injuries?" Sophie asked fearfully. "To heal?"

"My son is a pianist, a composer, Doctor Sanders," Joy said tensely. "His hands are his livelihood."

"His wrist is in plaster and his fingers are braced for at least six weeks. With physiotherapy, I don't see why he would have any problems returning to work," replied Doctor Sanders, before he took a breath, as though he needed to broach something difficult. "Now, as you haven't asked how Noah sustained these injuries, I'm sure you are somewhat aware. We believe an assault has taken place. Would you like me to call the police?"

Sophie wanted to say "yes". Every fibre of her being wanted Beck punished for everything he'd done. But a small, horrible, selfish voice in the back of her head told her, warned her that if Beck was arrested, would he start shouting to anyone who would listen about the bribery? Would that put Maddie at risk?

She looked to Joy and Tally, knowing that she wasn't in the right headspace to make that decision. She found that they were both looking at her for the same reason.

"Is Noah awake?" Joy asked Doctor Sanders.

"He is under a light anaesthetic to keep him comfortable, but it will be stopped in the morning," replied the doctor.

"Noah can decide then," Tally told the doctor, though looking at Sophie reassuringly.

"Are we allowed to see him?" asked Sophie.

"He will be moved to a ward in a few hours once he is weaned off the anaesthetic. You will be able to see him then."

CHAPTER 38

Noah blinked his eyes, again and again, as his vision cleared. It took a moment for him to register exactly where he was. What didn't take long to realise was the freaking hunchback that was ringing the bells of Notre Dame inside his skull. It felt seventeen times worse than any hangover he'd ever experienced in college.

He was in a hospital room and thank God for that. With a headache like this, he needed to see a doctor. Noah's logic then quickly set in. Why the fuck was he in hospital? What had happened? Was he okay?

He could hear the noise of monitors, the beeping and pinging of machines that were attached to him. A clear drip was dropping liquid in through an IV in his arm, and there felt like there was a wire brushing against his leg. Where the hell did that lead?

"Noah?"

He heard Sophie's panicked voice and he felt her hands latch onto his forearm. Her face appeared before him, brows furrowed, and brown eyes swollen and red. She looked like she hadn't had any sleep, like she'd been up all night worried sick about him.

"Sophie?" he said, his voice unintentionally sounding like a croaky groan.

"Oh my God!" cried Joy. "Oh, baby, you're awake!"

"Mom … what happened?" Noah grumbled almost incoherently.

"You don't remember, you big dope?" Tally asked angrily.

Tally was mad at him. God, what had he done? The last thing he remembered was … wait, what was the last thing he remembered? He remembered landing in London and seeing Sophie at Pete's. He remembered seeing Maddie at school … and that was about it. He wasn't sure how much time had passed.

"No," he mumbled, squinting his eyes. "What happened to me?"

"You went to see Beck," Sophie told him seriously, looking about as fragile as a china cup on the edge of a shelf. "You tried to fix things for me, and he antagonised you. He tried to pick, and fight and he punched you. You went down straight away."

Noah had no memory of going to see Beck. He didn't know what his purpose had been, but he could guess that it would have been to get the lowlife to drop his ridiculous case through any means necessary. He wasn't a man of violence. He'd never thrown a punch in his life, and he couldn't imagine that he would ever fight the guy.

Out of the corner of his eyes, he saw his mother press a call button on the wall. He could see that Joy wasn't happy. She had a lot of pent up yelling to do, and Noah knew that she believed whatever he'd done was stupid. As soon as a doctor cleared him, the woman would definitely try and ground her thirty-year-old son.

"I'm so sorry he did this to you," whispered Sophie, utterly ashamed.

Noah wasn't even aware of whatever it was that Beck had done to him, but he sure as well knew that it wasn't Sophie's fault. But he couldn't tell her that, as Joy beat him to it.

"It's not your fault, Sophie," Joy assured her. "My son was the big idiot who wouldn't listen to me." Okay, so maybe she wouldn't wait for the doctor.

The door to his small hospital room opened, and a middle-aged doctor wearing navy scrubs and carrying a tablet entered. He looked pleased to see Noah, and he stopped at the end of his bed.

"Good afternoon, Noah. My name is Doctor Sanders," he introduced himself. "How are you feeling?"

"Like crap," he answered truthfully. "My head is killing me." Noah lifted his right hand to rub his forehead, but instantly realised something was wrong. His arm felt different, heavy, and upon looking at it, he saw that his whole forearm was in plaster, and two of his fingers were in some serious looking splints. His eyes widened, which only worsened his splitting headache. "What the fuck happened to my hand?" Noah cried out in despair; his voice still raspy. "Oh my God, what happened?"

"Karma happened," retorted Joy. "That's what not listening to your mother looks like."

Noah glared at his mother. "Jesus, Mom, now it not the time. My whole freaking career is my hands!" Noah had been advised years ago to take out an insurance policy on his hands. He never imagined something would actually happen, and he would give all that money back if it meant he could play.

"Noah, calm down," instructed the doctor. "Mrs Bentley, please." The doctor went over to his drip and adjusted something, and Noah felt his pain nearly immediately dull.

"It's going to be fine," promised Sophie, rubbing his left arm.

"Noah, you presented last night with a compound skull fracture," began Doctor Sanders, who proceeded to tell Noah every detail about the last eighteen hours.

Noah was shocked to say the least. He'd never encountered anyone who'd had a skull fracture before. It was honestly an injury that sounded like something that could only happen in a movie or a TV show. But one punch to the head, right in the sweet spot, and he'd very nearly had a serious, traumatic brain injury.

He'd fallen apparently, and broken some ribs, his wrist, and two of his fingers. Simple fractures apparently, that would heal by themselves. Physical therapy would help him to play the piano again, and Noah would start researching therapists immediately.

To monitor the slight swelling on his brain, he still had a wire underneath his skull. One of the machines in the room was tracking this activity, and Noah was both alarmed and amazed that something like that was possible.

"Do you want to know how they got that wire in there, Noah?" remarked Joy sarcastically. "A neurosurgeon drilled into your skull. Drilled! Might as well have drilled a hole in my heart and slowly bled me to death. Would that have made you happy? My slow, painful death?"

Noah knew he would not hear the end of this. "How long until I get the wire out of my head?" he asked the doctor. "You said my brain is fine, swelling's not a concern. The fracture will heal by itself ..."

"You have a serious concussion as well, Noah, so I'm going to leave it in for the next twenty-four to forty-eight hours just to be on the safe side. You'll then be taken to theatre and sedated to have the wire removed comfortably."

"His shoulder's okay though, right Doctor?" Tally asked, concerned, motioning to Noah's left shoulder.

Doctor Sanders frowned. "Yes, there was no injury to his shoulder."

"Good," replied Tally, smiling, before she promptly punched him right where she'd pointed. "I oughta kill you!" she cried angrily, her face turning dark as she turned on her heel and stalked out of Noah's hospital room.

Sophie jumped in surprise, and Noah flinched as his shoulder throbbed. Joy followed Tally from the hospital room promptly. Noah had scared Tally, and he didn't want her to feel that way. He'd scared his mom, and he'd scared Sophie.

"I think there is obviously a lot to talk about. I will be back to check on you in the next hour, Noah. Please hit the call button if you need anything." He smiled grimly before leaving the room, closing the door behind him.

"I mean, would it be selfish of me to hope that you're not going to storm out of here, too?" Noah wondered half-heartedly.

Sophie's face softened as she sniffed and wiped one of her eyes with the back of her hand. "I'm not going anywhere," she promised, and Noah's painful chest filled with warmth. "I know why they're angry at you. They want you to be safe, as do I. But I know that you went to see Beck for me, and for Maddie, with nothing but pure and good intentions. You went to fight for us, and nobody has ever done anything like that for me before." Sophie chewed on her bottom lip to stop it from trembling. "I am so sorry that you were hurt, Noah, and I am so, so angry, so furious at Beck for hurting you like this. It could have been somuch worse, and I don't know what I would have done had your injuries been more severe than they were." Sophie rolled her eyes at herself. "Oh God," she complained, "I need to stop crying." She shook her head. "As it is, you have a bloody wire monitoring your brain!"

Noah didn't know what he'd said to Beck. He didn't know what Beck had come back with. Obviously they had not reached an agreement, but he wished he had managed to come away with something. All he'd succeeded in doing, it seemed, was putting the people that he loved through more stress.

"I'm sorry," he said sincerely. "God, I'm sorry for piling onto what you're already going through." He would make the same apology to his mom and to his sister when they decided to come back.

Noah actually couldn't recall a time when Tally had ever been seriously angry with him. He hadn't scared her before like he'd managed to now.

Sophie shook her head, as a small, emotional smile teased her lips. "I'm just glad you're okay. You don't know how glad." Taking a breath, she added, "But I need to ask if you want me to call the police. Beck assaulted you … he could have seriously hurt you … in fact, he did seriously hurt you."

Noah thought on it for a moment before he suddenly got an idea. "I obviously didn't achieve much when I went to speak to him. But what if I leverage this against him?" he suggested. "He drops the custody case; I don't file a police report."

Sophie suddenly stood up from the bed and stared at him, and Noah felt a rush of cold from where she'd been. "What? No!" she cried. "No, this is entirely separate from the custody petition," she insisted. "He doesn't get to walk away from this through bargaining. He could have killed you."

But Noah could see the conflict in Sophie's face as she said the words. She was tempted but didn't want to admit it. Noah didn't blame her at all. He held a potential ticket to making sure that Maddie stayed where she belonged.

"No!" Sophie said again, as though she was trying to convince herself.

There was a sudden knock on the door, and both Noah and Sophie turned their heads. He hoped it was his mom and Tally returning, but it wasn't. When the door opened slowly, Noah was shocked to see Beck awkwardly standing in the threshold.

"What the hell are you doing here?" Sophie demanded to know, her teeth clenching.

Noah was so used to a mixture of cocky and possessiveness from Beck, coupled with small man syndrome. Right now, he looked shattered. He, too, didn't look like he'd had a wink of sleep. Noah doubted it was through concern for him, but because he was worried about the repercussions.

"Look, I'm sorry to be interrupting ... the only reason they let me in here is because I told them I was your cousin," Beck said uncomfortably as he stepped into the room tentatively. Beck's eyes were filled with fear and anxiety as he looked over Noah in the hospital bed. He ran a hand back through his hair as he sucked in a tight, shaky breath. "Shit," he said under his breath, though loud enough that Sophie and Noah could both hear. "Are you okay?"

"What does it look like?" Sophie exclaimed. "No, he isn't okay! He has a skull fracture, and he could have had brain damage. And look at his arm, his hand! Look what you did!" Sophie positioned herself at the end of Noah's bed, creating a barrier between them.

"I'm sorry!" cried Beck. "I came to say sorry. I don't know why I did that ..." Beck stepped around Sophie so that he could look at Noah. "I don't like you, but the second I did it, I regretted it. I knew better, and I'm sorry."

Beck did sound very sincere. He knew he'd messed up badly.

Despite Sophie's objections, Noah was going to offer him the agreement. He would drop everything against Sophie, and Noah wouldn't file a police report. But Beck beat him to it.

From inside his jacket, he produced a folded document. He held it out to Sophie, who cautiously took it from him. Sophie unfolded it right away, and she began to read its contents.

"I, Kyle Becker, do hereby relinquish all parental rights to Madeleine Cartwright ..." Sophie trailed off as she read the rest of the document in pure shock.

"I had my lawyer send a copy to yours, and to the judge, but I wanted to bring a copy to you, Soph," Beck said quietly. "I don't know what's going to happen with the criminal case ... I hope it's dropped. Jeez, I'm sorry, Soph. It's no excuse for what I've put you through, but I hope that this is a start. It's the right thing to do. Maddie belongs with you. I'm no good for her, and I nearly took ... I nearly took her dad from her. I realise that now."

Sophie gripped the document tightly as her brown eyes found Noah. She was shocked and trying to get her head around what had just happened, as was Noah. He certainly hadn't expected remorse from the man, but then, Noah had never nearly killed someone himself.

"And what if Noah wants to make a police report?" Sophie rasped. "Will you take this back?"

"I can't take it back, Soph. It's signed. Maddie's yours, just like she always has been." Sighing, he added, "Look, I can't stop you from calling the police. I'd be lying if I said I wasn't hoping you'd forgive me. I don't want to go to jail."

"Neither did Sophie," said Noah tersely. He stopped himself from saying anything further. He needed to think for a minute. He'd gotten what he was going to bargain for without having to actually bargain. Sophie had Maddie, and she quite possibly was going to have the charges dropped against her.

Maybe it was a good thing that Noah couldn't actually remember the assault. He didn't want to drag things out. He didn't want to hang around, give statements, wait for a court date … not when everything could be finished today.

Noah had exactly what he wanted. Maddie was safe, and Sophie was going to be okay. They could start their lives together, and they could forget Beck after today.

"I don't want you contacting Sophie ever again," Noah told him sternly. "Don't call, text, email, nothing. You are not her responsibility, and she is no longer your punching bag, your object to make yourself feel better. You need to move on separately, and we will do the same." After a pause, he added, "I think you should also see a therapist. Someone to help you move on from this, to make better choices. You can't do this to another person, as they might not be as lucky as I am."

Noah saw Sophie cup her hand over her mouth as her eyes watered again. Could she see the light at the end of the tunnel, the same as he could? God, what he would give to never see pain, fear or anxiety on her face ever again.

Beck shuffled on the spot as he nodded his head. "I get it," he told Noah. "This is it." Beck took one last look at Sophie, exhaling as he did. "You take care of yourself, Soph. Take care of you both." And he left, closing the door behind him.

Sophie's arms dropped to her side, still holding the letter in a vice grip. "Are you sure?" she asked in disbelief. "Please, please, do not do this for me. Do not do another thing for me that you might live to regret."

Noah actually laughed, though his morphine drip wasn't strong enough to mask the pain in his ribs as he did so. "Sophie, trust me, I am doing this for me. I know what I want. I want you, and I want Maddie, and the life we talked about. I want to leave this behind and start fresh together. I know it's not going to be as straightforward as that, but so long as we're taking those steps together, I'm happy."

An elated smile spread across Sophie's face as an age of stress melted away. She raced around to his left side and knelt on his bed beside him. "I'm excited," she almost sang. "God, how good it feels to be excited."

Noah chuckled. "I love you," he said simply. "Now would you go and find my mom and Tally? I've got to suck up. Then you need to go and pick up Maddie. I want both my girls here together."

Chapter 39

May 30th

Five and a half months later

"Oh my Gosh, Sophie!" exclaimed Joy, as an envious groan escaped her throat. "Look at this master bath! Look at the tile! The bathtub ... oh, I always wanted a claw foot tub!" She panned the camera around the ensuite bathroom for Sophie to see, but the screen on her phone really didn't do it any justice.

Just like the dozen other houses she had shown Sophie on FaceTime this week, they all were enormous, luxurious, and ridiculously expensive. But just like London, prime real estate was worth a fortune in Los Angeles.

"And the closet is to die for!" she continued excitedly, bringing the camera into the walk-in-wardrobe which looked more like a high-end boutique then somewhere Sophie would store her jumpers and jeans.

Sophie had been very non-committal about making a decision on a place to live. It was very difficult choosing a home that she had never seen in person before. She really knew nothing about the neighbourhoods, and didn't really understand how the school districts worked and ... oh, who was she kidding? The price tags of these places were nauseating! Both Joy and Noah seemed to have no qualms with laying down a mid seven figure sum for a mansion in a gated LA community, but the idea made Sophie feel sea sick.

So much had happened since January and searching for a house was just the tip of the iceberg.

Beck had stayed true to his word, and the withdrawal of the C100 form made it simple for her criminal charge to be dismissed. Mediation was rendered unnecessary and Sophie received formal, full residential custody in writing that was completely iron clad, thanks to Olivia's thorough agreement.

Despite the fact that she didn't need to seek permission, she still informed Beck, through his parents, that she was moving to America with Maddie. Whatever bad blood, they were her grand-parents, and were the only relatives she had known up until Noah's family had come stampeding into their lives. She had promised to fly back once a year to visit, which had been her intention anyway. You could take the girl out of London, but you couldn't take London out of the girl.

Noah had been discharged from hospital six days after admission. After a repeat CT to be sure, he was medically cleared, and his ICP wire was removed in the surgical theatre. He had wanted to stay in London, but it made sense to go home once he was able to fly to begin his physiotherapy. He went home just as soon as Sophie's case had been dismissed.

Tally and Vanessa had flown home earlier as Tally had needed to return to work, and Maddie poignantly informed Sophie that she was excited to see them again in America. Despite the fact that

Sophie obviously wanted Maddie to bond with children her own age, the fact that her circle was widening was a win, and it warmed Sophie's heart.

Joy flew home with Noah nearly three weeks later, with Noah promising his mum that he would be okay at home, and she could definitely return home to Napa. Her fussing was driving him up the wall.

And life had returned to somewhat normal. Maddie went to school, and Sophie went to work. Maddie played on the piano whenever she was at Pete's, and she continued to achieve milestone after milestone in school.

But the moving date was approaching. Sophie and Maddie were booked on a flight in less than a week. Her intention had been for Maddie to see out the school year, but Sophie was pulling her out a few weeks early.

First and foremost, it had been announced in the American press that an eight-year-old girl from England was the co-composer for The Last Hope, the film that was tipped to be the major critical and commercial success at the summer Box Office. The buzz around Maddie was huge, and there were a lot of people who wanted a glimpse of such a phenomenal child.

Naturally, this idea frightened Sophie beyond anything, but Noah was an expert at this sort of thing, and he had arranged a few quiet and controlled interviews. Maddie had even been invited onto talk shows in anticipation!

Perhaps the most exciting event in the new few weeks was the premiere of the film. Noah didn't really like to go to these sorts of things. He liked to slip in the back and not be front and centre, but he was proud to stand beside Maddie. Sophie hoped that through the preparation with Maddie's psychologist, and her noise cancelling headphones, it could be an unforgettable experience for her.

For Sophie, it was exciting, too. The single that she had recorded for the film was being released in one week, fourteen days shy of the film's premiere. It was her own official launch into the industry, and part of the film's budget was dedicated to the heavy promotion of the song. This meant that Sophie would hear herself on the radio, which was just mind blowing to even contemplate.

They were going to be busy! Which was why they were forced to leave a little earlier than originally planned.

Maddie had a confirmed place with one of the most esteemed child psychologists in the city. She also had a place at an exclusive private school that were famed for their musical program. Maddie, apparently, already had a reputation. The smaller class sizes meant that Maddie would get more time with her teachers, and the private funding meant that the school employed several teacher's aides, who were there to specifically support students with additional needs.

Sophie had worked her last shift at the West End Piano Bar. She had cried. Pete had cried.Everyone had cried. It had been ten years of her life that she had spent there. She had been pregnant when she had first met Pete. She had promised to visit, and to stay in close contact. She had hugged and kissed Holly goodbye, and wished her luck as she finally finished uni, and she had wished Amy a safe journey back home to Australia.

She had then spent the next few days packing her entire life up into boxes and crates to be shipped to Los Angeles. It was amazing how much crap she had managed to hoard in her tiny flat, and she struggled to part with anything.

The very last decision that had to be made was a place to live. Sophie and Maddie were temporarily moving in with Noah and Tally. Vanessa, of course, was on tour in Europe, and Tally was flying over to join her as soon as her school broke up for the summer. Noah wanted to buy a house, his first house ... or theirs as he called it ... in the neighbourhood of Maddie's new school.

Noah was hopeless at looking. He'd never owned a home before and had lived his entire adult life in his sister's guest room. His mum had only been too happy to fly down to help.

"And this is the second master," Joy continued on her video tour. "Isn't it just stunning?" she exclaimed. "This would be perfect for Maddie. She would have her own bathroom ... oh and look at those bay windows! To die for!"

Sophie was sitting on the floor in Maddie's bedroom, having pulled out everything from under her bed and was sorting through what to pack into boxes, and what to donate.

From the shaky camera, she could see that the bedroom was indeed beautiful. It was also enormous and looked like it once again belonged in a six-million-dollar home. She had never imagined Noah to have such a fortune. He never behaved in such an entitled way, and he never made her feel awkward for their vast differences in financial circumstances.

Sophie knew that she wouldn't always have only a few hundred pounds in the bank. She was awaiting her pay cheque for the song ... and perhaps she was delaying choosing a house so that she could contribute to the purchase of a home.

"Aw!" cried Joy in a heartbreakingly warm tone. She took her phone into a little girl's bedroom.

Sophie looked closer at her screen as she saw the sort of bedroom that she had always wished she could create for Maddie. It was beautiful. Pink, with white plantation shutters on the windows. A beautiful, canopy bed with sheer white curtains tied to the posts with large, white ribbons. Toys were displayed beautifully on inbuilt shelves. A rocking chair sat in the corner beside a bookcase. There was a desk in front of one of the windows with white cups of pencils and pens. Sophie could even see a height chart stuck to one of the walls.

"Isn't this darling?" gushed Joy.

"It is," confirmed Sophie. "That's really beautiful," she added wistfully.

"You like this one?" Joy asked.

"I mean, I would have to see it for myself," Sophie clarified. "I can't decide where to live without having looked at it. But from what you've shown me, it is lovely, and I know Maddie would love to have a room like that one."

Joy chuckled. "Well, Maddie can have this room, and Grandma Joy can have the second master when she comes to stay," she said deviously. "No, I know what you mean. I don't think I could make this sort of decision from having seen it through a cell phone, but this is the best house I've been through. I know I lost Noah about five houses back, but I'll drag him into this one, and you two can make a decision when you get here."

Noah had given up. He knew Sophie wouldn't make a decision until she was there, and he couldn't stand touring another house until then.

"Well, we'll be there soon."

"Okay, everybody." Famed talk show host, Jenna Jackson, was addressing her studio audience in the ad break.

Noah, Sophie and Maddie were standing in the wings on the set. This was Maddie's very first press interview since arriving in America, and she was absolutely sweating bullets. Maddie was fine, excited even. Sophie had still insisted that she wear her headphones until she went out onto the stage just in case.

Maddie was holding up surprisingly well, and her new psychologist, Andrea Baker, had told Sophie that this was because she had been prepared so well for months for this move. She knew what to expect, and she knew it would all centre around the piano, her very favourite thing.

"I need to ask that you do not applause when Maddie Cartwright comes out," Jenna requested. Sophie had been the one to request this. She didn't know what the sensory overload would be like if five hundred people started clapping and cheering. "Maddie has sensory sensitivities, and her mom has said that smiling and waving is okay, but noise needs to be kept down."

Sophie knew to the audience that she probably sounded like the biggest helicopter parent. Maddie's autism wasn't public knowledge. It wasn't deliberately being hidden, but it wasn't anyone's business. People with keen eyes would probably be able to tell, but it was Maddie's business and Sophie wasn't going to advertise her personal information.

Jenna then quickly dashed back up on stage to her chair, and her producer signalled that they were back. Jenna smiled at the camera. "Up next I am joined by a musical prodigy. It was recently announced that an eight-year-old girl had co-composed the musical score for the upcoming film, The Last Hope. Of course, I had to meet her. All the way from London, England, please welcome Maddie Cartwright."

A stagehand then signalled to Maddie, and Sophie removed Maddie's headphones. There were a handful of claps from the audience, but the majority had heeded Jenna's request and were smiling and waving at Maddie.

Maddie looked so darling. She was wearing a white sundress, and by some miracle, had kept it clean in between putting it on this morning to now. She had a pale pink ribbon tied around her waist, which matched the ribbons in her hair. Her long, strawberry blonde locks were fixed into two plaits, and much to Maddie's delight, she had on a dusting of makeup.

They had rehearsed this before the audience had come in, and Maddie remembered what to do perfectly. She walked directly over to Jenna and gave her a high five, before taking a seat in the armchair next to her.

There was a monitor backstage for Noah and Sophie to watch, but Sophie's eyes were glued to Maddie from the wing. Joy was taping the whole show at home, or else Sophie would have had her phone out snapping insane amounts of photos.

"Welcome to America, Maddie!" greeted Jenna kindly. Jenna was aware that Maddie was autistic. Sophie would of course inform people privately who needed to know. She would need to carry the conversation if Maddie got stuck.

"Thank you," replied Maddie, remembering to smile.

Immediately there were "awws" from the audience as they heard Maddie's angelic voice.

"Now, I understand you just had your birthday! How old did you turn?" asked Jenna.

"Nine," replied Maddie. "My birthday is the fifth of June."

"Happy birthday!" Jenna beamed. "One more year before you turn double digits. Now, I understand that you're pretty talented on the piano. Is that right?"

"Yes," confirmed Maddie, almost bluntly. "I am very good." She received a chuckle from the audience. "Do you know how to play an instrument?"

Noah gasped as he squeezed Sophie playfully. "Reciprocal conversation," he quietly cheered. "That's my girl!"

Jenna chuckled. "Oh, I wish! I played clarinet in high school, but I gave it up quickly."

"I don't know what a clarinet is, but I could probably learn it because I learn instruments fast," replied Maddie matter-of-factly. Again, there was a rumble of laughter from the audience who interpreted Maddie's bluntness as humour.

"Now, what is really special is that you are a composer!" Jenna steered the conversation back on track. "You co-composed the musical score of a movie when you were onlyeight! That's amazing! Was it hard to compose the music?"

"No," replied Maddie, again, so bluntly. Sophie almost winced, but it was the absolute truth.

Jenna laughed lightly, as did the audience. "What did you like most about composing the score?"

"I liked when Noah would play and I would play it and make it better," she replied.

"And of course, Maddie is talking about Academy Award winning composer, Noah Bentley, who wrote the score with Maddie on this project," Jenna informed her audience. "I understand Noah is the one who taught you how to play the piano, is that right, Maddie?"

Maddie nodded. "Yes. But I learned in one day because my memory is good. Then me and Daddy made the music for the movie together."

"You are certainly a talented little girl, Maddie Cartwright," complimented Jenna.

Sophie's heart lurched when Maddie called Noah "Daddy". She was using his given name and Daddy interchangeably. Sophie knew that Noah was chuffed whenever Maddie called him "Daddy". He felt really proud, and Sophie was just as proud that Maddie saw Noah as her father.

"Now, we are lucky enough to have the whole family in the house today," Jenna told her audience. "I didn't warn them, but we're going to put them on the spot. Please welcome, Maddie's parents, Sophie Cartwright and Noah Bentley."

Sophie froze. She couldn't go on TV! She wasn't wearing any proper makeup! Her hair was in a messy bun! She was only in some daggy jeans and a plain white t-shirt as it was hot. But before she could even protest, a crewmember had attached a microphone to her shirt, and Noah had taken her hand and was leading her out on stage.

Without a reminder, the audience had started to clap, and Sophie gasped as Maddie's hands immediately went to her ears. Sophie quickly darted over to Maddie, still holding her headphones in her hands, and placed them comfortingly over her ears.

The crew had brought out an additional chair. Sophie sat down in Maddie's chair, holding Maddie on her lap, while Noah sat down beside her.

"Welcome," greeted Jenna, as though she hadn't already welcomed them backstage before the show. "Especially to you, Sophie, as I understand that you and Maddie had only both just moved over to the States."

"Yes," Sophie confirmed, before clearing her throat awkwardly. "We've only been here less than a week." She looked out into the sea of people in the audience, blocked by a barricade of cameras and technical equipment. Lord, it looked intense.

As the audience had settled, Sophie slipped the headphones off of Maddie again. She was okay and was sitting calmly.

"Noah, it's a pleasure to have you on the show," Jenna continued, turning her attention to him. "I've got to say, are you as amazed with this kid as we all are? I mean, composing is not easy, right?"

Noah chuckled, so much more at ease than Sophie was. "Well, I could say it comes easy but then I'd be in trouble when I turn a score in late," he joked, to which the audience all laughed. Sophie smiled too, feeling a little more relaxed. "But to answer your question, yes, I am amazed by Maddie. Every day she does something that impresses me, and I couldn't be more proud of her." Noah playfully pulled on one of Maddie's plaits. "Maddie picked up the piano in one lesson, and the next thing I knew, she was composing with me. Maddie wrote, she changed things, arranged some of the most beautiful melodies. I couldn't have done this score without her, and I'm so glad that she's being recognised as the talented kid that she is."

"And she gets it from Mama, right?" Jenna asked, smiling and raising an eyebrow at Sophie. "Your featured song in the movie is dropping this week." Turning to her audience, she said, "It truly is a family affair. Daddy and daughter wrote the music, and Mama is singing."

The sudden turn in attention made Sophie blush.

"Maddie definitely inherited her musical talents from Sophie. The first time I heard her sing I was floored," Noah replied sincerely. "I wrote the song "The Dream of Life" knowing she had to be the one to sing it."

"Well, I for one, can't wait to hear it," Jenna said enthusiastically, before she turned to the cameras. "When we come back, we'll hear a taste of what we are to expect in the upcoming musical score from Noah Bentley, and child superstar, Maddie Cartwright."

The producer let them know that they were out, and Sophie exhaled. As a piano was wheeled out onto the mainstage, another crewmember rushed over to them with a concerned expression.

"Was there supposed to be some sheet music or something?" he asked Sophie and Noah.

Noah shook his head. "She doesn't need sheet music. She remembers it all," he replied.

"Wow," remarked Jenna. "This kid … wow." She shook her head in amazement.

"That is pretty much how I feel all the time," assured Sophie. "Are you ready to play?" she asked Maddie.

Maddie was already on her feet, excited at seeing the piano.

Noah gasped. "Oh, kid, look at that!" he cried. "A Steinway. What do I always say about Steinways?"

"It's a holy instrument," replied Maddie.

Noah winked dand clicked his tongue. "You got it."

Noah was asked to play alongside Maddie for the first part of the piece, before stepping away and allowing Maddie to complete it by herself. Before the cameras were rolling again, Noah and Maddie were seated at the piano in the middle of the stage.

"Performing their musical score from the movie The Last Hope, Noah Bentley and Maddie Cartwright," introduced Jenna, before she turned to look at the pianists, just as Sophie was.

They looked so wonderful together, playing along the keys in perfect unison, their hands moving like a dance. Sophie recognised the piece from one of the many they had composed together at Pete's.

Sophie couldn't help but cry as she always did, but there were happy, happy tears.

And then Noah stepped away, and Maddie completed the piece by herself. She didn't flinch, or even hesitate, and played with skill, maturity, and composure beyond her years.

And as soon as she had finished, Noah swooped in with the headphones he had taken from beside Sophie and popped them on her head as she audience broke out into well-deserved applause. Noah took Maddie's hand and led her out in front of the audience, bowing with her, before clapping for her himself.

Maddie beamed excitedly, pinching the skirt of her sundress in each hand as she bowed again.

Epilogue

February 2022

Dolby Theatre

It was Oscar night. Sophie had been hoping, praying, wishing that Noah and Maddie would be recognised for their original score, and they had been. They were nominated, and up against some of the most renowned composers working in the business, including some of the musicians that Noah idolised.

The buzz surrounding Maddie had died down a little since the movie premiere, and she had been able to start at her new school relatively normally. She was loving her school, in particular the extensive music program, and the time she got during lessons to play and compose. She also was working beautifully with her psychologist, who had helped her to make some friends at school. Maddie had advanced in leaps and bounds in her ability to communicate her feelings, and this had dramatically helped her to control situations where she might become overwhelmed.

When the nominations had been announced, they watched together from the living room of their home in new home in Hidden

Hills, California. Of course, there was no way on earth that Sophie was going to be able to afford any sort of contribution to the purchase of the house itself, so she made do with decorating Maddie's new bedroom using the royalties that she earned from the release of Noah's song.

Sophie had been a little out of sorts at first. She didn't have a full-time job, and Noah had undertaken a new project, and was absolutely loving having his own studio in their home. She took driving lessons most days from a professional school, and managed to get her license, which greatly helped with ferrying Maddie to and from school.

But it took a little while for her to make some friends and to find her feet. She was able to get to know a few parents at Maddie's school, but she did need a purpose. Before having Maddie, it had been her dream to perform on the West End. She still loved theatre, she loved singing and pushing her voice.

To keep up with her love of theatre, Sophie joined a local company, which really put a fire in her belly to pursue her passion. She had never gone after anything for herself before. Noah was happy and successful, and Maddie was finally thriving.

As her song continued to chart really well, particularly with online streaming, Sophie did begin to catch the eye of some casting directors who contacted her through the movie studio asking for headshots.

A film remake of the Tony Award winning Broadway production of Shenandoah was being produced next year, and Sophie was asked to audition for the role of Jenny, the daughter of the main character. The director was after a fresh face, and unknown, and her voice and look were exactly what he was searching for.

Sophie had been training with a dialect coach for the last few months to help perfect her American accent, as she was perhaps "the most British sounding woman" the director had ever heard, and she needed to seem as though she was from Virginia.

The film was due to go into production in April, and Sophie couldn't have been more excited. And it felt good to be excited, optimistic, and not worrying or stressing about every little thing. Good things could happen.

Sophie was going to be filming for a few months in the city, so Joy was happily flying down to help out with Maddie. Maddie was still Joy's only grandchild; she loved any excuse to come down and dote upon her.

Of course, Maddie wouldn't be the only grandbaby for long. Haley was pregnant and had married Mark in the last Christmas holidays. She was due in September. Tally and Vanessa had also organised to start IVF after their wedding in July.

"Tonight you have heard the five songs that are nominated for Best Original Song."

Sophie's attention snapped back to the stage when she realised that this was Noah's big moment. They had performed together earlier in the evening, and Sophie and Noah had received a standing ovation from some of the most famous people in the world.

Sophie knew Noah's song was beautiful, but the four others that were nominated were also spectacular. One of them was from a new animated movie that Sophie had taken Maddie to see in the last summer holidays and she had been humming that tune for weeks after!

"The Academy Award goes to …" the resented opened the envelope and Sophie gripped Noah's hand.

He was squeezing her tightly. He was nervous, and he wanted this. Sophie sucked in a breath and held it tightly as she stared at the stage.

"Into the Night!" cried the presented. "Music by Derek Sharma, lyrics by Annette Lysander!"

The theatre erupted in applause as Noah's grip softened on Sophie's hand. He only allowed himself to be disappointed for a millisecond before he was applauding the two winners.

Both Noah and Sophie had practiced this with Maddie. The gracious loser face. Maddie was about as blunt as a human being could get, and she made no effort to hide her true thoughts or feelings about anything. Maddie knew that if they lost the next award, she would need to clap for the winner and smile.

But Sophie and Noah also wanted her to be excited, and Maddie was terribly. Noah had shown her the YouTube video of his award win eleven years ago now. Maddie had watched it at least a hundred times.

She had even written an acceptance speech by herself, and Sophie wasn't allowed to see it. Maddie had been working on it since the nominations had been announced. She had never worked so hard on something like a piece of writing before. This made her nervous, as Maddie could be quite capable of going up on that stage and bragging her little mouth off.

Okay, this was it. Best Original Score. Sophie took Maddie's headphones off. She wanted her to hear her name.

"Good luck!" Sophie whispered to her. "But remember your nice face if it isn't your name read out!"

Maddie looked so beautiful. Noah had treated them both to a glam squad ... at least, she thought that was what they were called.

They turned Sophie's ensuite into a hair and makeup haven and they were both glammed to the nines. Of course, Maddie was only wearing some lip gloss and a light pink eyeshadow, but it made her feel beautiful.

Their dresses were designer and borrowed. Under no circumstances was any food or drink coming near them. Maddie was wearing a tea length rose gold gown with matching slippers. Her hair was styled in sleek curls with some rose gold butterfly clips pinning any loose locks away from her face.

Sophie then turned to Noah, who looked like bloody James Bond in his fitted tuxedo. Once again, he was nervous, even more so, as this was the one that he wanted to win. He leaned in for a kiss and she pressed her lips to his lightly.

"Good luck," she uttered. "I love you."

Noah smiled nervously. "I love you, too."

The presenter began to read out the nominees, each receiving a clap.

"The Last Hope, original score composed by Noah Bentley and Madeleine Cartwright."

Sophie immediately clapped, and Maddie gasped excitedly when she heard her name. Sophie could practically hear Joy, and Noah's entire family, screaming with pride from home, where they were watching the show on television.

"And the Academy Award goes to ..."

Sophie bit down on her lip hard as the silence seemed to go on forever.

"The Last Hope! Original score composed by Noah Bentley and Madeleine Cartwright!"

So much for gracious losing, as Sophie needed lessons in gracious winning and she screamed in delight. She could practically hear the voice over now, telling the audience at home that this was Noah's second win, and Maddie's first. Maddie had now eclipsed Noah's record as the youngest person to ever win an Academy Award for Best Original Score.

Sophie kissed Noah again. "I'm so proud of you!" She squeezed Maddie tightly. Maddie was positively beaming as she and Noah worked their way out of their seats and into the aisle. They walked hand in hand down the aisle together, while people stood and clapped for the once in a generation feat that was before them. Sophie jumped on the spot, clapping for them both, and burst into happy tears.

They climbed up the stairs together, and a beautifully dressed teenage girl brought out their awards, handing them to the presenter before they were given to Maddie and Noah.

Maddie gripped her Oscar with both hands and bounced on the spot with excitement as Noah came up to the microphone.

"Thank you so much," he gushed gratefully, so clearly full of emotion. "I'll keep this brief because this is all her." He nodded down to Maddie. "Thank you to the Academy for recognising our work. Thank you to my family. And to Sophie." He looked out into the audience and found Sophie in the sea of faces. "You and Maddie are the best things to ever happen to me. I love you endlessly. This kid, Maddie, she wrote this score with me when she was eight." Noah smiled down at Maddie. "I'm in awe of you, and I am so proud of you." Noah stepped away from the microphone which then automatically lowered to Maddie's height. Noah took her statue from her as she pulled out her speech from her pocket.

Maddie unfolded it and took a breath. "I am very excited and thankful to win this award. I know how special it is and I am going to put it next to Daddy's trophy on the mantle at my Grandma and Grandpa's house."

Sophie melted, and a rumble of laughter sounded from the audience.

"Something you may not know about me is that I am special," Maddie continued. "When I was eight-years-old I was diagnosed with autism spectrum disorder."

Sophie clapped her hands together and held them against her lips. She had always promised herself that she wouldn't disclose Maddie's personal business. But she would never stop Maddie from speaking from her heart. To stop her would be like teaching her to be ashamed.

"A lot of you would hear that … and I … and it would make you think that I am disabled or limited. My mummy and my daddy helped me to see that I am special, but not in the way that I am limited. People with autism are only limited by the opinions of others. I am autistic, and I won this award, and I am an example of what people with autism are capable of when you free them from the limitations of your opinions. Autism is my superpower. Thank you so much for thinking that my daddy and me made the best score."

The applause was deafening. People were on their feet cheering, and Noah was down on his knees with his arms around Maddie. Hugging her out of pride, but also grounding her with the noise.

Sophie was an emotional wreck, but she couldn't have been prouder in that very moment.

"How I love you, my darling," Sophie said under her breath as she clapped louder than anyone.

12 Years Later

Carnegie Hall

New York City

"Accompanying the New York Philharmonic this evening is Madeleine Cartwright Bentley, Academy Award Winner, and senior at the Juilliard School majoring in piano."

The smooth voice of the announcer sent a chill down Sophie's spine as she watched Maddie gracefully walk out onto the stage at Carnegie Hall. She was ethereal in white, with her long, strawberry blonde hair worn straight down her back. She remained calm and bowed to the audience as she received their applause, before she took her place at the enormous grand piano.

It was a huge honour for Maddie to be invited to play at Carnegie Hall. And naturally, the entire family had flown out for it. She and Noah were flanked either side by Maddie's two younger sisters. Lena was ten years old and had been born the year before Noah and Sophie had finally gotten married.

Maddie had adored Lena when she had been born and thought that she was quite the best thing since sliced bread. Lena, in turn, idolised Maddie, and quite often stated that Maddie was who she wanted to be when she grew up. Lena thought that Maddie walked on water, and everything that she did was about the coolest thing ever.

Sophie supposed that Googling your older sister and finding hundreds of articles professing how amazing she was did pretty much confirm that. Lena was sitting forward in her chair, gripping the chair in front of her as she stared at Maddie in wonder.

Lena was taking piano lessons, only she was taking a little while longer to pick it up than Maddie and her dad. Penny, their five-year-old, was taking lessons, too. She had progressed as far as chopsticks and enjoyed beating the keys. Maddie had about freaked when she had seen this and had to have the conversation with her that Noah had given Maddie years earlier. A Steinway was a holy instrument, especially the one that had been so painstakingly repaired by Noah and John.

Joy and John, Haley, Mark, and their two children, Casey, Vanessa and Tally, and their son, were all sitting in their row, watching on at Maddie with pure pride.

Keith, Maureen, and even Beck were here somewhere as well. Sophie was sure that she would see them after the performance. Noah had flown them over. Sophie did not count them as family, or even friends, really, but they had managed to develop a civil relationship over the years. Beck had matured, and as far as Sophie knew, he had never engaged in any behaviour resembling the fight that he'd had once had with Noah. He was in a stable relationship now. He didn't have children, and Sophie didn't think he ever would. He wasn't interested in being a father, but he did care about Maddie, and he made efforts to take an interest in her life. Maddie thought of him like a distant relation. Her father was Noah. He was the one she called "Daddy".

Sophie and Maddie still flew over to England once a year for a visit, as well as to indulge in all things wonderful about home.

It was during these visits that she had started to see her parents again. Like with Beck's family, Sophie didn't count them as close relations, friends, or otherwise, but she didn't want to reject them as they had her. The publicity surrounding Maddie, and Sophie's acting and theatre career over the years, had brought them right back under the noses of her mum and dad.

They had tea one afternoon each year. It had become a routine. They didn't talk during the year. There were no phone calls or emails. Just tea. A few hours to catch up, before they saw each other again the next year. Sophie had invited them to Maddie's performance as well, but she didn't know if they were in the audience.

Maddie was performing Rachmaninoff's Piano Concerto No. 2. It was one of Noah's very favourite pieces and was nearly forty minutes in length. The moment Maddie put her fingers to the keys and began to expertly play the complex composition, Sophie was captivated.

But she was so often captivated. Maddie was extraordinary and had not met a hurdle that she could not jump in her twenty-two years. Lena wanted to be like Maddie when she grew up. Hell, so did Sophie.

She listened in awe, and the moment she played the final note, Sophie stood up, along with the rest of the audience, and applauded. Sophie looked up at Noah with tears in her eyes. He was as proud as punch, cheering on his eldest daughter like any doting dad would. God, Sophie adored him, even if he'd started to sprout some grey hairs around his ears now.

She could still vividly remember what it was like to feel defeated, to feel as though life had won, and there was no way through the fog. How much her life, their life, had changed for the better, all because of the piano man.